the Shul Boy

ISRAEL BOOKSHOP
PUBLICATIONS

the Shul Boy

A Novel

Meir Uri Gottesman

Copyright © 2014 by Israel Bookshop Publications

ISBN 978-1-60091-339-6

All rights reserved. No part of this book may be reproduced or transmitted in any form or by any means (electronic, photocopying, recording or otherwise) without prior permission of the publisher.

Published by:
Israel Bookshop Publications
501 Prospect Street
Lakewood, NJ 08701
Tel: (732) 901-3009 / Fax: (732) 901-4012
www.israelbookshoppublications.com
info@israelbookshoppublications.com

Printed in the United States of America

Distributed in Israel by:
Shanky's
Petach Tikva 16
Jerusalem
972-2-538-6936

Distributed in Europe by:
Lehmanns
Unit E Viking Industrial Park
Rolling Mill Road,
Jarrow, Tyne & Wear NE32 3DP
44-191-430-0333

Distributed in Australia by:
Gold's Book and Gift Company
3- 13 William Street
Balaclava 3183
613-9527-8775

Distributed in South Africa by:
Kollel Bookshop
Northfield Centre
17 Northfield Avenue
Glenhazel 2192
27-11-440-6679

In memory of my beloved wife

Susan Gottesman

Rachel Raizel bat Yaakov Tzvi Halevi a"h

My dear wife, Susan, passed away Erev Shabbos, Parshas Shelach 5774 (15 Sivan), and was laid to rest just before Shabbos like a great *tzaddekes*.

Susan read the completed manuscript of *The Shul Boy*, and her soul hovers over each sentence, as it does over all the other books that the Almighty has allowed me to write. She encouraged me, struggled with me; she was my partner in all that we accomplished together. Her kindness brought many under the wings of the *Shechinah*.

Oh, Susan, how I miss you! I still see you sitting at your chair by the living room window, *davening* Minchah, studying *Pirkei Avos*, speaking to the children and grandchildren, giving *chizuk* to so many!

Susan was an only child, orphaned at eight years old— yet she raised a holy empire.

I would ask a kindness from those who read my books—Susan's books, too—that you learn Mishnayos or recite Tehillim for the *neshamah* of Rebbetzin Rachel Raizel bat Yaakov Tzvi Halevi a"h, so together we can build a holy palace in her merit and the merit of all of Israel. Please contact me at meirurigottesman@gmail.com.

May we all know only blessings, good health, and *Yiddishe nachas*, and soon march forward to greet Mashiach, amen!

Meir Uri Gottesman

Part One

1

The Shul Boy

It was a warm summer day, and a young boy stood alone in his backyard, throwing a rubber ball against the back of his house. There was a tall, wooden, box-like protrusion that emerged from the back wall, and his game consisted of trying to bounce the ball off the top of the protrusion and then catch it quickly before it hit the ground. He felt a tiny flicker of childish guilt, because he knew that the protrusion was the back of an *aron kodesh*. But he made excuses for himself... The *aron kodesh*, after all, was inside the house, protected by a velvet curtain, and the shingles on the outside. The two *sifrei Torah* were covered in heavy mantles. Besides, he had nothing else to do all summer—no camp, no friends. His only pastime was throwing the ball over and over, running after it, catching it, daydreaming... He was the pitcher, he was the catcher, he was the hitter, he was Joe DiMaggio jumping up against the fence and catching the ball in one glove, cheered on by thousands of fans.

As he played, a shadow strangely flitted over his head. He gazed up and was so attracted by the sight, that he was drawn out of his daydreams. A flock of pigeons circled overhead between his house and the apartment house next door. They flew in perfect pattern, circling again and again, appearing and disappearing.

The boy, Lipa, ran down the driveway trying to follow the birds' flight. He looked up at the tall rooftop where the birds came from, but could see no one. The birds flew around and around, beating their wings in perfect rhythm, soaring upward, gliding down, like a fluttering banner against the blue sky. Lipa was mesmerized by the beautiful sight. Who was guiding those pigeons so perfectly? And in the deepest hollow of his heart, he envied the pigeons—they flew together—they were not lonely.

Lipa Wallerstein lived in a large rambling house that contained his father's shul, or *shtiebel*, and the family living quarters that were on the two upper floors. This was not just Lipa's house, but his whole universe. There were no Jewish friends, and his family left him to himself. All he had was the house, the rambling backyard, the back of the *aron kodesh*—and his fertile imagination where everything was possible. It was the early 1950s. Lipa dwelt in Jersey City, across the harbor from the Statue of Liberty. His father had started the shul a few years before, just after Lipa was born. Rabbi Wallerstein had come to Jersey City to be rabbi of the Willow Avenue Synagogue, only a block away. He served in that post for two years before he was dismissed—*fired*. His congregation expected that he would leave the city promptly, but his father had a handful of loyal followers. One wealthy gentleman, a jeweler, gave him the one hundred-dollar down payment he needed on a rambling house that was just a block away from Willow Avenue. There, Rabbi Nosson Wallerstein established his little synagogue.

There was no *minyan* during the week, just on Shabbos. The shul took up the entire main floor, except for Rabbi Wallerstein's office. The shul was long and narrow; the walls were painted sky blue, the dozen simple wooden benches a deeper blue. The *aron kodesh* stood flat against the front wall, and protruded out back. Every

Friday afternoon, Lipa had the task of preparing the shul. First, he took a wet rag and wiped down all the benches in the men's section and the side *veibersher* shul that was also the kiddush room. It was tedious, but it had to be done—too much dust gathered during the week. Then came his weekly game—covering the narrow tables that ran along two sides of the Torah *shulchan*, and the larger kiddush tables in the women's section.

The covering consisted of a heavy roll of white wrapping paper. He drew the roll out of the closet, reaching over a drawer full of tiny kittens, the size of little furry balls. The kittens hissed angrily at him whenever he opened the closet door. He tried to reassure them, reaching quickly over them, grabbing the roll and quickly shutting the door. He carried the roll to the edge of the first table, pulled out the end, and pinned it securely to the edge of the table with a thumbtack. Then came the race. He gave the roll a strong shove, and it began rolling toward the other end of the table. He needed to reach the other end of the table before the roll did. He ran quickly, and at the last instant caught the roll just as it was about to fall over. He sliced off the end of the unfurled roll, folded it underneath the other side of the table and pinned it firmly in. He did not always win the race. Sometimes he pushed too hard and it raced over the other side, falling over with a thud. Sometimes he pushed unevenly, and it careened over one side like a gutter ball in a bowling alley. It was a fun game, and it kept Lipa busy Friday afternoons—that, and preparing the herring.

Queen Shabbos descended on Rabbi Wallerstein's shul on shaky wings. There was barely a *minyan* for the Friday night service. The men arrived to shul painfully slow, one by one. The sky darkened, time grew late. Lipa stood in the back of the women's section, looking out the back window. Through an opening between two buildings, he could spy out the entrance to the Willow Avenue Synagogue on the next block—and see how *they* were doing. Willow Avenue Synagogue also struggled.

It grew even later—almost too late for Minchah. Lipa joined the men clustered up front near the window. There were just eight men. Lipa's father sat at his *shtender* next to the front window, looking out to the street so he could watch who was passing by, and perhaps call someone in. His siddur lay open on his *shtender*, and he recited *Shir Hashirim*, even as he peered out from time to time. The men sat near him, listening to his reading, growing impatient.

Rabbi Wallerstein grew very anxious. "Lipa, go out and see if anyone is coming."

Lipa stepped outside into the summer evening. It was almost dusk. He stood on the top of the staircase, grasped the corner of the building for balance, and leaned precariously over the side of the house so he could see up the block. Someone was coming!

"It's Gordon—Gordon is coming! And he has his son!"

Rabbi Wallerstein leaped up excitedly and grabbed a *tallis*. Lipa stood nervously, still watching carefully—was he right? It *did* look like Gordon. Yes, it was Gordon! Why did he always have to come so late! He beckoned him on faster—*Hurry up, Gordon!* Rabbi Wallerstein sighed with relief—they had a *minyan*!

―――

"Good Shabbos, good Shabbos, hey! Hey! Hey!" Rabbi Wallerstein raced up the stairs in a grand mood. It was a cloudy evening, the days were growing shorter at summer's end, and yet the shul had managed a *minyan*.

"*Shabbos shalom u'mevorach*! *Shabbos shalom u'mevorach*!" he greeted his wife and children.

For Lipa, Friday night was the highlight of his whole life. The whole week he barely saw his father, who hardly spoke a handful of words with him. Not that his father was away, but his father never had anything to say to him, no real reason to talk. Their house was simple, but it was large, rambling, with many rooms to hide. One could share a house and never see anyone except in passing. Lipa lived by himself, despite his family. His brother and sister hardly spoke to him, except to make some whispered commentary. *"You're a bag of bones,"* his older brother would observe, noting Lipa's slim frame. His sister would walk by and murmur: *"Lipa the Lipa…"* Like there was nothing more to be said after that. The name Lipa itself evoked ridicule.

But Friday night was different. They all sat together in their large kitchen, with the great wooden chopping table next to the stove, the oversized refrigerator in the corner. Lipa's father stood at the head of the kitchen table and chanted *Shalom Aleichem*. Lipa sang along loudly, louder than his brother Leon, who cast him a sour look, louder than his sister who tried to ignore him. He sang louder than them all, hoping his father would notice him, admire him. But only his mother seemed to appreciate his singing.

Rabbi Wallerstein made Kiddush with his usual flourish, closing his eyes and pronouncing each word loudly, with fervor. Lipa's father, who always seemed so angry and anxious during the week, seemed to be at peace in the Kiddush. He sat down, drank his measure, and distributed sips to each family member. *"Nu*, let's wash," he announced.

They all marched to the big sink near the back open window. From outside came the sounds of neighbors quarreling, cats fighting on the garage roof, sounds from the next street, the evening symphony of Jersey City. Lipa waited his turn, not without hearing a subtle whisper from his brother: "Hey, bag of bones…" Lipa accepted these comments stoically, like it was his lot in life. *Gefilte fish* was served, Rabbi Wallerstein complimented his wife on the challah, and the meal proceeded to its next, incendiary phase.

"*Nu*," his father ordered.

His brother Leon brought over a decanter marked "Crown Royal." His father filled the Kiddush cup full with the powerful blend of various leftover whiskeys, scotches, and ryes. "*L'chaim!*" he announced and quickly gulped down half a cup. Lipa dutifully dipped the edge of his challah into the cup and tasted a drop of the powerful liquid. It burned his tongue and lips, but he wanted to imitate his father in cleansing his mouth between the fish and chicken soup. His father took another hefty gulp, opened his old siddur and began singing *Kol Mekadesh*. Rabbi Wallerstein had a beautiful voice and sang fervently, lifting his hand piously at the start of each stanza, raising his eyes to the ceiling. From time to time, he took another sip from the cup, his eyes growing watery, his face redder and redder.

He finished the *zemiros* and closed his siddur firmly. His face had turned deep red. The whiskey had done its job and he was awash with courage and anger. He sat silently for a minute and gazed at his family. Then he pounded his fist on the table.

"No, they are not going to do this to me!" he shouted.

"What, dear?" his wife inquired, trying to calm him.

Rabbi Wallerstein pointed his finger angrily at Lipa. "They are not going to make me pay for *him* to go to yeshivah," he shouted. Rabbi Wallerstein glared at Lipa, as though *he* had done some terrible deed.

"They want me to pay five hundred dollars for him this year! Who can afford it? They are on the Jewish radio every week begging people to send them donations. They get money from everywhere, from rich people. Who is it for? But they said if I don't pay

Lipa's tuition, he wouldn't be allowed into class!"

Lipa cast his eyes down shamefacedly. Somehow, he was the cause of his father's anger.

"*I am not going to pay a penny*!" Rabbi Wallerstein roared. "You hear that, Chaya? *Not a single penny*! They ask for donations to help the poor, and then they want money from me."

"But what will we do?" asked Lipa's mother. "The child has to go to school."

Rabbi Wallerstein slammed his fist on the table, his face red with anger, fueled by a full cup of schnapps. He glared at Lipa angrily and pointed a trembling finger at his face.

"I'll tell you what we'll do! Lipa is going to march in front of the yeshivah on opening day with a signboard on his shoulders.

"'THEY WILL NOT LET ME INTO THIS YESHIVAH!'

"That's what it will say! I will have him march in front of the school just when all the children and teachers are entering. Then they will know who they are fighting with."

Lipa's face grew pale, and he looked down so they could not see that tears were falling from his face. Leon and Eva snickered audibly.

Pleased with his outburst, Rabbi Wallerstein took up his siddur and began the next of the *zemiros*. The soup was served and the meal continued uneventfully. Everyone seemed happy, but Lipa's heart sunk within him—he didn't want to walk with a signboard in front of everyone!

Jersey City lay across the Hudson River, a universe away from the yeshivah Lipa attended. The yeshivah was in the Lower East Side, and he had to travel an hour each way to attend. First, he took the Norway Avenue bus to the Hudson Tubes, traveled under the river to Lower Manhattan, then took the A train and the D train. He finally ascended a long escalator to the street, and from the isolation of Jersey City, he was thrust into the midst of the teeming Lower East Side. He did not know, could not understand, that the great cramped building with its narrow hallways and crowded classrooms, its poorer Lower East Side students and the more affluent Brooklyn boys, was a monument to the vast dedication and struggle to keep the school running, to pay the *rabbeim* and English teachers, to offer free breakfasts and *Mishmar* suppers. All Lipa knew was that it was the first day of school and his father had not paid tuition. Would he be sent home? Would he be embarrassed in front of the other boys? At least, his father had not followed through on his threat to make him march outside with a sandwich board sign.

Lipa was entering the seventh grade; at eleven years old, he was one of the younger boys in his class. It was a large class, more than thirty boys cramped into a small room. On one side of the classroom was a bank of tall windows, looking out to the tenement buildings outside. Their new *rebbi* stood at the front of his class, looking anxious. It was not so much a class as a collection of rambunctious yearlings, each set like a coiled watch spring set to burst out, ready to test their new teacher. The *rebbi* surveyed his new charges, and under his breath murmured a *tefillah* that he could control the huge, unruly throng. The *rebbi*, Reb Avraham, was a Holocaust survivor, a gentle *talmid chacham*, untrained in teaching, cast into the midst of this lion's den. Now he was in America, he had to make *parnassah* for his wife and children—and this was the only way. His whole life was Torah learning. He armed himself with a stern face, cleared his throat, and announced:

"*Everyone here show me his admission card!*"

There was a noisy rustling of chairs as each boy reached into his desk or school bag to produce the small green admission card that proved that his parents had paid tuition. He began walking down the aisles, collecting the cards from each student. Lipa, who sat near the back row, grew anxious. He had no card. The *rebbi* finished one aisle, then went up the next, then a third. Now he was in the fourth row, heading up his aisle. Each child handed his card proudly, showing that he indeed belonged. The *rebbi* drew closer, two before Lipa, next, the boy right in front—and finally he reached Lipa. Lipa looked up silently, cardless.

"Where is your card?" the *rebbi* asked, thinking that Lipa was slow to produce it. Lipa did not move, too embarrassed to speak.

Any distraction in the class was entertainment for the boys. They watched the little scene unfold.

"*Nu?*" the *rebbi* asked impatiently.

"I...I don't have one..." Lipa answered falteringly. He felt all eyes in the room on him.

The *rebbi* had been given strict instructions by the principal—every student must have an admission card, like a passport at the border.

"But, *bachur*, you *must* have an admission card to be in my class," he repeated.

A tear welled up in Lipa's eye—he did not have what to answer. Some of the boys were smirking and winking to each other.

The *rebbi* saw the tears welling up in Lipa's eyes. Despite his own strict instructions, he could not shame this *Yiddishe* child. The *rebbi* was a kindhearted man who had suffered plenty himself. Without a word, he moved on silently to another student, continuing his collections.

After class, Reb Avraham reported that one child, Lipa Wallerstein, had no admission slip. The executive director, despite his gruff manner, knew already that his father, Rabbi Wallerstein, would not—could not—pay. The director sighed and shook his head—but he could not send away a Jewish child. The admission card was overlooked, like every year, and Lipa remained in class.

The Shul Boy ೞ 17

Rabbi Wallerstein won his battle not to pay tuition, the *rebbi* and the yeshivah board emerged as truly righteous, and the only victim was poor Lipa. He wore his humiliation like a second pair of *tzitzis*. It was the same every year. He was allowed into class, but a misty cloud of peculiarity hovered over him. In the end, Lipa was alone at home, alone on the train, alone in school. His tender *neshamah* was forged by loneliness, and he sought comfort in his aloneness and endless imagination.

Lipa lived in two universes, his drab working-class neighborhood in Jersey City, with a mixture of Irish and Italians, and a gathering number of blacks who had started penetrating from nearby Ege Avenue, and a small scattering of Jews. But the Lower East Side where his yeshivah was located was a teeming wonder world of Jewish life. At lunchtime, which lasted an hour, Lipa wandered alone from the yeshivah and set out to explore the different streets. There was Norfolk Street with its glorious Beis Medrash Hagadol; Essex Street; Canal Street; and Rabbi Mordechai Lubart's *mocher sefarim* shop, Otzar Hasefarim Bookstore, where the pungent odor of freshly printed volumes wafted through the store. Lipa let his curiosity and imagination fly free. He drew his own map of the Lower East Side, like Treasure Island, the lofty tenement buildings that turned the streets into canyons, filled with the odor of baking bagels and freshly killed fish. There were the Brooklyn Bridge and Williamsburg Bridge, and the gloomy caverns where the streets ran underneath them. There were the projects on Lewis Street where the old Stretiner Beis Medrash once stood, and the newer apartments that overlooked the East River. Lipa wandered along East River Drive, inhaling the smell of the sea, and dreaming of casting off on a boat into the ocean. There was the Educational Alliance on

East Broadway, a haven for new immigrants a generation before. And there were the world-famous scholars who dwelt modestly on the Lower East Side, like the tiny Rabbi Yaakov Safsol who wrote sheaf after sheaf of brilliant *chiddushim*. There were shuls big and small, and the little *shtieblach*. All these places Lipa explored and imbibed, alone and yet not alone, for he shared his explorations with make-believe companions.

Lipa began each year with hope. He truly wanted to do well, to please his father, to be like his grandfathers who had been famous holy men. So, after his first day of near humiliation, he sat eagerly in his seat at the back of the crowded classroom, opened his new Gemara, and tried to pay attention as the *rebbi* began teaching. He tried to understand, ten minutes, twenty minutes. But he could not comprehend a word the *rebbi* was saying. The poor *rebbi* hardly knew English, and struggled to teach, half-English, half-Yiddish. Lipa followed along as best he could, his finger on the word, but in a few minutes, he was lost. The *rebbi* droned on, getting more and more frustrated.

Lipa's mind wandered. He looked out the window. Some boys were running along the tenement rooftop across the streets. Had they stolen something? Were they running away? Maybe the police would follow. They disappeared—no police. After a few minutes, an apartment window opened, and a woman hung out her laundry. Lipa watched her progress.

Lipa was not the only one growing restive. The poor *rebbi*, who never took teaching lessons, was having greater and greater trouble controlling the restless class; it was like controlling a corral of wild ponies. He was a new *rebbi*, and had been given the most difficult class that no one else wanted. Lipa felt sad for the poor *rebbi*, who had been kind to him. The *rebbi* taught, the buzzing in the room grew louder. The *rebbi* shouted for quiet, so the talking grew louder. What could the poor man do? He was a lamb among thirty wolves. It was frightening to watch the *rebbi* grow more and more frantic. He shouted, then shouted louder, and then his face began turning colors, like a lamp that changes hue. First his neck turned light pink, and then as the class grew more and more out of control, his whole face blossomed dark red. The *rebbi's* voice began to crack, so that he could barely speak. Lipa grew frightened as his face flushed from blood red to deep purplish blue. Poor *rebbi*! His neck veins began protruding dangerously, his face was purple, and Lipa was afraid that a blood vessel would burst open like an overheated pipe. Somehow, the *rebbi* was able survive until one o'clock, and the unruly class was dismissed.

The next morning, it all began again—a daily battle of who could outlast whom. There were a handful of good boys, bright boys, who wanted to learn. The *rebbi* directed more and more of his attention toward them, ignoring the others. As for Lipa, he sat quietly day after day, gazing out the window, lost in his own daydreams. He did not disturb the *rebbi*, the *rebbi* did not bother him. He did poorly on each test he took, but when he came home with a pitiful report card, it did not matter. No one cared. His father signed it without even looking at it, and that was that. Lipa's father had other serious matters to face—would his shul survive? How would he feed his family?

Lipa's home was a poor man's castle. Although simple, it was rambling and full of endless rooms and hidden alcoves. It had three stories, gabled roofs, plus a dank coal cellar below, with mysterious recesses and open bins. Multiple stairways led upstairs, some that ended mid-flight against a wall as though they were made only for ghosts. The synagogue was on the main floor, and to the side was the women's section, separated by a curtained wall. There were countless closets, cupboards, old iceboxes, and stuffed sideboards where the cats deposited their newborn litters. One could get lost in Lipa's house.

The heart of Lipa's home was Rabbi Wallerstein's office, downstairs. More cultured rabbis might term the room the "study" or the "library"—but for Lipa's father, it was simply the "office." It lay across the front lobby from the shul, looking out onto the street. There his father sat at his large desk, puffed on his cigar, and did his work. It was a high-ceilinged room, with two doors; one that led to the front lobby, and a narrower back door to the shul.

The office was lined on two sides with ceiling-high bookshelves that Lipa's father built himself. The shelves were filled with a cornucopia of books that his father had managed to accumulate; some from used bookstores, from shuls that had closed, some from Lipa's grandfathers. Among the volumes were hundreds-of-years-old antiques that were worth a great deal—but Rabbi Wallerstein would never sell his *sefarim*.

Despite the hundreds of books, *Shasim*, sets of *Chumashim*, *Encyclopedia Britannica*, there were still not enough volumes to fill all the shelves. But Rabbi Wallerstein, who did not like empty shelves, found a creative solution. He collected large cigar boxes, wrapped them in the same white paper used to cover the shul tables, and marked them in bold black ink…Volume I, Volume II, all the way to Volume XXVIII—as many volumes as he needed to fill the shelf. The volumes had no title—just the volume number. They looked impressive high above out of reach, and served their purpose. Rabbi Wallerstein's office looked properly rabbinical, his shelves full.

In the summer, Lipa found comfort in his backyard, throwing a ball against the back of the house and daydreaming. But as the days grew dark and cold, he arrived home from school late and had

The Shul Boy ∽ 21

no place to be by himself except downstairs. Everyone was upstairs doing homework or listening to the radio, so Lipa escaped below. Sometimes he entered the empty shul, the *ner tamid* casting a pale yellow light over the *aron kodesh*. He wandered about the room, but the ghostly darkness frightened him. What invisible spirits were seated on the benches, watching him? He retreated to his father's office, turned on the bright fluorescent light, and was suddenly cast into a wonderland of brightly covered volumes. From aloneness and rejection, he was encompassed by hundreds of books, like so many people hugging him. Lipa was no longer alone, but in a universe of holy *sefarim* and old English volumes. Like his daydreams, the books had no time, no place. He loved these books, he loved *sefarim*, he loved their covers and their thick pages and their deep, coal-black print. This room, this office, *was* his father, the smell of his cigars, his father's thick diary stuffed with papers that lay perpetually on his desk.

There were hundreds of volumes, but always he was drawn to one special set of Mishnayos. Carefully, not to harm its delicate pages, he opened one of the volumes to the first page, with its illustration of two pillars holding up the word *Mishnayos* etched boldly in red. The Mishnayos was a hundred years old, and its thick cloth-like pages had discolored into a pale, bluish white. But the letters were still boldly black, and stood out like they had been printed yesterday.

Lipa gazed into the Mishnayos, not understanding a word, but felt great love course through him. For this had been his *Zeide's* Mishnayos, left to his father when he died. Lipa's *Zeide* was the only person who ever showed him love, who thought he was special: "Lipa, you will be a tzaddik someday!" Lipa was just a little child, barely on the cusp of his first memories. Zeide balanced Lipa on one knee, and a volume of Mishnayos on the other. When Lipa wanted to grab at the pages, Zeide held his hand.

"Careful, careful, *yingel*! You are young and delicate, and the pages are old and delicate."

Lipa smiled and grabbed Zeide's white beard. "Zeide, you are also old and delicate."

Zeide smiled, then showed Lipa: "Look, here is the mishnah in the middle, and here the holy *Ovadiah Bartenura* on one side and the *Tosfos Yom Tov* on the other."

Lipa pointed toward the bottom of the page: "And who is that, Zeide?"

Zeide ran his finger down the page: "That is the *Yachin u'Boaz*."

"So much writing, Zeide!"

"There's more!" Zeide exclaimed. He carefully leafed through the volume, turning to the back. There were pages and pages of writing, in tiny letters.

"What is that, Zeide?"

"That is the holy *Mileches Shlomo*. It a great, difficult commentary."

Zeide turned back to the front of the mishnah.

"Did you learn all these words, Zeide?" Lipa asked, pointing to the *Bartenura* and *Tosfos Yom Tov*.

Zeide nodded. "*Baruch Hashem*, I have learned them many times, many times."

"What about down here?" Lipa asked, pointing to the *Yachin u'Boaz*.

"*Baruch Hashem*."

"And what about Shlomo, who's hiding in the back?"

Zeide shook his head disapprovingly. "Not 'Shlomo,' Lipa! *Mileches Shlomo*! I have learned much of it, but it is very long."

"But Zeide, when are you going to finish studying Rabbi Shlomo's words?" Lipa asked.

Zeide held his beloved grandson closer to his bosom, and sighed loudly. "Lipa, little Lipa, I am old! I am not well. My eyes are getting weaker and weaker. I do not know if I will ever learn it all."

Lipa looked up into the beautiful, loving face of his grandfather. "I will learn it!" he announced.

"Yes," said Zeide. "Someday you will learn all of them; the *Bartenura*, and the *Tosfos Yom Tov*, and even Rabbi Shlomo's *peirush*!"

Almost as an afterthought, Lipa looked up at Zeide and said, "But Zeide, I can't even read yet! How will I ever be able to learn all these hard little words?"

"I will tell you a secret," said Zeide. "If you want to really understand these words, you must imagine that these tzaddikim are right there in front of you, teaching you themselves!"

"But...are they still alive?" asked Lipa.

"Of course, they are alive!" answered Zeide firmly. "*Tzaddikim b'misasam k'ruim chaim*! A tzaddik is alive even when he leaves this world! If you want to learn the *Bartenura*, you must think: 'The *Bartenura* is sitting right across from me, listening to every word I say!'"

"And the others, too? Will they come to me?"

"If you study hard, with all your heart, and you want them to help you—they will come!"

Zeide died soon afterward, the only person who truly loved Lipa. It was just a few years ago, but a world away. Lipa remembered him but vaguely. But that one time that he sat on Zeide's lap, this ancient Mishnayos opened before him, that loving memory stayed deep. He did not remember the names of the great rabbis, but he remembered the ancient volume. He sat on Zeide's one knee, and the Mishnayos on Zeide's other knee—like Ephraim and Menashe. Each night he ended his lonely visit to his father's office by kissing the volume good night, and deep inside—he kissed his *Zeide* good night also.

Lipa had a delicate *neshamah* that grew more and more frustrated. He wanted to learn like his grandfather, who was a great tzaddik. On Shabbos Lipa sat among the older men, listening to his father tell parables from the *parshah* in the morning, or *Pirkei Avos* in the afternoon. Lipa wished his father would learn with him. But during the week, his father never had time for him—he was too busy with more important things. In the rare instance where his father finally sat down with him, Rabbi Wallerstein soon grew impatient that Lipa did not understand him. His father shut his *sefer* and ran upstairs to the kitchen.

In school Lipa sat quietly and tried to follow his *rebbi*, but he couldn't, try as he might. His *rebbi* spoke half-English, half-Yiddish, he explained everything quickly, and expected the boys to understand. When they didn't, he grew angry and the class grew unruly. There were spitball fights from one row to the other, or long distance from the back of the class to the front. Paper planes soared across the room in surprise attacks, landing on someone's yarmulke, to general merriment. The *rebbi* ran angrily in the direction of the plane's launching pad, grabbed a boy's papers and crushed them into a ball. Often, it was the wrong boy, who loudly screamed at the injustice—adding to everyone's fun. Lipa sat quietly day after day, not learning and not disturbing, so the *rebbi* tolerated him. He daydreamed, he gazed out the window, and was forlorn.

The unhappier he was in class, the more he sought out his *Zeide's* Mishnayos at home. Each night he opened a volume, stared at the words, thought of his *Zeide*, and wished he could learn from the Mishnah. But how could he? He couldn't learn himself; his father had no patience. Perhaps there was another way? Lipa's brother Leon was four years older than he was. Lipa loved his brother, looked up to him. Lipa was eleven, while Leon was fifteen, almost a grown-up. And yet, for some reason, Leon did not like Lipa. Leon had friends, was good in school, and was his father's favorite. There was no answer for Leon's dislike, but it was what it was—and Lipa learned to live with it.

Lipa so much wanted to learn from his *Zeide's* Mishnayos that he summoned his courage. He had no one else to ask. One night, Lipa approached his older brother, who was bent over his desk, doing homework.

Leon tried to ignore Lipa, but finally looked up. "What do you want, Lipa?" he asked.

"Leon, can you help me with something?"

Leon looked at him impatiently. "What do you want?"

"You know, we have a set of Mishnayos downstairs, in Daddy's office—"

"I know that. So?"

"Could...could you learn some Mishnah with me?"

Leon turned and looked at Lipa incredulously. "Lipa, Mishnah? Aren't you learning Gemara already? Mishnah is for grade three, for little kids!"

Lipa grew incensed. "But Zeide learned Mishnah—all the time! I saw him!"

Leon waved his hand impatiently. "Oh, so now you are Zeide? Zeide was a tzaddik. You are Lipa."

"But—"

Leon turned back impatiently to his work. "Lipa, don't bother me, please. Don't you see I have homework? Why don't you learn what you're supposed to so you don't get such bad report cards! Daddy says that your marks are terrible!"

"But—"

"Lipa—*out!*

But Lipa was determined. He had a delicate *neshamah*, but a stubborn will—a spark of *azuz d'kedushah*, holy boldness. He wanted to learn Mishnayos. The next evening, he slipped noiselessly downstairs, shutting the upstairs door softly behind him. He turned past the hallway and entered the dark shul. A shiver of fear coursed through him, frightened of what invisible *neshamos* might be sitting on the shadowy benches, watching him. He approached the front of the *aron kodesh*, and whispered a quick prayer:

"*Ribono shel Olam*, I so much want to learn Mishnayos, just like my *Zeide* did! There is no one who wants to help me. Can't *You* help me? I love You so much, and I so much want to learn Your Torah!"

He suddenly filled with panic. He felt a dozen pairs of eyes watching him from behind, staring over his shoulder, so he became terrified. In a panic, he quickly kissed the *paroches* and raced out of the shul for his life, afraid to turn around lest he glimpse the *neshamos* following him. He ran through the women's section, grabbed open the door to his father's office, and slammed it tight behind him. Lipa was breathing hard as he turned on the office lights and was momentarily blinded by the brilliant fluorescent lights that flooded the room. But his young eyes quickly focused, and he gazed around at the familiar walls. Here he was safe; here there were no invisible spirits, just books and books, Encyclopedias and Gemaras, *sefarim* upon *sefarim*, even disguised shoe boxes that were his friends, who surrounded him with their warmth. Just to reassure himself, he jammed the door to the shul closed even tighter, barring whoever lurked outside from getting in.

Lipa was determined. Leon had deeply upset him, insulted him—*Mishnah was for kids*. How could that be? Was Zeide a child? Like a cork that had been pushed deep into the water, his resolve to learn shot back up to the surface. Leon had pushed him down—now he rose up. Lipa was determined to learn Mishnah—to learn it, to understand it, to prove Leon wrong!

He headed straight to Zeide's Mishnayos and extracted the first volume. He did not even bother to carry it to his father's desk. He set a chair next to the bookcase, and opened the heavy volume on his knees. The pages were discolored and powdery, and he inhaled their fine grains. He opened to the first mishnah, the first word printed in great bold letters:

"*MEI'EIMASAI*"

Lipa had once studied this mishnah a long time ago, in the third grade, but had forgotten what it meant. He read the words carefully:

"*ko-koreen es ha-She-ma b'-Ar-vis mee-sheh—*"

He labored painfully through two, three lines. So far, so good. But what did they mean? He recognized just two words: *Shema…Arvis*—like Ma'ariv. But try as he might, he did not understand one sentence of the mishnah. His face drew dark with frustration. Next to the mishnah was the commentary of Rabbi Ovadiah of Bartenura, in small Rashi letters. That was even more difficult. Lipa placed his finger on the *Bartenura*, trying to unravel the meaning. *He couldn't even read it*! He tried to read the words, but he couldn't even make out the letters; they were too confusing. He tried once, twice. Nothing. Zero. He lowered the *sefer* down on his knees, and tears of frustration and disappointment ran down his face…

Leon was right. It was too hard. It was for Zeide, not for him!

But, *no*! Lipa was determined. He wanted to learn Mishnah, from this very *sefer* his *Zeide* had shown him!

Zeide, he cried to himself, *Zeide, can't you help me*?

But no one answered him. There was just silence in the room, and the buzzing of the fluorescent lights. *What to do…what to do?* He didn't understand anything, not the mishnah, not the *Bartenura* who was supposed to explain everything.

He remembered Zeide's admonition:

"*If you want to learn Torah, you must imagine that the rabbi is sitting right across from you, teaching you!*"

Lipa gazed angrily at the page he could not understand. Here was the mishnah. Here was Rabbi Ovadiah who was supposed to teach him. Lipa closed his eyes, and concentrated with all his might:

"*Rabbi Ovadiah,*" he cried, "*come teach me!*"

He opened his eyes hopefully, hoping that there would be standing the great sage, Rabbi Ovadiah. Lipa looked around. There was no one, just his father's office, the familiar *sefarim*, the heavy Mishnah on his lap.

Lipa sighed sadly, even bitterly. He did not understand the mishnah, he could not understand—and there was no one who wanted to teach him. Lipa, who had learned in his eleven years to live with loneliness, sighed and carefully returned the volume to its place on the shelf. There was nothing more to do than to go back upstairs, and to his daydreams where he was always a hero, a success.

Lipa was suddenly overcome with a weird childish terror. He realized he was all alone downstairs. Just outside his door was the dark, silent shul filled with invisible *neshamos*. He was suddenly very afraid; he just wanted to run upstairs to the safety of his family. He quickly shut the office light, casting the room into darkness, broken only by thin streaks of street light that seeped between the blinds. He hurriedly tried the doorknob leading to the front lobby, so he could avoid going back through the shul. The knob turned— but the door would not open. His father must have latched the door shut from outside. *He never did that—why did he have to do it tonight?* Almost in tears, Lipa twisted the knob harder and banged on the door, hoping the latch would fall open, even break. But it held firm like iron. Lipa was trapped between the office and the suddenly terrifying shul. There was no other way to escape but to run as fast as he could through the shul, past the *neshamos* staring at him. He caught his breath, and prepared to make his perilous escape when he stopped, frozen.

The Shul Boy ಆ 29

Someone was knocking on the shul door! Lipa stood frozen, too afraid to cry out, the hair on his neck standing stiff.

"*Lipa*," a voice called softly from behind the door. "*Lipa, open the door for me!*"

Who was it? Who was hiding behind the door?

Lipa shook so badly he could hardly speak. "*Go away! Go away!*" he cried to the mysterious voice.

"No, no," the voice implored. "Lipa, don't be frightened! You asked me to come, and I am here! But please, let me in—quickly! I am being pursued!"

"Who…who are you?" asked Lipa, his breath coming in frightened bursts, so that his voice quaked. Yet the voice on the other side of the door did not sound menacing. Lipa took a deep breath and mustered his courage. "Are you a ghost?" he demanded to know. "If you are, please go away!"

"Ghost? Ghost?" The voice sounded offended. "*Bambino*! Didn't you ask me, Ovadiah of Bartenura, to teach you Mishnah? Did you not?"

Lipa gulped. "I did!"

"So here I am! Lipa, I have no more time to argue! I am being hotly pursued! Open up quickly, or I will fly from here and be gone from you forever!"

Lipa stood motionless with confusion. He was so frightened, bewildered—and excited! Was it really a ghost outside? If he was, he seemed like a friendly ghost. But he had begged Ovadiah of Bartenura to help him! His *Zeide* had taught him to see the person he was learning from with his own eyes! Lipa could no longer resist—curiosity and intense loneliness overcame his fear. He could hear whomever it was on the other side of the door breathing heavily, like he was being chased. Lipa murmured a quick prayer to Hashem and ran determinedly to the shul door and pulled it open.

He ran back to the far end of the room and waited. In the darkness, it was hard to see anything. But slowly a figure began to appear in the narrow doorway. Lipa made him out bit by bit, like he was materializing right there before him, first the head and shoulders, then his chest, and then the rest of his tall frame. His face was in shadow; his clothes were rich—an ornate purple robe, a heavy mantle over his shoulders, and a large purple hat that flared out from his head like a sail. Lipa stared at the silent figure standing in the door, afraid to speak. Ovadiah was a very large man, and he filled the narrow entrance almost to the ceiling. Lipa felt a breeze on his face, and the office was suddenly filled with the tangy smell of the sea, like when one stood at the water's edge.

"May I come in, Lipa?" the visitor asked.

"Ye…yes, Rabbi Ovadiah… Is it really you?"

Even in the darkness, illuminated by thin streaks of silvery streetlight, Lipa saw Ovadiah nod. He stepped inside, and quickly shut the door behind him. The rabbi's great frame seemed to fill the room—Lipa did not know what to do. He was frightened and excited all at once.

Ovadiah addressed him. "A few minutes ago you prayed to Hashem that Rabbi Ovadiah of Bartenura should come and teach you Mishnah, did you not?"

"Ye…yes."

"Then why are you so surprised that I am here? Why are you so frightened? Do you not think that G-d hears, *chas v'shalom*?"

Lipa stood wide-eyed, speechless and afraid. He could hardly believe it. For once in his life, he wanted something, and received it! It really happened—Hashem listened!

Lipa gathered his courage. He had to do something for his visitor. "Rabbi Ovadiah, it is so dark in here. Shall I turn on the lights? I will take out the Mishnah so we can study?"

The Shul Boy 31

Suddenly, it was Rabbi Ovadiah who grew anxious. He lifted his finger to his lips to silence Lipa. "No, no, you mustn't turn on any lights, *bambino*! No one must see me here! I am being pursued wherever I go, and I must make my escape while it is still night! And you, Lipa, you must come with me. You must help me, please!"

Lipa's fear turned to excitement—the great Rabbi Ovadiah wanted his help!?

"But, Rabbi Ovadiah, who is chasing you? Is it bad people who wish to harm you?"

Even as they spoke, Lipa's eyes adjusted and he could see the great rabbi's handsome face clearly. He *looked* like a great sage, so impressive was his demeanor. Rabbi Ovadiah shook his head and a slightly amused smile lit his face. He gestured for Lipa to come close so he could speak in a whisper.

"No, Lipa, it is not bad people—it is...it is the good Jews of Palermo! They're pursuing me!"

Lipa face furrowed in confusion. "*Palermo*? *Palermo*? Rabbi Ovadiah, what is Palermo?!"

Rabbi Ovadiah leaned down and whispered. "Lipa, you asked to learn with me—and now you have caused yourself to enter my world. We are in the beautiful city of Palermo, in Sicily—"

"Sicily?"

"Yes, Sicily, by the great Mediterranean Sea! The city of Palermo is full of wonderful Jews, and they won't let me leave them! They won't allow me to go down to the port and find a boat!"

"A boat? Why do you need a boat, Rabbi Ovadiah?"

"Listen, Lipa! I am on my way to go to Eretz Yisrael. I set out from Rome, and I found a French vessel that could only bring me this far—to Palermo. I meant to stay here just for a few days until I found another vessel to bring me to Yaffo. But—" Rabbi Ovadiah sighed, a warm sigh, with just a touch of regret. "The Jews here—they are wonderful! They follow my every footstep. They beg me to speak on Shabbos, to learn with them, to teach their children…" He leaned down and whispered in Lipa's ear. "Lipa, they worship me! They beg me for a piece of my clothing for a keepsake. The women fight for the privilege of washing my clothing. But now, when I want to continue my journey to the Holy Land, they do everything to stop me. They will not let me know when a boat is heading for Egypt, so I can travel by camel to Yerushalayim. So now, I must slip by them—in the darkness."

Lipa was overcome—no one ever worshipped him like that, not even the tiniest bit. "So…why do you not stay here in Palermo, Rabbi Ovadiah, where everyone likes you?"

Rabbi Ovadiah's head fell back as though Lipa had struck him. Rabbi Ovadiah lifted his mantle from over his chest and pointed to his heart. Lipa looked—but there was nothing to see.

"Do you not see, *bambino*?"

Lipa shook his head, not knowing what to say.

"Don't you see, my child? My heart is not here—my heart is in Yerushalayim! That is where I belong—nowhere else! I have left my family, my fortune, my home—all for the Holy City. And now, tonight, I have made my escape! Will you come with me, *bambino*?"

"Rabbi Ovadiah," Lipa said boldly. "I so much want to study Mishnah with you! Where you will go, I will go!"

Rabbi Ovadiah beckoned silently to Lipa. Lipa quickly followed Rabbi Ovadiah's footsteps though the darkened doorway, entering a new, strange world filled with colorful spectacle and wonderful adventure—but lurking at his feet, terrible danger…

2 Palermo, Italy
Tammuz 5247 (1487)

Immediately, Lipa was thrust into the fragrant darkness of the Sicilian night. A glittering half moon cast silvery shadows amid the narrow lanes, while high above, a jewel box of twinkling stars shone brilliantly.

"Hurry," whispered Rabbi Ovadiah. "I see the first glimmer of light above the hills. Soon the city will be awake. We must move quickly."

They walked swiftly but cautiously, heading down steep, perilous lanes to the port below.

"Where are we going, Rabbi Ovadiah?" Lipa asked. Even as they ran, he saw that Rabbi Ovadiah pressed his hand to his cloak, clasping his chest.

"A boat, a boat, *bambino*," Ovadiah hissed. "We must find a boat that will take us to Yerushalayim."

Lipa flushed with excitement—did that mean that he, too, would reach Yerushalayim? The cloudless dawn spread quickly over the tall, rocky hills surrounding Palermo, and across the azure bay. Ovadiah took one last glance to see if he was being pursued by his adoring followers. He smiled wryly—they thought he was still in his lodging.

They reached the port, already bustling with rowdy crews, fishermen and sailors, merchants, and soldiers preparing to sail off to battle. The dock was ablaze with scores of colorful boats, smaller dinghies setting out to fish the rich Mediterranean waters, large boats ready to cross the sea to Africa, to Egypt, even to India. Lipa's eyes widened with wonder at the noisy, colorful spectacle, with sailors shouting to each other in a babbel of strange tongues. Their cloths were like a painter's palette, a rainbow of reds and greens, blues and yellows, and every color imaginable; their garments rough cut and sturdy. Ovadiah walked carefully along the docks, looking unsure. His rich, patrician attire made him stand out among the roughly dressed crews, and they occasionally glanced up at him curiously, but not for long.

Ovadiah slowed his step almost to a halt. "What are we looking for, Rabbi Ovadiah?" asked Lipa.

"We need, *bambino*...we need a ship that will take us to Eretz Yisrael, either Eretz Yisrael or somewhere close, like Alexandria. But we have to be cautious we are among strangers."

"*Pardone, pardone, Maestro Rabbino!*" It was the voice of a young boy, calling out to them.

Ovadiah halted, and closed his eyes in dismay. Had he been discovered, even at this last moment? They turned. A boy, not much older than Lipa, was running toward them, a big smile on his face. He wore no cap and had no side curls, and Ovadiah sighed in relief—he was not of the Palermo Jews.

The boy, short and stockily built, with apple red cheeks, was totally self-assured, approaching the two like an old comrade. He glanced briefly at Lipa, and then bowed respectfully to Ovadiah.

"*Bon journo, Maestro Rabbino*! I am Gustavi, and I am at your service. May I be of help to you?"

Ovadiah smiled at the boy's boldness. "And who told you that I am a *Rabbino*?" he asked.

"Oh, I have seen you! I have heard about you! My friends are very Jewish, and they tell me what a great man you are!"

Ovadiah laughed at his words. "I am no great man. I am a simple Jew, who wishes—"

"Who wishes to be a pilgrim to the holy places of Jerusalem!"

Ovadiah stared in amazement. "Who told you all this, Gustavi?"

The boy smiled triumphantly, lifting his finger for emphasis. "I am Gustavi, and Gustavi makes it his business to know everything in Palermo. When I saw you walking here by the ships, I knew that you are making ready to escape the Jews who worship you! And I am just the one to help you, *Rabbino*!"

Ovadiah stared skeptically at Gustavi, studying him, his demeanor sober. "So, Maestro Gustavi, how can you help us?"

Gustavi lifted his head defiantly and poked his chest with his thumb. "Because, this morning I am to set sail on a ship heading toward the Holy Land, just as you wish. I am going to be the captain's boy, help him run the ship! If the *Rabbino* is interested, I can bring you to my captain—perhaps he will take you aboard as a passenger. You will be the only passenger."

Ovadiah gestured to Lipa. "This lad must also come. He is my student."

Gustavi glanced at Lipa, an impatient frown darkening his ruddy face. "Well, if he is your student, I guess he must also come. I shall lead you to our ship!"

Gustavi led them quickly along the docks, passing boats and ships of all sizes and nationalities. Palermo was the hub of the Mediterranean, and ships anchored from every land. They came to the edge of a long stone jetty, alongside which was anchored a large Galleon, its great striped red and black sails unfurled to the wind, ready to lift anchor and sail off to sea.

"Hurry," urged Gustavi. "We are leaving at the second hour—I see the last barrels being hoisted up. Wait here!"

He burst away and ran up the steep gangplank like a sprite. Ovadiah laughed to himself. Here he had been wondering what he would find to take him east, and Hashem had sent him this lad to lead them. It was almost too easy.

"What are you thinking, Rabbi Ovadiah?" Lipa asked.

Ovadiah fell silent for a moment, and then answered: "Lipa, our rabbis teach: *Kabdeihu v'chashdeihu*—When you meet a stranger, be polite but be wary. This Gustavi, he is almost *too* nice."

"So, shall we look for another boat?" asked Lipa.

"Who knows if we will find one, little Lipa, and if it will be better than this? We must put our faith in *Hakadosh Baruch Hu*, and let things unfold. Who knows, maybe this Gustavi was sent like an angel!"

Just at the word angel, Gustavi appeared high at the side of the deck, gesturing to them: "*Veni, veni, Rabbino…*" he cried out. "The captain invites you to come up on the ship."

"*Baruch Hashem*," Ovadiah murmured, and turning to Lipa, he called out, "Come, Lipa, adventure awaits us!"

A narrow, wooden gangplank led steeply up to the deck of the ship. The gangplank shook to their step, and far below the green sea undulated dizzyingly. Lipa immediately felt sick, barely managing to reach the deck without heaving over.

The captain stood at the entrance to meet them. He was a powerful, broad-shouldered man, his face tanned leathery brown from the sun. He stood stiffly, his muscular arms folded tightly, and gave Ovadiah a bare nod of welcome.

"*Bon journo*," Rabbi Ovadiah greeted him respectfully.

"*Bon journo*," he answered curtly. "My name is Captain Antonio Vincente. Gustavi tells me you are a rabbi."

"At your service, my captain. I am a lowly pilgrim seeking to visit our holy places in Jerusalem."

The Shul Boy 37

"Who is the boy?"

"My student."

The captain was direct. "I understand you need passage east to the Holy Land, to Palestine. I am not going to Palestine. We sail only as far as the island of Rhodes."

The captain saw the disappointment on Ovadiah's face.

"Look, *Maestro Rabbino*," he said bluntly, "you will not find a ship sailing directly from the coast of Palermo to the Holy Land. It is too dangerous; the waters are full of privateers. But in Rhodes you can find ships that will bring you to Alexandria, in Egypt, which is but a few days' sail. From there, you will find a caravan to Jerusalem. That is the only way."

Ovadiah stood perplexed, unsure what to do.

The captain grew impatient. "Listen, *Maestro Rabbino*, I do not carry passengers. We carry cargo. But I wish to do you a favor, if it is worth my while. You must decide now. We have one small cabin, where we sometimes carry royal messengers. It is small, with barely room for one berth."

"But the boy?"

The captain glanced at Lipa disdainfully. Lipa was an afterthought, like human baggage. "He will sleep below in the hold, with the crew. I will find him a berth near Gustavi."

Lipa did not like the sound of that, but did not say anything.

"And the price?"

"Fifty gold ducats. Paid now."

Ovadiah's cheeks colored with anger. "Fifty ducats! That is an exorbitant sum, Captain."

Captain Vincente shrugged impassively, like it did not matter to him. "*Maestro Rabbino*, I told you. I am not in the passenger business. I am doing you a service, as you are a man of G-d." He pointed at Lipa. "And there is the boy. I will have to squeeze him below among the crew—they won't be pleased to have a Jew among them." The captain's face broke into a wry smile. "Besides, from the look of you, and from what Gustavi tells me, I believe you can well afford it. Do not the Palermo Jews adore you? They must have rewarded you handsomely." His face turned hard. "Our ship must leave shortly—what is your decision?"

Ovadiah was perplexed. He had no time to think. He needed to escape Palermo, and the boat was heading ever closer to Eretz Yisrael. He looked at Lipa as though seeking an answer, but Lipa stood there, tongue-tied and helpless. Ovadiah dropped his head into his hand, thinking hard and murmuring a silent prayer. He raised his head and nodded agreement—he had no choice.

"May the Al-mighty guide me on the voyage," he murmured. "I shall pay."

Captain Vincente grunted with satisfaction, having squeezed gold out of Ovadiah like the most seasoned highwayman. The ducats passed hands, and the deal was done.

Ovadiah turned to Lipa, almost embarrassed for what he had done. He tried to smile. "Whatever it cost, Lipa—we are sailing toward Yerushalayim!"

The warm orange sun rose over the waters, the ship raised anchor and set sail. Slowly, the coast of Sicily disappeared, and the ship headed into the blue green waters of the Mediterranean. Lipa stood alongside Rabbi Ovadiah, the intense heat bearing down on them. Ovadiah seemed deep in thought, his head resting on his hand across the railing. Lipa thought that Ovadiah would rejoice that he had left Palermo and was heading toward his beloved Eretz Yisrael, but he seemed apprehensive and lonely.

"Rabbi Ovadiah, you look sad," he said.

Ovadiah stirred himself and looked down at Lipa. "I am joyous that we are heading for the island of Rhodes," he said. "There are

Jews there who will help us. But *libi omer li*... My heart tells me that we are not safe here upon this ship." Ovadiah turned and watched the sailors, Greeks, Spanish, Italians, Germans, go about their work, fixing sails, securing cargo, climbing dizzying heights to the crow's nest. "We are the only Jews on board, and if they turn upon us, who will protect us except Hashem." Even as he spoke, Rabbi Ovadiah clutched his hand to his chest, as though he was guarding something, or perhaps his heart pained him.

"*Maestro Rabbino!*" Ovadiah almost leaped in shock. As stealthy as a cat, Gustavi appeared behind them, greeting Rabbi Ovadiah heartily. How long had he been there, and what had he heard? He showed no hint, but beamed his boyish smile at Ovadiah.

"Captain Vincente has sent me to show you your cabin. *Scusa*, we were very busy up until now securing the ship. But we are sailing well, aren't we? Look how the wind is caught in the sails, like the ship has wings!"

Gustavi's smile was infectious. Ovadiah bestirred himself and smiled. "Show me the cabin," he said. They marched across the deck to the aft of the boat, where a door led to the captain's quarters and the mizzen deck above. They walked down a few steps and Gustavi opened a narrow side door.

"*Entra, Maestro Rabbino,*" Gustavi said grandly. Ovadiah and Lipa squeezed their way inside. It was not so much a cabin as a large closet, with the bunk taking up half the space. There was a narrow porthole, but sufficient to flood the room with sunlight. The cabin was very warm. Gustavi smiled as though he had shown Rabbi Ovadiah a grand stateroom.

Ovadiah studied his new quarters with some dismay. He took a deep breath. "In Palermo, my quarters were twenty times this size, and at home even grander. But this tiny cabin will help me reach Jerusalem, so it is more precious to me than all of Rome and

Palermo. He lifted his hands: "*Baruch Hashem*! *Baruch Hashem*!"

He backed out of the cabin into the passage. "But what about my student? Where are his quarters?"

Gustavi glanced at Lipa, taking his measure. Although Gustavi was not much older than Lipa, he was stocky and broad, much more muscular than the slim Lipa. "He will sleep in a berth next to mine." He gestured to Lipa. "Come, I will show you."

Leaving Rabbi Ovadiah to his tiny cabin, Gustavi led Lipa back to the main deck until they reached a door that lay flat against the deck. He lifted the hatch, and Lipa peered hesitantly into the darkness below.

"Come." Gustavi looked up impatiently. "*Bambino*, what do they call you?"

"My name is Lipa."

Gustavi made a face. "Lipa? What kind of name is that?"

"What kind of name is Gustavi?" Lipa answered quickly.

Gustavi glared at Lipa for an instant, and then nodded, pleased at his sharp retort. "*Veni*," he ordered. "Now we go down to the hold."

A narrow wooden ladder led down to the gloom below. At first Lipa saw nothing in the darkness, but his eyes quickly adjusted and he peered around. The heat was intense, and the only light and air seeping into the hold came from small open portholes that lined the walls. It was a large chamber in the bowels of the ship, and rows of hammocks hung from the ceiling beams. As Lipa's eyes adjusted, he realized that some of the hammocks were filled with snoring sailors who had finished the earlier shift. The deep sound of their breathing sounded like wood being sawed. The mid-morning heat, the reek of the varnished hull, and the ripe smell of the sleeping mariners made Lipa feel ill. He wanted to run back atop deck, but Gustavi led him to the corner of the hold where two hammocks hung side by side, apart from the rest. A porthole opened right above the wall hammock, and a stream of sea air flowed above it.

"You see, I saved the best two hammocks for you and me," said Gustavi grandly. Suddenly, Lipa heard the sound of a bird chirping. He turned, and a little pigeon stood at the window, peering in.

"Where did he come from?" asked Lipa, amused.

Gustavi smiled. He stretched out his hand, and the little blue feathered bird flew onto his arm. Gustavi took him into his hands. "Oh, he is my companion, Maestro Blue Bird. Wherever I sail, he comes along."

Suddenly, the bird fluttered its wings and hopped straight onto Lipa's shoulder. Gustavi laughed in surprise. "Look, Hebrew *bambino*," he exclaimed, "he likes you better than me—already!"

Lipa stood at the ship's railing, gazing out over the glassy sea. The orange sun beat down fiercely, and only the canvas covering that stretched overhead kept Lipa from being overcome. Even the veteran sailors, used to the heat of the sun, had run for cover, and the deck was still. The sails barely billowed, and the air was listless and heavy. The ship tossed like in a dream, and the sky and the sea molded into bluish emerald canvas. For a day or two, Lipa could not eat; the endless rolling of the ship, the intense heat, the airless, heavy stink of his sleeping quarters, made him sick. But slowly he grew accustomed to the undulating waves that fell hypnotically and the sight of splendid giant albatrosses soaring overhead, and the realization that he was here, aboard ship with the famous Rabbi Ovadiah of Bartenura, gave him new strength.

Nothing was as he had expected. Why had Rabbi Ovadiah needed him to come on this voyage? He barely saw him on the ship. He thought the moment Rabbi Ovadiah settled in his cabin he would summon him and begin teaching him Mishnah. In fact, soon after they had departed he had implored Rabbi Ovadiah. "*Teach me… Teach me…*" But Ovadiah just looked at him with a far-away gaze.

"It is not time yet, my *bambino* Lipa. There will be a time when they will signal me from *Shamayim*—and then I will teach you."

Lipa learned that people were strange. His bunkmate Gustavi was really two Gustavis. When he was on deck, he went about his duties red-faced and cheery, climbing up the ropes to the crow's nest, or clambering fearlessly across yardarms to hoist sail, straddling the cross beam with his strong bare legs, indifferent to the sea passing far below. He tossed Lipa an occasional wave, and called for Lipa to climb the riggings behind him. But Lipa grew dizzy just looking straight up to the top of the mast, and the clouds skirting above. But as soon as Gustavi climbed into the hammock next to Lipa, he became sullen and distant, and watched Lipa suspiciously.

Captain Antonio Vincente was also a strange one, standing atop the mizzen deck watching his sailors, his face set like a mask. Since he had taken them on board and accepted Rabbi Ovadiah's money, he went out of his way to keep his distance, as though he were afraid of Ovadiah, as though he did not want to speak to a Jew. And yet, sometimes when Lipa turned suddenly from his place at the rail and he looked up, he saw that the captain was staring at him. The minute the captain saw that Lipa had noticed him, he looked away.

Rabbi Ovadiah rarely appeared on deck. A few times, Lipa visited him in his cabin, knocking politely and slipping into the small room. The room was like an oven, despite the open porthole. Rabbi Ovadiah did not seem to take heed of the heat. He had made himself a small corner near the bed where he sat immersed, his lips murmuring Torah. From time to time, he clasped his chest, as though he were in pain, but his face did not show any discomfort. He nodded to Lipa, acknowledging his presence with a little smile, but spoke little. He gestured with his eyes toward the deck, signaling to Lipa that he would join him later.

Rabbi Ovadiah had changed from when Lipa had first met him. Then he was friendly and cheerful, smiling a great deal. Now, upon this ship bearing them toward Yerushalayim, he had become quiet, even melancholy. In the late afternoon, when the heat bore down unbearably upon the ship, and the sails hung limply in the becalmed wind, Ovadiah stood next to Lipa and gazed out over the endless sea. He said little, but there was sadness in his face. Lipa looked up at the great teacher, the famous Rabbi Ovadiah of Bartenura, and placed his small hand over his, awakening him from his reverie.

"Rabbi Ovadiah," he asked, "why are you so sad? Here we are on a ship that is bringing us to Eretz Yisrael, to Jerusalem. I thought you would be happy, but you look sad."

Rabbi Ovadiah placed his other hand over Lipa's, so that his small hand was sandwiched in his. They were soft hands, the hands of a *talmid chacham* who labored with his soul, with his brains, not with his hands. Rabbi Ovadiah looked down at him.

"You ask good questions, *bambino*. We are sailing toward the place of my heart, and I am joyous. But look around—do you not see the sailors of the ship? Do you not know they are watching us every moment? They are envious of us, of me. Who knows what they plan, even on this ship? That is why I stay in my cabin, to be out of their gaze."

"What about Captain Vincente? Are you afraid of him also?"

"Who knows? Perhaps he is honest, but a person who craves money like he does—who can tell?" Even as Ovadiah spoke, he clutched his chest protectively.

Lipa's question had opened a door in Ovadiah's heart. Suddenly, he lifted his hand and waved it over the sea, like he was trying to make it disappear. He looked down at Lipa.

"Lipa, Lipa, Lipa," he sighed, "what is going to be with you? What is going to be with all the young boys and girls, and all the beautiful Jewish families who live near this great sea they call the Mediterranean? Now we live in comfort, in luxury, in Spain and Portugal and Italy. We have great wealth, we have comfort, we have honor. We are blessed with many *talmidei chachamim*. But the eyes of our enemies are upon us—just like on this ship, envious eyes. I see a storm coming, like terrible dark storm clouds coming up from the sea in a sudden! I see our enemies rising up and driving us out of our homes, driving us out of Spain, out of Portugal, wherever the hand of the Church touches, not letting us live as Jews, not studying our holy Torah. No one sees it—but I see it! That is why I sail now to Jerusalem, our true home—fleeing there before we are driven out of our homes in lands that are not ours! But even—"

Ovadiah wanted to continue, but just then Captain Vincente approached within hearing distance. Ovadiah greeted him politely.

"Good evening, Captain Vincente," Ovadiah greeted.

The captain grunted a response. He stood alongside Ovadiah, frowning. "The weather is just terrible. We are caught in a doldrums, the worse I have encountered in all my years! *Rabbino*, you have brought us bad luck! I should have never taken you on board! The men are not happy with you on ship—and with this Jewish boy sleeping down in the hold with them. I may have to find him a place on deck, or even keep him in your cabin."

Ovadiah grew ashen at the captain's cross words. "I am sorry, Captain Vincente, truly sorry. I shall pray for favorable winds for the ship."

"Your 'sorry' doesn't help us, *Rabbino*," he answered harshly. "As for your prayers—pray for yourself."

Without a further word, Captain Vincente strode off, leaving Ovadiah deeply uneasy.

That brief encounter was a turning point in their voyage. Captain Antonio Vincente had drawn away the veil of cold politeness that he had shown until then. Perhaps the other sailors had overheard his comments, or just sensed their captain's feelings, for now they looked upon Ovadiah and Lipa with undisguised repugnance. They spoke the tongue of many nations, Italians, Greeks, Spanish, Arabs, Turks; they often quarreled with each other, but they shared their dislike for the only two Jews aboard. Ovadiah spent even more time in his cabin, only exiting in the late afternoon when the heat became unbearable. But Lipa had no place to hide. He could not stay below in the dark hold with the sailors who slept below at all hours, he could not stay in Rabbi Ovadiah's tiny cabin, barely enough for one. So he stayed atop deck, trying to stay out of the way, watching the sailors go about their duties, washing the deck, securing the cargo, climbing the rigging to haul up sail, trying to catch whatever wind they could. The best climber was little Gustavi. He climbed up the ladders like a monkey, fearless of the heights, clambering into the crow's nest above the tallest mast, straddling the yardarms that held up the sails. He was the favorite of the sailors, their mascot, the captain's favorite. But the bolder Gustavi became, the more he began tormenting Lipa.

"Hey, Jewish *bambino*, come, I am climbing up to the mizzen sail. It is not so high. Come, climb up with me!"

Lipa, who grew dizzy from the sea below, and the heights above, declined. But Gustavi did not relent. Seeing Lipa's fright at climbing, he tormented him even further.

"Come, I'm going up to the crow's nest, right above the whole ship. You can see for miles—you might even see Jerusalem. Come on, climb up with me!"

Lipa shook his head.

"Are you afraid? Don't be a coward! Be brave like me—aren't we the same age? Come, Lipa!" Again Lipa refused, pulling away angrily when Gustavi tried to grab him by the arm. The sailors watched the scene of Gustavi taunting Lipa, and drew great amusement.

Lipa was miserable. *Why did Rabbi Ovadiah bring me on this journey?* he wondered.

Baruch Hashem, Rabbi Ovadiah's prayers bore fruit. A few days after the sharp encounter with Captain Vincente, a strong north wind blew down from the European mountains, sending the ship hurtling forward. It was almost too powerful, causing the ship to roll endlessly in the rising and falling waves, making Lipa queasy stomached. He hung over the railing, his face pale, trying to breathe in draughts of evening air. The condition aboard the deck was still unfriendly, but Lipa's mood brightened as they sped toward their destination. Soon they would escape the hostility that surrounded them on every side. Rabbi Ovadiah had promised that he would begin teaching Lipa Mishnah before the ship landed. The queasiness of his stomach began to settle, and a glimmer of hope lit his child's soul. Here he was—Lipa, sailing to Jerusalem with Rabbi Ovadiah of Bartenura! Just as Lipa was losing himself in pleasant reveries, Gustavi suddenly appeared next to him against the railing, an eager glint in his eye.

"Hey," he greeted him with unusual warmth. "*Come estu, bene?* Are you feeling good?"

Gustavi's unusually friendly greeting startled Lipa.

"Yes, *baruch Hashem*," he answered instinctively.

Gustavi snickered, mimicking Lipa's "*Baruch*" under his breath. "Well, *bambino*, hold on to that hat you always wear! You're going to see something that you never saw in Palermo or Rome or where you Hebrews come from!"

The Shul Boy 47

Lipa followed Gustavi's gaze to the upper deck above the captain's quarters. From somewhere, a boatswain's bell rang, summoning all the crew on deck. They climbed out sleepily from the hold and stood there waiting with the sailors on duty. Even the hardened sailors cowered. Suddenly, from below, a sailor appeared, hands bound behind him by cords. He was bare to the waist, his head thrown forward. Behind him strode an immensely tall sailor, blond hair shaven close to his skull, giving him an even more menacing, bear-like appearance. He had a huge barrel chest and arms that rippled with iron muscles. Lipa shuddered just looking at him. In his right hand, he held a huge whip, a cat-o'-nine-tails like a multi-headed serpent, with lashes knotted at each end. The huge man took his captive, and bound him against the bottom of the mast.

"What is happening?" asked Lipa in a whisper, very frightened.

Gustavi sneered excitedly. "That's what happens when you don't follow orders! He disobeyed the first mate's orders, and even cursed at the captain."

The huge man with the whip bent the sailor's head down, and with an enormous blow brought the whip down ferociously against his bare back. The sailor's back burst open in bright crimson strips, and blood flowed down his back. The sound of the lashes whistled though the vessel, mixed with the shrieks of the sailor being lashed. He was whipped again and again mercilessly, until his screaming stopped and he fell mercifully unconscious to the deck. Two other sailors ran to the victim's side, and threw a bucket of seawater over his open wounds, stopping the bleeding. His eyes fluttered open. The huge man beat his cat-o'-nines noisily against the railing, eying the crew as he did so. Then he collected it into his hands, wrapping it around almost lovingly. He addressed the ship's crew, a terrible look on his swarthy face.

"Let it be a warning to the rest of you—that's what's in store for disobeying commands!" he bellowed. He paused, and seemed to search the deck until his gaze fell on Lipa.

"And that goes for you, too, my fine voyager who does no work! I have a cat-o'-nines waiting just for you!"

Lipa's face turned white, and some of the crew watched Lipa slyly, a smirk on their faces.

Gustavi leaned close to Lipa. "Better be careful, Jewish *bambino*," he whispered. "Henzel has eyes to whip you, too!"

Three days, just three days to Rhodes—that was what Captain Vincente had told Rabbi Ovadiah. The ship made good progress, but the closer they reached to their destination, the greater unease Lipa felt. He felt like a pigeon in a cage, and the closer he came to escaping, the more he noticed the furtive glances of the crew, always sly, always bitter. The ship felt like it had a heavy, dark cloud hanging over it. Rabbi Ovadiah had not left his cabin once since the day before, and now Lipa stood at the railing, peering listlessly down upon the foamy waves breaking alongside. It was mid-morning, the sun ascended into the fiery, cobalt sky, when Rabbi Ovadiah appeared unexpectedly on deck. Rabbi Ovadiah never appeared on deck so early in the day. All eyes watched as the great rabbi, dressed in his regal wardrobe, strode to Lipa's side. He walked with his usual strange manner, arm clutched to his chest like he was in pain—or guarding something.

"Good morning, Rabbi Ovadiah," Lipa greeted him respectfully, standing straight. Ovadiah appeared very agitated.

"Lipa, dear Lipa, *boker tov*," Rabbi Ovadiah answered in a voice hardly above a whisper. "Listen, *bambino*, it is not safe to talk here! There are eyes all around us—even Captain Vincente is watching us from the deck."

"What is the matter, Rabbi Ovadiah?" Lipa asked, alarmed.

Ovadiah leaned close to Lipa, shielding his mouth. "I cannot talk here! I am going to return to my cabin. In a few minutes, follow me below."

Ovadiah strode back to the door leading to his cabin just below deck. Captain Vincente stood above on the poop deck directly over the door. Ovadiah bowed respectfully to the captain, but was met with a blank, steely nod. Lipa waited a few minutes, and then as unobtrusively as he could, followed Rabbi Ovadiah below.

"Close the door tight," Ovadiah ordered Lipa.

The cabin was terribly hot, but despite the heat, Ovadiah still wore his heavy vestments. He gestured for Lipa to sit close by him, so that his voice might not rise above a whisper. Rabbi Ovadiah appeared fearful that someone might be listening behind the door, or that the very ship walls had ears or that a little bird at the window might carry his words to the deck above.

Ovadiah spoke quickly. "Know, dear little Lipa, that it was Hashem Himself who sent you to me to share this journey. Do not think, *bambino*, that I am traveling to Jerusalem on some personal whim, or to fulfill some vow. I have a sacred purpose in going there, that will touch the hearts of all Israel for ages to come! For this purpose I abandoned my home, my wealth, my exalted position—all for this holy mission."

"What mission, Rabbi Ovadiah?" asked Lipa with grown-up seriousness. "Please, please tell me!"

Ovadiah gazed upon his young companion, saw his earnestness, and a small smile crossed his face. Lipa had raised his voice, and Ovadiah lifted a cautionary finger to quiet him, nodding at the door.

"In time, Lipa, in time! I promise, before we leave the ship in Rhodes, I will share with you my mission, just as I promised to teach you Mishnah. But listen, Lipa! I am in grave danger that my whole mission will fail—and only you can help me! Know, that I carry a precious parcel from my brothers to bring to Jerusalem— only with it will my mission succeed. Without it, my entire journey to Jerusalem will be wasted. Here, I will show you."

Ovadiah opened his ornate robe and lifted the shirt underneath, revealing his long, snowy white *arba kanfos*. Ovadiah gazed at the door anxiously one more time as though afraid that someone might burst in, and then lifted his *arba kanfos* garment. There, clipped on to his undershirt, was a leather pouch, about two handbreadths square. The pouch was stuffed very tightly, and now that it had been released from its bonds, bulged outward. Ovadiah reached down, painstakingly undid the pouch from his shirt, dressed, and displayed the pouch to Lipa.

"There are two precious articles I bear on this voyage. My *tallit* and *tefillin*, and this parcel. I know that the crew aboard will have no interest in the *tallit* and *tefillin*, but I was afraid that they might steal this leather packet—that is why I hid it under my garments. I tried to leave my cabin as little as possible, to keep it out of sight, even under my garments. But I have not succeeded. My great caution was my undoing. The crew watched me closely each time I walked outside, and grew suspicious that I was guarding something. They began following my every footstep above deck. Two days ago one of the sailors 'accidentally' tripped against me, falling against my chest. He was trying to feel if I was hiding something, and I am sure that he pressed against the parcel. Yesterday I did not leave my cabin once, to stay out of sight. I have been counting the days and hours until we will disembark in Rhodes and escape this crew. I do not trust Captain Vincente either—he watches me constantly, and I don't know why."

"He watches me, too—" murmured Lipa.

"Strange, strange man. Listen, *bambino*… Last night I finally went to bed. The moon shone through my small window. I prayed to Hashem that we should safely reach our destination of Rhodes, that we should eventually reach Jerusalem. But I was troubled, and my thoughts kept me awake. I lay there, my eyes open, when I heard someone prying at the door, undoing the latch from outside. It was child's play. I heard the latch lift, and from the corner of my eye, I saw two dark figures enter. *They are going to kill me*, I thought. In my heart I prayed to Hashem to guard me. They were in their stockinged feet, and made not a sound. They approached my bed. I knew what they were searching for. If I made a sound, they might kill me right there. I feigned that I was asleep. They approached my bed, and I felt a hand upon me, searching my cloak. I did the only thing I could do. I made myself appear like I was sleeping deeply, and rolled over toward the wall, embracing my packet in my arms. There was no way they could find it except by waking me, and they would have been discovered. That, *baruch Hashem*, they were afraid to do. I lay there, praying to Hashem in my head, guarding my precious parcel. I heard them arguing in whispers. Maybe they were deciding whether to murder me right there and then. But they were cowards. I heard more whispers, and then their footsteps retreated—and they were gone."

Rabbi Ovadiah grew silent. "I had wondered, little Lipa, why Hashem sent you to me from so far away, but now I understand. In less than three days—*just two more nights*—we shall end our journey. The sailors are onto me. I don't know if it was just two, or all of them. Lipa, you must help me conceal this packet, not for my sake, but for Klal Yisrael—"

"What do you wish me to do, Rabbi Ovadiah?"

"*Bambino*, you must hide this parcel under your clothes—tight as you can, mind you! No one must suspect. They are onto me, ready to pounce. I will take some rags, and stuff them under my robe, in place of the parcel, and pretend to guard it as before."

Ovadiah stared at Lipa earnestly. "Will you do that for me, *bambino*?"

Lipa nodded proudly. *Finally*! Finally—someone finally needed him, wanted him! He stood up, lifting his finger dramatically. "*Na'aseh v'nishma*!" he murmured. "I will do whatever Rabbi Ovadiah wants!"

Ovadiah smiled ruefully at Lipa's childlike eagerness. "Do not be so quick to answer, little Lipa. They may catch on to our ruse. You might even face danger."

"Hashem will protect me."

"Hashem will protect you. He will protect all of us, and all of Israel! All Israel depends on what is hidden in this packet. Here—"

Ovadiah handed the parcel to Lipa. Lipa lifted the bottom of his shirt, his dingy *arba kanfos*, and carefully squeezed the packet inside the waistband of his trousers. Ovadiah frowned with concern. Lipa grimaced in distress as he pressed down the bulging package against his skin. But once it was pressed down evenly, it became more bearable. Lipa covered himself and looked up at Rabbi Ovadiah triumphantly. He remembered at least one phrase from his learning:

"I shall be your *shomer chinam*, Rabbi Ovadiah," he announced proudly.

Ovadiah laughed. "May Hashem make you a *shomer sachar* by rewarding you to become a *talmid chacham*," he murmured.

Lipa was proud—he was finally helping Rabbi Ovadiah. After waiting a few minutes, he left Ovadiah's cabin and returned to his place on deck. The sailors went about their duties, and no one seemed to take notice of him. Even Gustavi seemed to be in a playful mood, and kept on challenging him to climb up the rigging with him. "It is easy, Lipa," he urged.

Lipa shook his head, but not so vigorously. He watched Gustavi climb up the ropes to the tallest yardarm and wave down. It did not seem so difficult. At that moment he refused Gustavi's offer, but wished he would ask him again. The air had cooled, the ship sailed out at a fast clip, the wind blew strongly against Lipa's face, almost blowing away his cap. It was only two days until they landed, and the mood on the ship seemed to lift. That night, Lipa retired to his bed early. Gustavi, who lay in the next hammock, even seemed more friendly than usual, the bad-tempered look gone.

"Good night, Gustavi," Lipa murmured sleepily.

"Good night, Hebrew *bambino*," Gustavi answered almost cordially. Lipa fell peacefully into a deep, dreamy sleep, with white clouds and blue sky, the white capped waves passing sweetly below. Above, the white sails swelled in the wind, and in the far distance he spied tall, green-covered mountains. He snored slightly, peacefully, unaware that Gustavi was watching him all the time, and signaling to the two sailors who stood in the shadows behind him.

Morning came, and Lipa was soon up on deck. This day was warmer, the hot morning sun blazing down. Still, the ship moved on at a steady pace, heading toward its destination of Rhodes. There were more crew on deck than usual. There was a great deal of work as they prepared to reach port the next day. Some cargo was already lashed up on deck for quick unloading—merchants were waiting on shore. In the great heat, the mood was not as jovial as yesterday, and the sailors sweated and complained loudly as they worked. There was special resentment toward Lipa, who stood there like a prince doing nothing, while they labored so hard. He felt increasingly uneasy—but there was no place to hide. He just tried to keep himself as unobtrusive as he could, glad, at least, that no one suspected what a precious article he had hidden on him.

Captain Vincente stood solemnly on the stern deck observing his men, but when Lipa looked up at him suddenly, he saw that he was watching him also, closely. *I'll be glad when I'm off this boat*, Lipa whispered to himself.

Suddenly, Gustavi appeared alongside. He seemed especially cheerful this morning, despite the heat. He was the pet of the ship, and besides running errands for the captain and some of the crew, or climbing the mast to fix the sails, he did not seem to have to work much.

He approached Lipa cheerily. "*Bon journo*, Lipa! I see you slept like a baby last night!"

"I am happy that the journey is soon ending," he answered. "Rabbi Ovadiah and I will find a boat for Jerusalem."

Gustavi smiled, but did not respond. He looked up at the sails fluttering above. "They're not catching enough wind," he remarked. "Come on, *bambino*! It is your last day on board. Come, let me show you how to climb the riggings."

"They rise up so high," Lipa answered. "Look, they are almost four stories tall!"

Gustavi reassured him. "Who says you have to climb to the top? When I started, I just climbed halfway. Come, I will go first, and you follow."

Lipa thought he saw crewmen watching him out of the corner of their eyes. He did not want to appear as a coward. He took a deep breath and nodded.

"*Bono*—follow me to the mainmast."

The mainmast stood in the center of the ship. It reached high into the sky, with two huge, white sails hanging from its yardarms. A series of cable ladders rose from on the deck, leading to the wide yardarms above.

"Come on, Lipa!" Gustavi yelled cheerily. Gustavi climbed the

The Shul Boy 55

riggings swiftly, like he was born to them. He reached hand over hand, slipping his feet into the rope footholds. Lipa followed uncertainly. His feet became tangled in the footholds, and he had trouble grasping the swinging rope ladder. He climbed slowly, but each step brought him higher. Gustavi, who was already just below the first yardarm, urged him. He waited for Lipa to reach him. Lipa drew upward, and Gustavi climbed even higher, and then again waited. Lipa had not planned to climb so far up. He looked down and saw the sea passing dizzyingly below him. His boyish excitement overcame his fear. Here he was, Lipa Wallerstein, scaling up the mast of a clipper ship, the wind in his face, the sea racing below, the sails billowing alongside, his companion Gustavi urging him ever higher! He was halfway up the rigging, just below the bottom yardarm, forty feet above the deck below.

Gustavi stood above the yardarm, holding on with one hand, one leg grasping a foothold, his other arm and leg dangling rakishly over the void, urging Lipa on. He was as carefree as a bird in a tree.

"Come on, Lipa, climb on to the yardarm—you'll help me fix the sails!"

There was a foot-wide gap between the rigging and the huge yardarm beam. Lipa reached forward, grasped the yardarm beam and mounted it like it were a horse, straddling it with both legs. He sat there, the wind whipping his face, the sail flapping noisily. He looked down and grew afraid—the deck was so far below. Gustavi came down from his perch, and straddled the yardarm behind him.

"Go on, Lipa," he yelled. "You're doing great! Move to the end of the yardarm so we can fix the sails."

Lipa looked down and was suddenly filled with panic. The green waves raced far below. He wanted to climb back down, but now Gustavi blocked his escape.

"Go on, *bambino*," Gustavi yelled into his ear. "Move down to the end of the yardarm!"

Lipa could not contain himself. "Gustavi, I can't do this. I'm afraid! I want to go back down!" He was almost in tears.

Gustavi moved closer to him. "Don't be afraid, Lipa. Look, I'll hold onto you."

He drew close to Lipa, shoulder to shoulder, and wrapped his arm around him, holding him. As he did, Lipa could feel Gustavi's hands feeling down his shirt, until it felt the pouch jammed into his clothes. He felt Gustavi run his hands rapidly over the bag, and then raise his hands to Lipa's shoulders. His voice changed suddenly. "So are you really afraid, Hebrew *bambino*?" he whispered mockingly.

Lipa was ashamed and confused—but above all, he was frightened at the great drop below.

"Yes," he yelled angrily. "Gustavi, I want to go back down!"

Gustavi was perfectly calm. "So, who stops you, Lipa? Go down if you are afraid—I shall climb back myself later. I'm not scared like you."

Gustavi pulled away so abruptly that Lipa almost slipped off the yardarm. Lipa slid backward toward the mast, until he could reach out toward the rigging. He looked down, and saw the crew watching him from below, laughing. Carefully, he climbed out of the yardarm, and began the long descent below.

It had all been a trap, Lipa realized. *Gustavi had me climb up the yardarm so he could search me!*

So now they knew he was carrying Ovadiah's treasure. What was next? Lipa leaned pensively against the railing, staring into the sea, feeling foolish. He dared not look around. Who was watching him now? Gustavi had descended from his high perch on the yardarm, and disappeared somewhere into the ship. Lipa did not want to see him—he was frightened of Gustavi. It was Gustavi

The Shul Boy ~ 57

who had lured them onto this ship, knowing that Ovadiah was wealthy, probably carrying gold. It was Gustavi who observed his every move, day and night. And now, it was Gustavi who had slyly lured him up the riggings, onto the yardarm, so that he could feel him. Lipa was naive, unworldly, a lamb among wolves, an innocent among hardened thieves. What should he do now? He was certain that they would come after him again, and grab Ovadiah's precious parcel from right under his clothing.

Lipa hoped that Rabbi Ovadiah would appear on deck just as he did each afternoon. He waited and waited—but Ovadiah did not appear. Perhaps he was playing decoy, trying to make the crew think he was still hiding the parcel under his clothing. He did not know that Lipa had been found out, parcel and all. Lipa must go and tell Ovadiah, ask him what to do. Lipa discreetly wandered toward the stern deck, entered below, and knocked quietly on Ovadiah's narrow entrance. There was no answer. Lipa knocked more firmly, but Ovadiah still did not come to the door.

"Rabbi Ovadiah, Rabbi Ovadiah," Lipa whispered desperately. No answer. Lipa had no choice. He opened the door a notch and peered inside. He was blown back by the heat. The cabin was like a furnace—how could Ovadiah stand it? But what Lipa saw startled him even more. Rabbi Ovadiah stood in a corner, facing toward Jerusalem. His face was fiery red, and sweat and tears rolled down his face like a stream. He clasped his hands tightly, swaying from side to side, his eyes clenched tightly, his lips moving in intense *tefillah*. No wonder Ovadiah did not hear or see him. Lipa saw that this great tzaddik was no longer on the ship, even in this world, but flown away into Heavenly worlds. Was this the Ovadiah who had taken him on this voyage? Ovadiah, always so calm, so courtly, so good-humored, so *Italian*—was really a flaming fire, consumed in Hashem. The furnace heat of the cabin came not from the hot sun, but from Ovadiah's *neshamah*.

Ashamed and frightened, Lipa quickly closed the door silently. He knew that Ovadiah was frightened for *him*, praying for *him*. What more could Rabbi Ovadiah do? His *tefillos* were more important than anything, and Lipa dared not disturb him again—unless Ovadiah summoned him.

Lipa's fright and confusion turned to resolve. He had to do something. He touched under his shirt, the precious parcel that Ovadiah had put into his hands. What could it be? Ovadiah said: *The future of Klal Yisrael depends on it*. And Lipa held it on himself! How long would it be before Gustavi and his companions fell on him and grabbed the parcel away? And there was nothing he could do to fight them. Even now, as he stood at the railing, he saw that he was being watched secretly. He must do something—anything to fight back. Then came a desperate plan… Lipa gazed out over the warm waters, yawned, and shook his head. He blinked wearily in the afternoon heat. He yawned once again, stretched tiredly, and made his way to the hold below to nap.

The heat and smell of the afternoon was intense. Some of the hammocks swayed with sleeping crewmen snoring loudly. Lipa looked around, and saw that everything was quiet—no one had followed him. The dark belly of the ship was divided into two holds; one for the crew to sleep, and deeper within, for cargo. A wooden barrier divided the sections. Lipa opened the narrow door and entered the crammed cargo hold. The air was so thick Lipa could hardly breathe. A horde of rats scurried away at the sound of his footsteps, squeaking loudly at his intrusion. Lipa squeezed his way through the stacks of wooden crates, bales of clothing, barrels of oil—headed for Rhodes. He knew that he and Rabbi Ovadiah would be long gone from the ship before the crew lifted the cargo at port. Lipa crawled deeper into the cargo hold, so crowded that it

The Shul Boy 59

was almost impossible to see. One large box had a yellow streak, conspicuous even in the deep gloom of the hold. It would be his beacon. He lifted his shirt and removed the parcel. Looking back one last nervous time to see that no one was stalking him, Lipa slipped the packet under a crevice of the box. Lipa stood up, took a deep breath and smiled, pleased with himself. They could gang up on him, they could search and press him skinny—but they would not find Ovadiah's packet!

Night descended quickly aboard ship. Most of the crew retired to their beds, exhausted from a day of working under the blazing sun. Only a handful of sailors were left on deck to keep watch for trouble. Lipa looked up at the glistening galaxy of stars above, brilliant planets and streaking meteors exploding through the heavens. What a beautiful world Hashem made! If people could just be kind and nice, honest and faithful!

Rabbi Ovadiah never came out of his cabin. Lipa knew for certain that the holy man was praying intensely, praying and learning that they could reach their destination safely. They were so close to escaping. He wanted to stay up on deck, in the cooler night air, not descend below to the dark hold where devious Gustavi slept in the very next hammock. Since climbing the riggings together with Lipa, Gustavi had disappeared, hiding. The nocturnal hours passed, the stars moved majestically in their great heavenly court, and sleepiness overtook Lipa. His eyes drooped, and he had to shake himself awake from falling down. He could not stand there any longer, nor could he sleep on the deck in front of the crew. No one was allowed to lie down on deck lest someone trip over him. He had no choice but to go to bed. He made his way to the hatch, and down the narrow stairs to the great, dark hold. Everything was quiet except for the snoring of the crew, like a gang of men, sawing wood. Good—everyone was fast asleep. He approached his hammock, and saw

Gustavi safely fast asleep, his eyes closed tight, his arms wrapped around himself like a baby. Only a few hours to dawn, and then they would be safe. Standing in the porthole was little Maestro Blue Bird, watching him solemnly like a monitor. Lipa smiled. For the first time, he felt at peace. He gazed around one more time at the room filled with sleeping men, climbed into his hammock, recited *Hamapil*, and fell into a deep, sweet sleep.

When did he know that he was being grabbed at? Lipa's eyes opened wide, and he realized that a group of men were running their hands over his body, searching for the packet. He wanted to cry out in alarm, but one of the men had his hand clamped tight over his mouth. He could do nothing. They held him tight. From the corner of his eye, he could see Gustavi standing behind them, directing everything like an overseer. The men lifted him up over the bed, so that every part of him was open to their searching hands. Over and over they felt, squeezing him painfully, pulling his shirt up, checking everywhere. Lipa was frightened but excited. *You won't find it!* thought Lipa clearly. *Do what you want, search as hard as you can—you won't find Rabbi Ovadiah's treasure!* They probed him over and over—but they could find nothing—because there was nothing there! One sailor led the search. He was tall and gaunt, raw boned and angry, with a foul odor. He grew angry.

He lifted his hand from Lipa's face and hissed angrily into his ear. "Where is it, Hebrew boy? What did you do with the bag?"

Lipa was too frightened to speak. He just shook his head, trying to see the man's face. Raw Bones squeezed his hand even tighter over Lipa's mouth. "Where is it!" he hissed. "You had it on you! What did you do with it? Where did you hide it?"

He lifted his hand. Lipa trembled in pain. "I don't have it! I don't know where it is. Please, leave me alone!"

"I'll leave you alone!" He squeezed Lipa's face with his long, bony fingers, so that Lipa's mouth squeezed into a doughnut. Lipa cried out silently in pain, but he shook his head stubbornly. He would not betray Rabbi Ovadiah—he would not betray Klal Yisrael, whatever he suffered.

"He wants to be a hero," muttered the other sailor, who they called Giovanni. "Let's just throw him overboard and be done with it."

"Fool, there's no profit if he's gone and we don't know what happened to the money!" hissed Raw Bones. "First he'll tell us, and then we will be rid of him!"

Gustavi placed his hand on Raw Bones' shoulder, drew him close and whispered in his ear. Raw Bones nodded, glanced at Lipa, and smiled in agreement. All this time, his long, spidery hand did not leave Lipa's mouth, squeezing his lips shut like a vise. All Lipa could do was look with wide eyes like it was happening to someone else. He was terrified, but he would not give in.

The sailor lifted his hand from Lipa's mouth and smirked cruelly.

"So you won't tell us, aye, *bambino*? You want to be a hero? We'll see what you'll look like when Henzel is finished with you! You'll talk then, my brave lad—you'll jabber like a monkey!"

He lifted Lipa out of his bed like a doll—despite his appearance, he was very strong. He released his hand from Lipa's mouth, but warned him with his finger not to utter a peep. Lipa was frozen in fear, but stubborn—*azuz d'kedushah*. He was very frightened of these men, especially his "good friend" Gustavi. But they still did not have Rabbi Ovadiah's bag. They didn't know where it was, and he would not tell them, no matter what. Klal Yisrael depended on it—and he was willing to endure whatever it took! They crept silently to the other side of the room where a huge hammock drooped heavily like a great haystack. They approached the bed, and Raw Bones tapped the sleeping man cautiously.

"Henzel! Henzel!" he hissed. "Wake up quick, we need you!"

The huge haystack shifted on its side. Henzel opened his eyes and blinked, angry to be woken in the darkness.

"Who's that?" he muttered, and then suddenly fully awake sat up violently like a volcano. "Giovanni, is that you? And you, Raw Bones? Even young Gustavi... *What do you all want?* Can't you see a man's trying to sleep?"

His eyes focused, and for the first time noticed Lipa trussed up in Raw Bones' arms like a chicken.

"Shh, Henzel," Giovanni hissed. "This Hebrew lad knows where a treasure is hidden on board—the rabbi brought it on with him. Remember? The crew is supposed to share in everything that the ship carries—that's what the captain promised. But the Jews held out on us—they didn't declare their goods! It's in a leather pouch somewhere on ship, and this lad won't tell us where it is!"

Henzel turned his heavy gaze at Lipa, and Lipa shook in fear. "Where is it?" he grunted angrily.

"I...I don't know," answered Lipa, his voice quavering.

"He knows," Gustavi insisted. "He knows... He had the money on him, I felt it! Now he's hiding it somewhere."

All the men glared at Lipa angrily, demanding the parcel. Lipa, despite his great fear, was steadfast. He stayed stubbornly silent, defiantly pursing his lips. The men were furious, but also impressed by his courage.

"Listen, Henzel," Giovanni whispered. "The boy is stubborn. Maybe he thinks he will get a better seat in heaven if he's quiet! He won't talk to you or me—but he will talk to your cat-o'-nine-tails, right quick."

The giant gazed hard at Lipa, and snorted. He reached deep into his bed, and retrieved a leather object—his coiled, black whip.

The Shul Boy

He held it in front of Lipa's face. "Do I have to use this on you, *bambino*?" he asked. He sounded almost reluctant.

Lipa looked at the whip fearfully, but remained silent.

"He doesn't know what it means," Giovanni snickered impatiently. "Don't waste time, Henzel—it's almost morning! We'll carry him on deck, and after one lash he will tell us everything!"

From behind Giovanni, Gustavi urged Henzel on. "Hurry, Henzel—it's almost morning. This is our last chance!"

The moon had set; the deck was pitch black and almost deserted. The few men on watch were either asleep, or knew enough to mind their own business with Henzel roaming about. A strong gust blew off the waters, and the sails snapped violently overhead. The thieves did not waste time. Raw Bones bore Lipa, bound firmly in his gaunt arms like a lamb to the slaughter, to the mainmast where he was set down behind the riggings.

Giovanni whispered into Lipa's ear. "This is your last chance, Hebrew *bambino*. You've played the hero well enough. Now tell us where the rabbi's parcel is."

Lipa looked up at his tormentor. "No," he uttered firmly. "No—never!"

"Whip him now!" urged Raw Bones, eager to watch Lipa being whipped.

Giovanni turned to Henzel. The huge man approached Lipa, who was held fast against the riggings. The cat-o'-nines lay furled in his fist, like a curled-up cat. He addressed Lipa.

"Laddie, you are a brave boy! I don't *want* to hurt you. If this cat-o'-nines touches your back, you'll bear its scars for the rest of your life—if you live to survive it. Bigger men than you have fallen under my lash, never to rise. Please don't make me hit you—just tell them what they need to know."

Despite his enormous size and ominous appearance, he spoke very gently. Lipa looked up and saw that this terrible brute had an inkling of softness in his eyes.

"I *can't* tell them, Henzel," he pleaded. "I gave my word."

Henzel's tone suddenly changed. "Then your blood is on your own head!" he growled.

He unfurled the long whip with its terrible knotted cat-o'-nines, raised his hand high over his head, and struck down with a thunderous crack that could be heard for miles over the sea—but on the ship's deck, not on Lipa. It was so powerful that even Giovanni fell back in fear.

Henzel waited for the echo of the crack to disappear, and then spoke to Lipa again.

"I gave you one last chance, *bambino*. You heard that crack—I almost cut the deck in splinters. The next one will be against your little back. It'll slice right through you! Where is the parcel?"

Lipa trembled, too frightened to speak. He managed to shake his head one last time. Henzel lifted his hand, the whip rose high in the air—Lipa closed his eyes.

"*Stop!*"

A voice called out from the stern of the ship. Everyone turned, even Lipa. Rabbi Ovadiah stood on deck.

"Don't strike the child!" he shouted. "Don't touch the child!"

Henzel lowered his hand, the whip dragging alongside him. Rabbi Ovadiah approached the men hurriedly.

"Why do you want to strike him—strike me!" Rabbi Ovadiah shouted angrily. "He was keeping his word to me."

After the first shock at seeing Rabbi Ovadiah, Giovanni regained his boldness. "So, will you take his place before the whip, *Rabbino*?" he shouted.

Ovadiah answered boldly. "Sailor, are you not ashamed? Did I

The Shul Boy 65

sign on to a pirates' ship that you wish to rob me of my most precious belongings?"

"You are robbing *us*," Giovanni answered angrily. "We have a compact with the captain that we get a share of all the valuables that are brought aboard—that includes what you brought on board! And you hid it from us."

Ovadiah laughed bitterly. So now he was the thief and they were the tzaddikim! He thought of Pharaoh. He thought of Bilaam. He thought of Haman. He thought of all the wicked who had good reasons why they were the righteous! Henzel began stirring with his whip again, slithering it across the deck like a serpent. There was utter silence on deck as everyone waited for the next move.

"Lipa, come here!" Rabbi Ovadiah called out. Lipa slipped out from under Raw Bones' hands and ran to Ovadiah, hiding under his cloak. Rabbi Ovadiah covered him with his sleeve, protecting him. Under Ovadiah's clasp, Lipa's face grew warm. It was the first time that anyone held him, cared for him.

Ovadiah turned to the gang. He spoke contemptuously.

"You thieves claim a share of my fortune, do you? Indeed—I will reveal it to you and the crew—but only before the captain! He can decide how to dispose of it!"

"The captain?" hissed Giovanni. "Why the captain? It is not his business."

"*It is my business!*"

Everyone looked up in astonishment. There, standing on the stern deck gazing down, was Captain Antonio Vincente. He, too, had been awoken by the thunderous crack of Henzel's whip. He stood silently, glaring, and walked solemnly down to the deck, approaching the group.

"Is it true, Rabbi," he asked, "that you have brought on board a parcel containing precious valuables?"

"Precious to me," Ovadiah answered.

"You should have told me."

"It is my own property which I am bringing to the Holy City."

"It is ours to share," Giovanni demanded.

The captain seemed dispirited, unhappy with what was transpiring on his ship. "Will you show me the parcel, *Rabbino*?" he asked. "Then I will know how it should be divided."

"If I can show it to you privately, Captain Vincente," Rabbi Ovadiah answered. "Then we will see how the matter falls."

The captain nodded. "So be it!" The captain addressed the men, who looked at him, swallowing their great anger.

"Leave these two Hebrews alone!" he ordered. He addressed Lipa who still hid under Ovadiah's cloak.

"*Bambino*, do you know where the parcel is?"

Lipa looked up from under the cloak at Ovadiah, questioningly. Ovadiah placed his hand on Lipa's soft brow. "Go, brave child—go and fetch the treasure. Hashem will protect us."

Lipa climbed down to the hold. The crew still slept soundly, snoring peacefully in the dark room. Lipa felt peculiar, unreal, like this was not really happening. He had put his life at risk, refusing to reveal where the precious parcel was, and now he was going down to bring it to the captain. Rabbi Ovadiah would not let him go alone, and Gustavi was sent to accompany him in the darkness, carrying a small ship's lantern. They crossed the room to the door leading to the cargo hold.

"It's in here," Lipa told Gustavi. He opened the door. "Come on," he urged.

Gustavi hesitated at the door. "It's inside," Lipa repeated, "come on!"

"I'm not going in," Gustavi said firmly. "There are rats crawling around there, and mice, and who knows what else."

The Shul Boy

Brave Gustavi! "Are you afraid?" asked Lipa disdainfully. "You, brave Gustavi?"

But Gustavi would not move. Lipa entered the black cargo hold alone. The rodents held sway in the heavy darkness, scampering and squeaking among the huge bales and wooden crates. Gustavi stood at the door, casting a faint glow from his lantern. Lipa made his way carefully among the bins, searching for the sign of the yellow streak. Even now he wished he could run from Gustavi, hide deep inside the hold behind some pile of boxes, so that no one could find him until the morning—and then run off with the precious parcel. But Rabbi Ovadiah had told him to retrieve it. He felt a soft body slither around his foot and run off. He hurried his steps, frightened. *There!* He spotted the yellow-streaked crate ahead. He ran over, reached down and groped for the bag hastily, hoping he wouldn't be bitten. He felt the leather-covered parcel that had slid further under the crate and pulled it out, standing up quickly.

"Have it!" he murmured to himself triumphantly—for a while he was afraid he would never find it in the dark. He retraced his footsteps back to the doorway, where Gustavi waited with his lantern, which now seemed so much brighter.

Gustavi spied the precious bag. "Let me hold it," he said to Lipa. But Lipa clasped it tightly—he would only surrender it to Rabbi Ovadiah. Lipa sealed the door behind him, and Gustavi turned to him.

"Hebrew *bambino*," Gustavi said, "you are braver than I thought."

"Gustavi," answered Lipa, "I think you *smell*!"

Before Gustavi could respond, Lipa ran off and dashed back up to the deck.

The captain's cabin was a large room at the stern of the ship, behind a narrow corridor and up four steps. Unlike Rabbi Ovadiah's tiny cabin and the crew's dank hold, there were airy portholes that allowed in fresh breezes. A large lamp hung from the ceiling over the captain's round table where various maps and documents were scattered. Through the windows, the first pale light of dawn streaked the sky.

The three entered the room, Captain Vincente, Rabbi Ovadiah, and Lipa, still holding the precious parcel. The captain closed the door behind them. The three stood silently, and the captain signaled for the packet. Lipa looked up to Rabbi Ovadiah for what to do next.

Rabbi Ovadiah gestured for Lipa to stay still. He turned to Captain Vincente solemnly:

"Know, Captain, that I carried this package all the way from Rome, a gift from my brothers. They were blessed by the Al-mighty, and this was their offering to Jerusalem, so I could serve the Al-mighty in peace. I did not bear its precious contents for glory, or wealth, or honor, but to serve the Al-mighty in the only way I can. I plead with you one last time—please leave it sealed."

"What is the value of the treasure inside?" asked Captain Vincente.

"In truth?" answered Ovadiah. "In truth, Captain, the treasure contained in this small leather bag is worth more than all the cargo you have on your great ship."

The captain remained silent, staring intensely at Rabbi Ovadiah. He glanced down at Lipa, still grasping his precious charge.

The captain shook his head, almost sadly. "It is too late, *Rabbino*," he answered. "Henzel is a terrible beast—even I fear him. No one recovers from his cat-o'-nines—certainly this poor lad would not have! He spared him because of my orders, and now I must keep my word to the crew and expose its contents."

He stretched out his hand to Lipa. "Let me have the bag now, *bambino*."

Lipa looked up at Rabbi Ovadiah, who nodded solemnly. "Give it to the captain, Lipa."

The captain took the leather parcel and studied its tight seal. There were two metal signets over its fold, and thick leather stitching that sealed the bag tight. He took a sharp blade from his desk, and still staring up at Rabbi Ovadiah, sliced the seals, and cut through the leather stitching. He grasped the bag by its closed mouth, and pulled it firmly open, forcing its contents upward.

The captain grasped the contents, lifted it clear of its leather container, and held it before him in his two hands. He looked at the contents, perplexed.

"What is this, a trick?" he asked angrily. "There is nothing here but—paper!"

"The finest paper," said Ovadiah calmly. "The finest paper that money can buy."

"But it is just paper!" the captain replied angrily, almost shouting. "Empty sheets that are worthless."

Rabbi Ovadiah laughed bitterly. "To you, they are worthless, Captain Vincente. For me they are the most valuable object that you can imagine, worth more than your ship, more than your cargo!"

"Are you mocking me?" demanded the captain angrily. "Is this some sort of a trick? Where is the real treasure that you have been hiding? You have switched it!"

Ovadiah shook his head. The more agitated Captain Vincente grew, the calmer and more resigned Ovadiah became. "I give my sacred word, Captain, that this is it, Captain! There is no other treasure, no gold, no jewels. I will explain, but you will not understand. I am bringing these fine sheets to Jerusalem, for there I plan to write a commentary on a holy book—a book we Jews call the Mishnah. It is the basis of our whole Law. I am writing the commentary so that future generations of my people will be able to study and understand this sacred book, the Mishnah. I myself stood there when the paper was prepared by pious workmen, and watched over it closely every step so that its very fibers be imbued with great holiness. I prayed that only Jewish hands would touch these sheets, but it now appears that G-d's will is otherwise."

There was silence, and then the strangest thing happened. Two tears welled up in Captain Vincente's eyes. He wiped them away quickly, ashamedly. He ran suddenly to the door and opened it quickly, making certain that no one was hiding behind the door listening. He closed the door, and locked it. He returned to Rabbi Ovadiah, and then, in a voice hardly above a whisper, said:

"*Rabbino—I am a Jew.*"

Ovadiah gazed at the captain in shock, unable to speak. The two men stared at each other, bound silent, made speechless by intense emotion. Lipa watched them, not comprehending how profound was this revelation.

Finally, Ovadiah found his voice. "I ask you, Captain Vincente—is it true what you are saying, or is this some joke that you are playing on me?"

Captain Vincente shook his head, and answered firmly: "*Rabbino*, you gave me your sacred word about the contents of this packet that it was mere paper, and I believed you—now you must believe me. Know, Rabbi Ovadiah, that you are the only one I have revealed this secret to for forty years—that I am a Jew! If my ship owners would know, if my crew would know—"

The captain drew a thumb across his neck.

"Then why are you telling me now?" asked Ovadiah.

"I don't know," answered the captain. "But when you told me that you wanted only Jewish hands to touch these holy papers, and I was the one who held them in my hands—I knew that G-d wanted me to reveal who I am to you!" He glanced down at Lipa. "And

The Shul Boy ᛜ 71

especially in front of this brave *bambino* here—*he* is the real reason that I could not conceal myself from you any longer."

Rabbi Ovadiah glanced down at Lipa, and then up to Captain Vincente.

"The boy, Lipa? Because of him you needed to reveal yourself?"

"I watched this *bambino* with his Jewish cap and little strings peeping out of his shirt, and I saw myself just like him, when I was a young boy. But I was all by myself—I had no one to watch over me. No one cared about me, what I did, or where I went, not my father, not my mother, no one! I saw other Hebrew boys my age, children of wealthy merchants, dressed grandly, so proud, and so loved. And I was a castoff, deserted by the other, rich boys. So I escaped—"

"Escaped? Where?"

"I escaped everything! I escaped my home, my family, and my faith. I ran off to sea, to be a sailor. There I was wanted and I was able—I was willing to work hard, and I was honest. I went from rank to rank until I became captain of my own ship. And so all these years at sea, I hid everything—even my name. I took my new name from the first ship I sailed. It was called '*Vincente*—Victory'— because I triumphed over all those who had cast me away."

"But now, after all these years, you decided to reveal yourself— that you are a Jew."

"I did it because I know that you are a truly righteous man. And I did it, because of this child—he is the good Hebrew lad that I could have been."

Lipa flushed at the captain's words. He felt such pity for him. The same loneliness that he knew, the captain had also endured.

Rabbi Ovadiah's face turned from shock to sadness to resolve. "Captain, tell me, what was your Hebrew name—do you still remember?"

"Of course I remember," answered the captain, bristling. "They called me Gershon."

"Gershon, Gershon," said Ovadiah. "It is still not too late! G-d sent me aboard this ship; it was no accident. Little Gustavi was His angel! We had to suffer all these travails so that you finally revealed yourself. Do you know who you revealed yourself to?"

"To you, Rabbi. To you and the precious *bambino*."

"No, Gershon! You revealed yourself to *yourself*! You could not hide any longer from the holy *neshamah* that is in you, pining to be revealed. My sheets of paper meant to write the Mishnah awoke the sparks in your *neshamah*—for they are the same letters… Listen, Gershon! Your ship docks today in Rhodes, in just a few hours. I know a pious scholar, a tzaddik, who resides there. He will be so happy to welcome you! You've brought the ship to safe port. Leave it, leave the ship and these low men—and become a Jew again!"

The captain shook his head. "It is too late, *Rabbino*—too many years and too many sins. I dug a pit for myself that I can never climb out of."

"It is never too late, Gershon!" Rabbi Ovadiah insisted. "Wherever you were, however far you fell, the Al-mighty was there, waiting for you to come back."

Captain Vincente shook his head fiercely. "I sinned in so many ways, *Rabbino*. I sinned with my body."

"*Hashem was there—waiting.*"

"I ate foods that no Jew would eat."

"*Hashem was there—waiting.*"

"I did things, I said things, I went places—places and things and terrible things that no Jew could ever imagine."

"And each time you sinned, the Al-mighty was there—waiting for you to return. It is called *teshuvah*. The power of *teshuvah*—to transform your angry, wild deeds into sparks of holiness. Come with me, Captain Vincente! Come with me, Reb Gershon, to a new beginning! The rest of your life awaits you! The whole Soul of Israel is waiting for you! *Veni*, Vincente! Victory is in your grasp!"

But Captain Vincente shook his head firmly. He began making ready to rejoin his crew. "*Rabbino*, I have great respect for you, but it is something I cannot do. I cannot change now. Perhaps I am a coward, but Captain Vincente will stay who he is and who he will always be."

There was absolute silence. Rabbi Ovadiah gazed upon the captain sadly, and sadness also crept over the captain's face.

Suddenly, little Lipa broke the silence.

"Captain Vincente—*shame on you!*" he said in a firm whisper, just barely loud enough to be heard. "If I, Lipa Wallerstein, was ready to feel the lashes of Henzel's whip—can you not have the courage to change? I was a castoff just as you were—but I was not afraid! Don't be afraid, Captain Vincente! G-d will protect you like He protected me!"

Lipa folded his arms grandly—like *he* was the captain. Captain Vincente stared at Lipa, a tiny smile lighting his face.

"Come here, *bambino*," he ordered. Lipa approached the captain who bent down and planted a kiss atop Lipa's cap.

"Some day, *bambino*, maybe we will meet again—and then, perhaps, I shall be a better Jew."

—⚡—

Bright morning sunshine poured cheerily through the cabin windows. From outside, great bustle could be heard, shouts of the crew unloading cargo, hawkers offering their wares loudly, the clamor of horses and wagons. The ship had dropped anchor, and Rabbi Ovadiah and Lipa would soon disembark and continue their voyage. But for now, Captain Vincente had offered them his cabin so that Rabbi Ovadiah could finally study with Lipa.

Lipa had been awake almost all night, and drowsiness weighed heavily over his eyelids. But Lipa was determined. This was his one chance, just as his *Zeide* had promised. He had pleaded for Rabbi Ovadiah of Bartenura to learn with him, and now, finally, here he was, right across the table! There was no *sefer*, nor was any needed—Rabbi Ovadiah knew all of the Mishnah by heart. He looked at his beloved *talmid*.

"Are you ready, Lipa?"

Lipa nodded wearily, his eyes drooping.

"You must pay close attention! Do you know how holy the Mishnah is? The Al-mighty Himself taught it to our teacher Moshe at Sinai. Every word is *Kodesh Kadashim*—Holy of Holies. Are you *sure* you are ready to start—you look so weary?"

Lipa forced his eyes wide open. "Please, Rabbi Ovadiah, I so much want to begin."

Rabbi Ovadiah looked at Lipa doubtfully, but in the sweetest sing-song melody, like a sacred lullaby, he began:

"*Mei'eimatai korin et Shema b'Arvit?*

"*Mi'sha'ah shehakohanim nichnasin le'echol b'terumatan...*

"*When do we begin to recite the Shema at night...from the time that the* kohanim *enter to eat the* terumah..."

"*Lipa...Lipa! Lipa, come with us...*"

Lipa's eyes drooped, and then closed. He smiled to himself happily. All around him he saw the *kohanim* rushing at nightfall to eat their *terumah*—they had nothing else to eat all day.

"*Lipa...Lipa! We're waiting for you to find a tenth man.*"

Now he saw his father's shul, and the men waiting for a *minyan*. His father sat anxiously at his window seat, searching for a tenth man...

"*Lipa, Lipa, wake up...*"

From somewhere far away, like the other end of a long tunnel, he heard Rabbi Ovadiah calling out to him, trying to make him stay awake, to listen. But his head spun in a dizzy whirl, and Rabbi Ovadiah's voice faded further and further away. Lipa made one last desperate attempt to stay awake, to learn the holy Mishnah.

"Rabbi Ovadiah, Rabbi Ovadiah…" he cried out. "*I so much want to learn!*"

But it was too late. Rabbi Ovadiah's voice became a distant murmur, a faraway whispering brook, while all around *kohanim* appeared and disappeared, and the men in his father's shul were begging him to find a tenth man…

Lipa fell fast asleep…

Lipa awoke, and he was in his own bed. How he got there, who carried him to his room, he did not know—his father, his mother, Rabbi Ovadiah? But it was over. He was back in Jersey City, back in his house, back alone. He had missed his chance to learn with Rabbi Ovadiah of Bartenura.

But now—what was next?

3. The Kol Nidrei Appeal

Rabbi Wallerstein sat in his corner office, deeply engrossed in thought. He drew on a great Havana cigar, sending up puffs of smoke like an Indian smoke signal, but no one answered his signals. He was left alone to ponder his future. He drew comfort clasping an ancient Talmud *Menachos* printed in Brandenburg, with the permission of the Latin censor. He looked in the frontispiece and made out the date of its printing in *gematria* code—5459, 1699. He gently ran his fingers over the cloth-like paper, now turned brown with age. The black letters, set with ancient wooden type, were still legible. A person could still learn from this Gemara. But the dark covers were fraying, and the volume's spine was shedding little crumbs. The precious volume had to be protected. Rabbi Wallerstein found an inexpensive solution. At the nearby Woolworth's Five and Dime store, he bought sticky contact paper, embellished with bricks on one side, sticky backing on the other. Lovingly, he shaped the contact paper into strips and covered the fraying covers with sturdy contact paper overlay—nothing would fall apart after his cover. He took a white label, etched the name of the *sefer* in large black letters, and placed it carefully onto the spine of the *sefer*. He lifted the *sefer* and admired his handiwork. He came to these rare volumes in secondhand *mocher sefarim* bookstores on the

Lower East Side, or given away by old shuls that did not know what to do with their old *sheimos*. So now they stood proudly on Rabbi Wallerstein's shelves, a wonderful display of contact-paper artwork.

Rabbi Wallerstein puffed hard on his cigar, gazed out the large windows at passersby walking to the corner, and frowned deeply. It was a very difficult time—how could his shul survive when there was not enough money to pay the mortgage or food? Another person would have thrown in the towel long ago, folded his shul tent, and moved on. There were shuls all over America where he could be rabbi. But Rabbi Wallerstein would not surrender. His pride and hurt would not allow it. He had been dealt an injustice, and his anger was like the fuel that made a car run, a plane fly, and Rabbi Wallerstein stay on Ulysses Avenue. He had come to Jersey City to serve as rabbi of the Willow Avenue Synagogue just a block away. He tried his best, he gave speeches, taught a rowdy class of children, his wife attended Ladies Auxiliary meetings. But, he could not accept the orders of the synagogue board. They wanted him to do things a certain way, and he insisted on doing them his own way. If they spoke to him impertinently, he answered them back sharply.

One synagogue official in particular, the first vice president, was the bane of Rabbi Nosson Wallerstein's existence—a lawyer named Harry Kattel. He dogged Rabbi Wallerstein's every move; how he dressed, how clean his shoes were, how well he preached, how much time he actually spent on shul work, the freshness of the *kichel* at the Shabbos kiddush, the dresses the *rebbetzin* wore—nothing missed his attention. He had a sharp, grating voice, like nails on a chalkboard, and he let his opinions be heard all over the shul. The rabbi had a handful of followers who liked his simplicity and directness—but they were not lawyers like Harry, and not officers.

One day, when Rabbi Wallerstein sat in his apartment reading the Yiddish paper, there was a sharp knock on the door. The rabbi opened the door, and a postman held in his hand a registered letter from Willow Avenue Synagogue. The rabbi signed for it nervously, and opened the envelope.

Rabbi Nosson Wallerstein:

This is to inform you that at a meeting last night of the synagogue committee it was voted to terminate your post as rabbi of our Willow Avenue Synagogue.

Your personal belongings will be delivered to your home, and it is no longer necessary for you to enter our synagogue.

Sincerely,
Harry Kattel, First Vice President
Willow Avenue Synagogue

And that was that. Kattel had been working behind the scenes for weeks to get rid of the rabbi, and despite some feeble dissent, it was done. Rabbi Wallerstein was given one month's salary, and it was expected he would be out of Jersey City in weeks—if not days.

But Hashem in His kindness did not let Rabbi Wallerstein fall. Whether because of his *zechus avos* going back hundreds of years, or the special spark of kindness which swirled around his troubled soul—the Al-mighty sent a rescuer to his cause.

Morris Struhl was an elderly jewelry merchant who prayed at Willow Avenue Synagogue. Quiet, not mixing in to shul affairs, he watched with sadness as poor Rabbi Wallerstein was left jobless and adrift with his young family. A block away from Willow Avenue, right in sight of the shul between two buildings—was a large ramshackle house for sale.

"I will help you buy the house," he said. So, with a down payment of one hundred dollars, Rabbi Wallerstein acquired the house at 97 Ulysses Avenue. With Morris Struhl as his main support, and a handful of men from Willow Avenue Synagogue who followed him, Rabbi Wallerstein started his *minyan*. Here, there was no board, and no bosses. Here, Rabbi Wallerstein could be himself—warm, outspoken, friendly, argumentative. But it was a struggle, a struggle to survive, a struggle to find a *minyan*, a struggle with no clear destination. Mr. Mernick, a carpenter, made the wooden benches and narrow wooden tables. Old Mr. Ingber, who remembered the Oklahoma Indians from back in the 1880s, was a regular. And so the shul was launched. There was a *minyan* only on the Sabbath, but that was sufficient.

One weekday morning, Rabbi Wallerstein stood alone in his shul, leaning over his rough *shtender*. He puffed on his cigar and recited Tehillim, which he completed each week. It was an old Tehillim, with aging pages and large letters, and it gave Rabbi Wallerstein great comfort. The lights were shut, the shul was dark, and the windows were thrown open. Rabbi Wallerstein recited his Tehillim, puffed on his cigar, and gazed out the window all at the same time. Suddenly, from down the street, Harry Kattel walked past with another gentleman. Rabbi Wallerstein hid in the shadows, seeing but not seen. The men stopped, surveyed the new shul, and then with a snicker, Harry remarked loudly, "This shul won't last six weeks!"

The two men laughed and marched off. Rabbi Wallerstein blew huge black smoke rings out of his cigar. The Tehillim shook in his hands and he trembled with anger. Bad enough that Harry Kattel drove him out of Willow Avenue—now he was trying to drive him out of Ulysses Avenue also! Rabbi Wallerstein lay down his cigar in the heavy glass ashtray, looked heavenward and cried out for help—

"*Ribono shel Olam*, please don't let me fail."

He ripped through the rest of the Tehillim angrily, determined that Harry Kattel would be proven wrong.

That was six years ago. The synagogue survived, but it was a struggle, week by week—and getting worse. Old Mr. Struhl passed on. His family still attended, but only on holidays. People came to shul, but there were no wealthy congregants to give generous donations. Rabbi Wallerstein was too proud to go pleading to outsiders—his father didn't do it, and he wouldn't. One ray of hope lay ahead. It was the end of the summer, and the High Holy Days would soon arrive. That brought in some extra money, and would keep the shul going another few months.

Rabbi Wallerstein lay down the Gemara he had just covered, swiveled in his chair, and gazed out the large office windows at the passing street. Soon it would be Yom Tov—they would survive. He puffed contentedly, thanking the Al-mighty for his family, his dutiful wife, his children. A gleam of joy came to his eye thinking about them. Leon was the oldest, now turned fifteen. He was tall, handsome, great at sports, had a good head for learning. He would make a good living someday. He always made the principal's list of outstanding students. There was twelve-year-old Eva, the apple of his eye. Her light brown curls, her mother's eyes, her happy smile—warmed everyone's heart. She had endless friends and did well in school. Then—there was Lipa. Rabbi Wallerstein frowned to himself, blowing a feeble smoke ring upwards. Two out of three was not bad. Even the best baseball hitters hit only three hundred. Rabbi Wallerstein shrugged—what could he do with his youngest? If there would be a profession of banging a ball against a wall and daydreaming all day, he would do well. In school, he did poorly. He had no friends. He was always by himself, in his own world. Rabbi Wallerstein blew a great smoke ring to the ceiling. At least Lipa was good at cleaning the shul. Maybe he could become a *shamash* in some synagogue. He sighed resignedly—the *Ribono shel Olam* needed all types, even a Lipa.

Summer ended and Rosh Hashanah approached quickly. The phone rang regularly, neighborhood Jews looking for a *minyan*. In Rabbi Wallerstein's shul, everyone was welcome. There were no tickets—there hadn't been in his father's *shtiebel*, nor his grandfather's before that. Tickets were for Broadway shows, not for praying to the Al-mighty. A Jew wanted to come to shul, let him come—no charge or toll. There was one appeal on *Kol Nidrei* night, and those who gave, gave.

Lipa had the job of preparing the shul for the extra people. He wiped down each bench twice, rolled out fresh wrapping paper to cover the tables, searched the shelves to find whatever old *machzorim* were available. He checked the closets to see that no kittens were nesting there, and that the sink towel was clean. His father kept a list of all those who arranged seats, writing their names on office labels. Lipa carefully pasted the labels on the back of the benches so everyone had an assigned seat, the regulars who came every Shabbos—Huss, the "President"; Yeitlen, the coal merchant; Mr. Ingber, the Indian agent; Volker, the cholent maker—and the visitors who attended only three days a year. A special place was reserved at the front table for Mr. Abe Ravitz, the courtly insurance broker, who made the *Kol Nidrei* appeal.

Rabbi Nosson Wallerstein looked forward all year to these three days. If he had been brought up differently, he might have been a professor, or a bookbinder, or even a surgeon. But that was not his lot. He was raised, he was bred for only one thing—to be a rabbi, to have a shul, to show warmth to others. His blood flowed *Yiddishkeit*, his golden *yichus*, generation after generation of tzaddikim.

He had no choice in life, no more than an eagle *must* fly and a lion *must* roar—he was born to be in a shul. But this was not the Europe of his ancestors, not Galicia or Hungary, with hordes of pious followers. This was Jersey City, where even children of observant Jews abandoned their roots, and the people who attended his shul were simple and unlearned. So Rabbi Wallerstein struggled to earn a living, to keep his shul alive, and see that his children remained religious. It was so hard, and sometimes a little extra robust *l'chaim* on Friday night soothed his path. He was a great man, undiscovered and unknown, like a blossom trapped in its shell.

But three days a year, the blossom broke through its shell, and Rabbi Wallerstein could reach out to his glorious past, his holy *Zeides* whose holiness pulsed through his veins. For it was Rabbi Wallerstein himself who *davened Mussaf* on Rosh Hashanah, no *chazzan*, no hired person, but he himself. Rabbi Wallerstein was not a cantor, but a beautiful *ba'al tefillah*, with a clear, sweet voice and a *nussach* that he had inherited from his father and grandfather. He did not race, he did not perform, but *davened* with childlike purity. For those few hours, all his worries and all his cares blew away like smoke rings.

He stood at the *bimah* wrapped in his *tallis*. Leon stood alongside him, and his whole congregation surrounded him just a few feet away in the small room.

Rabbi Wallerstein closed his eyes, and began praying:

"*Hineni he'ani mimu'us...*"

"*Behold I stand here, so poor in good deeds...*"

"*Nir'ash v'nifchad mi'pachad yosheiv tehillos Yisrael...*"

"*...Trembling and frightened before You*, Ribono shel Olam, *Who rests upon the praises of Your people Israel...*"

That was all. His voice choked and his eyes filled with tears, and his heart was flooded with memories of things past and present. It

The Shul Boy ❧ 83

was so hard, so hard, his life was so difficult! He remembered the grand world of his father and grandfathers, and here he was lost on Ulysses Avenue in Jersey City, with his tiny congregation. The congregation waited silently, some wept with him secretly—for everyone had his own heartaches.

Rabbi Wallerstein knew this would not do. People were waiting for him; they wanted to go home. He must move on—it was late. He brushed aside an emotional tear, sighed, and moved on with the *Hineni* prayer. Then, mustering his strength, he began chanting Kaddish with great sweetness.

The long *Mussaf* followed, interrupted three times by the blasts of the shofar. Rabbi Wallerstein began the *Chazaras Hashatz*, the sacred *U'nesaneh Tokef*, the holy *Kedushah*, the blessings of *Malchiyos*, *Zichronos*, and *Shofaros*, verse after verse after verse, so many prayers, so many melodies, some joyous, some longing, more sounding of the shofar—the *Mussaf* went on and on. Some of the men dozed peacefully at the sound of Rabbi Wallerstein's voice. Others slipped out discreetly, not accustomed to such long praying. Many secretly flipped their *machzor* to see how many pages were left to finish. Even Leon left his father's side to mingle with his friends in his father's office. Rabbi Wallerstein paid no attention to all of this, his soul bound up in his prayers. Was it little wonder, then, that he did not notice Lipa standing next to him, following every word, looking up from time to time to the father he loved so much?

Rosh Hashanah passed, and the Ten Days of Penitence. Lipa was moved to a different class, not promoted but not quite left back. This new class was of younger boys who were not so rough. A glimmer of hope filled him—perhaps this year he could do better.

An exhilarating hope filled Rabbi Wallerstein as *Kol Nidrei* night approached—the night of the great appeal. Only forty men had reserved seats, but on *Kol Nidrei* night, strangers suddenly appeared at shul. Word had spread that there was no charge for praying on Yom Kippur at Ulysses Avenue shul, no ticket checker. Rabbi Wallerstein did not mind the unexpected visitors. He watched, pleased and proud, as his little shul filled up with worshippers. Who knows—maybe Ulysses Avenue Shul had a bigger *minyan* than Willow Avenue! It did not matter—let them all *daven*, let them come to shul.

The clock struck seven, and sunset neared—it was almost time to begin. The last few minutes, and the most distinguished families poured in, children and grandchildren, bearing fancy leather-bound *machzorim* with gilded pages, and wearing fancy blue and white silk *talleisim*. Lipa sat on a bench near the front, alongside the *mechitzah*, watching proudly as the crowd filled his father's shul. He envied the white silk yarmulkes and *talleisim* that the rich Struhl boys wore.

Last to enter was Mr. Abraham Ravitz and his son-in-law, finding their way up to the front table. For although Rabbi Wallerstein would be the *chazzan*, it was Mr. Ravitz's appeal that would make all the difference. He was a courtly man, avuncular and dignified. He strode by Lipa, winked, and pinched his cheek affectionately.

"Good *Yuntiff*, Lipa."

Lipa looked up shyly, smiled and answered good Yom Tov. He was always fascinated by Mr. Ravitz's many chins that bounced up and down like jelly whenever he spoke. But he was always very kindly, and Lipa liked him a lot.

Sundown approached, the Torahs were removed from the ark, and Rabbi Wallerstein began *Kol Nidrei*. Rabbi Wallerstein's voice was sincere and tender, the congregation was his only choir. They sang together, rabbi and congregation, simply and longingly, so that not the greatest cantor with his finest choir could match the holiness and wonder of those few precious minutes, a rabbi blessed

The Shul Boy 85

with his people, with his Torahs, with his problems, with his longing for forgiveness.

Kol Nidrei was completed, the *Shehecheyanu* blessing was recited joyously, and the Torahs were marched back to the holy ark. The shul returned back to earth, and a hush fell on the room. Rabbi Wallerstein took a seat alongside the ark, leaning over his *shtender* nervously. Mr. Ravitz rose to speak. Lipa sat in his seat near the front and waited eagerly for the appeal. Lipa loved to hear Mr. Ravitz speak. He always said nice things about his father, and he spoke not like Jersey City, but with Churchillian eloquence, pronouncing each word elegantly.

"Ladies and gentlemen," he began, "I begin with wishing everyone here a good year, healthy and prosperous—"

The congregation murmured "amen."

"Once a year we come to this lovely little shul to pray for a good year, for us and our children. The rabbis say that the Book of Life is opened in Heaven, and we are here to make sure that our names are inscribed there for good health and for prosperity.

"Tonight, you can earn your place in that Book of Life, right now! Our shul needs your help—desperately! We are very fortunate that we have as our rabbi, Rabbi Nosson Wallerstein, a man of great sincerity, a kindly man, a man of G-d."

He paused to let his words sink in. Lipa looked at his father proudly.

"Let me tell you a story about our rabbi—one that someone told me recently. Rabbi Wallerstein recently visited a patient at Jersey City Medical Center, and the man complained to the rabbi that he never knew what time it was. Do you know what your rabbi did? He took off his watch and gave it to him—no questions. That is the type of man your rabbi is!"

Mr. Ravitz paused dramatically, clearing his throat. The

congregation turned to gaze at Rabbi Wallerstein admiringly, nodding their heads. Rabbi Wallerstein, embarrassed, stared down humbly at his *shtender*.

"Some of you are here only a few days a year, and some of you are here every Shabbos. But Rabbi Wallerstein is here in this shul three hundred and sixty-five days a year to help anyone who needs his help, and to keep the shul going! But Rabbi Wallerstein cannot do it alone, ladies and gentlemen! The rabbi needs help—your help and mine, to keep the shul alive, and to feed his family!"

Again, Mr. Ravitz paused, letting his words sink in. He surveyed the crowd with a long, knowing gaze. The congregation hung onto his every word.

"Now look here," he continued. "Sitting right in front of me is a wonderful young boy, the rabbi's son, Lipa—"

He lifted his hand and gestured dramatically toward Lipa.

"Look at Lipa—what a fine boy he is! But look at his suit! Look at his shoes!"

Like passengers on a tour bus, the whole congregation leaned over to get a better view of Lipa. Lipa's face reddened.

"He's a wonderful boy, our Lipa. But you see, Lipa needs a new suit, new shoes, boots for the winter, a warm coat for school! Who will help dress Lipa for the winter, and help Rabbi Wallerstein keep up this wonderful synagogue? Only you can help—and tonight! Remember, that Book of Life is open above—and now is the time for you to write yourself in by making a pledge!"

Finally, he turned toward Rabbi Wallerstein, who looked up appreciatively. Mr. Ravitz gestured grandly at the shul people. "Rabbi, you have a wonderful shul and a wonderful family—and I know that this congregation will do right by you!"

He turned back to the people. "Ladies and gentlemen, we will begin the appeal now—please speak up and give generously!"

The Shul Boy

The appeal began, but many eyes were still on Lipa, studying his outgrown suit and scruffy shoes. Louis Huss with his brassy, high-pitched voice went from person to person and loudly announced each pledge.

He started at the front. "Mr. Abraham Ravitz—two hundred dollars!

"Mr. Louis Yeitlen—two tons of coal." Mr. Yeitlen never gave money, he always gave coal.

Some of the announced pledges were not made in earnest, just meant to spur others to give more. Mr. Huss moved from bench to bench down toward the back of the shul, and the pledges grew smaller and smaller, fifty dollars, twenty-five dollars, ten dollars, five dollars—and a few who remained silent. Rabbi Wallerstein sat at his *shtender* and recited Tehillim, waiting for the appeal to end. He could tell that it was successful, *baruch Hashem*.

Meanwhile, Lipa sat red-faced with embarrassment, the subject of everyone's gaze. But there was nothing he could do. It was the *Kol Nidrei* appeal, he was the rabbi's son—the Shul Boy.

Rabbi Wallerstein was a happy man. It was the day after Yom Kippur, and he was busy carrying out the odd collection of old doors that would form the walls of his sukkah. It was heavy work, but it made him feel like a young man again. He had a hammer in one pocket, nails protruding out of his shirt pocket, and *s'chach* poles leaning against the back wall like an Indian teepee. He sang a little song to himself, for he loved this work, and for the first time in months the threat of money did not hang over his head. The Yom Kippur *davening* was beautiful, the shul was full of people, and the appeal had gone well. Even if only most of the people who spoke up actually brought their pledges, the shul could survive yet another while. He was a new man, relieved, and he breathed in the crisp autumn air.

Suddenly, his wife Chaya appeared at the bottom of the long flight of stairs leading from the kitchen upstairs. Rabbi Wallerstein frowned. It must be a phone call, he thought, and he didn't want to talk now.

"Nosson," she called, "I need to talk to you."

Rabbi Wallerstein stopped what he was doing, suddenly concerned. His wife was a quiet, obedient woman who let him have his way in everything, and it was rare that she addressed him like that. Rabbi Wallerstein set down the door he was carrying against a tall hedge, lay his hammer down on a table, and approached his wife.

"Yes, Mrs. Wallerstein," he answered a bit impatiently. "Is everything all right?"

"Everything is all right, Nosson, but I must talk to you about Lipa."

Rabbi Wallerstein's frown grew deeper. *Lipa?* What was there to talk about?

"It is his Shabbos suit, Nosson. *Kein ayin hara*, Lipa is growing out of it."

"It looks fine to me," said Rabbi Wallerstein impatiently.

"Because you don't look close enough, Nosson. Do you not see how short his sleeves are? His wrists are sticking out, so you can see his shirtsleeves. His jacket is tight, and his pants are almost over his socks."

Why did Abraham Ravitz have to talk about Lipa's suit? Rabbi Wallerstein fumed to himself. *That's what started all this.*

"But can't you see that I am busy making the sukkah?" Rabbi Wallerstein answered. "He went this long in that suit; let's wait for after Sukkos, when some real money comes in."

"But Lipa is begging me for a new suit," Mrs. Wallerstein

The Shul Boy 89

answered firmly. "He says he's ashamed to go to shul in his suit—everyone will look at him like Yom Kippur night. Didn't you tell me that the Struhls brought you some money this morning?"

Why couldn't I be quiet? Rabbi Wallerstein thought to himself.

"Besides," continued his wife, "we got the *Jersey Journal* today, and the Manhattan Shop advertises that it's having a sale on boys' suits."

"The Manhattan Shop—are you sure?" asked Rabbi Wallerstein in surprise. The Manhattan Shop was the most expensive men's shop on Jackson Avenue, and they rarely had sales.

"Yes, just today and tomorrow. Please, Nosson—our boy needs a suit really badly."

Rabbi Wallerstein sighed—easy come, easy go. A sale at the Manhattan Shop was not something to be dismissed. He finally got in a few dollars, and before it could grow warm in his wallet, he would have to spend it—on Lipa, no less.

"All right," he answered resignedly. "If they're having a sale. Tell Lipa I'll go with him this afternoon. But please, please let me get some work done now, Chaya."

"Thank you, Nosson," the *rebbetzin* answered, pleased. "But be careful putting up the sukkah—don't hurt your back like last year."

Later that afternoon, Lipa and his father marched together the two blocks to the Manhattan Shop. Rabbi Wallerstein had changed from the clothes he wore to build the sukkah, and donned his dark rabbinical suit and gray Homburg hat. They walked silently, not exchanging a word the whole time. Rabbi Wallerstein walked with a glum, almost angry look on his face. Here a few dollars finally flowed in, and now he would have to spend it on a new suit. Lipa looked up silently at his father. They rarely ever walked together. *Why is Daddy always so angry?* he wondered.

They reached the Manhattan Shop. There was a huge vertical

neon sign outside dominating the street, the smell of freshly lacquered floors when you entered, impeccably dressed salesmen—the store had an atmosphere of refinement and wealth that made Rabbi Wallerstein nervous. It was owned by Harry Solomon, president of the Jersey City Merchants Association. Rabbi Wallerstein looked around self-consciously, and spotted a sign for boys' suits.

"Follow me," he ordered Lipa. Lipa followed eagerly. His old suit had been tight on him for months, and entering the boys' suit department was like entering a wonderland. He ran from his father's side straight to a rack of beautiful charcoal gray suits. Lipa felt the sleeves of a jacket—he loved these suits! They were the same suits that the Struhl boys wore to shul. He would look neat in them. He fingered the suits longingly. A salesman approached.

"Can I help you, young man?" he asked. "These are really fine suits."

Lipa's face glowed.

Rabbi Wallerstein approached quickly. "How much are these suits, sir?" he asked.

"They start at seventy dollars, plus alterations," the salesman said.

Rabbi Wallerstein's face paled. "Seventy dollars? But I was told that you have suits on sale—in the twenty, thirty-dollar range."

"Ah, yes," the salesman answered quickly, as though he had just recalled that fact. "They are on the other rack—a discontinued line, if you get my drift. We just want to get rid of them, make room for new merchandise. You can find something at a real bargain."

"Good," answered Rabbi Wallerstein, "we'll take a look at them."

Lipa protested, raising his voice. "But Daddy, these suits are really nice. The Struhl boys wore them on Yom Tov."

Rabbi Wallerstein grew embarrassed in front of the salesman.

The Shul Boy ఞ 91

"We are not the Struhls, Lipa, do you understand?" he said, trying to sound reasonable. "Do you want a new suit or not?"

The salesman stood silently, waiting for the little drama to play out. Cowered by his father's anger, Lipa nodded to his father silently. Rabbi Wallerstein looked knowingly at the salesman, and the three marched directly to the discounted sales rack. There were a dozen brown plaid suits on sale, with little belts in the back that had not been in style for two years. The sign atop the rack read:

"Suits on Sale: $29.95"

"Try on a jacket for fit," Rabbi Wallerstein told his son. Lipa hated these suits. Nobody wore suits like that. If he were not ashamed, he would have cried. Lipa did not move. The salesman took a jacket off the rack to help him.

"Good afternoon, Rabbi, can I help you?"

Rabbi Wallerstein turned, surprised. Harry Solomon himself approached, his hand extended. He had been watching the little drama of the rabbi and his son from his mezzanine office above, and came down to greet them. Rabbi Wallerstein was flustered that Harry Solomon himself had come down to serve him.

"*Shalom aleichem*, Mr. Solomon. I've heard so many fine things about you. Beautiful store you have here."

"Thank you," Solomon answered. "But I really came down to speak to this young lad." He looked down at Lipa warmly. "Come, sonny, come with me."

He led Lipa back to the rack of charcoal gray suits, Rabbi Wallerstein following in tow.

"Tell me," he said to Lipa. "Do you like these suits?"

"I *love* them," answered Lipa with childish honesty.

"Well, then you shall have one," Mr. Solomon pronounced.

Rabbi Wallerstein cleared his throat nervously. "Er, Mr. Solomon, the suits are really beautiful, but I am afraid they are above our price range."

Harry Solomon turned to Rabbi Wallerstein firmly. "Rabbi, I will make you a special offer. I will sell you one of these suits that your son craves for forty dollars, including adjusting cuffs and sleeves." Lipa's face glowed with joy.

Rabbi Wallerstein flushed. "It's still a bit—"

"Wait—hear me out. You don't have to pay it all at once. You'll pay it off on credit, a dollar a week until it's all paid off."

"A dollar a week! That is very generous of you!"

"But one condition, Rabbi. I want this boy himself to bring me the dollar each week." He looked down at Lipa whose eyes gleamed with happiness. "You understand, my boy? Don't give it to the cashier or the salesman—but me alone! If you don't see me on the floor, bring it up to my office. Is that clear?"

Lipa nodded, his face flushed with joy. "Yes, Mr. Solomon. Thank you, Mr. Solomon."

Harry Solomon smiled and shook Lipa's hand firmly, sealing the deal. He turned to the salesman. "Arthur, look after this young gentleman, please."

Harry Solomon returned to his office, and Lipa was fitted with the nicest suit he ever had. Rabbi Wallerstein and his son left the Manhattan Shop delighted, Lipa with his new suit, Rabbi Wallerstein that he still had money in his wallet. He still hardly shared a word with Lipa, but some of the anger had left his face.

———

Afterward, Arthur the salesman, who had worked at the Manhattan Shop for thirty years, approached Mr. Solomon.

"Harry, you never give discounts like that— it was less than we paid for it. Why did you do that now?"

The Shul Boy 93

Harry Solomon did not look his salesman in his eye for fear of embarrassing himself. He cleared his throat. *"Arthur, when I looked into that little boy's eyes, I saw myself."*

4 The Coal Bin

The holidays passed, and a new school year began. Lipa was shifted into another class, with a new, untried teacher, Rabbi Pesach Levy. He was young, he was inexperienced, and he was excellent. The children he taught were precious to him, each and every one, including Lipa. He introduced them to Gemara, Chapter *Eilu Metzios*. Using props, poppy seeds and wheat sheaves, dried figs and date cakes, he played out the Gemara's questions like a child's game.

"*Kav b'arba amos*... A measure in four amos..."

"How big is a *kav*?" he asked. "And how wide are four *amos*?"

The children raised their hands, full of enthusiasm, but poor in real knowledge.

"Come," Rabbi Levy said, "this is no good. We must see how big four *amos* by four *amos* is!"

At recess, he hauled down his class to the black-top basketball court, gave each boy a piece of white chalk, and then told them to draw four *amos* by four *amos*. The sizes varied, some tiny, some much too wide. He went from drawing to drawing, shaking his head, pointing out their errors. When he was done, he brought out a *sefer*, explained to them the different opinions about the size of a *tefach* handbreadth, times six for an *amah* and then times four — and then drew them a clear outline to the inch — this is four *amos* according to the Chazon Ish, and this according to Reb Chaim Na'eh, and this according to…

And so he taught creatively, whether illustrating the size of the Mishkan courtyard, 50 by 100 cubits, he traced it all out in chalk on the basketball court, so that the lines of Gemara and Mishnah and *Chumash* rose magically from the paper and came alive. Lipa, who lived for imagination, loved it. But the new *rebbi* did something that Lipa had never known before—he gave each boy a *chavrusa* to study with—and Lipa's life was suddenly changed.

Young as he was, inexperienced as he was, Rabbi Levy had a keen eye for each boy. He saw Lipa's great shyness, so he matched him up with a lively East Side boy named Shmuel Praguer. Lipa was delicate and shy, while Shmuel was robust and outgoing. After the *rebbi* gave his *shiur* for an hour, the boys broke into *chavrusos*. For Lipa it meant simply turning around in his seat, tucking his legs under Shmuel's desk, and reviewing what the *rebbi* taught. Lipa was the leader in this review, reading the lines they had learned. Shmuel sat and listened to Lipa explain. He smiled a lot, and really seemed to like Lipa. It was not the most comfortable seating, as their knees often banged against each other, but for Lipa it was heaven. Finally—someone who paid him attention, listened to him, appreciated him. Just as his ancestors had taught Torah before him, now he was the *rebbi*—to Shmuel. When the brief half hour of *chazarah* was over, Lipa turned around, feeling happy. He looked forward each day to his *chazarah* with Shmuel, and in anticipation, paid very special attention to the *rebbi's* every word, so that he could be a good teacher.

Still, even that friendship had its limits. The half hour they spent together was heavenly, but then came an hour's lunch recess, and Lipa was cast back into his own lonely world. Shmuel ate lunch and played punchball and football with his friends, while

Lipa wandered off on his own, too shy and not knowing how to ask to be counted in. No one knew of his loneliness, of his wandering the Lower East Side by himself, daydreaming. His only consolation was the knowledge that for a half hour each day, he studied with Shmuel.

The days grew shorter, darkness fell earlier, fall passed swiftly. Suddenly, the days grew cold, and the first swirling snow drifted down. Lipa bundled up and wandered daily around the East Side like an explorer, so different from Jersey City. Every block was a new world—Essex Street, East Broadway, Delancey, Pitt, Norfolk. Above, great flocks of gray pigeons soared gracefully between the tall tenement buildings, guided by some unseen hand. His walks took him further and further away from the yeshivah, but he was limited in how far he could wander, for he had to be back by two o'clock for English. His northern limit was the south side of Delancey Street that ran along the Williamsburg Bridge to the East River. He had an urge to explore north of the bridge, where his *Zeide's* shul once stood, but he had no time.

That year, Chanukah fell late in December. The vice principal, Mr. Nehlman, came in and announced that there would be no English for the next two days. A loud roar rose from the class. On the first day of Chanukah, the class was let out at one, and all the boys rushed home. Lipa was in no such rush—he had nothing to do at home, and no one to do it with. Instead, he decided to wander past his usual haunts, pass under the Williamsburg Bridge, and walk north to where his *Zeide's* shul once stood. He loved his *Zeide*. He had sat on his lap, tugged childishly at his great white beard. His *Zeide* smiled at him indulgently, told him stories, and even sang with him some Mishnayos. Lipa did not know that he was *sitting* on a living set of Mishnah, for his *Zeide* knew the whole Mishnah by heart, word by word, and the holy *Zohar* inside out, and much more

Torah. To Lipa he was just his *Zeide* whom he loved, who fed him spoonfuls of love, until one day Zeide was gone.

Lipa walked under the gloomy, frigid underpass of the Williamsburg Bridge and came out on the north side of Delancey. He had never seen his *Zeide's* shul since he was a little boy. He wasn't even sure of the address—he just knew the street, Lewis Street. He headed north, crossing street after street, looking for Lewis Street. But all he found on every side was a maze of tall apartment buildings, with littered playgrounds and a labyrinth of walkways. Where had Lewis Street gone? He saw two men huddled at the entrance to one of the buildings, smoking. He approached them bashfully.

"Pardon me," he asked, "but do you know where Lewis Street is?"

The men shrugged sourly, not even looking up. "Never heard of it," one said, and they turned away.

Despite this setback, Lipa was determined. When he set his mind to something, he did not give up. So it was that he continued exploring through the unknown neighborhood, searching for street signs, not finding anything. These were low-income projects, and there were few Jews living there. The wind lifted harder, and Lipa's face turned cherry pink from the cold. After almost an hour of trying to find the street, he was ready to give up, when an old Jewish man popped out of one of the buildings. He was stooped over and walked slowly with a cane, a felt cap pulled over his head. He had a small, wispy beard, and looked down as he walked. He seemed to be holding on to This World by a hair—but maybe he would know.

Lipa ran to him, happy to see a Jew. "*Shalom aleichem,*" he greeted him. The old man stopped in his tracks and looked up at Lipa.

"*Nu?*" he answered.

"Mister, could you tell me where Lewis Street is?"

The old man looked at Lipa for a brief second, shrugged, and shook his head impatiently, eager to move on.

"Please," begged Lipa, "it is so important that I find that street. My *Zeide* used to be a rabbi there once!"

The old man raised his cane impatiently. "Sonny, there hasn't been a Lewis Street here in years. They tore it all down—all you have are these buildings."

He lifted his cane and pointed down a walkway between two buildings. "You see there—there was where Lewis Street used to be. It's gone. Everything is gone! I have to go now, sonny—have a *freilichen* Chanukah." He hobbled off quickly, wiping his nose with his scarf.

Lipa gazed in the direction the old man had pointed to. There was a row of buildings, fronted by a labyrinth of walkways and playgrounds. His *Zeide's* shul had been somewhere there among those apartment buildings. Walking slowly, Lipa followed the walkway. Where had Lewis Street been; where was his *Zeide's* shul? He suddenly remembered the address, 115 Lewis. Was it a block away, or two blocks or three? How could he tell? The sharp wind blew across his face, daring him to continue. But somewhere, somewhere here his *Zeide* had had his shul, had *davened*, had held him on his lap. But where? Everything was washed away.

Suddenly, Lipa was engulfed with an eerie warmth. Where was it coming from? The bitter wind blew across his face, but he was no longer cold. He looked around—was there a sign, some marker: *Here stood Zeide's shul?* There was nothing, just row after row of buildings, yet as he walked, he grew warmer. He knew he was getting closer and closer—closer to what? There was no sign, no street, no *siman*, no nothing—it was all washed away years before. But he knew—part of his *Zeide's neshamah* was still here, hovering over what had once been his street, his shul, his holy *makom*! For the building was gone, and Zeide was buried far away, but the miracles he performed, the prayers he recited with such fire that the

The Shul Boy 99

walls shook, the *Nishmas Kol Chai* he recited each Shabbos word by word with his chassidim—they were still here, like a flame that could never be extinguished, bursting with holy sparks right here in the midst of the frozen walkway. No earthmover could uproot it; no twenty-story building could bury it. Lipa glanced around to make sure that no one was watching him, and like a little child, he opened his palms flat to collect the holy *nitzozos* that poured down from his *Zeide's* old shul like snowflakes.

The afternoon grew dark, and the snow fell heavier. It was time to return to Jersey City, back to the lonely house. Lipa had drawn down great sparks of holiness from his *Zeide*; they danced invisibly around him, lighting the way for strange and wondrous events yet to come.

―❦―

It was the last night of Chanukah. The family stood in the kitchen, lit the flaming menorahs at the window, and sang *Ma'oz Tzur*. Rabbi Wallerstein watched with satisfaction. He was sure that the people from Willow Avenue Shul could see the candles burn between the buildings even as they left shul, despite the snow falling outside. This was real *pirsumei nisa*—Rabbi Wallerstein wanted everyone to see, especially his nemesis, Harry Kattel, that Rabbi Wallerstein and his shul were still here, burning brightly. It was chilly in the house; the furnace must have burned low. Leon and Eva went about their business, Lipa's mother peeled potatoes, and Rabbi Wallerstein went about his favorite hobby of baking potato latkes. The room soon heated up with the cooking.

Lipa had his own secret pursuit. Since the last time that he had sneaked into his father's office and peered into his *Zeide's* Mishnah, he dared not try it again. He remembered the frightening adventure he had with Rabbi Ovadiah of Bartenura, Gustavi, and Henzel with his terrifying cat-o'-nines. Then he had been trapped in his father's office with no way to escape but through the dark, empty shul. But now he was more careful. The holy sparks from visiting his *Zeide's* old shul flew round and round his head, and gave him no rest. Like an itch that had to be scratched, he needed to go back and peer into Zeide's Mishnah. But this time he took precautions. The family was busy, and did not notice him slip downstairs. Instead of circling through the darkened shul, he turned straight from the front hall to his father's office. He checked the outside latch over and over. It was open. He even opened the door and closed it a few times to make sure he would not be trapped again. He finally entered the office and closed the door firmly behind him. The shades were open, and outside, the snow swirled brightly like a white curtain. The street lamp shone through the office windows, casting a white glow, so that it was hardly necessary to turn on the ceiling lights. Even by the light from outside, Lipa could make out the letters on the volumes. He was afraid to take out the first volume, *Zera'im*—it reminded him of his near disaster with Rabbi Ovadiah. He pulled out the second volume, *Moed*, and held it cautiously in his hands— still, his hands trembled slightly.

Just to make certain that he did not run into Rabbi Ovadiah again, he opened the Mishnah from the back. There were pages and pages of tiny print, a commentary on the Mishnah. *Who wrote all this? It must have been so difficult! In the old days, a writer had to dip a feather quill in ink every few lines. How many dips in the inkwell did it take to write all these pages? A thousand, five thousand? It must have been a great* talmid chacham *sitting in his study, surrounded by many holy* sefarim.

On top of each page was the name of the author:

"Meh Mah Mal..." He could not make it out. He tried the second word:

"*Sh… Shl… Shlomo…* Shlomo!"

Lipa raised his head, gazed out into the snow and smiled. He was so proud! He had read out the name, "Shlomo," even without dots.

He gazed with fascination at the pages and pages of holy commentary on the Mishnah. So much, so much he wished he could understand these tiny words, this mighty commentary! But he knew that he could not even understand the plain Mishnah itself! Lipa sighed. So much he wished—

"*So there you are!*"

Suddenly, the front office door burst open and his brother Leon appeared. He quickly shut the door behind him, trapping Lipa. He seemed unusually friendly. "Lipa, where were you hiding?" he asked solicitously. "I was looking for you upstairs and down. What are you doing here by yourself?"

"I was looking at Zeide's Mishnayos," he answered, quickly closing the *sefer*. "Why were you looking for me?"

"Lipa, my good friend," Leon said, "I need you to do me a big favor. It's freezing upstairs, and we have to put more coal in the furnace. Daddy asked me to do it, but I'm busy—I have a project due. Do me a favor, Lipa, and go down and start the fire for me."

"I don't like to go down to the cellar by myself at night," Lipa argued. "It's too dark."

Leon made a face. "Come on, Lipa, you're a big boy now! What are you afraid of—ghosts?"

Seeing Lipa's continued reluctance, Leon sweetened the pot. "Look, Lipa, Daddy made really great latkes with onions. You go down to the furnace, and I'll give two extra latkes from mine. Please, Lipa, I really need the favor, and you know, doing a favor is a big mitzvah! I'll remember it a long time."

It was too strong an argument for Lipa to resist. His older brother usually ignored him and now he was actually begging for a favor—maybe he would treat him better. And it *was* a mitzvah. Besides, there was the matter of the two extra latkes, and Lipa was hungry.

"Okay," he agreed. Leon rushed up and patted him on the back. "You're a good man, Lipa Wallerstein! But hurry, it's really freezing upstairs!"

All Lipa's escape plans had come to naught. He had planned to look into Zeide's Mishnayos, close the *sefer*, and run safely back up to the family. Now he had to go through the back door, pass through the women's section, and slide open the heavy door to the cellar below. He flipped open the staircase switch and a light came on below, casting a faint yellow glow. He ran down the narrow, steep staircase. He wanted to get out of the dank cellar as quickly as possible—he was scared. By day, light came through the small cellar windows. As a child he played in the cellar, climbing the coal bin like a black mountain. But at night, the unlit, dusty cellar was a dark, scary place, with hidden recesses and black, open shafts. All sorts of discarded items, old iceboxes from the past owner, broken furniture, rusty tools, littered the floor, and the smell of coal ashes was everywhere.

At the heart of the cellar were two coal furnaces—one for the shul, and the other for the upstairs floors. The shul furnace was left cold all week until Friday. But the big upstairs furnace had to be constantly fed coal like a hungry beast; otherwise the heat would not rise upstairs. Lipa walked quickly toward the furnace. He looked up to the window and stopped short, frozen. A pair of yellow eyes was staring at him, watching him. Lipa caught his breath—it was one of the stupid cats watching him, hoping he brought something to eat. Lipa grew very afraid—he regretted agreeing to Leon's request, mitzvah or not. The cellar was dark and very spooky. But it was too late—his family was freezing upstairs, and he had agreed to go down.

He opened the iron furnace door, and saw that the last coals had almost burned out, covered in gray ash. He would have to start the fire all over from the beginning. He took a shovel from the coal bin and shoveled out the gray ashes, pouring them into a large barrel that stood next to the furnace. Near the wall was a pile of old newspapers. Lipa squashed a thick weekend edition of *Jersey Journal* into a large ball, and threw it into the furnace. Immediately, the paper exploded into flames. Moving quickly, Lipa took a handful of kindling, split furniture legs, sawed off boards, and cast them in carefully one by one like an Indian teepee, until the flame set fire to them. Lipa was so intense on feeding the furnace that he did not notice that the one light bulb had gone out, casting the cellar into complete darkness except for the fierce glow of the furnace door. Satisfied that the fire had taken to the wood, Lipa grabbed the shovel and headed for the coal bin with its huge pile of black coal. His pupils had grown tiny staring into the furnace, but now, turning, everything was pitch black. Lipa wanted to finish as fast as he could. He was nervous in the pitch-black room, not even sure he could find where the staircase was to go back upstairs.

The coal bin contained a huge mountain of coal that reached almost to the ceiling. In the darkness, he groped his way to find the bin opening and scoop up the coal before the wood burned down. He felt his way like a blind man, hand outstretched, feeling along the wooden wall that surrounded the bin. He finally found the opening, and pressed the shovel deep into the coal.

"*Lipa—*"

Lipa stopped short. *There was someone else in the coal bin*! The hairs of his neck stood straight up. Someone was climbing up the bin on the other side, the coal rustling under his feet. Lipa stopped and listened closely, his whole eleven-year-old body trembling with fear. Whoever it was stopped also, hiding silently. Was it just his imagination? Lipa dug the shovel noisily into the coal and then stopped abruptly. Footsteps scampered up the other side, and then stopped when Lipa paused, waiting. Lipa could not stop shaking.

"*Lipa—*"

"Who…who is there?" Lipa cried out in a shaky voice.

There was silence.

"Please, who…who is there?" Lipa repeated, almost in tears. "Are you a ghost? Please, please go away!"

"Lipa…don't be afraid!" a voice whispered reassuringly from behind the coal. "It is just I, Shlomo!"

"Who…*who*?" Lipa repeated like an owl, the shovel trembling in his hands.

Suddenly, a figure materialized right atop the coal pile, like Moses atop the mountain. Everything was so black, the coal so pitch black, the bin so windowless, that Lipa could not make out anything. But slowly, Lipa's eyes adjusted and he beheld his unexpected visitor.

"Who…who are you?" asked Lipa, truly frightened.

The visitor lifted his hands, almost pleadingly. "Lipa! Just a few minutes ago you opened a Mishnah and peered into my commentary. I was so happy! So few people study my words, but you did! So I have come to study Torah with you! I looked for you upstairs, but you are here, hiding in the coal bin!"

Lipa's eyes widened with astonishment. "You are the one who wrote that—" Lipa's tongue stumbled. "*Mah… Meh…*"

His visitor's face was darkly Yemenite—but his amused grin shone even through the darkness.

"*Milechet Shlomo*," he said. "My commentary is called *Milechet Shlomo*."

"*Milechet… Shlomo,*" Lipa repeated uncertainly, trying to remember.

"Lipa," Shlomo suddenly pleaded, "please! I need you to come with me! I am very lonely where I am. Every day I wonder if I will survive to the next! Come, be my companion! You will be like my little brother, and I will teach you Torah! Lipa, please—hurry! Climb up on the coal and follow me!"

Lipa did not know what to do. He wanted to follow Shlomo—he, too, was lonely and desolate. "But what about the furnace, Shlomo? My mother and father are freezing, and they are waiting for me to pour coal into the fire!"

"You are a good son, Lipa!" answered Shlomo. "Quickly… quickly finish your work and then *maher*! Up the mountain and follow me!"

Bewildered but excited, Lipa dug the shovel deep into the coal and ran back and forth, feeding shovel after heavy shovel of coal into the furnace until it glowed hot like Molech. Each time he ran back to the bin, he gazed up to see if Shlomo was still there—or if it was just his imagination. But no—Shlomo stood there patiently in the darkness watching him shovel, waiting for Lipa to finish his work. Finally, Lipa stood the shovel alongside the furnace, rubbed the coal dust off his hands and ran back to Shlomo.

5 Dung Gate, Jerusalem
Teves 5343 (1583)

It was much harder climbing the coal heap than Lipa had ever remembered. Shlomo stood atop the black mountain as Lipa struggled to climb up, almost on all fours. The coal kept sliding underfoot, so that he constantly slipped back downward. Lipa gazed up, and saw that the pile had suddenly grown much taller, way over the cellar, so it was transformed into a mountainside. The coals fused into rocky earth. Lipa found his footing, and suddenly caught up with Shlomo, who now walked alongside him briskly. It was still pitch black, night, and the desert cold froze Lipa to the bone, leaving him shivering. Shlomo slipped off one of wrappings and wound it over Lipa's shoulders. Still Lipa trembled with cold. Above, in the clear night sky, a thousand stars sparkled in their celestial orbits, shining silvery light over the rocky landscape.

Shlomo observed Lipa's trembling and tried to encourage him. "Look," he announced, pointing eastward, "there, over Har Hazeitim! You see dawn beginning to rise over Hebron, just like in days of the *Mikdash*. Soon it will warm up, Lipa—hold on!"

Above, the morning star shone majestically, and even as they climbed higher the sky grew pale and the first streaks of orange sunlight spread their wings over the mountaintops. All around were steep canyons, and straight ahead above, a great stone rampart.

"Where are we?" asked Lipa.

The Shul Boy ✑ 107

Shlomo stopped abruptly, surprised at Lipa's question. "Lipa, you don't know? We are about to enter Jerusalem!"

Jerusalem! Lipa was overcome—a few minutes ago he was on Ulysses Avenue in Jersey City, and now he was entering Jerusalem! Despite the cold, his face reddened with excitement and gladness and he quickened his steps, so that it was hard for Shlomo to keep up with him. Now that it was daylight, Lipa turned and saw his companion clearly. He stopped short, staring at him.

"Now what is the matter?" Shlomo asked impatiently.

"Rabbi Shlomo...Shlomo—I thought you were a man, a great rabbi. But you are not much older than my brother Leon."

"And how old is your brother?"

"Fifteen."

"I am sixteen. So...now that you know how old I am, and that I am not an old rabbi, can we please keep on walking! I am late for *tefillot*, and then I must to go straight to my rabbi's *shiur*. He will not be pleased if I am late! Come, Lipa, if you are going to be my helper, then you must hurry!"

Lipa kept his mouth shut, not revealing his great astonishment. Shlomo was nothing he expected, not like the great Rabbi Ovadiah of Bartenura. Shlomo was just a boy, just a few years older than Lipa. Unlike Rabbi Ovadiah, who was dressed in royal garments, Shlomo wore a patchwork of clothing, a patched robe, a jumble of rough woolen wrappings to shield him from the cold. He wore a dun-colored turban about his head, and his long black *peyos* twisted unruly down to his thin shoulders. His skin was dark and Yemenite, and he had coal-black, piercing eyes that looked right into Lipa.

As they neared the rampart to the holy city, a terrible stench began entering Lipa's nostrils. The closer they approached the small gateway, the stronger the smell grew. Lipa's face recoiled with disgust and bewilderment—was this the holy city of Jerusalem he had heard about? He saw that Shlomo also was overcome with the smell and he covered his face with his shawl. They entered the small entrance, and Lipa saw where the terrible odor was coming from. A huge mountain of garbage, rotting food, animal dirt, all matter of debris was piled high up against a huge stone wall that seemed to stretch forever. Here and there a tiny bit of the Wall, smashed and uneven stones, could be seen above the debris. A narrow lane lay between the mountain of garbage and a row of flat-roofed stone houses that stood on the other side. Even now as morning broke, Arab women were leading their donkeys to the Wall, and dumping the night's garbage. Lipa could hardly breathe in the stench. He wanted to run away from this terrible place as fast as possible, but Shlomo suddenly paused and bowed toward the Wall.

Shlomo, please, let's get out of here, Lipa begged silently.

But Shlomo just stared at the mountains of garbage and the little bit of wall that peered over it, and sighed. He turned to Lipa. "Do you know where you are?"

"No," answered Lipa, hardly able to speak.

Shlomo sadly lifted his hand toward the Wall. "Here, Lipa, is the *Kotel Hama'aravi*, the only thing we have left from the holy Bet Hamikdash!"

"It is so holy—why is it all covered in garbage?" asked Lipa.

"It is by the sultan's orders," answered Shlomo. "The gate we entered is called the Dung Gate. The sultan commanded that all the garbage in Jerusalem or anywhere near Jerusalem must be brought here and dumped against the Wall."

Shlomo grew silent, and he seemed near tears. Then he spoke very quietly so that no one nearby should hear him. "But someday, Lipa, this Wall will be washed clean and revealed for the world to see! Its stones will shine from one end of the earth to the other—and then—Mashiach!

The Shul Boy

Above, flocks of pigeons flew round and round silently in the azure morning sky, like a white veil fluttering over the wall. They circled high over the great wall, led by a little bird.

I can't even breathe here, Lipa thought.

Shlomo turned and saw Lipa's confusion and dismay at the terrible odor.

"Lipa, it is not right to be so sad your first morning in Yerushalayim!" he said. "Come, my teacher is waiting, let us hurry to *tefillot*."

They passed through the alley and crossed a narrow gorge, climbing up rough-hewn steps to the other side of the hill. Suddenly, it was another world. Unlike the desolation of the Kosel, this western quarter of Jerusalem was buzzing with dark-skinned Jews in robes and long *peyos*, Arab hawkers, Christian pilgrims, Armenian peddlers. The morning air was fragrant with the smell of freshly baked pita breads, tangy spices, honey-layered pastries. Shopkeepers stood in their small doorways, loudly announcing their wares. The lanes were narrow and stone paved, and Lipa had to tread carefully to avoid ill-tempered donkeys that tramped alongside. Shlomo hurried amid the flow of people and animals, Lipa in tow, turning corners into ever more hidden lanes, until they reached the entrance to a synagogue.

They slipped through the portal into the *bet knesset*, whose sky blue plastered walls glistened from the morning sun that poured though great open windows. As Shlomo promised, the day grew warmer quickly. Lipa looked around; he had never seen a shul like this—nothing like his father's shul. There were no chairs or benches, just a mosaic of colorful carpets scattered on the stone floor upon which men sat, cross-legged, their backs to the wall. Only the *chazzan* stood at a *bimah* before the *aron kodesh*, leading the prayers in a sing-song melody. Lipa stood there transfixed, absorbing the strange synagogue. Suddenly, Shlomo yanked him by his arm, warned him to be still, and drew him to the furthest back corner of the room. Shlomo donned his *tefillin*, passed a small siddur to Lipa, and sat down cross-legged, joining the prayers. Lipa followed the unfamiliar melodies as best he could. From time to time, he lifted his head and peered at his exotic neighbors. They were all dark-skinned Jews, Sephardim and Yemenites, like the few who he had seen sometimes on the East Side. But here, they filled the room. Besides himself, there was only one other Ashkenazi in the synagogue, a distinguished-looking man who sat alongside the *aron kodesh*, his back to the wall, eyes closed, praying fervently. Lipa wondered how he came to be here among all the Sephardim and Yemenites. Suddenly, Lipa felt Shlomo's finger tapping heavily on his siddur. He looked up, and saw Shlomo looking at him sternly, shaking his head, as if to say: "*You are not here to look around the room!*"

Frightened by Shlomo's stern look—he reminded him of his own big brother—Lipa frowned and began swaying with all his might, praying especially loudly, all the while nervously observing Shlomo through the corner of his eye.

The prayers took a long time with Hallel, but finally they ended with the mid-morning sun beating warmly into the crowded room. Shlomo wrapped his *tefillin* closed and whispered to Lipa, "Come, Rabbi Betzalel will begin his *shiur* in a few minutes—there is a small room next door."

Lipa could no longer contain himself. "Shlomo," he said. "I'm starving. Is there any breakfast?"

It was like an afterthought to Shlomo. He was so thin, he looked like he never ate any breakfast. Shlomo apologized. "I am sorry, Lipa. I am so busy thinking of today's lessons, I forgot that you need to eat. Come, there is a little kitchen near the *bet knesset*, and I shall find you something."

The Shul Boy

They walked through a narrow hall to a small room. Some of the worshippers were already there, sipping dark coffee in tiny cups. Shlomo had a little shelf. He reached in and took out a small cake covered in honey, and a few dried figs.

"Here," he said graciously, as if offering Lipa a feast. "Make a *brachah* and refresh yourself."

Lipa stared at the tiny piece of stale cake and dried figs. *That was breakfast*? He looked up at Shlomo questioningly—is that all?

Shlomo saw his disappointment. "I am sorry, little Lipa, that is all I have. But it will make you feel full for the day."

Lipa had no choice. He made a *brachah*, quickly gulped down the honey cake, and then began chewing on the figs. Their sweet contents oozed into his mouth, and as Shlomo promised, the hunger pangs left him. He felt bad—because he saw that Shlomo just had two little dried figs for himself. For the first time he realized—the great tzaddik who wrote *Mileches Shlomo* was terribly poor, even poorer than his father.

"Come," he urged Lipa, but then stopped abruptly. "Listen, Lipa, it was a miracle that Rabbi Betzalel allowed me to listen to his *shiur*. I am the youngest of all his students—they are all great scholars. He…he had pity on me. I will slip you in behind me—I hope he will not notice. Just please, Lipa, just sit alongside me by the wall and be absolutely still."

Across the hall from the synagogue was another room. Already the other students had gathered. They sat there like a hungry pride of lions, waiting to be fed Torah. Some whispered among themselves, nodding and waving their thumbs in discussion. Others peered into the large, torn volumes they held on their laps, studying the words silently. Again, they were almost all Oriental Jews, except for one or two. But even the Ashkenazim were dressed up like Sephardim, as though they did not want to stand out. Suddenly,

Rabbi Betzalel appeared, and the students rose with a rush. It was the same rabbi Lipa had seen sitting alongside the *aron kodesh*, Rabbi Betzalel Ashkenazi.

The students sat on low carpets, while Rabbi Betzalel was raised up on a small bench, covered with pillows. He looked around and surveyed his class, eyes flitting from one to the other. His gaze turned onto Shlomo, and then for a second rested on Lipa. He frowned, and Lipa slipped behind Shlomo's robe, trying to hide. Shlomo brushed him back to his place. Rabbi Betzalel's gaze was still on him, but he had the slightest amused smile. Lipa looked back shyly, not sure whether he should smile back. Suddenly, Rabbi Betzalel turned back to the class.

"*B'siyata d'Shmaya*," he announced, "we begin the chapter of *Chezkas Habatim*…"

And that was all that Lipa understood for the next five hours. For the next five hours, the great Rabbi Betzalel, author of the *Shitah Mikubetzes*, lectured his students without once looking into the Gemara, or looking at notes, or hesitating—just Torah and Torah and more Torah. His handpicked students were like a pack of lions, falling on their prey. Rabbi Betzalel began his lecture, and a half-dozen students began arguing back, raising their voices. Rabbi Betzalel fended them off, shouting back, waving away their arguments with a sweep of his arm, quoting passage after passage. When one student backed down, another took up his cause. There was so much shouting going on, Lipa was afraid there would be a real fight, with punches. But it was not, for they were *ba'alei treisin*, warriors of Torah, debating and searching for the truth. Rabbi Betzalel's forehead gleamed with perspiration, his face creased with concentration, but the students kept up. When Rabbi Betzalel finished his *shiur*, Lipa saw that his face shone with happiness, and he beamed at his students who had just fought with him so stubbornly.

"*V'hu k'chassan yotzei mei'chupaso; yasis k'gibor larutz orach...*"

"For he is like a groom coming from his bridal chamber; rejoicing like a warrior to run his course..."

All the students took part in the fierce arguments—except for Shlomo. He sat timidly in his corner, listening, writing down notes inside the fold of his Gemara. His handwriting was very small, but beautifully clear. Rabbi Betzalel rose, and his students rose respectfully in his honor. Only Lipa did not rise—he was fast asleep.

Darkness came quickly in Jerusalem, one moment daylight and few minutes later, deep darkness. There were no more stars to be seen. Heavy clouds rolled in from the sea, and there was the smell of snow in the air. It grew bitter cold, and as Shlomo and Lipa walked back across the city, Lipa felt hungrier and hungrier. Shlomo had slipped him a few more fruits, figs and dates, and one small *ugah* during the day—but it was not enough to satisfy Lipa's gnawing hunger. Yet Shlomo seemed in a cheerful mood, and glanced at Lipa good-naturedly from time to time.

"Where are we going?" asked Lipa, as they crossed back through the valley, and then past the alley that ran alongside the huge covered wall.

"We are going outside the city wall," Shlomo explained. "Down the hill to where I sleep." He suddenly paused and looked at Lipa. "Lipa, you are a very lucky boy, you know?"

"I am?"

"Yes. I slipped you in with me during Rabbi Betzalel's *shiur* and tried to hide you, but Rabbi Betzalel saw you anyway. For some reason, you caught his eye and he was *pleased* you were there! I don't know why—he must see something in you. Anyway, he sent word to me with one of the other students that you may return tomorrow.

It is a big *kavod* for you, Lipa! He is very strict with who he allows to sit in his *shiur*."

Lipa was happy at Shlomo's words, happy and hungry. They exited through the Dung Gate, escaping the terrible odor, and began descending the steep hill toward the Shiloach fountain. Halfway down the hill, Shlomo turned up a stony path and entered a small abandoned building without even a door. There was no lamp, no fire, no furniture—just a pile of straw in one corner.

"This is where you live?" asked Lipa in wonderment. *This is where the famous Mileches Shlomo lives?* he wondered to himself.

"This is where I must live now," Shlomo answered apologetically. "It is too costly to live in Jerusalem. Many of the Jews who escaped from Spain came to Jerusalem seeking refuge. The Arabs who own the houses charge high rent. I have no money—so I stay in this abandoned house."

Lipa gazed at the rough stone walls. It was like living in a cave, except for one small window in the back wall.

Lipa could no longer contain himself. "Shlomo—I am *starving*! Is there nothing to eat except figs and dates?"

Lipa's eyes adjusted to the darkness, and saw that Shlomo was downhearted.

"I am sorry, Lipa," he said ashamedly. "I do not have much, no meat, no fowl. But I have some pita, and I ground up some seeds to make a paste. Yes! Yesterday, I picked some wild pomegranates—they will fill you. Come, let us sit down and eat."

Shlomo had water stored in a barrel. They washed with a small earthen cup, sat together cross-legged, and ate the simple repast, pita, *humus*, pomegranates, more figs and dates. There was nothing else to eat. Although Lipa was no longer starving, he was not full. They finished their meal, and intense blackness descended outside. The bone-chilling Jerusalem cold turned the house's stone walls into ice blocks and Lipa shivered with cold.

"Lipa," said Shlomo, "I know that you are very cold and you are not used to sleeping like this. But I shall try to make you comfortable. *Chazak*, Lipa—be strong! The *Ribono shel Olam* wants that you be with me, otherwise you would not be here now. Something wonderful will happen—of that I am certain! But meanwhile, poor Lipa, you are shivering. Here, I will make a bed for you."

There was a heavy pile of straw in the corner that Shlomo used as his bed. He took a few armfuls of straw and smoothed them down in the corner across from his bed. He found a few old cloths, and piled them into a pillow.

"Lie down," he said to Lipa tenderly. "Lie down and I will cover you."

Lipa removed his shoes and lay down on the rough straw. Shlomo took cloth after cloth, whatever he could find, and covered Lipa tightly, until Lipa felt warm. The bed of straw was uneven and prickly, the old clothing he was wrapped in were rough and a little smelly, but as Shlomo covered him so painstakingly, Lipa thought:

Nobody in Jersey City ever covered me with such love like Rabbi Shlomo, the famous Mileches Shlomo!

Lying under layers of clothing, Lipa listened as Shlomo sat cross-legged on his bed, reviewing the day's *shiur* in his beautiful Yemenite song. Despite the cold, the darkness, the sparse supper, Shlomo sounded so happy reciting Torah. Lipa's eyes drooped, and he thought about his father's latkes with onions, with sour cream and applesauce on the side. He was still hungry—but he had made himself such a wonderful companion with Shlomo. Finally, Lipa fell fast asleep.

It was sometime in the middle of the night when Lipa opened his eyes in fright. Someone had slipped into the house through the open door—he could hear heavy, warm breathing.

"Shlomo, Shlomo," he called out in fright, "there is someone in our room!"

Shlomo sat up, glanced at the intruder, and waved his hand wearily. "Do not worry, Lipa. It is the donkey who lives down the road—he came in to sleep."

Lipa lay with his eyes open nervously, and then shrugged. The room certainly had warmed up. So the three poor creatures shared the simple room, Shlomo on one side, Lipa on the other, and the donkey nestled comfortably between them, snoring peacefully.

...*V'rachamav al kol ma'asav*... *His mercy is upon all His creatures*...

Lipa woke the next morning. The donkey had disappeared, but outside heavy snow swirled around their heads as Shlomo and Lipa trudged up the mountain back into the city. It was cold, and despite being wrapped in one of Shlomo's scarves, melting snow leaked down Lipa's neck. He was hungry and he felt very lonely. Shlomo was kind but he was in his own mystic world. His lips moved in Torah, he didn't even think about eating—while Lipa couldn't stop thinking about food. *Why did Shlomo need me to come to him?* Lipa wondered.

Again, they passed the great Wall hidden by garbage, and back to the same *bet knesset* to pray. Rabbi Betzalel sat in front of the synagogue just like yesterday, but this time there were fewer men at prayer because of the heavy snow that swirled outside. Afterward, there was hardly anything to eat in the kitchen. Shlomo tried his best to find something for Lipa, but all he found was a stale piece of cake, and a few old dried figs. Lipa was worried that Shlomo was giving away his own meager breakfast. No one was missing at the *shiur*, though. Rabbi Betzalel sat upon his chair and surveyed his students. Again, his gaze fell on Shlomo for a longer time, and then on Lipa, who tried to hide. Rabbi Betzalel glanced at Lipa briefly, a slight smile on his face, and Lipa looked back bashfully. *I wonder if he has any food to eat?* Lipa wondered. The *shiur* began, fierce like yesterday, even as outside the snow fell like a white curtain, and the room was so cold that everyone was wrapped in heavy robes and scarves, even Rabbi Betzalel. The room grew dark.

Jerusalem had not seen such snow in many years. Shlomo and Lipa walked back under the Dung Gate; the snow reached Lipa's knees. Walking was difficult, and Lipa's pants were soaked. They cautiously climbed down the hillside to Shlomo's forlorn quarters. Shlomo tried to keep Lipa's sagging spirits up, humming a Yemenite melody, telling him how lucky he was to be in Jerusalem during a snowfall that so few had ever seen. It did not help. Lipa was cold, hungry, and unhappy.

They finally reached Shlomo's dwelling, almost slipping on the rocks to his entrance. Shlomo led Lipa inside, and tried to raise his spirits.

"You are cold and wet, poor Lipa," he consoled him. "Tonight we will make a fire, and even eat something hot."

Lipa watched as Shlomo made a small pile of dried leaves and branches in the middle of the room. He rubbed two sticks together vigorously, until a small flame sprung out from beneath them. He quickly blew the flame onto the pile, and a cheerful, warm glow filled the room. Shlomo placed an earthen pot filled with water upon the fire, threw in a handful of beets and turnips, and turned happily to Lipa. "Tonight, you will eat like a prince."

Lipa warmed himself near the fire, hoping his clothing would dry off. He was tired and very hungry. Shlomo sat across from him, trying to be cheerful in these dreary circumstances. He sang a melody, reviewed the day's happenings, smiled at the fierce arguments that took place in *shiur*, marveled at the pure snow that cast a holy white mantle over Jerusalem—anything to cheer Lipa up. Lipa sat silently, wondering when the soup would be ready. Shlomo peered into the pot, waited a few minutes more, and, satisfied, doled out a large bowl of watery soup to Lipa. His own portion was much smaller. Shlomo found some old pita, and made a repast. To top off the feast, Shlomo gave Lipa a whole pomegranate for himself. Lipa finished the meal, pomegranate and all, but he was still hungry—but there was nothing more. They recited *Birkas Hamazon*, and like the night before, Shlomo tucked Lipa lovingly into his bed of straw, covering him with layers of clothing. The dying embers gave little warmth. Shlomo sat in his corner, reciting the day's *shiur* in his sing-song style. Lipa, who lay huddled in his dark bed, began crying.

Shlomo grew silent. "Lipa," Shlomo called, "are you crying?"

Lipa did not answer, but his sobs grew louder. Shlomo rose, and approached Lipa's bed—Lipa turned away.

"Come, Lipa," he said softly, "I want to talk to you."

Lipa sat up from his bed, tears rolling down his cheeks. Shlomo put more wood on the fire, and the room grew brighter. Lipa sat silently, watching the fire burn.

"Come," said Shlomo, "sit next to me here by the fire. I want to talk to you."

Lipa didn't move. He didn't want to talk. Shlomo's voice grew firmer. "Lipa, come here now, sit near me by the fire!"

Lipa, still tearstained, rose and sat near the fire, still huddled in Shlomo's castoffs. Shlomo looked at Lipa, who tried to hide his tears. "Why are you crying, Lipa?"

"I want to go home," Lipa answered. "I want to go home to my family."

"But you are here, Lipa, you are here in Yerushalayim! You are here where the Bet Hamikdash once stood, and where the Kotel still stands. Are you not fortunate to be here?"

The Shul Boy ꙮ 119

Lipa began crying again. "I am hungry and cold!" Lipa answered sharply. "I want to go home—can't you send me back?"

Shlomo looked at Lipa understandingly. He stoked the branches so the flames grew higher, driving away some of the cold wind that blew in through the open doorway.

He spoke quietly. "Lipa, listen—do you remember why I came to you in the first place? It was from the *Ribono shel Olam* Himself! It was a reward! You went yourself and opened the pages of the holy Mishnah, and tried to read the words of my explanations—the *Milechet Shlomo*! No one looked into my words written in that book of Mishnah for a hundred years—until you, wonderful Lipa! Do you know what a *zechut* you had? That is why the *Ribono shel Olam* sent me to meet you, to come into my world, and to learn!"

"But why am I here, Shlomo?" Lipa sniffled, drying his face. "I have not learned any Torah from you yet. I don't understand a word that Rabbi Betzalel teaches. I am hungry all the time—and last night I had to sleep next to—a donkey!"

Shlomo laughed at Lipa's words, and even Lipa had to laugh amid his tears. The mood lightened. They both sat silently, and then Shlomo spoke, gazing earnestly at Lipa.

"Lipa," he began, "do you know what *bitachon* means?"

"*Bitachon*?" He had heard the word, but wasn't sure what it meant—exactly.

"*Bitachon* means when you trust in Hashem. Do you trust in Hashem, Lipa?"

"I trust in Hashem," Lipa answered quickly. Of course he did.

Shlomo shook his head. "No, Lipa. There are many people who *say* they trust in Hashem, that they have *bitachon*. But they just say it—they don't mean it. The minute things are not good, things are bad, things are terrible—they worry and complain. They even cry like you—"

Quickly, Lipa rubbed his scarf over his face, trying to wipe away the tears that fell just a few minutes ago.

"*Bitachon* means that whatever place you are, Lipa, you believe that Hashem is there, and that He is guiding you—and you are *supposed* to be right there! Do you understand? *Bitachon* means that even if you are standing at the edge of a cliff, even if there is a terrible *rasha* who is holding a whip over you—you do not lose your *bitachon*—do you understand?"

Lipa nodded his head. He had never seen Shlomo, who was always so quiet, speak like this. Shlomo raised his voice even higher.

"So why are you crying, Lipa ben Nosson? You are here in this little house without a door, and you don't have enough to eat? You are in Gan Eden compared to what I have had to endure. I am here alone in Yerushalayim, Lipa! I have gone through Gehinnom, terrible, terrible things to get here. But I have not lost my *bitachon*—do you understand?"

Shlomo stared at Lipa fiercely, studying his face to see if he really understood his words. Lipa looked down speechlessly, ashamed of his recent tears. Shlomo stoked at the fire, trying to awaken the rest of the dying embers. He knew he had said enough.

Suddenly, Lipa looked up. "Shlomo, what terrible things did you go through?"

Shlomo stared into the fire and shook his head. "It is late, Lipa. You have to go back to bed. It is too awful a story for a young boy like yourself."

Lipa sat straight up and faced Shlomo. "So, Shlomo—you have no *hitachon* in *me*, that I am brave enough to share what you went through? Didn't Hashem send you to me—maybe just that I hear your story?"

Shlomo half smiled, half frowned, pleased by Lipa's stubbornness—for it was a spark of his own stubbornness. He dropped the branch he played with, crossed his legs, and pointed at Lipa to sit like him, cross-legged, Yemenite style. Lipa tucked his legs under himself, and as the fire burned low, and the freezing wind blew in through the open door, Shlomo told his incredible tale.

"Lipa, do you know where Sanaa is, in Yemen?"

Lipa shook his head.

It is a city far away, far from Eretz Yisrael, far away from anywhere, in the middle of the Arabian Desert. Lipa—you live in a city. How long have your parents lived there?"

"Ten years," answered Lipa, "since just after I was born."

"Well, my family lived in Sanaa for two thousand years! Since Nebuchadnezzar sent the Jews into exile when he destroyed the Bet Hamikdash. Listen, Lipa—our family made a terrible mistake! When Ezra the Scribe called for all the exiles to return to Eretz Yisrael, our family refused to go. They were too comfortable in their new land. Ezra cursed the Jews of Sanaa to remain always poor, and so we remained. But my grandfathers and their grandfathers remained faithful Jews, *yirei Shamayim*! They were *melamdim*, teaching children Torah. So they bore a second 'curse'—that *melamdim* should always remain poor—otherwise they might abandon their sacred task of teaching Torah."

Lipa frowned. "My father is not a *melamed*, but he is poor, anyway."

Shlomo ignored Lipa's interruption. "Listen—my father, Yehoshua was a truly pious Jew, with all his heart. He struggled to raise our little family—my older sister, my brother, and me—we had just enough. But one day, my father came home excited, called my mother and us together, and announced: 'We had enough of *galus*! I have heard from an emissary from Jerusalem—many Jews have returned to Eretz Yisrael. It is the beginning of the Redemption.

Now it is our turn to go back!'

"I was just a boy of four then, but I remember my mother pleading with my father. 'Yehoshua, Yehoshua! It will take months to reach Eretz Yisrael! The roads are full of robbers, and wild beasts roam the desert by night. Why can't we stay here, like my own sisters, and serve the Al-mighty!'

"My father listened to my mother's arguments, long arguments, but all he could answer her was with tears. 'Rachel, my precious lamb—I can't stand to remain in exile any longer! My soul pines for the Holy Land. I must go, I must! *We* must go. You will see—Hashem will watch over us! Have *bitachon*!'

"And so, soon after Sukkot, we left Sanaa and headed across the great Arabian desert. We were not alone; we went with a small caravan. A few other families also wanted to travel to Tzfat. Some were traders, and others were weavers and silversmiths who heard that there was a need for their craft in the Holy Land. But my father went just for the love of the Holy Land: *Ki ratzu avadecha et avaneha…* 'For your servants have cherished her stones…'

"The whole city went out to escort us and shower their blessings. There were flutes and drums, and much singing. We felt like heroes, like the warriors of Menashe, who marched at the head of the Children of Israel when they entered to conquer the Holy Land. Nothing could stop us from our great journey. I remember how proud I felt that day; even I, a little child, was looked upon as special—"

Suddenly, Shlomo stopped, and a tiny tear flowed from his eye.

"*Ay yay yay!*" he cried. "If only I knew what heartache lay ahead! The first few days, when we passed villages that had a few Jews, we were safe—under their protection. But then we entered the deep, empty desert. There was no road, no people, just small oases, where Arabs pitched their tents and demanded ransom from all passersby. They watched us like hawks set to strike, and we trembled as we

The Shul Boy ↩ 123

passed them. Every time, my father recited Tehillim loudly, crying out to Hashem. Perhaps they saw his holy face, and his long *tzitzit* hanging about him, and were afraid to harm us. So we passed in peace. But nothing could protect us from the endless desert itself. By day it glowed red like an oven, with no inch of shade. Then, when the sun went down, it suddenly turned bitter cold to the bone. My mother wrapped us in her cloak to keep us from becoming sick. Water became scarce, our food grew stale and moldy, we suffered— but my poor mother suffered the most. Each day she grew thinner and weaker. My poor father looked at her in despair and tried to encourage her. He gave her the cleanest water and food we had, whatever she asked for. He made her a soft donkey saddle so that she would not have to walk even one step. But it was not enough. Just weeks before we reached Rabbat Amman, my mother lost her last drop of strength. It was the middle of the open, barren desert, not a tree, not a cloud, not a human being anywhere—except us. It was the loneliest place on earth. My mother could go no further. My father laid her down on a blanket, and made a fire to warm her. I remember standing beside her, my little brother next to me, my older sister trying to feed her some water. My mother could not take anything. She could hardly speak. My father kneeled next to her, and he was crying:

"'Rachel, Rachel, I am so sorry—forgive me! I should have heeded your warnings. Listen, perhaps we can go back to Sanaa, even now, back to our family! They will make you better—'

"My mother shook her head and closed her eyes. She reached up and touched my father's face. 'Yehoshua, Yehoshua,' she whispered. 'When father Jacob returned to Eretz Yisrael from the house of Laban, his wife Rachel gave birth to Benjamin, and she died by the road.' She opened her eyes and looked at us. 'I have given birth to three Benjamins, beautiful children who will live in the Holy

Land. If I die, I will be buried on the way just like Mother Rachel. Whatever Hashem decides, Yehoshua, my *neshamah*, my *neshamah* will travel with you. I am the *seh*, the lamb that was offered up to Hashem.' She looked up at us children and said, 'Dear children, my only joy in *Shamayim* is—' And then, with the word *Shamayim* on her lips, she closed her eyes and was no more. We buried her there in the lonely desert, with only Hashem to watch over her. We sat *shivah* and my father set a stone as a mark. But who would ever see it? I wish, Lipa, that some day I could visit her grave, but I have no idea where it is, for the sand has covered up the marker."

Lipa wiped a tear from his eye. It was so sad. He looked at Shlomo, ashamed that he had wept over a little food and a freezing bed. Shlomo saw his tears and lifted his hand to quiet him.

"But, little Lipa, this was only the *start*—"

Lipa stared—*only the start*?

Shlomo continued. "We left my poor mother buried there in the middle of the desert like Mother Rachel, to pray for those who pass by that lonely wilderness. We traveled by Rabbat Amman, until with Hashem's *chessed* we finally crossed the Jordan at Jericho. I cannot tell you what joy my father had! He lay down and kissed the stones, and threw dust over himself—*v'et afrah yechaneinu*… 'and favored her dust…'

"But even there we were still not safe. It was a wilderness, with leopards, bears, and packs of wolves—and Arab highwaymen ready to steal all we possessed. We made our way through the hills of Samaria, until we reached the holy city of Tzfat. It took us many days of weary travel, but finally, we were there—the city of our holy masters, Rabbi Moshe Cordovero and the Ari Hakadosh!"

Lipa heard the joyfulness in Shlomo's voice at the very mention of Tzfat, and the holy teachers who resided there. Lipa leaned forward excitedly, wanting to hear more. But Shlomo suddenly stopped, his face fell, and he sighed deeply.

"*Ay vay vay!*" he groaned, "*ay vay vay!* Tzfat, Tzfat, how beautiful you are in the mountains, like a holy dove nestled in the cleft of a rock—but how cruel you were to my poor father..." A tear dropped from his eye, and he murmured under his breath, "*Kol mah d'avid Rachmana, l'tav avid...* Whatever Hashem does is for the good..."

Lipa saw that Shlomo was deeply overcome, and let him remain silent. But finally, he asked, "What happened, Shlomo?"

Shlomo frowned, ashamed of his despair. "We are not allowed to question Hashem's will, Lipa. We entered Tzfat like a proud family, my father, my sister, my little brother, and I. We had nothing but the clothing on our backs, and a little food. At first we had no place to sleep, until kindly people took us into their homes. My father prayed in the synagogue of the holy Ari, sitting humbly by a corner.

"But in a few days, the holy men of Tzfat realized that my father was truly special, a sincere, righteous Jew. They themselves were tzaddikim, and a tzaddik can smell a tzaddik. They watched him pray, they heard him chant Tehillim sweetly like Dovid Hamelech himself, they heard him recite whole chapters of Mishnah by heart—and they poured out their kindness upon him. They heard how my mother had died on the terrible journey and that we were orphans. Suddenly, we had everything we needed. They gave us wool to make us clothing, they found us a house to dwell in, they made certain that we had plenty to eat. My father gathered young boys and taught them Torah in our house.

"And I, I was so happy. I sat in the Ari's synagogue and listened to tzaddikim who had known the Ari, and even Rabbi Moshe Cordovero. I studied Mishnah and Talmud with them, and even overheard them whispering secrets from the Kabbalah. I looked into the eyes that looked into the eyes of the Ari Hakadosh!

"But then—the hand of Hashem's judgment reached out on us and everything turned over."

Again, Lipa saw Shlomo pause and murmur, "*Hashem natan*

v'Hashem lakach, yehi shem Hashem mevorach—'Hashem gave and Hashem has taken—blessed is the Name of Hashem!'

"My sister married and gave birth to two beautiful children. My father rejoiced, for he knew that my mother's *neshamah* was comforted in Gan Eden. But then—the plague came to Tzfat. Many died, one after the other. There was no escaping. Those who hid in their houses, the plague pursued them there, even to the neighboring villages like Biram and Meron. My poor sister died, and then her two little children—and then my younger brother, who was innocent like a *malach*. They all died, one after the other, like the *Malach Hamavet* had a list with their names written on it. My father lost all that was precious and joyful. Only I was spared by Hashem's mercy, before bar mitzvah—just like you. We spent hardly seven years in Tzfat, barely one *shemittah*, and my father had everything—and lost everything, like Pharaoh's dream."

Lipa sat sadly, watching the great pain on Shlomo's face as he remembered. *I should not have asked him to tell me his story*, he thought. Lipa was terribly ashamed of his own childish complaining.

Shlomo sighed, and then sat upright. He saw the sadness in Lipa's face. "Wait," he warned, "this is not the end of my story!

"My father rose up from his final *shivah* and said, 'Shlomo, Tzfat is no longer the place for us. *Meshaneh makom meshaneh mazel*—He who changes his dwelling, changes his *mazel*...' So, with the few possessions we had, we loaded our donkey and set forth for Yerushalayim. My father was hopeful—we will go *el hanachalah*—'to our inheritance...' he said. 'Here we will start again, Shlomo. We must not lose faith.'

"We finally reached Yerushalayim after a difficult, dangerous trek through the mountains. My father tried so hard. He ran here, he ran there, he tried his best. He looked for students. No one knew my poor father in Yerushalayim, or saw his greatness. It was too much—my father was heartbroken. He lost his wife, his children, his grandchildren, his only family lived far, far away in Yemen. He wasn't even sure that I would live. Too much, too much for one man! The *Malach Hamavet* came from Tzfat to seek my father here in Jerusalem. He was buried at the bottom of Har Hazeitim among the poorest of the poor."

"You were left alone?" asked Lipa.

"All alone."

"But—who took care of you?"

"Hashem took care of me, no one else. But I was not completely lost. I knew where I belonged. All my mother and father wanted of me was that I grow to be a *talmid chacham*. You see how easily I started that fire before? I have quick hands, skillful hands! I could be a silversmith, or weave delicate carpets. But for two thousand years my grandfathers were *talmidei chachamim*, teachers of Torah. So, I knew what I had to do. I sought to sit at the feet of great scholars, and to drink in their words. That is where I belong. Without Torah, I am a fish out of water—I cannot breathe. When I heard that the great Rabbi Betzalel, who wrote the *Shitah Mikubetzes*, arrived in Jerusalem, I ran straight to him and begged him to let me be his student.

"'But you are too young,' he said. 'All my students are much older, and have studied many years. You need…another teacher.'

"But I was insistent. 'Rabbi Betzalel,' I pleaded, 'I wish to study only with you! What I will understand, I will understand. I shall copy down faithfully your words and review them over and over. What I don't understand, I will ask the other students.'

"At first he remained silent. But when he saw that there were nearly tears in my eyes, he could not bear it. He gave me a *brachah*: 'May you grow to a great *talmid chacham*, Shlomo Adani, and may your Torah light up the whole world!' So, since then, I have sat at his feet, learning his Torah, and copying his words—*baruch Hashem*!"

Shlomo grew silent. He completed his story, his face a mixture of sorrowful memories and glimmers of hope. He leaned back wearily, exhausted from his harrowing tale.

Lipa was not convinced by his hopeful words. "But you live so poorly here, Shlomo. It's terrible! This is not even a house, not even a barn! It is freezing cold, there is no light, no windows, not even a front door to stop the wind. You have nothing to eat except figs and dates, dates and figs—and old pita bread!"

Shlomo sat up, and waved Lipa's complaints away with a wave of his hand. "Lipa, you don't know—I am doing good now!" he shouted. "Before, I didn't even have this, not a roof over my head! After my poor father died, I had no place to go! I slept on the ground, under the sky, amid ash heaps and refuse, like the poorest of the poor! Sometimes I had nothing to eat—even on Shabbat! I went hungry when no one invited me. Now, at least I have a roof over my head, a bed to sleep on. And at Rabbi Betzalel's yeshivah I can always find something to eat, even if it is just some fruit—but it is enough!"

Despite himself, Lipa started crying again. Was this to be *his* life also? *I want to go back home*, he whispered to himself. *I don't want to live like this…*

Shlomo moved to Lipa's side and lifted his face in his hands, so that Lipa had to look straight at him. "Lipa, Lipa, do not cry. Have *bitachon*! Do you not know—'*Teshuat Hashem k'heref ayin*… 'Hashem's help can come like the blink of an eye!' Who knows—tomorrow we may have everything, plenty of food to eat, a warm room to sleep! We must have *emunah* that in one moment Hashem can turn everything upside down! Where is your *bitachon*, little Lipa—did you leave it at home? My father had *bitachon* even when my mother died, even when my sister and my brother were taken; he believed '*Teshuat Hashem k'heref ayin*!' Even when he lay there at his last moments, he held my hand in his and whispered, 'Shlomo, Shlomo, do not despair! Have *bitachon*—all is *for* the good, and all *is* good, and all *will be* for the good!'

"Lipa, Hashem sent you to be my new little brother. Now you must have *bitachon* just like my father had—do you understand, Lipa?"

Lipa looked back at Shlomo, confused, bewildered. He was glad that he had become Shlomo's new brother, but he was still hungry and cold. He did not know what to think, what to answer.

Shlomo held Lipa's face firmly in his hands and commanded, "Lipa, recite these words: *'Teshuat Hashem k'heref ayin…'*"

"*Teshuat Hashem k'heref ayin,*" Lipa intoned, half awake, half in a dream. Shlomo fell back content, releasing Lipa. The last fiery embers grew black, and a chill wind blew in through the open doorway.

"Now go to sleep, Lipa," said Shlomo. "Soon it will be *neitz*—and we shall see what tomorrow brings."

Morning broke. The air had warmed, and above the city walls, billowing gray clouds blew quickly overhead, tiny flashes of sunlight glinting through. The thick mantle of snow had melted to wet slush, flowing swiftly down the hill toward the Siloam. Shlomo and Lipa trudged upward through the streams, their feet growing numb in the icy waters. They were both silent. Shlomo did not try to entertain Lipa; Lipa did not ask any childish questions. Last night, a curtain had fallen away between them. Until last night, Lipa had not truly known Shlomo. He had peered into his commentaries, he had been allowed to sit next to him during Rabbi Betzalel's long *shiur* for some reason. But now he looked up and saw a different Shlomo, a Shlomo who was brave, who was a real hero, not make-believe, who suffered so much and yet had iron *bitachon*. And this holy Shlomo, this great Shlomo, said last night that he, poor little Lipa, could be his little *brother*. Lipa adored Shlomo—he wanted to be with Shlomo and like Shlomo, even if he had to sleep on wet straw and always feel hungry. For the first time, someone really cared about him—and Lipa felt *safe*.

They prayed Shacharis, and Shlomo scrounged through the synagogue kitchen, looking for something for them to eat. Lipa saw that Shlomo's bearing to him had changed. Now, he treated him like a real little brother, in charge of him. For the first time, Shlomo was not satisfied with the little food he found himself, but begged some of the other men if there was anything more to be found. But there was very little. Everyone made do with what there was, some bread, a little cheese, and dates—dates and more dates. *I wonder if a date tree will grow out of my ears*? Lipa wondered.

Rabbi Betzalel seemed in an especially good mood this morning. He surveyed his class with a pleased look, letting his gaze rest upon Shlomo—and then gazing longer than usual at Lipa, like he was thinking some private secret. For the first time, Lipa looked around the room of scholars in a different way. Shlomo had told him his terrible story. How many other terrible stories were there in this room? Who were these other *talmidei chachamim* who debated fiercely each day with Rabbi Betzalel? What great *mesiras nefesh* did each one of these students have to sit here, amid cold and hunger, and dedicate themselves just to Torah! He realized now—he was sitting in a room full of heroes, of holy lions—and he hadn't even realized until today! What was he, Lipa, doing here among them? Why had Hashem brought him here?

The clouds rolled in by afternoon, and the room darkened, almost like night. Outside, the rain clattered noisily on the stone pavement. Still, Rabbi Betzalel did not let up. He seemed to be in an especially elevated mood, and he continued teaching even longer than usual. Meanwhile, Lipa, who had eaten little since breakfast, felt a gnawing emptiness in his stomach. He was hungry—*really* hungry. But he would not let on—if the others could wait, if Shlomo could wait—so could he.

Finally, the *shiur* ended. Rabbi Betzalel rose, and everyone stood in his honor. He headed for the door, past Shlomo who sat at the very back, and then suddenly stopped. He leaned down, and addressed Lipa: "What is your name, *yeled*?"

Lipa was so frightened, he could barely speak. "Li…Lipa," he finally stammered.

Rabbi Betzalel looked at him and wagged his finger reprovingly. "*Zeh lo shimecha*—that is not your name," he said firmly, and then left. Everyone looked at Lipa, wondering at the extraordinary encounter. Lipa stood silently, bewildered and embarrassed, and he looked at Shlomo pleadingly to save him. Shlomo grabbed Lipa's arm and led him quickly outside, escaping the curious gazes.

The narrow lane was dark, and though the rain let up, there was still a cold drizzle. The stones were extremely slippery, a mix of rain and icy slush, and they made their way carefully. Standing at the side of the lane was a short, elderly man, cane in hand, his hand outstretched. He stopped them.

"Young man," the gentleman called out to Shlomo, "could you please help me."

Jerusalem was full of beggars, hands constantly outstretched. Shlomo reached into his pocket. There was nothing there. "I am sorry, father," he apologized. "I have really nothing—not even a fig to give you."

"No, no," the old man shook his cane. "I don't need your *tzedakah*. I have another favor to ask of you! I have invited a guest into my humble home, a righteous man. It is just he and I who are eating at our small repast. He asked me to find a third man to join us, so we can recite *Birkat Hamazon* with a *mezuman* of three. You are welcome to share whatever little we have."

Shlomo was not eager to accept. "I live outside the city walls, revered sir," he answered. "It means that we will have to walk down the steep hill when it is deep night. I have also this young boy to look after."

The old man looked down at Lipa and nodded understandingly. "Oh, he, too, is welcome to join us for our modest *seudah*. I even have a small room where you can lodge tonight."

Food, thought Lipa, *food!*

The old man was dressed simply, in a modest dun-colored cloak and a simple brown turban. He did not appear that he had enough supper even for himself.

"Perhaps you can ask someone else, old man," Shlomo said. "We will be an extra burden on you, the boy and I. Your invitation is a very great *kavod*, though. Thank you for your kindness."

Shlomo took Lipa's hand and was about to walk off, when the man raised his cane, blocking him. "Tell me, young man," he said. "Is your name not Shlomo Adani, whose family comes from Sanaa?"

Shlomo looked at the old man in amazement. "Yes, my father—how do you know?"

The old man nodded. "I spoke to your teacher, Rabbi Betzalel. When I told him of my desire for someone to join us, he told me that I may invite you."

Shlomo was flustered. "Invite me? Why me?"

The old man, whose skin was dark and wrinkled from many years in the scorching sun, responded almost mischievously. "Shall we go ask him? Did I not know your name?"

"Yes."

"So, Shlomo Adani, I beg of you. Do not argue anymore—my guest is waiting. It will be a *kavod* for me to have you join us." He looked down at Lipa. "And you, too, *yeled*. Rabbi Betzalel said I

The Shul Boy 133

should invite you also! Come!"

Shlomo followed the old man as he led them through the maze of streets and narrow lanes. He was puzzled—who was this old man? From his deeply bronzed face and simple robe he seemed to be a plain old Jew, perhaps a farmer. Yet he knew his name and where he came from. And he had spoken to Rabbi Betzalel, who had told him to invite him. Why would Rabbi Betzalel even speak to such a plain Jew? They went from lane to lane, wending far away from the neighborhood of the yeshivah, to the western quarter of the city. The rain had stopped, but the streets were still slick and treacherous, yet the old man walked with a firm, confident step.

"Tell me, father," asked Shlomo finally, "what is the name of your guest?"

"Chaim."

"Oh. And is he visiting?"

"Yes. He will be staying in Yerushalayim for a time. I have offered him my modest home to sleep."

"Oh. And where is he from?"

"Tzfat..."

Shlomo's footsteps suddenly slowed so that the old man looked at him impatiently. "Come, come," he urged, "it is getting late!"

But Shlomo stopped in his tracks, growing suspicious. "And that is his only name—Chaim?"

"Rabbi Chaim."

"Just Rabbi Chaim?"

The old man turned to Shlomo impatiently. "Rabbi Chaim of Tzfat—Rabbi Chaim *Vital*."

Shlomo stopped short and stared at the old man in disbelief. "Your guest is *Rabbi Chaim Vital*! You did not tell me!"

"You did not ask until now."

Shlomo lifted his hands and his face darkened with anguish.

His body shook, his knees knocked together—*v'arkubatei da l'da nakshan…*

Shlomo faced the old man head on. "Dear sir, what is *your* name, if I may ask?"

The old man bowed modestly. "I? I am…Moshe…Moshe Al'chami—"

"Reb Moshe, what have you done to me? Do you not see that I am just a young man, not married? I am the poorest of the poor, the youngest and most unlearned of Rabbi Betzalel's students. How dare I sit alone together with the holy of holiest Rabbi Chaim Vital, who sat at the feet of the holy Ari! Everyone has heard of him! The holy Ari himself brought Rabbi Chaim to the Sea of Galilee to drink from Miriam's Well, so that he was able to acquire wondrous knowledge! He…can gaze at man's forehead and see everything he has ever done! Please, I beg of you—let me and the boy return home! You can find someone else, surely!"

Shlomo grabbed Lipa's hand, preparing to escape. The old man quickly lifted his cane and held him. The old man spoke quietly but very firmly to Shlomo, carefully choosing his words.

"Shlomo Adani! On your forehead Rabbi Chaim will see only holiness and courage, *bitachon* and *emunah*—of that I am sure! And if you are not convinced, hear me out—*Rabbi Chaim himself commanded me to invite you tonight*!"

Shlomo looked at the old man uncertainly. Reb Moshe stood patiently, waiting for Shlomo to digest his words. "Come," he finally ordered, "enough modesty! Rabbi Chaim is waiting!"

He turned and looked at Lipa. "You, too, *yeled*," he said. "I am sure that you must be hungry!"

The old man led them through a maze of stone lanes and alleys, until they reached his house. It had a plain stone face, with iron doors enclosing its entrance. Reb Moshe knocked with his cane against the door, and presently the door swung open, held by a servant. With great politeness, Reb Moshe bowed toward Shlomo. "It is my great *kavod* to welcome you into my humble dwelling."

Shlomo and Lipa followed the old man into the house, and then stopped short—in awe. From the outside it was plain—inside, it was a palace. They entered a high-ceilinged hall, with so many lanterns hanging from its walls that it turned night into day. They passed quickly into another great room, with tall marble walls, and elaborately decorated tapestries hanging from every wall. The two guests, used to sleeping on straw beds in a dingy hovel, gazed at all the splendor wide-eyed, as though they had entered a king's palace.

"You *live* here, Reb Moshe?" Shlomo blurted out, overcome.

"I reside here temporarily," answered the old man, smiling. "Until the *Ribono shel Olam* will find me a more permanent dwelling on a higher floor. I moved to Yerushalayim a year ago from Egypt, and I was able to find this abode, *baruch Hashem*. You understand, young Shlomo, that I am an old man. What do I need? I do not need such a large dwelling, but—but I am able to perform a few good mitzvot with it, especially *hachnasat orchim*—and for that I am pleased! Now, I have Rabbi Chaim as my guest—and now I have you."

He turned toward Lipa, who hid timidly behind Shlomo. "And you, *yeled*—I have the pleasure of having such a sweet child in my home."

In the first shock of seeing such a magnificent dwelling, one that he had never seen in his life, Shlomo temporarily forgot his fear of meeting Rabbi Chaim Vital. But he soon recovered his senses and gazed around anxiously. Had he overlooked greeting the great tzaddik in his first excitement? But there was no one else there.

"Where is Rabbi Chaim?" Shlomo asked anxiously.

"This room is much too large for us to dine in," answered

Moshe. "I have never grown accustomed to such grandeur, even though Hashem allowed me to acquire this all. Come, we will go into the smaller dining room—we will meet him there."

Moshe pounded loudly with his cane on the marble floor, and immediately two servants appeared, bowing respectfully. They held the doors open to a side room. The ceiling was lower, and there were no elaborate hangings on the wall. One door looked out upon an inner garden, and Shlomo could hear the sound of a fountain running, and the patter of raindrops. There was a dining table, set with four chairs.

"One more chair, for the boy," the elderly host ordered.

"I am waiting for Rabbi Chaim to arrive," explained Reb Moshe. "You and the boy are very weary. Why don't you sit."

Shlomo shook his head firmly, his lips moving in prayer. Lipa looked up, and saw that Shlomo was truly frightened—afraid of meeting Rabbi Chaim Vital. Reb Moshe saw that Shlomo was immersed in preparations for meeting Rabbi Chaim, and did not disturb him further. He was pleased that Shlomo took this encounter so seriously.

What will I say to Rabbi Chaim? wondered Shlomo, *and what will he say to me?*

Although it was his home, the old man remained standing—out of respect for Shlomo. As they waited, he bent down and whispered to Lipa.

"And what is your name?" he asked.

Lipa looked up at him, afraid to answer. Just then, a door swung open, and Rabbi Chaim Vital appeared.

Shlomo and the old man bowed respectfully. Lipa tried awkwardly to imitate them. Shlomo looked up anxiously, gazing into the face of the great tzaddik. He was struck by Rabbi Chaim's eyes. Rabbi Chaim gazed at the assembly, and smiled ever so slightly, enigmatically.

"*Shalom aleichem,*" he greeted his host. He glanced at Shlomo and nodded ever so slightly, but said nothing. Lipa—he didn't seem to notice Lipa at all.

"Rabbi Chaim," announced the host formally, "it is my great honor to welcome you to dine with us tonight. This young man is Shlomo Adani, from Yemen. He shall make our *mezuman* tonight."

Rabbi Chaim turned and stared piercingly at Shlomo. Shlomo felt his whole body tremble. Rabbi Chaim did not say a word, but an awesome aura flowed out from the tzaddik, summoning Shlomo's soul to him. Shlomo felt his whole *neshamah* drawn out of his skin. He suddenly felt helpless, his body trembled, and he dropped his head in surrender.

Rabbi Chaim saw Shlomo's fright.

"Why are shaking so, Shlomo Adani?" he asked. "Did I not know your saintly father, Yehoshua? I have waited long to meet you—and now you tremble! Lift your head, Shlomo Adani!"

Shlomo lifted his head and gazed into the tzaddik's face. Rabbi Chaim was pleased, the calm, enigmatic smile still on his thin, ascetic face. Shlomo dared not smile back, for it would be disrespectful, but he no longer looked away, either. His trembling stopped, and he stared straight at the tzaddik, drinking in the holy countenance.

There was a moment of hanging silence, and Reb Moshe tapped his cane on the floor, summoning his servants to begin the meal. He pointed to the table.

"Rabbi Chaim, you asked me to set one extra chair for our meal, which I have done. I have added another one, for the child."

Rabbi Chaim nodded, giving Lipa the tiniest glance out of the corner of his eye, from which Lipa tried to hide. He acted as though Lipa was not there.

The guests proceeded directly to the table. It was a strangely silent, almost surreal, meal. Rabbi Chaim Vital sat at the head of the table, directly across from the empty chair—as though he was expecting another guest. But there was no other guest—just an empty seat. To his right sat Reb Moshe, who did not take his eyes off Rabbi Chaim, anticipating his every need for a washing cup, salt for *Hamotzi*, handing him a knife and spoon as was needed. The host also washed for bread, and like Rabbi Chaim, ate just a minimum *Hamotzi*, and took just a bite or two from the courses that were served; fish, lentil soup, veal smothered in onions and garlic.

Despite Rabbi Chaim's reassuring words, it was difficult for Shlomo to eat even one bite. Here he sat, just a few inches away from Rabbi Chaim Vital, the greatest disciple of the holy Ari! Shlomo wanted to ask Rabbi Chaim so many questions, the miracles he had witnessed from the Ari, his famous journey into the Sea of Galilee where the Ari gave him to imbibe from Miriam's Well, so he could absorb the teachings of his holy master. But he was afraid to open his mouth and interrupt Rabbi Chaim's holy meditations. If he were not ashamed, Shlomo would have laid down his knife and fork and just gazed at the tzaddik who sat so close to him. But he had to pretend that he was eating—although he could barely swallow from nervousness. Only one person at the table was having a grand time—Lipa! With complete lack of self-consciousness, he cleaned out his plate, helping himself to whatever condiments were before him. Poor Lipa had not eaten in days, and he was famished. Reb Moshe watched Lipa furtively, deriving great pleasure at his eating.

Shlomo now watched Rabbi Chaim openly, plainly. It did not matter now, for Rabbi Chaim seemed so much caught up in his own *kavanot*, that he could have been a thousand miles away. The meal was completed, but still Rabbi Chaim stared at the empty chair across from him, a look of growing consternation on his face. Reb Moshe tried to awaken his guest from his reverie:

"My honored guest, shall we bring wine for the *mezuman*?" he suggested.

Just at that moment—Rabbi Chaim's eyes suddenly opened wide and he lifted right out of his chair. He stared at the empty chair wide-eyed and frightened, and a powerful shudder coursed through his whole body. Shlomo and the old man watched Rabbi Chaim with awe. Rabbi Chaim's face turned fiery red, and his eyes bulged out. Even Lipa finally looked up from his food and watched in amazement. Rabbi Chaim's face was on fire as he sat transfixed, half seated, half suspended over his chair. He stayed in that bizarre, immobile posture for a number of minutes. How long, Shlomo could not tell—all time seemed to have stopped. And then, abruptly, it was over. Rabbi Chaim fell into his chair with a great, happy sigh. He hid his face in his hands and began to weep. Reb Moshe and Shlomo stared at him with great concern—and wonder. Reb Moshe did not know what to do. He poured a cup of water and offered it to Rabbi Chaim, who did not even respond. Reb Moshe and Shlomo sat there helplessly, listening to Rabbi Chaim's quiet weeping. Shlomo looked down and recited Tehillim silently. After a few minutes, the weeping stopped. Rabbi Chaim lifted his head, his eyes awash with tears. He had a great smile on his face.

"Please, Reb Moshe," he asked his host. "Please give me some water to cleanse my face, and a towel."

Reb Moshe himself rose swiftly and ran to a side table, carrying a basin of water and a towel. Rabbi Chaim cleansed his face, then wiped himself dry. He returned the towel, and looked around, as though he had woken from a dream. His face glowed.

"*Hodu laShem, ki tov!*" he proclaimed. "Tonight we had a holy guest at our table!"

He turned to Moshe. "Happy is your lot, Reb Moshe Al'chami, that you merited such a holy visitor in your home!"

Then he turned to Shlomo: "Happy is your lot, Rabbi Shlomo Adani, for he came here for your sake!"

Rabbi Chaim leaned over, and placed his hands heavily on Shlomo's shoulders—like *semichah*. Shlomo could not contain himself any longer—astonishment and fear made him forget his awe of Rabbi Chaim.

"Rabbi Chaim, *who* came for me?" he cried out in bewilderment. "What is happening, Rabbi Chaim? Why do you call me 'Rabbi Shlomo'? I am just a boy, a poor orphan. I know so little! You *frighten* me, Rabbi Chaim!"

Rabbi Chaim sat calmly, absorbing Shlomo's intemperate outburst. He lifted his hands to calm him, the enigmatic smile never leaving his face. Shlomo caught control of himself, and realized he had spoken disrespectfully to the great tzaddik, and was overcome with regret. He looked down shamefacedly.

Rabbi Chaim reached out and raised up Shlomo's head. He gazed at Shlomo with such warmth, that Shlomo was comforted—he was forgiven.

Rabbi Chaim gazed down, ran his finger across the table, then lifted his head and spoke:

"The verse says: *They have eyes, but they see not...*

"Did you not see, Reb Shlomo? Seated in that chair was Rabbeinu Hakadosh, Rabbi Yehudah Hanasi, who authored the Mishnah. He sat right there across from you, his face shining like the sun, with such holiness—and such sadness! Did you not see? He spoke to me—did you not hear?"

Shlomo shook his head helplessly.

"He sat crying, heartbroken! 'Why, holy master?' I asked. And he answered, 'I did what no one dared do before—for it was an *et la'asot laShem*, a time of great desperation. I gathered the teachings of our *Tanna'im*, I inscribed them in ink and parchment, so

The Shul Boy ~ 141

that Jews scattered far across the mighty Roman Empire would not forget our *Torah sheb'al peh,* taught to Moshe at Sinai!' And then his face darkened and he cried out, 'And now my holy Mishnah has been cast aside!'

"I was astonished by his words. I asked him, 'Our holy teacher! How can you say that of our holy people? The *yeshivot* are full of students who dwell on the Talmud day and night!'

"Rabbi Yehudah shook his head and his visage darkened further.

"'Yes, what you say is true—they dwell deeply on the subjects upon which Rav Ashi wrote his holy Talmud. But if a father has six children and only four are cared for, and two are left to be neglected and lonely—will that be sufficient? Tell me, Rabbi Chaim: Who is learning *Nega'im?* Who is learning *Ohalot?* Who studies *Kinnim,* Rabbi Chaim, holy *Kinnim!* The pillars of heaven and earth shake without *Kinnim!*'

"I was in great fear, for I saw that Rabbi Yehudah's face was black with despair. But then I saw his face suddenly begin to shine brighter and brighter, for he was gazing upon you, Rabbi Shlomo— he was pouring out his holiness on you!

"Rabbi Yehudah said: 'Here sits a holy young man, Shlomo Adani—the sweet fruit of two thousand years of *mesirat nefesh* of Yemen! And now he has returned to the Holy Land. He bears the holy *zechut!* He will author a commentary that will teach my Mishnah for all generations—even *Kinnim!* Rabbi Chaim! You must see that he lacks for nothing!'

"And then Rabbi Yehudah vanished before my eyes, and I could breathe again. He came in a blink and disappeared in a blink! That is why I set a chair for him tonight, for I knew that you, Shlomo, would be here."

"How did you know, Rabbi Chaim?" asked Shlomo.

"You appeared in my dreams, Shlomo, alongside your father, Yehoshua. Your father begged me—'Rabbi Chaim, watch over my poor son whom I have left all on his own!' And I saw the words of the Mishnah emblazoned upon your forehead! That is why I prayed that Rabbi Yehudah Hanasi should appear tonight—for your sake. For it is I who summoned you here!"

Shlomo looked down, as though trying to hide. Could it be true—that the holy Mishnah was inscribed upon his forehead? That the holy Rabbi Yehudah Hanasi had appeared for his sake?

Rabbi Chaim read his thoughts. He bent close and whispered, *"It is true, Rabbi Shlomo—it is true!"*

Then Rabbi Chaim Vital turned to his host. "Reb Moshe Al'chami! How blessed you are that you had such a holy guest in your home! The Al-mighty has given you great fortune, and I plead with you—make this young Shlomo a member of your household like he would be your own son! See to his needs—shelter and food and clothing. Someday, he will write a holy commentary on the Mishnah and your name will be blessed for all time! Do you accept?"

Reb Moshe rose with alacrity and bowed before Rabbi Chaim. Glancing at Shlomo, he responded, "I shall fulfill the great mitzvah that I have been granted."

He turned to Shlomo. "Rabbi Shlomo Adani! As long as the Al-mighty gives me strength, you will never again want for anything! My home is your home, my bread is your bread!"

Shlomo did not know what to say. Despite himself, he wept—*Teshuat Hashem k'heref ayin*!

The guests proceeded to *Birkat Hamazon*. Rabbi Chaim lifted a cup of wine, and his face shone with incredible joy. He had seen Rabbi Yehudah Hanasi, he had set Rabbi Shlomo Adani on his great mission in life—to explain the most difficult secrets of the Mishnah. The Grace ended, and Rabbi Chaim rose. Everyone stood. He proceeded toward the door, when he suddenly stopped, leaned down, and addressed Lipa.

"What is your name, *yeled*?" he asked.

"Li...Lipa," answered Lipa.

Rabbi Chaim leaned very close, shook his head firmly, and whispered, "*Your name is Petachiah!*"

Then he turned and left hurriedly.

Lipa lay in bed, his eyes wide open. How things had changed, just as Shlomo had said. Last night, they had been sleeping in a broken house, on wet straw, with a donkey wandering in. Now he lay in a warm bed, with a cover filled with goose feathers. But Lipa could not sleep. An intense feeling of loneliness descended upon him—he knew not why. Shlomo sat on the other bed, reviewing the day's *shiur* in a sweet Yemenite song. It was like a mother's lullaby that usually sent Lipa drifting peacefully to sleep—but not tonight. Something was troubling him, and he was suddenly very afraid.

Rabbi Chaim had whispered something in his ear:

"*Your name is—*"

But try as he might, Lipa could not remember the name he gave him—*Pi-ta... Pi-tu... Pa-pa... What was it*? No one else heard it except him.

"Shlomo," he called.

Shlomo interrupted his singing. "Yes, Lipa?"

"It happened, just like you said. Everything changed in one day. *Teshuat Hashem k'heref ayin*."

"*I* did not say it, Lipa—our rabbis said it. I just taught you to truly believe it."

Shlomo returned to his learning.

"Shlomo—"

"Yes?"

"Now that we are no longer poor, and you will live in this great house—will you still be my big brother, or will you forget me?"

"Forget you? Never! How can I ever forget you? Every time you study the *Milechet Shlomo* you will know that I am your big brother forever, teaching you—"

Shlomo's words lifted some of the loneliness that Lipa suddenly felt.

"Shlomo—"

Shlomo sighed. "What now, Lipa?"

What does '*Kinnim*' mean? Rabbi Chaim kept on mentioning it."

Shlomo patiently laid down his *sefer*. "*Kinnim* are the two birds that a woman brought to the Holy Temple after she gave birth to a new child."

"Why birds?"

"You are asking a lot of questions tonight, Lipa. A new *neshamah* is like a bird that flies down from *Shamayim* to the earth below. Don't you know that a person's *neshamah* can fly, Lipa? Every night when you go to sleep, your *neshamah* flies up to *Shamayim* and the Heavenly angels inspect everything you did that day. Lipa—it is late and I must review what I learned today. Now—go to sleep!"

Lipa turned over wearily on his side, and Shlomo continued with his learning. Lipa was happier now. He remembered the birds he saw flying over the Kosel and the pretty little bird that led them. He thought of the flock of pigeons that flew high over his house, guided by an invisible hand. He imagined he was also a bird, Lipa with beautiful golden wings, *v'evraso yerakrak charutz*... He beat his wings and began soaring into the starry night sky. He flew higher and higher, further and further away, so that Shlomo's voice grew fainter and fainter. Suddenly, he was frightened. He wanted to fly back, return to his beloved brother Shlomo—but it was too late. Lipa

The Shul Boy ∽ 145

was swept downward by a mighty wind into the deepest sleep, like a deep well...

Lipa awoke. Outside the window, snow fell drearily and a cold draft blew in from under the windowpanes. He was back home in Jersey City, back in his room, alone and lonely. Shlomo Adani was gone, Yerushalayim was gone, Reb Moshe's glorious palace had disappeared.

Lipa looked up at the bare ceiling. *What happens next?* he wondered.

6

JVK

Rabbi Wallerstein puffed on his cigar and stared glumly out the office window. The game was nearly over. He had tried; he had started a shul, it had survived longer than anyone had imagined—but now there was no more money left. It was mid-January; the money raised on Rosh Hashanah and Yom Kippur had almost run out, and there was very little income coming in. He would have to begin scouring the Jewish newspapers to see if some congregation was advertising for a rabbi—and start all over.

He looked morosely at the stack of bills in front of him—threatening letters from the city tax department, water and electric bills, reminders from the children's schools of unpaid tuition. Besides, he owed money at Goldberg's grocery and at the butcher. It was Friday afternoon and Shabbos would start in a few hours—but how much longer could he keep the shul going? He dreaded the smile of satisfaction that would cover Harry Kattel's face when he heard that he had closed down the shul. But what more could he do?

The office door opened, and Lipa entered. Rabbi Wallerstein frowned at his son.

"*Nu?*" he asked.

"Abba, I need a dollar to bring to Mr. Solomon for my suit. I'm going to Goldberg's to buy herring, and I'll bring him the money on the way."

Rabbi Wallerstein laid down his cigar. This was the last straw. "Lipa, I don't have money this week. You'll pay next week."

"But Daddy—we're supposed to pay Mr. Solomon a dollar a week. That's what we made up with him."

"It doesn't matter what we made up," Rabbi Wallerstein answered impatiently. "I have no money, do you understand, Lipa? I never told you to buy such an expensive suit! Just go in to Mr. Solomon and tell him that your father can't pay this week, and you'll bring two dollars next week!"

"But—"

Rabbi Wallerstein raised his voice angrily. "Lipa, I have no time for this! It's late, and you still have to clean the herring for Shabbos. Go into the Manhattan Shop like I told you and tell Mr. Solomon we'll pay him next week—if we can."

Rabbi Wallerstein retrieved his cigar and began puffing angrily, sending a billow of heavy white smoke to the ceiling. *If he had taken the twenty-nine-dollar suit it would have been all paid up already*!

Lipa stood wordlessly, silenced by his father's shouting. There was no further arguing. Rabbi Wallerstein returned to his stack of bills and Lipa ran out quickly, to avoid being yelled at further.

For the past months, Lipa had a weekly ritual every Erev Shabbos. He collected a dollar from his father, turned the corner at Ulysses and headed down Jackson Avenue, on the way to Goldberg's Appetizer to pick up herring. He would dodge the cars, cross Jackson, and enter the Manhattan Shop. It was so different from his own ramshackle house, with its shul on the first floor. The Manhattan Shop was an elegant men's store with gleaming mirrors and thick carpets. On every side hung racks of beautiful suits, sport coats, wool slacks in all colors, exquisite overcoats, tables laden with expensive knitted shirts and Italian ties. There was a refined atmosphere inside the store, like a courtroom or public building.

The salesmen spoke in hushed, respectful voices to their customers and each other. Mr. Solomon himself was not to be seen. He sat high above the sales floor in a mezzanine, observing the floor below. When an invoice or receipt had to be sent up to his attention, a long pulley wire sent the papers sliding up or down.

At Mr. Solomon's instructions, Lipa was not to give the money to anyone except Mr. Solomon himself. There was a wide flight of stairs leading up to the mezzanine. Lipa climbed up and knocked quietly on Mr. Solomon's door.

It was always the same ritual. "Come in," Mr. Solomon called.

Lipa entered timidly, like an acolyte entering the royal court, dollar in hand.

"Hello, young man," Mr. Solomon greeted him formally. "Thank you for coming."

Lipa handed him the dollar, and Mr. Solomon slipped it quickly into his vest pocket. Then he smiled ever so slightly and gave Lipa a pinch on his cheek, the same place each week.

Then he would say, "Thank you, young man. I shall see you next week."

"Good Shabbos, Mr. Solomon," Lipa answered politely.

Mr. Solomon never returned his "Good Shabbos" greeting, but instead returned quickly back to his desk. Lipa left quickly and quietly, closing the door carefully behind him. He did not know that often when he left, Mr. Solomon wiped away a sentimental tear from his eye.

Now, Lipa walked down Jackson Avenue without any money. He walked on the west side of the street, while the Manhattan Shop was across on the east. Usually he timed the traffic, and ran across to Mr. Solomon. But now, he had nothing to give. He was in a quandary—what should he do? His father had told him to go across the street, speak to Mr. Solomon and tell him he would pay next week, if

The Shul Boy ∽ 149

he could. Lipa was in awe of Mr. Solomon. Mr. Solomon was a very rich man, a famous man, head of the Hudson County Merchant's Association. Mr. Solomon never had to raise his voice. His clothing was elegant, his white handkerchief always folded perfectly into his breast pocket. Walking into his office was scary, like walking into Dr. Weiss, the principal's office. How could he knock on his door, walk in and tell Mr. Solomon—"I have no money this week." He was afraid. After all, they had *promised*. Lipa was ashamed and fearful. He glanced guiltily at the front of the Manhattan Shop and walked past as quickly as he could on the far side, heading for Goldberg's for the herring. Next week his father would give him money and he would apologize—but how could he walk in now with nothing?

The week passed, and again Lipa entered his father's office, looking for his weekly dollar to pay Mr. Solomon. His father was not even there—he wasn't home, gone out to visit someone. Should he wait? Goldberg's closed at three, and without herring, there was no kiddush. What would Mr. Solomon think now? Would he be angry? Lipa had no choice—he couldn't wait. Kiddush without herring was unthinkable. So again, he was forced to march down Jackson Avenue on the far side, walking as fast as he could past the Manhattan Shop. In truth, he missed visiting Mr. Solomon, whom he admired. He didn't even have the heart to glance at the Manhattan Shop as he walked by—someone inside might spot him. Later, as he stood at the women's shul table, gutting out the long white milts inside the raw herring, he daydreamed that he had two dollars in his pocket, and he proudly brought it up to Mr. Solomon who gave him his weekly pinch on the cheek. But it was just a daydream. Instead, he cut the milts into pieces, carried it out, and fed the nine stray cats that lived in the backyard, waiting for handouts.

A gloomy cloud rested over the Wallerstein household. Rabbi Wallerstein was constantly nervous, shouting more than usual—especially at Lipa. Leon in turn grew surly, picking on Lipa also. Eva spent hours in her room, talking on the phone. Rebbetzin Wallerstein coped as best she could. Only she knew how bad the situation was, and tried to appease her nervous husband. They were in great debt. A shul in Connecticut had answered Rabbi Wallerstein's application, and he might go there in a few weeks for a trial Shabbos. He had to start off again like a young rabbi, and the family would be uprooted.

The next Friday afternoon, Lipa knocked nervously at his father's door and entered. His father looked angry.

"Yes?" demanded his father.

"Abba, I'm going out now to Jackson Avenue and—"

"Lipa, I have no money for you, do you understand?"

"But, Mr. Solomon—"

"Didn't you tell Mr. Solomon we would give him money when we could?"

"No."

"Well, go tell him now, Lipa!" his father shouted angrily. "The suit was for you, wasn't it? I didn't tell you to buy a seventy-dollar suit, did I?"

"But, Abba—"

"Lipa, I am busy now. I have no money. Go to Goldberg's and leave me alone!"

Lipa left the office, totally bewildered about what to do. Rabbi Wallerstein sat at his desk, puffing heavily, miserable at himself for being so impatient, even if it was just Lipa.

Very sadly, Lipa marched down Jackson Avenue for the third week. Should he cross the street and go to Mr. Solomon? He was very ashamed. This was already three weeks that they had not paid. Mr. Solomon must be wondering what happened to him. Lipa glanced from afar at the Manhattan Shop that he missed so much, but decided to head straight down his side of the street, passing it as fast as he could. He walked quickly by it, when a voice called out to him:

"Hey, sonny! You—the rabbi's son!"

Lipa turned. It was Arthur, the salesman who had sold him his suit. He was calling to him from the front of the store.

"Sonny," he shouted. "Come over here! Mr. Solomon wants to see you!"

At those words, Lipa's face flushed with shame. For an instant he wanted to run away, but he knew he couldn't do that—it was like being a thief. Arthur ran across the street to Lipa.

"Come on," he said. "I'll help you cross."

Arthur grabbed Lipa's hand and stretched out his arm like a crossing guard, stopping traffic. He held on to Lipa's hand until he was safely inside the Manhattan Shop. Lipa had not been in the store for almost a month, and he forgot how beautiful the store was. Having fulfilled his mission, Arthur regained his professional composure.

"Go upstairs, sonny. Mr. Solomon wants to talk to you. He's waiting."

With great dread, Lipa walked up the stairs to the mezzanine like a man headed to the gallows. He had just been yelled at angrily by his father, and now he faced Mr. Solomon being angry at him—and it was all not his fault. He had no money! With great trepidation, Lipa knocked on Mr. Solomon's door.

"Come in," Mr. Solomon said.

Lipa entered. Mr. Solomon was sitting at his desk as usual, but this time he did not have a pen in hand. Instead, a chair was placed alongside Mr. Solomon's desk, near him.

"Sit down, Lipa," Mr. Solomon said. *At least he wasn't yelling.*

"Where have you been, Lipa?" Mr. Solomon asked. "I missed you."

"I couldn't come."

"Oh, and why not?"

Lipa remained silent.

Mr. Solomon turned and leaned close to Lipa.

"Why couldn't you come, Lipa?"

Lipa looked down, and despite himself, tears flowed down his cheeks. "I didn't have any money to give you."

"And your father—didn't he have any money, even a dollar?"

Lipa looked down and shook his head, wiping away his tears. He felt like a baby.

"So, Lipa, why didn't you come to me anyway? Why didn't you come and tell me?"

Lipa shook his head without answering. He couldn't talk.

"Were you afraid?"

Lipa nodded.

"Lipa, look at me—"

Lipa looked up. His face was tearstained. Mr. Solomon addressed him firmly. "Young man, you must never be afraid to tell me when you don't have enough money, do you understand? Never do that again. Whatever it is, you must act like a man! You come and tell me: 'Mr. Solomon, I don't have money.' Do you understand?"

Lipa nodded. He addressed Mr. Solomon: "Mr. Solomon, my father has no more money. He said that when we get some, he would pay you back. We may even have to close our shul."

Mr. Solomon leaned back, startled at that news. He played with his pen.

"I am sorry to hear that, Lipa. I hope things work out better for your father. But do me a favor, Lipa, since we are friends."

"Sure." Lipa nodded.

"Whether you have a dollar or not, I want you to come to me every Friday afternoon and wish me a good Shabbos, okay?"

The Shul Boy ☙ 153

Lipa looked up, smiling through his tears. "Good Shabbos, Mr. Solomon."

For the first time, Mr. Solomon returned his greeting: "Good Shabbos, Lipa. Please send my regards to your father."

Lipa almost danced down the wide steps. He was so happy that Mr. Solomon had not yelled at him.

―⁓―

Rabbi Wallerstein stood in his darkened shul, a pale light coming from the shadeless windows. He stood at his *shtender*, his father's old Tehillim open before him, with its browned pages. He gazed out at the cracked pavement, at the occasional passersby huddled against the cold. The shul was chilly. He took one last puff on his cigar, lay it down in an ashtray, and began reciting Tehillim. It was the one strength he had in his life, reciting the whole Tehillim each week. His own father had never spoken to him much, but he was sure that he also struggled aplenty with his little *shtiebel* on 91 Hart Street, running out to the street to find a tenth man, making a *melaveh malkah* twice a year to pay the mortgage. But at least his father's shul had not closed down. Rabbi Wallerstein ran his finger under the words and began reading. Maybe some miracle could save his shul.

Suddenly, the door opened, and Rebbetzin Wallerstein stood at the doorway, a look of panic on her face.

"What is it?" he gestured anxiously, trying not to interrupt his Tehillim.

"Mr. Harry Solomon is on the phone," she whispered, as though he might hear her from the other side of the house.

Harry Solomon! Harry Solomon never called him before—he had only met him once. Rabbi Wallerstein's face grew ashen. *It's that stupid suit! If Lipa had taken that cheaper suit he wouldn't be after me now!*

Why does Lipa cause me so much trouble all the time!

For an instant he was tempted to tell his wife to say that he was not available—he was praying. But it was just putting off the inevitable demand for money. He might as well face him now, and explain their circumstances.

He marched quickly through the front hall, sat down at his desk and picked up the phone. Even before Mr. Solomon could speak, Rabbi Wallerstein was on the offensive.

"I'm sorry, Mr. Solomon, that I haven't kept up on the payments for the suit. I told you then, it was too costly for—"

Harry Solomon cut him short. "Rabbi Wallerstein, it's nice to speak to you again. Actually, I am not calling you about your son's suit."

Rabbi Wallerstein let out his breath. "You're not?"

"No. Your son was here the other day, and told me that things are difficult for you now—"

"Yes—"

"He told me that you are even thinking of closing your synagogue."

"He told you *that*?" Rabbi Wallerstein's face grew livid with shock. His closing the shul was an absolute secret that no one was supposed to know. *Lipa went and told Mr. Solomon!* Smoke came out of Rabbi Wallerstein's ears.

He could only stumble an answer. "Oh, I am...not sure. We... don't know. Maybe—"

Mr. Solomon cut him off. "Rabbi Wallerstein, listen. I understand your difficulty. I had a talk recently with JVK, and he told me that he is interested in installing a Jewish chaplain for Hudson County, like there is a Catholic and Protestant one. I told him about you, that you would make a fine rabbi for the post—and he wants to talk to you."

The Shul Boy ₪ 155

"The mayor wants to talk to *me*?" Rabbi Wallerstein answered, stunned.

"Yes. I'll give you his secretary's private number. Please make an appointment to meet him right away. You know, there are a few other rabbis who would give their right arm for the post. So don't waste time!"

Rabbi Wallerstein could hardly speak, he was so stunned. Finally, he found his tongue. "Well, thank you, thank you *very* much, Mr. Solomon!"

"Don't thank me. Thank your son, Lipa. He is a fine young man!"

Rabbi Wallerstein copied down the number Mr. Solomon gave him. He wasn't sure what to do next. Call up the secretary's number right away? Run upstairs and tell his wife the news. No, he must go back to the *shtender* and finish the day's Tehillim. He remembered Mr. Solomon's words. *There are a lot of other rabbis who want that post.*

There was no guarantee that he would get the job. He recited the rest of the Tehillim with all his heart, kissed the *sefer* closed, and prayed:

Hashem, I need this job so much! In the merit of my holy ancestors, please—please let me get it!

Rabbi Wallerstein called the mayor's secretary, and made an appointment for the next Tuesday. Rabbi Wallerstein was extremely anxious that Shabbos. Who knew if he would get the post—other rabbis wanted it also. He tried to carry on as best as possible, blessing in the month of Shevat at *Mussaf*, singing *zemiros* joyously at the Shabbos meal. Sunday morning he was back at his shul *shtender*, gazing out the window, reciting chapter after chapter from his father's Tehillim. He counted the days and then the hours until he would meet the mayor of Jersey City.

Jersey City had its own version of democracy. The Republican

Party did not exist. Instead, the city was ruled by party bosses who ran everything. First there was Frank Hague, who delivered New Jersey to President Roosevelt for four terms. But then he was overthrown by a new cadre of job seekers, led by John V. Kenny, who took over city hall. JVK was the boss—and what he said was final.

Tuesday came. Rabbi Wallerstein's appointment was for eleven. He brushed back his long smooth locks, now quickly turning silver. He had his best suit cleaned, his shirt freshly washed and pressed. He was so anxious, he could hardly knot his tie, his hands trembled so. He looked at himself impatiently in the mirror. *Why are you so nervous*, he berated himself. *The mayor is just a person, a human being*!

He realized he was putting too much into this meeting, too much into JVK. He had to put his *bitachon* in Hashem—what G-d wanted, that's what would be. He slipped on his coat, waved a final goodbye to his wife, and set out to find his fortune, taking the Norway Avenue bus.

Jersey City city hall was an ornate, Jeffersonian building, with a tall cupola topped by a bronze statue. Rabbi Wallerstein had never been to the building before. He walked up the steep steps and entered an enormous marble-floored lobby. He gazed around, lost in the huge space. A guard gave him directions to the mayor's office, which was on the second floor. He walked up the grand marble staircase, down the hallway whose polished floor gleamed like a mirror, and knocked at the mayor's door, five minutes early.

A secretary greeted him.

"I am Rabbi Wallerstein," he said. "I have an appointment with the mayor."

"He will be with you in a few minutes," she said. "Please take a seat, Rabbi."

Rabbi Wallerstein sunk into a richly cushioned chair, semi-dazed. He felt lost. He could do only what he knew to do. Under

The Shul Boy 157

his breath, out of the secretary's earshot, he recited *Mizmor l'Dovid Hashem ro'i...* The clock turned eleven, then eleven fifteen; still he waited, growing ever nervous. The phone buzzed on the secretary's desk. She picked it up, then turned to Rabbi Wallerstein.

"The mayor will see you now, Rabbi. Please go right in."

Rabbi Wallerstein rose, and took a deep, deep breath. *He is only basar v'dam—flesh and blood*, he told himself. *You are not allowed to be so nervous!*

Reinforced by his own words, Rabbi Wallerstein opened the door and entered the inner office of Mayor John V. Kenny.

The mayor rose from his desk and came forward to greet Rabbi Wallerstein. He looked just like his newspaper photographs; short, extremely neat, with a head of snowy white hair. He nodded courteously at the rabbi, showed him a seat in front of his huge mayoral desk, and circled back to his own large chair. On the wall above the mayor were photographs of him with the governor, senators—and even the president. A single sheet of paper lay in front of him.

"I am very glad you were able to come today, Rabbi. Harry Solomon spoke nicely about you."

"Thank you, Mr. Mayor," Rabbi Wallerstein answered. "I have heard many good things that you are doing for the city."

The mayor looked up, silently appraising Rabbi Wallerstein. He had cold, gray eyes that hid whatever was going on in his mind behind them.

"Please call me, John, Rabbi—"

"Thank you, John—"

"You know, we have a number of hospitals and prisons run by the city and Hudson County. Up until now, we have had a Catholic priest and a Protestant minister to serve the people. But we have never had a rabbi for the Jewish community. I would like to put one in place—"

Just then a piercing screech erupted from the corner of the room, interrupting the mayor in mid-sentence. JVK, who until then had sat with a fixed smile, suddenly broke into a chuckle.

"Oh, sorry, Rabbi," he apologized. "I must have missed feeding time. Tell me, Rabbi, would you like to meet my two presidents?"

Rabbi Wallerstein was bewildered by the suggestion, but agreed readily.

"Come, I will introduce you." JVK briskly rose from his chair and proceeded to the office window.

There hung a large birdcage, three feet high, with two colorful birds inside. One of them actually seemed to have *peyos*, with its head feathers swept forward like side locks.

"These are my two presidents," explained the mayor, "Truman and Roosevelt. Aren't they beauties?"

"Are they parrots?"

"No, no way parrots. These are pigeons."

Rabbi Wallerstein was sincerely astounded. "I never saw pigeons that look like these."

"I know. But they are. Most people know the plain pigeons that roam the streets. But these are a special breed. Truman, here, with his turned-back head feathers is a trumpeter. Roosevelt is a pure pouter."

"Very interesting," Rabbi Wallerstein said. "I never saw anything like that before."

The mayor reached behind a curtain, and retrieved a brown sandwich bag. He took out a half-eaten roll, broke it into tiny pieces, and scattered the crumbs on the floor of the cage. The pigeons leaped down from their perch and began gobbling up the crumbs.

"What are you feeding them?" asked Rabbi Wallerstein.

"My leftover roll from breakfast," answered JVK, not taking his eyes off his beloved birds. "No use letting good food go to waste."

Rabbi Wallerstein stood, uncertain whether to speak or not. Perhaps silence was wiser—but he couldn't contain himself.

"Mr. Mayor…John, I wish you had met my father."

JVK looked up. "Oh, really?"

"You see, what you are doing, my father did also. There is a verse in our Hebrew Psalms… *V'rachamav al kol ma'asav*… 'G-d's mercy is on all His creatures…' When we were growing up, we were never allowed to throw away leftovers. There were stray cats on our street, and my father insisted that we take out the leftover food and leave it for them. A lot of cats lived in our backyard—but that is the way we thanked the Al-mighty for our own bounty. And here you are, the mayor of Jersey City—doing the same thing as my father!"

Mayor Kenny did not answer. For a moment Rabbi Wallerstein regretted his outburst—perhaps he had said the wrong thing. The mayor finished distributing his roll, and led Rabbi Wallerstein back to his desk. The mayor sat down and picked up his pen.

"Tell me, Rabbi," the mayor asked. "What is that verse you said?"

"'His mercy is upon all His creatures.'"

Very carefully, in small precise lettering, Mayor John V. Kenny copied down Rabbi Wallerstein's words. Then he looked up and smiled. "Rabbi, I think that you are going to do a very good job as Jewish chaplain of Hudson County. The job of a chaplain is to show mercy, and I see that you are a man of mercy. I am putting you on the county payroll starting next week—Jewish Chaplain of Hudson County. I'll have my assistant give you a list of the hospitals and jails you need to visit."

The mayor stuck out his hand. "Congratulations."

Rabbi Wallerstein accepted the handshake, his face flushed with excitement. He had no idea what he would be paid, or when.

It didn't matter.

"Thank you, John, thank you very much," he managed to blurt out.

"Rabbi, just keep me in mind in your prayers."

The mayor rose, signaling the end of the meeting. Rabbi Wallerstein quickly left the mayor's office, tears of joy in his eyes.

Teshuas Hashem k'heref ayin, he whispered to himself. ...*Baruch Hashem...baruch Hashem...*

That Friday night, Rabbi Wallerstein was in great high spirits. He practically danced up the steps after shul. There had been an extra man at *minyan*, and now he was celebrating his new position, Jewish Chaplain of Hudson County. He sang *Shalom Aleichem* and Kiddush joyfully, recited *Hamotzi* with great flair, and relished his fish. Then he filled his Kiddush cup with a hefty measure of whiskey, and began singing *Kol Mekadesh*. Rabbi Wallerstein's face beamed with joy and gratitude, growing more colored with each taste of scotch.

Kol Mekadesh ended. Rabbi Wallerstein could not contain his exultation. His shul was saved, his *parnassah* was saved, he would not have to go to Connecticut to be appraised by some committee!

"All from a *pasuk* in Tehillim," he announced triumphantly, hardly believing his good fortune. "Harry Solomon called me today to congratulate me. He said that the mayor had planned to meet two or three other rabbis also, but then I quoted him the Psalm, *V'rachamav al kol ma'asav*—'His mercy is upon all His creatures...' He was so taken by that, that he decided right there to give me the post! *Baruch Hashem, baruch Hashem!*"

Rabbi Wallerstein took another hefty gulp from his cup and his face turned bright red. Suddenly, he lifted his finger and pointed

The Shul Boy 161

straight at Lipa. "It was all your doing, Lipa! Because you *schnorred* that suit from Harry Solomon, he took an interest in our family! My little *schnorrer*—you saved everyone!"

Rabbi Wallerstein laughed broadly at his *schnorrer* remark. Leon smirked, Eva giggled in ridicule. Lipa looked down with embarrassment—*was he a* schnorrer? Only Rebbetzin Wallerstein looked at her youngest son sympathetically, but remained silent.

But poor Rabbi Wallerstein was not correct. His shul, his parnassah, *his whole life had indeed been saved by Lipa—but not because of the suit. But each Friday afternoon when Lipa visited Harry Solomon and wished him a good Shabbos, some sadness in Lipa's eyes, in Lipa's voice, touched Harry Solomon to the core. The lonely child in Harry Solomon finally found a soul mate—in Lipa Wallerstein.*

7
The Maggid

Like a bird soaring through blue skies, like a fish gliding through turquoise waters, like an elk skipping nimbly atop mountains—Rabbi Wallerstein took to his new post as chaplain. It was a job Hashem had made special for him. His natural warmth, his simplicity, his good-natured humor—won him hearts everywhere. Here he had no boss, no committee overseeing his performance, no Harry Kattel. There was a roster of hospitals to visit, the county jailhouse, occasional shut-ins. He went about his duties with a joy, like a young man. For a river of kindness flowed through Rabbi Wallerstein's soul that he had inherited from his pious ancestors, a living stream of *ahavas Yisrael*. *You see a Jew, you love a Jew, you help a Jew*. Every smile he gave was a mitzvah. If he could help someone, make someone laugh at a silly joke, bring a siddur or Tehillim, lend a watch, scribble down a name for a *mi shebeirach*—that made his day. It was a job that was no job—it was just mitzvos. But—he also began receiving a salary. Suddenly, he no longer had to struggle to survive. The salary he received was not huge, but together with donations from the shul, an occasional call to a funeral—it was enough, it was plenty. He heard word from Harry Solomon—JVK was pleased with his performance.

On Fridays yeshivah ended early, and Rabbi Wallerstein let Leon accompany him on some of his chaplaincy visits. Later, at the Friday night meal, Leon proudly recounted his experiences, especially the jailhouse visit where he met the notorious gangster, Lefty Lefkowitz, whose picture had been on the front paper of the *Jersey Journal*.

"Daddy gave him *mussar*," Leon boasted proudly.

Lipa begged his father to be allowed to come with him on his visits to the hospitals and jail, but his father pushed him off with different excuses—he was too young, they wouldn't allow him on hospital wards, a jail was no place for a boy. Above all, someone had to take care of cleaning the shul and cutting the herring while Rabbi Wallerstein went about his duties.

"Lipa, you are my shul boy," he said. "Someone has to clean the shul and make the herring. You're doing a great job!" In truth, Rabbi Wallerstein had no interest in having him tag along.

Friday afternoon was the loneliest time for Lipa. During the week, he sat in the desk in front of Shmuel Praguer and listened eagerly as Rabbi Levy explained the Gemara. Then, for one precious hour a day, he would turn around, face Shmuel knee to knee, and teach the Gemara to Shmuel, who listened earnestly.

"You really know your stuff," he praised Lipa, who basked in Shmuel's admiration. Shmuel was the only one in the whole world who liked him. Unbeknownst to his parents, Lipa's marks soared in Gemara. But they did not notice. For them, it was just—Lipa.

During the week, Lipa had one hour a day of friendship, and he lived for it. But Fridays there was no *chazarah*. The days grew longer, Shabbos came late. After visiting Mr. Solomon, buying the herring, wiping down the benches and cutting open herring, he nothing to do and no one to do it with. He shared the backyard with the cats, throwing a ball up against the back of the house, dreaming he was center fielder for the Yankees, hitting four hundred-foot home runs like Johnny Mize.

One Friday afternoon, Lipa returned from yeshivah to a frightening scene. There were two police cars outside his house, lights flashing. A policeman stood outside his car, talking into a radio. Lipa ran quickly toward his house. The policeman stopped him.

"You live here, son?" he asked.

"Ye…yes…" Lipa answered, frightened of the officer. "What happened, sir?"

"Someone tried to break into your house from the back. We have him. Your father is the city chaplain, right?"

"Yes."

"He was called. He's on the way here."

Lipa's mother and Eva must have gone shopping for clothing, and Leon was with his father. Lipa stood at the car, waiting, very afraid of someone breaking into their home. In a few minutes, Rabbi Wallerstein's black Chevrolet sped down the street, stopping behind the police car. Rabbi Wallerstein jumped out of his car, threw on his black Homburg and ran to the policeman.

"What happened?" he asked anxiously.

"Your neighbor, Lieutenant Bradley, spotted this guy climbing through your open back window. He ran out and grabbed him and then called us."

Lieutenant Bradley, who had been sitting in one of the cars with the suspect, jumped out. "It's lucky I spotted him, Rabbi," he said. "You should keep your windows locked."

"Who is it?" asked Rabbi Wallerstein. "There's nothing to steal in my house except prayer books."

"You want to see if you could identify him?" asked the officer.

Rabbi Wallerstein followed the policeman to the car and he opened the door. Rabbi Wallerstein peered in. "It's the Maggid!" he cried out.

"*Vos villen zei fun mir*?…What do they want from me?"

Inside the back seat was the little Litvish Maggid who came to their house once a year.

"I know this man," Rabbi Wallerstein explained. "There was nobody home, so he probably decided to climb in by the back window. Please, let him go."

"Are you sure?" asked the rabbi's policeman neighbor. "I almost shot him."

"Please, Lieutenant," said Rabbi Wallerstein. "Please don't shoot the Maggid!"

It took a few minutes and some explaining, but the matter was finally straightened out. The poor Maggid was finally released from his confinement in the back of the police car; he straightened out his battered black hat, and Rabbi Wallerstein escorted him into the house—this time, safely through the front door.

That night, the story of the Maggid's arrest caused great amusement at the Wallersteins' Shabbos table. The poor Maggid never knew what struck him. He tried to crawl into the locked house by the back window, and the Lieutenant grabbed him by the legs. The next thing he knew he was in the back of a police car, under arrest. *Please don't shoot the Maggid*! became the catch phrase of the meal.

The meal ended, but the Maggid had not yet arrived in their house. He ate his meals at the home of Mr. Joe Gross, a wealthy member of the Norway Synagogue, and then walked back the half mile to their house. It was late, nearly eleven. Rabbi Wallerstein was weary from the heavy meal and his busy rounds at the hospital. Leon disappeared after *bentching*. Rabbi Wallerstein turned to Lipa.

"Lipa, the Maggid should be here soon. Stay up and listen to his knock and let him in."

Lipa agreed, which pleased his father. Lipa sat in the upstairs kitchen reading a book, waiting for the Maggid's knock. It took almost a half hour, but finally he heard the muffled sound of the

Maggid knocking outside. He closed the book and rushed down, opening the door for the guest.

The Maggid entered. He was a very short, old gentleman, bent over gnome like, with a prominent black birthmark on his forehead. He didn't speak much, and when he spoke it was hard to make out what he was saying.

"We have the room ready for you on the second floor," Lipa told him. "The bed is all made."

The Maggid glanced at Lipa and shook his head. "I can't sleep yet," the old man said. "I'll go into the shul for a few minutes and learn. Come with me."

The shul lights were left on the whole Shabbos, so that the shul looked cheerful and warm, unlike the weekdays when it was pitch black and scary. The Maggid shuffled to the narrow table in the front of the shul alongside the *bimah*, diagonal to the *aron kodesh*. The Maggid squeezed himself onto the bench, tired from his long walk. Lipa could not leave the guest alone—besides, he had to show him his room.

The Maggid looked up at Lipa, who was staring with fascination at his birthmark that had little hairs growing out of it.

"You are a good *bachur*," the Maggid said. "You'll grow up to be a great tzaddik someday."

He looked around as though searching for something.

"Tell me, *bachur'l*, maybe you can find me a *Mishnayos Shabbos* so I can study."

"Which book of Mishnayos is that in?" asked Lipa.

The Maggid looked at Lipa and frowned.

"An *einekel* of the Tosfos Yom Tov doesn't know how to find *Mishnayos Shabbos*? The second volume—*Beis*."

Lipa went to fetch the Mishnayos in his father's office. How different and bright it was on Friday night, when all the lights were

The Shul Boy 167

left on. The room was a rainbow of colors from his father's contact-paper covers. Although there were a number of sets of Mishnayos, Lipa went straight to his *Zeide's* set, so that the elderly Maggid would study from it—he was sure his *Zeide* would be pleased. He brought the volume to the Maggid and laid it before him on the narrow wooden table.

The Maggid lifted his hand and indicated the seat next to him. "Come, *bachur'l*," he said, "come sit next to the old Maggid."

Lipa walked around the table and slid alongside the Maggid, who had opened the *sefer* and began learning aloud: "*Yetzios haShabbos shtayim sheheim arba bif'nim…*"

His finger ran quickly down the page, and then over to the commentary on the inside fold—*Bartenura*. His lips moved silently as he read the commentary. Then his finger shifted to the larger outside commentary. He paused and turned to Lipa. "*Bachur'l*," he asked. "Do you ever study the Tosfos Yom Tov?"

Lipa shook his head. "I can't understand it," he explained.

The Maggid made a sour face. "*You* can't understand it—*you*? You are an *einekel* of the Tosfos Yom Tov! Aren't you a *levi, bachur'l*?"

"Yes."

"And your family name is—what?"

"Wallerstein."

"Wallerstein! You are a *levi* and a Wallerstein! Do you know that the Tosfos Yom Tov was born in a town called Wallerstein, and it was once the name of his family? You are a *ben achar ben* of the holy Tosfos Yom Tov! Tell me—who was the Tosfos Yom Tov's teacher—do you know?"

Lipa shook his head. He hardly knew who the Tosfos Yom Tov was.

The Maggid shook his head. "The *rebbi* of the Tosfos Yom Tov was the holy Maharal of Prague, who made the *Golem*! The Tosfos

Yom Tov was his closest pupil. Who knows—maybe the Tosfos Yom Tov even met the *Golem*! The Tosfos Yom Tov was your *Zeide*, and you don't even learn him! *Ay yay yay!*"

"I don't understand his words," Lipa apologized.

The Maggid tried to calm him. "*Bachur'l*, someday you are going to be a tzaddik, and you will learn the Tosfos Yom Tov. He will even come and help you."

The Maggid returned his finger back to the mishnah. "At least listen, *bachur'l*, while I read."

In a sweetly accented *niggun*, his thumb twisting happily through the air, the Maggid began reciting: "*Peirush harav, hotza'ah she'mereshus l'reshus…*"

Lipa never heard any further. His head dropped and he fell fast asleep right onto the table. Rabbi Wallerstein himself had to come down a few minutes later and rescue Lipa and the little Maggid, who was still twisting his thumb happily.

A gray cloud of loneliness hung over Lipa. It was nearing June. Although he still had his precious hour of learning with Shmuel, the term ended in a few weeks. Shmuel would go away to camp, he wouldn't see him for two months, and Lipa would be confined to the loneliness of his backyard. There was nothing he could do— it was what it was. This particular Monday afternoon, the Wallerstein's house was especially still. It was Decoration Day and Rabbi Wallerstein was invited to give the invocation at the city's observance, together with the mayor and other dignitaries. It was a great honor, and Rabbi Wallerstein took along his mother and Eva to hear him speak. Leon had a baseball game with his friends. Lipa returned alone from his half day at yeshivah to an empty house. He made himself lunch, and tried to figure out what to do next.

Since the Maggid's visit to the house a few weeks before, Lipa had developed a great interest in his famous ancestor, the Tosfos Yom Tov. He wanted to go back down to his father's office, retrieve the volume *Beis* that he had lent the Maggid and peer into the commentary—even if he didn't understand the words. But Lipa wasn't stupid. Twice before he had opened the holy volumes and been plunged into all sorts of situations—he didn't want that to happen again!

But that was then and now was now. Before, he had sneaked down at night, when it was dark and scary and he was alone. In the dark, anything was possible—Rabbi Ovadiah of Bartenura knocking on the door, Rabbi Shlomo Adani hiding in the coal bin. But now it was a warm afternoon, with the sun shining brightly over Ulysses Avenue. Cars ran down the street, he heard voices of kids playing—it was safe.

So, with utter privacy, with no one home to watch, Lipa went downstairs to his father's office. For good measure, he checked out the front window whose blinds were raised. The street was there, people walked by—everything was normal. He found the second volume of his *Zeide's* Mishnah, pulled it out, and lay it on his father's desk. He opened to the first folio of *Shabbos* and saw how the page was laid out, the bold letter mishnah in the middle, *Bartenura's* commentary on the right, and then his *Zeide's Zeide*, the Tosfos Yom Tov, so much larger than any other section of the page. He could not understand the words, but he turned page after page, from *Shabbos* to *Eruvin*, and it was almost always the same—a little mishnah, a bit of *Bartenura*, and then lots and lots of his *Zeide's* words. Sometimes his commentary alone took up a whole page, with nothing else but his commentary.

Someday I am going to learn these words, promised Lipa.

Lipa was so immersed in turning the pages and admiring his

ancestor's commentary that at first he did not notice the sound of pebbles striking the front window. But as the sharp tapping continued, it finally caught his attention and he looked up. Lipa walked to the window, looked out, but saw no one. Maybe it was some birds banging against the window. He went back to his *sefer*, but the tapping started again. He looked up quickly and saw that someone was throwing small stones at the window. There were a number of wild boys on the block, Irish and Italian teenagers, who liked to make trouble for the rabbi, and they were probably at it now. Lipa was especially frightened of them now as he was all alone in the house. He tried to ignore them and hoped they would just grow tired of their game and go away. But the sharp rapping grew louder and more persistent, almost like a drum beat. Finally, despite his timidity, Lipa lost his patience. He ran to the window, raised it slightly and yelled out: "Get away!"

But there was no one there.

There was quiet for a few minutes, and Lipa hoped they had run away, but then the pebbles began striking sharply against a window that stood behind his father's desk. That window faced a narrow alleyway that ran along the far side of the house, and its blinds were always closed. A high, narrow wooden wall separated the alley from the street, and there was no way they could hit that side window unless they either climbed over the wall, or worse, ran around the whole house and invaded the alley. The situation grew scarier—it meant a gang of them was in the back, attacking him. Lipa ran to the covered window, pulled back the side of the blind slightly—afraid to be seen—and banged hard in the window, trying to scare them away. There was quiet for a moment, and then the window banging started from the back side room which served as the shul storeroom. They were taunting him, going from window to window! Despite his fear, Lipa followed the sound of stones tapping loudly against the windows—they must have thrown a hundred stones. There were no shades on the storeroom windows, and Lipa peered cautiously out to the alley. There was no one there—they must have fled.

He was about to return to his father's office where the Mishnah still lay open, when he heard a terrible crack against the window at the back of the women's shul. They were in the backyard now! The sound of stone smashing against the window was so loud that Lipa was sure they broke the glass. He ran nervously into the women's section, fearful that the bunch of boys might even try to break in. The blinds were pulled down over the window, and even the shade covering the back door was lowered, so the room was cast in shadow, and Lipa could not tell who was out back. He approached the back window carefully. There was no broken glass on the floor and the banging had stopped—maybe they had gotten scared and ran away.

Suddenly, a voice called out. "Lipa Wallerstein, come on out!"

Lipa stopped short, and the hairs on the back of his neck rose. Those Irish and Italian boys didn't know his name—who was calling him?

"Lipa Wallerstein, don't be afraid!" the voice called loudly. "Come on out—we're waiting for you!"

Who was waiting for him?

"Who is there?" Lipa answered, hiding behind the door.

"Don't be afraid—come out!"

Lipa *was* frightened. Who was calling him? Who knew his name? The voice sounded…almost friendly. Lipa was bewildered—what should he do? He was afraid. But—here he was, alone in the empty house with absolutely nothing to do. What did he have to lose? What could they do to him? With a sudden burst of courage, Lipa threw open the back door and gazed out.

Lipa looked out, absolutely astonished. His dreary concrete backyard was gone! Instead, he gazed upon an open field dappled with a rainbow of wildflowers. A road ran through the field and wended over a far hill. Standing facing him were a half-dozen young men. They looked like yeshivah students, large three-cornered hats set rakishly on their heads, *tzitzis* peering out from under their vests. One of the men stepped forward, his hand outstretched.

"*Shalom aleichem*, Lipa," he introduced himself. "My name is Shmuel."

Still confused, Lipa took his hand and shook it limply.

"Who—who are you?" he asked.

"Why are you so surprised, Lipa Wallerstein," Shmuel answered. "Weren't you just inside, looking at my father's *peirush*?"

Still Lipa was speechless, and Shmuel lost his patience. "The Tosfos Yom Tov—weren't you just studying the Tosfos Yom Tov all by yourself?"

"Ye…yes."

"Did you understand it?"

"No—not a word."

Shmuel stood up proudly. "The Tosfos Yom Tov is my father! I haven't seen him in four years and now I'm going back home to visit him. Come along with us —you'll meet him! Maybe he'll teach you himself!"

Lipa was dumbfounded. He stood there uncertainly. The other men began shuffling impatiently, eager to move on.

"Is it far?" asked Lipa.

"Yes, it is far," said Shmuel. "But what do you care? It will be the greatest walk you ever had! You'll see all the great sights! We have plenty of places where we can find food and places to sleep. Come on, Lipa, don't be afraid! You can be part of our *chevrah* and even meet my father."

There was such optimism and joy in Shmuel's voice. The other students also seem spirited and happy, eager to run like young deer, so that Lipa's spirits were suddenly lifted. He was off to see the Tosfos Yom Tov!

He shut the door tightly behind him and announced:

"Shmuel, wait for me—I'm coming along!"

8. Vienna, Austria
Tammuz 5389 (1629)

Lipa had never known such fun in his life. Unlike his other adventures, when he was swept onto a boat with a dangerous crew, or suffered with Shlomo Adani in a poor hovel, the band he had attached himself to now was full of joy and confidence—heading home. Shmuel was their leader. He walked a little ahead, showing the way, deciding when to rest at the side of the road or turn off to a village for the night. They marched jauntily, their backpacks hanging from poles slung over their shoulders. Lipa walked alongside Shmuel, who watched over him like a big brother. He was very talkative. The students, he explained, had just ended a long *zman* at the Yeshivah of Metz in France, studying with the famed Rabbi Mordecai Luria. It was not easy—there were wars going on all over the countryside. Now they were heading home to see their parents, maybe even find a wife. Shmuel hadn't seen his famous father, the Tosfos Yom Tov, for four years, since his bar mitzvah. He had become tall and grown up; he doubted his father would even recognize him. He would have stayed longer in yeshivah, Shmuel said, but his father had sent him a letter begging him to come home.

"Didn't you miss him?" asked Lipa.

"Yes and no," answered Shmuel. "I knew he loves me, and I love him. He sent me ten silver pieces each month, so I had more money than any other student in the yeshivah. I helped out the others. And then he sent me letters every month, full of the latest news at home, all the honor he received from the people in Prague—even the gentiles—and his *chiddushim*. And I sent him back some of my *chiddushim*. So we were really very close. You don't have to see someone face to face to be close, Lipa—you can be far, and still be very close. I felt my father near me wherever I was."

And you can be close and still very far, thought Lipa. *I wish I had a father like that.*

Shmuel was right—it was a long trek that Lipa had never known before. They marched steadily on the long road, passing ox-carts carrying families escaping battles, peddlers tramping from town to town hawking wares, soldiers on horseback riding fiercely toward them, causing them to scramble off the road for safety. But there was a *simchah* in this band of students that Lipa had never known before.

"We're going to see our parents," explained Shmuel. "Every step we take is a mitzvah—why shouldn't we be in good spirits?" Then he counted off gaily, "*Step one, mitzvah—step two, mitzvah—step three, mitzvah…*"

Often they broke into a song or *niggun*, or someone mentioned a verse from the *parshah*, or a line in Rashi, and there would be lively argument. The boys spoke Yiddish, but also a half-dozen other languages: German, Polish, Russian, a smattering of French. They followed the Rhine River south, and then crossed over by raft, heading east.

There was no problem finding a place to eat or sleep. After all, they were yeshivah students. In every city or town they lodged for the night, they were welcomed like royalty—for they were the *talmidei chachamim* of the future. Shmuel received special attention. Whenever the local community heard he was the son of the author of the *Tosfos Yom Tov*, he was treated like a celebrity. The whole of

Europe marveled at his father's brilliant, encyclopedic commentary. They stopped in small villages and great cities like Frankfurt, Salzburg, Regensburg, Linz. In each community, however small, there was a shul, a *beis medrash*, a *hachnasas orchim* for visitors.

Lipa was used to the colorless streets of Jersey City or the drab tenements of the Lower East Side. The trek through the Rhineland was like a journey through an enchanted forest. Here, great castles overlooked the Rhine, with ornate parapets and soaring steeples. Huge, gray fortresses clung to cliff tops, keeping watch on the valley below. Sun-drenched orchards and vineyards lined the road, with lush fields of ripened grain. The road traversed through dark, foreboding forests that turned day into night.

"It is so beautiful here," Lipa murmured to Shmuel with childlike admiration. "The farms are so full of fruit, I see so many deer in the forest, the castles are so big and beautiful."

Shmuel, who was usually so ebullient, did not answer, and his face clouded. He shook his head. "We are walking on German ground, Lipa. So many Jews were killed here by murderous rabble, and who knows what they will do in the future. I will be happy when we are out of this land."

"Where are your father and mother?" asked Lipa.

"My father is *rav* of Prague, in Bohemia," answered Shmuel. "But I haven't seen my uncle since I was ten years old. He lives in Vienna. I owe him a visit; who knows when I'll ever get another chance to see him. I'll go to him first, and then go home to Prague."

It was many days since they set out from Metz until they reached the banks of the Danube. From there the road led to Vienna.

"You traveled so far away to study Torah, Shmuel?" Lipa asked wonderingly. "Are there no other *yeshivos* that are closer?"

Shmuel pointed to the boys following. "Others here have traveled even further than I, from Poland and Russia and Hungary.

There are many good *yeshivos*, but we all wanted to fulfill the Mishnah's admonishment: *Hevei golah l'makom Torah*—'Go into exile to study Torah.' That is why we wandered so far away."

Indeed, like birds abandoning a flock, one by one, the students began leaving the troupe. They reached main crossroads heading north or south, and each one took his leave. It was a sad moment. A student proclaimed: "Here I must leave you, my worthy *chaveirim*." He embraced each one of the students in turn, and they poured fervent blessings on each other—a blessing to last a lifetime. For the roads were dangerous, sundered by wars, threatened by highwaymen, bands of hooligans looking for victims. Each student now went his own way in life, and they might not ever see each other again. The partings were very sad, for once a friend was gone—he was gone. In the end, Shmuel and Lipa were left by themselves, walking the main road to Vienna.

They had just passed the town of Tulln, a two-day trek from Vienna, when the pastoral scene they had enjoyed changed dramatically. Before, the road had been sparsely traveled and peaceful, but now companies of Austrian soldiers suddenly appeared, heading out to battle. There were army camps surrounding the capital, and the soldiers were heading out to confront the enemy. Meanwhile, wagons were heading back toward the camps, carrying wounded soldiers in heavy wooden carts. The sheets that covered them were stained with blood. It was a chaotic scene, horses dashing down the road, hoof beats thundering, carrying commanders racing to the battlefield. From a far distance came the deep rumble of heavy cannon, the echo rolling over them like muffled thunder. It was difficult to walk on the road with all the military traffic. Shmuel led Lipa up onto a small rise that ran alongside the road, out of the way of the marching soldiers. But even that did not spare them the sharp stares of the soldiers who watched them as they marched by.

Shmuel and Lipa were obviously Jews, not Austrians—maybe they were spying for the enemy. The closer they marched toward the city, the longer and more suspicious were the looks they received.

Shmuel suddenly sensed danger. "Come," he urged Lipa, "we have to get away from here."

They left the side of the road, passing over the rise that took them out of sight of the soldiers. In the distance beyond thick brush, they spied the waters of the Danube River.

"We have no choice," Shmuel told Lipa. "The roads are too dangerous now to change plans and go to Prague. We'll just have to follow alongside the river until we reach Vienna."

What had been an easy jaunt until now turned into a great challenge, just to move ahead. Occasionally, there was a narrow trail along the riverbank pounded smooth by travelers, but mostly the riverbank was a tangle of thorny bushes and thick underbrush. The ground was uneven and slippery, made slick from rain and waves from the river that lapped up alongside the banks. The trek was slow and treacherous, but there was no other choice. Shmuel led, bending back bushes, seeking footholds, while Lipa followed close at his heels. Sometimes Shmuel had to lift Lipa past obstacles, or over treacherous gaps where the riverbank had collapsed. Even from this distance they could hear the sound of the cannon, and soldiers marching to the beat of war drums. Baruch Hashem *that we are hidden*, thought Shmuel. Meanwhile, Lipa was having the adventure of his lifetime! The river ran to their left, and occasional large ships sailed downstream toward Vienna.

The sun began sinking westward, casting long shadows. The air grew cooler. There would be no comfortable resting place tonight—they were lucky just to be safe. It was time to *daven* Minchah. Fortunately, they entered a small clearing where they could at least stand upright. There were high grasses to the right that shielded them

The Shul Boy 179

from the road, and the only intrusion were two boys fishing alongside the river. The boys seemed more frightened of Shmuel than Shmuel was afraid of them. He waved to them in a polite manner to show that he meant no harm, and ascertaining which way was Yerushalayim, he lent Lipa his small siddur, and they both began praying with great earnestness, swaying like tall grass.

Hashem, Shmuel prayed, *I am suddenly afraid—please help us*!

They finished praying, even as the day grew to a close. The two boys who had kept their distance now stood up and approached them. They were not much older than Lipa, dressed in straw hats and rough peasant shirts.

"Are you Jews?" asked one of them, a freckle-faced boy with tousled red hair.

Why is he asking? thought Shmuel.

"Yes, we are—" he answered cautiously.

"I never saw Jews pray before. Are you Jews allowed to eat fish?"

Shmuel laughed. "Why are you asking?" he asked.

"We caught a really big carp, and we will sell it to you if you want to buy it. You want to see it?"

Half amused, half bemused, Shmuel followed the boys to the river bank where their fishing poles lay on a small wooden platform, which bobbed in the water. The boys pulled their line out of the water, showing off the fish that was still alive, caught in a hook. It was a good-sized fish. As they stood on the platform, it swayed under them. Shmuel realized that they were standing on a raft hauled up halfway onto the side of the bank. A sudden idea struck him.

"How much do you want for the fish?" he asked.

The boys looked at each other uncertainly. Obviously, they had no idea what to ask for.

"What will you pay?" asked the boy with the tousled head.

"I'll make you a deal," Shmuel said. He took out his purse, and extracted three silver coins. The boys' eyes grew wide—they had probably never seen so much money in their lives. "I will pay you three silver coins for the fish—and for this raft. It's not going to last very much longer anyway; the wood is old. What do you say?"

The two young fishermen looked at each other in amazement. For them, it was the deal of their lifetimes—three pieces of silver was a small fortune. At first, they couldn't answer.

"Okay," said Shmuel, "forget it. We'll just move on."

"You can have the raft," they answered quickly in chorus.

Shmuel smiled to himself, extracted the three coins and handed it to them. They grabbed the money and were gone in a blink, running up the thin path that led through the grass. They were probably afraid that Shmuel might change his mind.

Shmuel turned to Lipa. "You see, Lipa, how Hashem helps! We won't even have to walk to Vienna. We'll ride the raft right down to the city."

Shmuel reached down and cut the poor carp free from the raft, carefully extracting the hook: *v'rachamav al kol ma'asav*. It swam off almost as fast as the boys, slipping deep into the dark waters. Shmuel settled Lipa next to him in the middle of the raft, pushed off the riverbank with the oar the boys had left, and they were immediately carried by the strong current into the middle of the great Danube, just as the sun set and darkness fell.

Shmuel took out a shirt from his bag, folding it under Lipa's head like a pillow. He himself lay down against his backpack. They had enough food for the night, and when they reached Vienna there would be plenty to eat at his uncle's house. The night was pitch black and moonless, and they gazed up to a dazzling sky filled with endless shimmering stars.

Lipa was awestruck. "I never saw so many stars in my life," he exclaimed to Shmuel excitedly.

"*Mah rabbu ma'asecha Hashem*—'How great are Thy works, Hashem,'" Shmuel answered. "Do you know any of their names?"

"None."

Shmuel pointed heavenward. "You see that bright star there on the east?"

"Where?"

"*There*, right over those trees! That is not a star—it is a planet, *Shabtai*. The gentiles call it Saturn. And you see there, in the west, that shiny star?"

"Where?"

"There—Lipa, can't you see?"

"I see."

"That is *Nogah*, Venus. Isn't it beautiful—look how it glistens, almost like the moon."

"What is that red star, right above us?"

Shmuel frowned. "That is *Ma'adim*, Mars—the star of War."

Just as he pronounced the word "war," they heard the boom of a cannon, thundering in the distance.

"The sky is full of wonders, Lipa—you just have to look up. Look—there is the North Star, and there is the Great Bowl. Look at the three stars in a row; that is the belt of Orion, the Hunter."

"How do you know so much about the stars?" asked Lipa.

"My father taught me. He is a *gaon* in astronomy. There are millions of stars, and each star sings its own song to Hashem. Can you hear them singing?"

In the absolute stillness except for the waves lapping against the raft, Lipa listened closely. Above, the stars danced in their heavenly hosts, Gemini and Capricorn, Vega and Sirius, the Scorpion and the Bear; they all sang praise to Hashem.

"Do you hear them, Lipa?" Shmuel demanded again.

"I hear each star *davening* to Hashem," Lipa responded.

Pleased at Lipa's response, Shmuel continued his lecture on the stars. "Stars are *mazel*, Lipa. Every person has a *mazel*. If he's lucky, he has good *mazel*." Shmuel paused, contemplating his next words. "Can I tell you a secret, Lipa, just between you and me, since I made you my little brother?"

"Tell me," urged Lipa.

"I must have been born under the brightest *mazel* in the sky, like *Nogah*, for I don't know a person in the world who is luckier than I! Look how many Jews are so terribly poor, have no homes, are sick, sold like slaves, driven from their homes like the Spanish Jews. And here I am, I have all the money I need! I am the son of the famous Tostos Yom Tov. I don't mean to show off, Lipa, but we are *really* rich. My father has money and *sefarim* and a beautiful house. My father is the Rabbi of Prague, a student of the Maharal of Prague!"

"Did your father ever meet the Maharal's *Golem*?" asked Lipa.

Shmuel grew coy. "I'm not allowed to talk about that—not even to you, Lipa. But look here—I am just sixteen years old and I have learned the whole *Shas*, all of the Talmud!"

"Every word?"

"Every word—with Rashi and Tosafos. Now, I am going back to visit my father like royalty. He won't even recognize me, I grew so tall. Oh, what a greeting I am going to get! I bet the Prague synagogue makes a special kiddush to welcome me back."

"You are so lucky," said Lipa enviously. "What about my star, Shmuel?" asked Lipa. "How bright is my star?"

Shmuel was silent at first, not certain what to say. "I don't know, Lipa. You are still young—but I read a lot of loneliness on your face. Your star isn't shining so brightly yet. You yourself have to make your star shine, Lipa! Your star is like your name—you make your name shine by how you act. Lipa, do you know—your *neshamah* is

The Shul Boy ↩ 183

hidden inside your name, your star shines over your name. Do you want to hear a joke about a name, Lipa?"

"Tell me."

"What is your family's name?"

"Wallerstein."

"And do you know the name of the great general who is leading the fight for our Kaiser?"

"No."

"*Wallerstein*—General Von Wallerstein! He is a great field marshal, and someday you must be a great field marshal—of mitzvos! You hear me, General Lipa Von Wallerstein!"

Lipa laughed, laughed—but absorbed everything, gazing dreamily upward. The vast constellations moved majestically across the skies. Lipa tried to count the brightest stars, and his eyes began to droop. With the murmur of waves lapping around them, Shmuel and Lipa both fell sound asleep as the raft carried them silently toward Vienna.

Little did Shmuel know that even as he slept, his father's star had darkened to deepest black...

The two voyagers woke at the same time with a firm bump. The raft had been carried by a turn in the river to the riverbank, and it became ensnarled in branches. Shmuel leaned over carefully, hauling the raft alongside the shore, and with Lipa in tow, they climbed up to higher ground. They climbed a small hillock and Shmuel searched the horizon.

"I can't believe it!" he proclaimed happily. "Look, Lipa, you see the skyline over there, those spires—that's Vienna. The raft must have carried us fifteen miles during the night. It would have taken us two days by foot."

Lipa gazed in the direction of the city. It seemed to grow out of the forest, with mighty buildings, spires that reached into the sky, great palaces. It floated in the distance like a beautiful canvas.

"We're still not there yet," warned Shmuel. "It will still be a good day's walk. We'll *daven*, have something to eat, and then set out. I don't hear any cannon explosions here—the battle must be far away."

They prayed quickly and Shmuel broke out breakfast. In truth, they were growing low on food, and Shmuel kept back some bread and cheese for lunch. They finished eating and set out on the last leg of their long trek to the capital city.

They neared the outskirts of the capital; there was no trace of battle. The soldiers had all departed, and the road was peaceful, even deserted. All along were signs of the Hapsburgs' mighty reign, beautiful formal gardens, ornate palaces hidden behind great iron gates and long entranceways, an occasional government stagecoach drawn by magnificent white horses. Vienna appeared closer than it really was—there were still a few miles to go. The hot sun rose high in the sky and the day grew extremely warm, hotter than any other day of their long journey. Even Shmuel, who was usually tireless, grew exhausted. They were still a few hours from the edge of the city, and then they would have to find the Jewish Quarter along the river. They came alongside a shady park, a Royal *Lustgarten*, with a formal path that led deep inside a shaded forest. There was still plenty of time to reach Vienna before nightfall, and Shmuel decided to stop.

Lipa, who suffered silently but was even more exhausted, agreed happily. They turned down the path and immediately Shmuel felt revived. The path had been laid out skillfully, leading them through a pleasant walk beneath leafy oaks and elms. Interspersed among the trees were small grassy clearings, bordered with multi-colored wildflowers, watered by little brooks that ran over stones. This was one of Vienna's renowned pleasure gardens, meant for the nobility. Perhaps Jews were not even allowed here, but there was no one to stop them. It was a little Gan Eden, and Shmuel decided to take a short nap in the shade.

They entered an attractive clearing, bordered with fragrant wildflowers. A stone frog poured constant cool waters out of his mouth into a scalloped fountain. Birds fluttered in the branches. One little bluebird squirted water over himself happily in the fountain, chirping in welcome. Shmuel laid down his knapsack, indicated to Lipa to lie down alongside, and wearily closed his eyes.

"*Help! Help! Help!*"

Shmuel's eyes opened wide. Terrible screams were coming from the path, and an earsplitting bellowing that frightened Shmuel to the bone.

"*Help us! Oh, please someone help us! Please!*"

The terrible screams mixed with the ear-piercing growling. Without thinking, Shmuel jumped up, pulled Lipa after him, and ran in the direction of the screams. On the road were two young women and a little boy. Between them and Shmuel stood a huge bull that had emerged from the woods. His head was down, he bellowed and snorted in rage, his horns lowered, ready to charge. The women stood petrified, screaming hysterically. They saw Shmuel, and their pleas grew more desperate.

"Lipa," Shmuel ordered, "listen to me! Start yelling, '*Hayn! Hayn!*'"

Lipa looked at Shmuel, confused. "What are you waiting for?!" Shmuel screamed angrily. "Yell '*Hayn, hayn*' and wave your arms—quick!"

Totally flustered, Lipa obeyed, screaming, "*Hayn! Hayn!*" as loudly as he could, waving his arms furiously. For just an instant, the bull was distracted and turned his head toward them. Shmuel leaped around the bull, raced in front of it, and grabbed a bright red bonnet that one of the women was wearing. He tore it off her head, threw it right before the bull, and chased the women behind a tree. The bull spotted the red garment and charged furiously, gored it with his sharp horns, and stomped on it repeatedly, totally crushing it to shreds. The women watched in horror, trembling in their hiding place. Meanwhile, Shmuel and Lipa ran for shelter behind trees.

It was not necessary. Having totally demolished the red piece of material to his satisfaction, the bull calmly turned and sauntered back into the woods, totally pleased with himself.

There was a moment's stunned silence, and then a man's voice called from a distance. "Marguerite! Marguerite! Where are you?"

The women ran out of their hiding place toward the voice. "Pierre! Pierre!" screamed the older woman. "We're here, help us!"

In a minute, a man appeared, racing down the road toward the women and the little boy. He was dressed in a glistening white uniform adorned with gold braids and medals. The woman embraced her husband, and the officer lifted his young son high in the air.

"What happened?" he asked anxiously. "I heard your cries all the way down from the road."

Her voice shaking, she quickly unfolded the events. They had been walking, their son and his sitter. The young maid had been wearing a bright crimson bonnet she had brought to Vienna. The bull came raging wildly out of the woods from nowhere, spied the red hat and was ready to gore them all.

"We would have been killed, Pierre," she sobbed, "but—" She turned and pointed to Shmuel and Lipa who were still back down the path, watching the drama from behind the trees. "Those boys—those Jewish boys, they ran and saved us! They saved our lives, Pierre!"

Her husband tried to calm her, looking toward Shmuel and Lipa. He placed his wife and son back in the arms of the maid who was still shaking, kept his hand close to his holster should the bull reappear, and walked quickly toward Shmuel.

Shmuel was anxious. He had never seen such a bemedaled soldier before, and he did not know what to expect or say. The officer gestured to them:

"Come here, boys," he called out, in French.

"We are coming," Shmuel responded—in perfect French.

The officer was astonished. They approached slowly, timidly, unsure of what to expect.

The officer would have nothing of that. "Come here," he shouted impatiently. "Why are you so fearful?"

They approached more quickly, and he ran to meet them, embracing them together in his strong arms. "You saved my wife and my son's life, you two," he exclaimed gratefully. "And that sitter with her silly crimson bonnet! You saved my whole life!"

"We did what we had to do," Shmuel answered humbly. "There wasn't even time to think. It just happened! Thank G-d everyone is safe."

"Never mind 'it just happened,'" answered the officer roughly. "You are heroes—especially you! You ran right in front of the angry bull and saved everyone! Without you, he would have done to my wife and son what he did to that hat."

With those words, his faced turned ashen, realizing how close his wife and child had come to death. What had been a beautiful bonnet moments before, now was a pile of shattered red fabric, caked in dust.

He stood there for a moment, stunned into silence, then turned to his wife, trying to put on a brave face.

"Come, Marguerite," he said tenderly, "the coach is right on the road. We'll head straight for Vienna."

They began walking back toward the park entrance, the boy in his father's arms, the two women, still shaken, embracing each other. Suddenly, the officer stopped and turned: "What are you lads waiting for?" he shouted. "You're coming with us to Vienna. Hurry up!"

He turned toward the road, and Shmuel followed well behind. He turned to Lipa and whispered: "I can't believe this—we're getting a coach ride to Vienna! I told you—I'm under a bright star."

They reached the road. The women climbed into the coach. Shmuel had never seen such a beautiful carriage in his life, drawn by a team of four matching white horses. The coach was large, its black sides polished like mirrors. A painted coat of arms was emblazoned on its door. The officer stood at the foot of the carriage, waiting for Shmuel and Lipa. "Get in, get in," he urged. "We are late."

It was not easy for Lipa to reach the floor of the coach, and Shmuel had to help him up. The officer jumped in last, and one of two coachmen closed the door behind him. The interior of the carriage was as opulent as the outside, with satiny flowered benches, silk curtains to keep out unwanted glances, and even a small lantern that hung from the ceiling. With an abrupt lurch, the coach started moving. The two young women and boy sat on one side facing Shmuel and Lipa, while the officer sat diagonally along the wall between them.

The officer had regained his composure. He was an extremely imposing man, tall and very handsome. Although he was young, he radiated authority. He looked at Shmuel for a long time, not saying anything, like he was studying him. Shmuel look down, unused to this special attention. Lipa, meanwhile, was having a grand time, enjoying the coach ride.

The Shul Boy ∽ 189

Finally, the officer broke his silence. "You are a Jew. Where did you learn to speak French so well?"

Shmuel answered softly, respectfully. "I studied in a Jewish school in Metz for four years. I learned French just from speaking to the townsfolk."

"You speak a more refined French than half my own countrymen. Why did you go to study in Metz?"

Shmuel could not restrain his pride. "My father is the Chief Rabbi of Prague. He sent me there to learn my faith and now I am returning. I have not seen him in four years."

"You are a very impressive young man," the officer answered. "It is a shame…"

A shame? Shmuel was confused by the officer's words, and it showed on his face. *What was a shame*?

The officer explained, somewhat apologetically. "If you weren't a Jew, I would take you under my wing and send you to a French university, even to the court in Paris. You have the making of greatness, but you are Jew. Pity."

Pity? Shmuel would have liked to answer—that being a servant of the Al-mighty was greater than all the royal court with its dissoluteness. But he was wise enough to keep his mouth shut.

The carriage traveled quickly, and they grew closer to the capital. The officer reached under his jacket, took out a pouch, and extracted a fist full of gold coins.

"You saved my wife and child's life, Samuel. I want to reward you. Please take this, for you and your little brother." He reached over to hand Shmuel the money, but Shmuel refused.

"I do not want the money," he said firmly.

The officer was taken aback—he held the handful of gold ducats in his hand, a fortune. "Why not?" he asked.

"Your Excellency," answered Shmuel, "what I did before was

what we call in our Jewish faith a good deed, a mitzvah. I did it because it was the right thing to do. I cannot accept payment for a good deed."

The officer was astonished. "I never heard of a Jew who would not accept money."

Shmuel's face reddened. He tried to suppress his anger, but he couldn't. "Your Excellency, I mean no disrespect, but you have been told falsehoods all your life about Jews! Jews are wonderful people! They are G-d-fearing, and honest and hardworking. They are loyal to their homeland and to their king. And yet, out of jealousy and hate, people make up fabrications about us—we are greedy, that we are full of trickery, we are dishonest. We are not, we are not!"

By themselves, tears began streaming from Shmuel's eyes. *Why do Christians always speak so badly about us?*

The officer stared at Shmuel for a long time without speaking, and his face reflected deep regret. No one, no Jew, had ever spoken to him like this before. Shmuel, embarrassed at his tears, wiped his face dry with his sleeve.

"Samuel," said the officer soberly, "I wish I had a son like you."

They entered the cobbled streets of Vienna. Soon they would have to depart, the officer to the Hapsburgs' Court, and Shmuel to the Jewish Quarter. Until this time, Shmuel had no idea to whom he was speaking. The coach stopped alongside a narrow street that led to the Jewish Quarter. Shmuel made ready to leave together with Lipa, who had been silent the whole journey. Perhaps he had spoken too boldly but it did not matter; he had said what he had said and the words could not be returned.

The officer addressed Shmuel. "Samuel, you informed me that you are the son of the Chief Rabbi of Prague. Now, I will introduce myself. I am His Majesty, the King of France's ambassador to the royal court of the Hapsburgs. France and Austria are together

The Shul Boy 191

fighting a great war against the Protestants, but we hope to sign a peace agreement. My post is very important to both countries, and I have great influence here. If you are ever in need, Samuel, you must come to me! Do you understand? We owe you everything."

Shmuel's face colored with joy. His star was shining even brighter. *The ambassador of France to the royal court*!

"Your Excellency," answered Shmuel, "I thank you sincerely, but I ask of you just one favor. If ever you can help our people, please help them in their great distress. That is all I ask."

"Even so," the ambassador answered sternly. "You never know, Samuel, when even you, the great rabbi's son, might need my help. Here—"

He extracted a richly embossed card from his jacket and scribbled a few words on the back.

"Here," he said, handing the card to Shmuel. "This card bears my name and ambassadorial seal. "If you ever run into trouble, show it. And may your G-d watch over you."

He leaned over and embraced Shmuel warmly. Then he gave Lipa an affectionate pinch on his cheek, so heartily that it hurt. *Why does everyone have to pinch my cheek*? thought Lipa.

The coach sped off, and Shmuel and Lipa stood at the roadway leading to the Jewish Quarter. *Did this really happen to me*? wondered Shmuel. It seemed like a dream. But he held the ambassador's gleaming white card in his hand, and that was no dream. He slipped the card into his inner pocket next to a thin siddur. He was filled with joy—meeting the mighty French ambassador, and now—onward to his uncle's house!

Night fell. Shmuel and Lipa walked through the darkened streets of the Jewish Quarter, near the riverbank. The night was still, the air warm. Although he was tired from his long and adventurous day, Shmuel was eager to see his uncle and aunt. He had an address, but no idea where the street was. A lone soul walked the dark road, and Shmuel accosted him:

"My master, would you know the house where Reb Baruch Zatruner dwells?"

Shmuel had chosen well. The stranger was a kindly person. "You will never find it yourself," he said. "Come, I will take you there." Again, Shmuel's bright star led him.

The stranger led them through a labyrinth of cobbled streets and twisting lanes until they stood in front of a narrow, tall building with a gabled roof. Shmuel thanked the stranger for his kindness, and he left them there before the dark building. No light shone from any window, and the house had a somber, mournful look, dampening Shmuel's spirits somewhat. But it did not matter. It was an uncle he had not seen since childhood. He imagined with what joy and excitement he would be welcomed, despite the late hour. Shmuel knocked on the door. There was no answer. He tried again, pounding loudly until finally a window opened above and a head appeared.

"Who is there?" a man's voice called out from above.

It was his uncle, Baruch. "It is I, Shmuel!" Shmuel's voice rang out loudly.

"*Who?*"

"Shmuel—your nephew. Uncle Baruch, open up!"

The man above looked down at him mistrustfully. "I don't recognize you!"

"Reb Baruch, I am Shmuel, your sister's son from Prague. Please, come down and open the door for us!"

"Wait."

The window slammed shut and there was silence. Darkness reigned over the street. It was no surprise that his uncle did not

The Shul Boy 193

recognize him. The last time he saw Shmuel, he was a young boy. Finally, the door opened a crack, guarded by a chain. A face appeared in the opening.

"Who are you?" the man asked.

"Uncle Baruch, don't you know me? I am your nephew, the son of Rabbi Yom Tov Lipman Heller! I have come all the way to Vienna to see you."

The door closed, there was a rattling as the chain was undone, and the door opened. Shmuel recognized his uncle, but his uncle looked at him in astonishment.

"Little Shmuel, is it really you? You are…you are a man already!"

"But you are still the same Uncle Baruch after all these years— *shalom aleichem*!" Shmuel cried joyously.

His uncle finally recognized him, and he cried out emotionally, "Shmuel, I can't believe it is you! How did you know to come here now?"

Shmuel did not understand what his uncle meant by "now," but something in his voice caused him a tiniest tinge of uneasiness. His uncle welcomed him quickly into the house, making sure there were no intruders lurking outside. He didn't even see little Lipa who was almost locked out, but Shmuel dragged Lipa inside behind him. His uncle lit a candle and led him upstairs to the main room, all the time shouting for his wife, "Esther, Esther, we have a surprise guest! Come quickly!"

He led Shmuel to a dining table and sat him down, setting the candle in the middle of the table, and went to fetch some refreshments. In a few minutes, his aunt appeared, took a few minutes to recognize him, and cried out with happiness. His uncle returned with a large fruit bowl, a bottle of wine, and cups. He set them down.

"Eat, eat," his aunt urged. "You must be hungry from your trip. Who is the boy?"

"He is a child I met, a distant relative of ours. I am watching after him until he returns home."

Shmuel and Lipa each took a fruit from the bowl, made a *brachah*, and sliced off a piece. The candle cast a weak glow into the room. *There is something not right here*, Shmuel sensed. Despite his uncle's warm greeting, he felt that there was something going on behind the scenes. He looked down at the fruit he was peeling. He looked up suddenly, and saw that his uncle and aunt were talking to each other with their eyes, *hiding something*. Something was not right.

He looked at his uncle, and saw that hidden on his face was great anxiety. Shmuel could no longer conceal his concern.

"Uncle Baruch, something is troubling you and Aunt Esther. Tell me, what is the matter?"

His uncle seemed almost relieved by Shmuel's question—and his astuteness.

"Tell me, Shmuel," he asked, "why did you come to Vienna?"

"I was heading back home to Prague at the end of the learning *zman*. I knew that I had not seen my precious uncle and aunt for many years, and I wanted to see you once more before I head home. So I came—it was a great adventure."

"And do you know where your father is?"

"In Prague, I imagine."

"Shmuel, I wish you to remain calm, but I must tell you awful news. Your father is not in Prague. He is here in Vienna."

"*Vienna!* Here?" Shmuel stood up in surprise. "Where is he, tell me?" Shmuel was shocked and excited.

His uncle raised his voice. "Sit down, Shmuel, sit down and listen to the terrible thing that has happened. Your father has been imprisoned. He is in the Vienna fortress, a prisoner, bound in chains."

"Imprisoned, imprisoned for what? My father is...he is a tzaddik, he is world famous!"

"Listen, Shmuel—it is worse! He faces, G-d forbid, a sentence of death!"

"A *what*?" Again, Shmuel leaped out of his chair, not believing the incredible news. *His father, imprisoned, facing a death sentence*!

"Not only is he in mortal danger, but because of your father, the whole Jewish community of Prague may be driven out of the city."

Shmuel stared at his uncle, and shook his head in disbelief. *This must be a dream. This can't be happening.*

Shmuel grew very agitated. He was in shock. He collapsed into his chair, unable to speak. His uncle and aunt looked at each other in fright. Shmuel sat like a stone, staring straight ahead. Lipa, who was very frightened, tugged at his sleeve, but Shmuel did not respond.

"Baruch, give him some wine," his aunt cried.

His uncle poured a cup of the strong wine and forced it into Shmuel's hand. "Make a *brachah*," he commanded Shmuel. "Drink."

Dazed, Shmuel followed his uncle's command, recited the blessing, and gulped down half a cup. His color returned, and he began to revive.

"Finish the cup," his uncle ordered. Shmuel drank down the cup, and grew calmer. *What happened to his shining* mazel?

"Tell me, uncle," he asked. "Tell me how this came to be."

His uncle did not answer directly. His eyes were downcast as he carefully considered his words.

"What is the matter, Uncle?" Shmuel asked.

Baruch sighed. "I am ashamed to say what I have to say, but—" He grimaced like he had just tasted something rotten. "But I must tell you. Your father was imprisoned because of a *malshin*, a Jewish informant. A certain prominent Jew in Prague went and reported him to the government."

"A *Jew*?" asked Shmuel, incredulous. "Why? How? How can that be? My father is such a tzaddik; he is kind and forgiving to everyone."

"It does not matter," answered his uncle quickly. "You can be a Moshe Rabbeinu and still have enemies! The short of it is, it had to do with war—and money. Ten years ago there was a rebellion against the Austrian Kaiser, Ferdinand. An assembly of Bohemian barons chose a king of their own, from their own, and a bitter war followed right outside the gates of Vienna, on White Mountain. *Baruch Hashem*, our Kaiser overcame them, and the Jews remained loyal. But the Hapsburgs accumulated great debts in their victory, and they laid a tax on the citizens of Vienna to pay back the huge debt they had accumulated. They laid an especially huge sum on the Prague Jewish community—protection money—and left it to the officials of the Jewish community to apportion the tax each according to his means. Your father was part of that committee, since he is the *rav*. They assessed a certain prominent person in the community a large sum—"

"Who?" demanded Shmuel.

"That's not for me to say," his uncle answered sharply. "It doesn't matter now. That man, anyway, carried a grudge against your father since childhood. He was angry and argued that his assessment was too high. He especially blamed your father, out of envy. Your father sent emissaries to placate him, tried to make peace. But your father was too trusting, like Gedaliah in the Tanach—he never expected what would happen. Behind his back, this man went to his powerful friends in the Austrian court and reported that your father had insulted the Christian religion."

"My father never insults anyone," Shmuel said. "He respects everyone."

"Your father published a new a *sefer*, *Ma'adanei Melech*. The informer went and told the officials that it contained passages that insulted Christians. When the Kaiser was told of this he became furious—he is supposed to be the great defender of the Pope. He had your father brought to Vienna and imprisoned in the great fortress, held in chains. His trial is to be held in a few days. If he is found guilty, *chas v'shalom*, he will be executed and the whole Jewish community of Prague will be exiled from the city. They will lose everything—their homes, their businesses, their shuls, everything!"

At these words, Shmuel gave out a great wail. "But my father is a tzaddik—how could any Jew do this to him? He just writes Torah! Who studies his books but great *talmidei chachamim*? What business does he have with royal courts or insulting Christians? He lives in peace, he is honest with everyone. Who could have done such a terrible thing to my poor father?"

At Shmuel's terrible outcry, his uncle and aunt began weeping also, for the Tosfos Yom Tov, for the poor Jews of Prague, and for the shocking state their nephew suddenly found himself in. He came to Vienna dancing, and instead he sat there now in mourning. Lipa watched the drama unfold, but did not know what to do—he did not understand what was happening.

The tears flowed hot, but they were also a balm. Out of hot tears, grew determination. Shmuel's tears slowed, his breath came furious, and he raised his head in anger. He rinsed his tearstained face, and dried himself clean. They had a surprise to tell *him*—and he had a surprise to tell *them*. Shmuel addressed his uncle and aunt.

"Uncle Baruch—I did not understand what happened to me earlier today, something so strange, straight from Hashem's hand. But now I see: *Hashem makdim refuah l'machalah...*—'Hashem sends the cure before the illness.' Listen—"

Very quickly, Shmuel recalled the amazing incident that occurred earlier that afternoon with the wife of the French ambassador—he had saved her life. The ambassador had offered him a great reward but he refused. The ambassador was very impressed, and told him: *Whenever you need my help, come to me.*

"That is why such a wonderful thing happened," said Shmuel. "It was all from Hashem. Now I have a friend in a high place—the French ambassador to the Austrian court! I shall go to him first thing in the morning and implore him to help my father."

Shmuel's uncle and aunt listened to his story in amazement, and they were filled with hope. But Shmuel's uncle advised him:

"Listen, nephew, it is certainly the hand of Hashem. But listen—before you run to the ambassador, first visit your father and speak with him. He will tell you his whole story and tell you what to say to the ambassador."

"Will they really let me see him?" Shmuel asked excitedly.

"There is no guarantee. The warden of the prison is not a bad man. He knows that your father is a holy man. Some relatives have been allowed to visit your father for a very brief time. Tomorrow, we will pray Shacharis in the synagogue, then you will try to see your father. Just seeing you will give him great strength. Listen to what your father has to say, and then, armed with his words, go to the ambassador. And may Hashem be with you."

Lipa, who had been silent during the whole discussion, suddenly spoke up: "Can I come also?"

The uncle looked down at the timid child and smiled. "Surely you may. How could anyone refuse you entry—with such innocent eyes!"

Shmuel wanted to stay awake all night and recite Tehillim for his father—but he could not. He was utterly wearied from the long, tumultuous day. His uncle showed him and Lipa a quiet room with two large beds. Shmuel fell asleep in a wink. He dreamed… A thousand stars glistened overhead, but one by one they went out. New stars appeared in their place, shone brilliantly for an instant, but they, too, were snuffed out by an invisible hand. The flickering constellations turned in their heavenly orb, but for all their infinite numbers, his father's star was not among them—*had his father's star gone black*, chas v'shalom?

Shmuel's uncle woke him early the next day, otherwise he would have overslept. "Come, nephew," he urged, "we'll go to pray and then you will eat something. With G-d's help, perhaps you will be able to see your father today."

Shmuel dressed quickly and followed his uncle to a small synagogue set among a row of narrow, tall houses. There was just a tiny Hebrew shield, otherwise the shul looked like every other building on the street.

"It is better that we be discreet here in Vienna," his uncle explained. "We were exiled from this city before, and it can happen again. Better that the synagogue does not stand out."

The Shacharis prayers were recited quickly, quietly—like men who are anxious not to be overheard. They left discreetly, in twos or threes, and hurried home. Even Lipa was subdued, and walked close behind Shmuel.

They ate a breakfast with their uncle, said Grace, and it was time to set out. His uncle gave Shmuel a final word of caution.

"We are living in very dangerous times. You are going to the most guarded fortress in Vienna, where those who are charged with the most serious offenses—death sentences—are held. Our *shtadlan*, Reb Henna, received some permission for relatives to visit your father. But it is hit and miss. It matters what mood the warden is in, or his aides, or the guards on watch. Don't talk too much to the guards—they are a mean lot. Ask politely for permission to visit your father. If, with G-d's help, it is granted, he will certainly be overjoyed to see you. Then, leave as soon as you can. I was in the fortress once. It is a fearful place. It is a place of meanness and cruelty, cruel guards, cruel prisoners. Your father sits there, a lamb among wolves. May Hashem watch over you."

With that, his uncle whom he barely knew kissed him on his forehead. When he retreated, Shmuel felt the wetness on his forehead from his uncle's tears. He embraced his uncle, thanked him and his aunt who watched his departure, and grabbing Lipa in tow, headed for the dreaded Vienna fortress where his father lay bound in chains.

They crossed the bridge that led from the Jewish Quarter to the Inner City. Vienna was laid out like a jewel, with large formal gardens, replete with fountains and exquisite flower displays, ornate palaces and government buildings. Shmuel followed his uncle's direction that led them toward the center of the city. It was a warm summer day, and from a distance a violin could be heard playing from one of the numerous outdoor cafés. Lipa followed along excitedly, wide-eyed. He had never seen such glorious boulevards and buildings in his life.

Although his father lay imprisoned, Shmuel was full of hope. Less than twenty-four hours before, he had saved the French ambassador's wife's life, and he pledged to help him if he ever was in trouble. At the memory of the ambassador, Shmuel felt into his inner coat pocket where he had laid the ambassador's card, emblazoned with the French crest, right next to his thin siddur. He felt through the pocket but he could not find the card. Where was it? He stopped in his tracks, and checked the pocket again thoroughly. The card was missing. How did it fall out? Had he put it into another pocket? He was so tired yesterday, last night, that anything was possible. Like a pious Jew searching his pockets for *chametz* on Erev Pesach, he went through all his pockets, again and again. He searched that inner coat pocket a dozen times, removed his siddur wrapped in a thin paper, and pulled his pocket inside out. It was gone! Where

The Shul Boy

was it? He must have dropped it somewhere. Maybe when he took off his coat to go to bed, or maybe when he prayed Shacharis in the morning, and had undone his coat to put on *tefillin*. He was angry with himself. How could he have been so careless? It had an address for the ambassador; it was a calling card with his seal. Now he would have to approach the French embassy cold and try to convince someone that he really knew the ambassador. Perhaps Hashem would have mercy on him and he would still find it back home, or in that shul.

Lipa watched his mentor search frantically over and over, wishing he could help. Shmuel saw the worry on Lipa's face, and reassured him. "I lost the card, Lipa, but I did not lose Hashem."

They continued walking toward the prison. *Why has this happened?* wondered Shmuel. Nothing happens for nothing. *I know,* thought Shmuel. He addressed his young protégé: "Lipa, do you know why I lost that card?"

Lipa shook his head.

"Because I put too much *bitachon* in that card and in the French ambassador. The ambassador is not going to save my father. Hashem will save him. I put too much faith in a person, in a *basar v'dam*, and that is wrong. Listen, Lipa, we still have a way to go. Do you want to stand there, just staring at everything? We should be *davening*. I will say a few words, and you recite after me, like we are in shul, do you understand?"

Lipa nodded brightly, wanting to help.

"*Mizmor l'Dovid—*"

"*Mizmor l'Dovid—*"

"*Hashem ro'i—*"

"*Hashem ro'i—*"

And so Shmuel and Lipa went through the twenty-third psalm, word by word. Shmuel felt stronger, and Lipa beamed with pride.

Instead of wasting time, they had *done* something. They turned a corner, and there, suddenly looming before them, stood the fortress. Shmuel stopped in his tracks, overwhelmed. It was a massive building, black faced and foreboding, towering over the district like some great beast. It had no windows, except small barred portals for air. The building did not seem an inanimate structure, but a living, breathing creature that threatened to gobble up all who dared approach it. Somewhere in that terrible fortress was his father, lying in chains.

"Let's go," Shmuel urged Lipa.

But Lipa couldn't move. Shmuel turned to him impatiently. "Lipa, we have to go in! My father's there, the Tosfos Yom Tov! Remember, you were studying his words."

Lipa stood frozen. "Shmuel, I am afraid," he whimpered.

Shmuel bent next to him. "Listen, Lipa. I am also afraid. But did you never hear. *'yeshuas Hashem k'heref ayin?'* Hashem is greater than any prison and He is with us. Don't be afraid. We have a mitzvah to do—so come!"

Without further discussion, Shmuel took Lipa firmly by the hand and dragged him along until they reached the great wooden doors that served as the entrance to the prison. Two tall guards stood at the entrance, razor sharp pikes in hand. The minute Shmuel approached the steps leading to the doors, they crossed pikes, blocking him.

"What do you want here?" one of the guards demanded.

Shmuel was very frightened. He took a deep breath and tried not to shake. "My father, Rabbi Heller, is here in the prison. I was told that we might visit him. May I be allowed to enter?"

"You need permission from the warden. He is not here now. Come back another time."

"Please," Shmuel pleaded. "I have not seen my father for

four years. He is a holy man. Is there no else that can grant us permission?"

The guards looked at each other questioningly. Shmuel was no more than sixteen, and Lipa—was Lipa. They did not seem to pose any threat. They unlocked their pikes.

"Walk straight ahead inside," the guard said sternly, staring straight ahead. "Maybe the section captain will grant you permission."

"Thank you, sir," Shmuel answered humbly. The guard unlocked the wooden door, and Shmuel and Lipa slipped silently into the prison. They were immediately thrust into darkness. All the sunlight and beauty of outdoors disappeared here. The walls were the same dismal black pilings, blotting out any glimmer of light or hope. The hallway was arched and narrow, cave-like. They passed narrow, barred passageways that branched off the main walkway and led to cells. Shmuel walked straight ahead, not knowing exactly where he was going or what to expect. The fortress was a mammoth structure; it felt like the inside of a mountain. Presently they approached another barred gate, where two other guards stood vigil.

Because they had already penetrated the prison, Shmuel felt less terrified. He was inside, not outside. The sentries watched their approach suspiciously, keeping their hands on the hilt of their swords.

One guard stepped forward. "What is your business here?"

Shmuel tried to speak with confidence. "We are here to visit my father, Rabbi Heller, who is being held here. I was given permission by the guards to enter. Can you tell me where he is?"

The guard studied Shmuel for a long time, silently. His interest was piqued. "Your father is the rabbi?" he asked, as though he didn't believe Shmuel.

"He is."

"I didn't know that rabbis had children. He had a few visitors the last days, but it requires the permission of the warden. Do you have it?"

"The warden is away now. I was told that the captain of the guards watching my father could give permission to visit if the warden is not here. I ask you, please, that I might be allowed to see my father. I haven't seen him in four years."

The guard stared at Shmuel wordlessly, as though he was trying to make up his mind. He glanced down at Lipa.

"Who's he?"

"He is…a grandson. I am in charge of watching him."

The slightest look of amusement crossed the guard's face. Lipa looked away, afraid of his sharp look.

"Well, if a grandson is here, I will let you go through. Your father is in a special secured section on the third floor, in the far corner of the building. Go straight ahead until you find the stairs and go to the third floor. Turn right and walk down the hall until you will reach the door to your father's cell."

He opened the gate for Shmuel and Lipa to pass through. Shmuel thanked him with great excitement—he was getting closer and closer to his father. The guard locked the door behind them. When they were out of earshot, the first guard turned to his companion.

"I bet he'll never get to see his father. Heinz is on duty. He is Meanness itself. Even the warden shakes when he sees him."

In his own way, the guard felt bad for Shmuel and the scared little boy.

Shmuel and Lipa reached the base of the staircase. It was in a dark corner of the walkway, along the back wall. Hardly any light penetrated the deep recesses of this prison. The narrow staircase spiraled upward steeply, each step very high. The guard had said

The Shul Boy

the third floor. But as they climbed higher and higher, there was no doorway or floor. Each "floor" was the equivalent of three or four normal heights. They reached the second landing. Shmuel peered down the center of the stairwell. They must have been forty feet up. They continue climbing upward. His father must be on the very highest landing, under the roof. Despite the shadows, there was no moving air in the stairwell. The heat accumulated like an oven. His father must be suffering terribly.

Finally, they reached the "third" floor, the top of the staircase, under the prison's roof. The heat was intense. A row of small openings allowed in some light, and following the guard's directions, they followed the narrow walkway to the far end, where they met a great wooden door with a small barred window in the upper half. Was his father inside? Shmuel peered in hopefully. No. It was not a cell, but some sort of anteroom, a guardhouse. Shmuel knocked quietly. There was a moment's silence, and then a door opened somewhere, and suddenly a face appeared in the small window.

"Yes?" the face demanded.

"I am Samuel Heller, the son of Rabbi Heller who is being held. I was told that I might visit my father. Could you please let me see him?"

"Did the warden grant permission?"

"The warden is not here. I was told that the commander of the watch could grant permission. May I please speak with him?"

"He is busy."

Shmuel had come so far. His father was only a few feet away. All self-control fell away. Shmuel raised his voice. "*Please*, please, sir. I beg of you. Let me speak to the commander. If I have to wait, I have to wait. *Please!*"

Somewhere, a spark of mercy was kindled in the guard's soul. After a moment's hesitation, there was the sound of a key turning a latch, and the wooden door swung open. "Come in," the guard said grudgingly.

Shmuel and Lipa slipped in quickly, and the guard locked the door behind them. For an instant, Shmuel was overcome with panic—now he was also a prisoner. But he cast the thought aside. On the other side of the room was another door, a door that led to his father. For a moment, he even thought of rushing past the guard and throwing that door open, just to glimpse his father for a second. But he knew that it would bring disaster.

There was a rough wooden bench along one wall. "Sit down and don't move!" the guard ordered. "You stand up without permission and I'll throw you out in a second."

"Yes, sir," Shmuel answered submissively. He took Lipa's hand and sat him next to him. They sat and waited, who knows how long, five minutes, ten minutes. Even a few minutes seemed like forever—imagine his poor father, chained in his cell for weeks.

There was absolute silence, no voices, no sound from the outside, nothing—just the ticking of a clock. Suddenly, a thunderous, deep voice bellowed from the other room.

"THROW THEM OUT!"

Despite the guard's orders, Shmuel jumped up in fright. It sounded like some beast, not a man. Lipa, completely terrified, grabbed Shmuel's hand for protection.

There was a sound of discussion inside, and then the voice roared again, a deep rolling sound that made the doors rattle.

"I DON'T WANT THEM HERE, JOHANNES, DO YOU HEAR ME? THROW THEM BACK DOWN THE STAIRS!"

Again, there was a sound of discussion. Suddenly, there was the thunderous echo of footsteps approaching quickly and the door was thrown open wide. Shmuel, who had regained his seat, stood up in utter fright. He had never seen such a giant person in his life.

The Shul Boy 207

The captain filled the whole doorway with his barrel chest, and his head almost brushed the lintel. He glared down at Shmuel and Lipa angrily.

"What do you Jews want here?" he roared.

Shmuel could hardly answer, but he had no choice. In a stuttering voice, he tried to answer. "Sir…my father, Rabbi Heller, is being held here. I have not seen my father in four years. I ask you, please, sir, may I visit my father, even for a few minutes."

"You haven't seen your father in four years?"

"No."

"So, come back in four more years and maybe I'll let you see him." With that, the giant roared a deep laugh, amused at his own humor.

Shmuel did something that he never thought he would do. He fell on his knee and bowed down like a slave. "Please," he pleaded, "please, for the sake of Heaven, please let me see my father! He is a holy man."

"No Jew is holy," the guard responded roughly. Shmuel kneeled there like a supplicant, giving great pleasure to the immense guard. The first guard peered from behind the door. He was also terrified of the giant.

The captain stood there, considering. In fact, he was in a jolly mood. He had finished a half-dozen steins of Vienna beer, and he was slated to go off duty in a few hours. He looked at the pathetic Jewish boy kneeling helplessly in front of him, and he felt like a cat playing with a mouse. What pleasure was there in just throwing him down the stairs?

"Stand up, laddy," he ordered.

Shmuel, tears wetting his face, stood up. The giant's attitude had changed. His round face was suddenly wrinkled in a warm smile.

"I am a Christian," he announced proudly, "and we Christians know what mercy means. The warden is not here, and I'm going to use my authority as chief guard to help you. I will let you see your father—"

Shmuel's face lit up with joy. "Oh, thank you, thank you."

"But, I can only give you permission to visit him for one hour, no more—do you understand? Not one minute longer! You see that clock over there?"

He grabbed Shmuel and turned him around forcibly, facing him toward the clock that stood near the entrance door. You see the time? Do you?"

"Yes, sir."

"It is almost three o'clock. I will allow you to visit your father for one hour, but—if you are late by even one minute, I will whip you myself, one lash for every minute you are late! I am putting myself out for you out of pure Christian kindness. But you will never forget those lashes if I have to lay them on you! Do you accept or not—otherwise, get out of here now!"

An hour with his beloved father… Shmuel was overcome with joy. A whole hour! He could see his father, and then leave the cell in time.

"But how will I know when the hour is over?" asked Shmuel.

"There is a clock in your father's room." Suddenly, Heinz grew impatient and his visage turned angry again. "Look, I don't have all day—yes or no?"

"Yes, yes," answered Shmuel gratefully. "I will watch the clock closely."

The giant grunted with satisfaction. "Wait here," he ordered. "I have to get everything secured. Sit down and wait."

Shmuel and Lipa sat down and waited. Shmuel was overjoyed. There were just five minutes to three, five minutes until he saw his father.

Meanwhile, Heinz and Johannes huddled in the middle room,

between the Tosfos Yom Tov's cell and the anteroom where Shmuel waited. Heinz laid his great wide hand on Johannes's bony shoulder.

"Johannes," he whispered. "Go into the rabbi's room, and set his clock *back by five minutes.*"

Johannes looked up at his captain. He wanted to argue. He liked those boys outside. They had courage to enter the terrible prison, even climbing all the way upstairs to the most guarded section. Heinz saw his hesitation, and began squeezing Johannes's shoulder in a viselike grip.

He stared straight into his face menacingly. "Johannes, do what I tell you, do you understand?"

Johannes had no choice. Just as ordered, he slipped into the rabbi's dim cell, went to the clock, and set it back. The rabbi, engrossed in his learning, didn't notice a thing. The trap was set, and the mouse was ready to be caught.

Johannes returned. Satisfied, Heinz sat down for yet another pint of beer, and Johannes led Shmuel and Lipa to the cell door.

"Go in," he said. "The door is open."

Shmuel took one last glance at the clock—it was three o'clock exactly. He stepped into the shadowy cell, and saw they had played a cruel trick on him. There was a prisoner—but it was not his father. An old man sat on the bed, learning from a *sefer*. His father was just fifty years old. When he last saw him, he was in the prime of life, youthful, full of energy. Why had they sent him in here to visit this old Jew? At least, he was a Jew. With no choice, he approached the white-haired man with the pale, thin face. The old man put down his *sefer* and stared at him. They gazed at each other for a minute.

"*Abba?*" asked Shmuel. "Is it *you?*" Shmuel was stunned—was that old man his father?

The old man stared at him and frowned. "Are you my Shmuel?" the prisoner asked in disbelief. The father and son stared at each other in shock—they barely recognized each other. But it was—father and son!

Shmuel fell down onto the bed and embraced his father, tears streaming down both their faces. Was this his father? He had become a white-bearded man overnight from his travails, and Shmuel, who had left a little boy, was now a grown-up lad. Lipa watched silently as the two held each other for the longest time, weeping unashamedly, tears of joy, tears of sorrow. But the clock was ticking. Shmuel released himself from his father's embrace, but he clasped his father's hands tightly the whole time he was there.

He is holding his son's hand in one hour more than my father has held my hand my whole life, thought Lipa.

"Abba," he said, "I have only an hour to visit, and time is running out. Tell me, what has happened?"

But his father just stared at him. He looked proud. His little boy had grown into a handsome young man. He brushed aside Shmuel's question.

"My son," he said, "what gift have you brought your father?"

Shmuel looked at his father in anguish. He had not thought to bring anything—he had come completely empty-handed.

"I am sorry, Abba…I had no time. I—"

The Tosfos Yom Tov swept his hand impatiently, cutting off Shmuel. "I asked you—what gift did you bring me, my son? You have studied in yeshivah for four years. Tell me something you have learned—that's all I want from you."

"Do you want to hear a *dvar Torah* now, Abba? We have so little time."

"What else matters to me?" answered his father, his voice rising. "What real gifts do we have in life but Torah and *yiras Shamayim*? Look at me, Shmuel! A month ago I was the *rav* of Prague. I had everything! I had honor and *sefarim* and *parnassah* and everything a man could want. They took it all away, the position, the honor, the fortune—everything was taken away! But they could not take away my Torah, or my *emunah* in Hashem. So tell me—what gift of Torah have you brought me?"

Shmuel looked at the clock. Nothing seemed to matter to his father, his imprisonment, his coming trial, the heavy chains on his legs—just what he had learned. As succinctly as he could, he said over a *chiddush* he had made on the mishnah: *When a Jew is in torment, the holy* Shechinah *cries out...* He explained a question he had, a contradiction, possible answers, and his own, original answer.

The Tosfos Yom Tov listened to his son's recitation with his eyes closed, and there was immense pleasure on his face. He opened his eyes, and he gazed proudly at the son who he was now rediscovering. The chains, the bed, the cell were forgotten—his soul was comforted. His son was indeed a *talmid chacham*.

Shmuel grew nervous—time was running out. There was only a half hour left. "Abba, I can only stay for a few more minutes. Tell me, why did they bring you here on these terrible charges? What happened?"

Briefly, the Tosfos Yom Tov explained his "crime." He had extolled the *kedushah* of the Talmud—the very same Talmud that the Pope had ordered burned. No one would have noticed his few words, interspersed among various difficult *halachos*—except for the *moser*, the informer.

The informer, angered at his tax assessment, went to the Hapsburg palace where he had acquaintances among one of the royal ministers and complained that the rabbi had insulted His Royal Highness's Christian religion. The informer meant just to have Rabbi Heller fired from his post, but his words were made to sound like an even greater slur. The Kaiser, who was the chief champion of the Pope, was infuriated—and instead of being ordered removed from his post, Rabbi Heller faced the death penalty.

"That is why I am here," the Tosfos Yom Tov concluded his tale.

Time was running out quickly. There were only twelve minutes left.

Shmuel wanted to give his father hope. "Abba, a wonderful thing happened yesterday," he began. He quickly recounted how he had saved the wife and son of the French ambassador, and that he had promised to help Shmuel if he was in distress.

"It is clear as day, Abba. That is why Hashem sent me to save his wife and child—just that I could help save you."

The Tosfos Yom Tov listened to his son's amazing story, his eyes cast down, nodding. Even as he spoke, Shmuel watched the clock.

Finally, the Tosfos Yom Tov lifted his head and spoke: "Shmuel, my son, listen! Do what you can. Go to the French ambassador and tell him that your father is innocent. Nowhere did I write or say anything against their religion just that we Jews must be faithful to our Torah. But remember one thing. If I escape death, it will not be because of this or that ambassador. Hashem will save me, or *chas v'shalom*—not. It is in His hands. We all leave this world eventually."

His father sighed. "But only this deeply distresses me—that because of something I wrote, I will cause the Jews of Prague to be banished from their homes, from their livelihoods. Why should Yom Tov Lipman Heller be the one who caused this!"

Shmuel looked up. There were only three minutes left. He must leave now, or face terrible lashes.

Shmuel stood up quickly. "Abba, I must go. Give me a *brachah* that I succeed in freeing you."

The Tosfos Yom Tov raised his hand, placed it on Shmuel's head and blessed him: *"Yesimcha Elokim k'Ephraim v'chi'Menashe."*

For the first time, he took notice of Lipa. He smiled, and Lipa smiled bashfully back.

The Shul Boy ೨ 213

"Someday I am going to learn the *Tosfos Yom Tov*," Lipa blurted out.

The Tosfos Yom Tov smiled. "You will not only learn it, my child, you will know Mishnah better than anyone—like little birds know how to soar in the sky!"

Only two more minutes to go! Shmuel kissed his father's hands, grabbed Lipa, and ran out of the cell, shutting the door behind him. There in the anteroom stood the towering Heinz, glowering angrily at him. "Look at the clock," he roared. "*You are four minutes late!*" Shmuel looked at the clock in shock. How could that be—he had been so careful to watch the time. "There...there must be some mistake—" he sputtered.

"No mistake!" Heinz bellowed furiously. "You gave me your word, and you broke it—like you Jews always break it!" He grabbed Shmuel by the scruff of his neck and dragged him out back to the front room. Meanwhile, he winked to Johannes, who slipped back to the cell and readjusted the clock to the proper time. All the while, Lipa skipped behind Shmuel in anguish, like a puppy behind its master.

Heinz waited for his assistant to catch up. He spun Shmuel around and addressed him face to face.

"Didn't I do you a favor in allowing you to visit your father?"

"Yes—"

"And wasn't the rule that you had to be out within an hour or you would be lashed for every minute you were late?"

"Yes—" admitted Shmuel, resignedly. The giant held him in his vise-like grip—there was nothing he could do.

"Well, law's the law! Rule are rules in this prison—and you broke them. We're going down to the dungeon floor, and you will learn that you don't break our rules here!"

"Maybe the clock in the other room was slow!" a voice called out. It was little Lipa. He could not bear to see his beloved Shmuel having to endure a whipping. The giant glanced at Lipa for a second, startled by his outburst. Then his face grew even redder. "*You, be quiet!*" he thundered, so loudly that the walls shook. Lipa, terrified, ran for cover behind Shmuel, who himself shook with fright.

Heinz put two fingers to his mouth, and gave an ear-piercing whistle, summoning help. Quickly, a handful of guards appeared.

"I am taking this Jew downstairs to the dungeon floor to administer punishment," he announced proudly. "Watch the prisoner in the cell closely until I come back. Make sure to watch him carefully—he will be a rich prize for the hangman."

With that, he grasped Shmuel harshly by the back of his neck and began leading him down the hallway to the steep staircase leading below. Meanwhile, his assistant, Johannes, kept a hand on little Lipa's arm, although lightly. They began marching down the spiral staircase, each with his own thoughts. Heinz was ecstatic. He had set a neat little trap, and the Jewish lad fell right into it. Heinz hated Jews. Why? Because his father hated Jews, and his father before him. The only one who hated Jews more than Heinz's father was his mother. Heinz imbibed hate for Jews from his mother's milk. But now, he could really do *something*—whip this Jewish lad, and it would be like whipping all Jews. He would carry the scars of these lashes the rest of his life.

Shmuel walked ahead, Heinz's powerful hand grasping his neck like chicken to slaughter, and recited Tehillim. His lips moved, but not a sound was heard. *Hashem, please give me strength to survive*, he prayed.

Lipa walked down very sad. His beloved Shmuel was going to suffer for no reason—what difference did four minutes make, anyway? Whom did he hurt? And yet, he found a strange comfort. His guard, Johannes, who held him, was actually stroking his arm, trying to comfort him. Johannes followed last. He was very angry at Heinz—and mad at himself. He was a coward for going along with this injustice.

They walked down the steps until they reached the main floor. Another staircase further down the hall led to the dungeon. The dungeon was always black as midnight, lit up by a few thin torches. There, in the almost total darkness, Shmuel would receive his terrible whipping.

As the group reached the main floor and started crossing toward the dungeon staircase, they were confronted by a guard who worked in the warden's office. "Heinz," he announced, "the warden has returned and is in his office. He wants to see you."

Drats, thought Heinz, *drats and more drats*.

The prison rules were that a guard could only administer corporal punishment on his own if the warden was not present. But now that the warden had returned, he had to first seek permission. Heinz had little regard for this warden, who was too soft and did not know how to run a prison with proper discipline. If Heinz ran the prison, there would be fewer prisoners alive to make trouble, and those who were there would wish they weren't alive. He breathed a deep, impatient sigh, and grumbling to himself, led his prey to the warden's office, not far from the main prison entrance.

"Don't worry," he warned Shmuel. "This will be just a short reprieve. You're not going to escape my lashing, I guarantee you! This will just make me hit harder." He sniggered with pleasure at the thought.

The doleful group marched to the warden's office. The warden kept them waiting in his anteroom, which infuriated Heinz even more. Finally, a guard appeared, and they were ushered into the warden's ornate office. Heinz surveyed the office with silent contempt. It was all soft, not fit for a prison.

The warden surveyed the odd group before him; the giant guard, the innocent-faced teenage boy, the little boy, and poor Johannes, who was more frightened of Heinz than of any prisoner.

Heinz was indeed an intimidating figure, filling the room with his towering, powerful figure. Even the warden was fearful, like he was confronting a tamed lion.

"What is happening here, Heinz?" he asked.

Heinz spoke self-assuredly. "This lad was visiting his father, the rabbi, who is up in the most guarded cell in the prison. He asked me for permission to see his father, and I showed him some slack—out of Christian kindness, you know. I told him that the rules of the prison were that he could visit for one hour—no longer. Those are the rules, are they not?"

"Yes," agreed the warden, watching Shmuel the whole time.

"Well, whether deliberately or whatever, he went past the hour. I warned him clearly—for every minute past an hour, he would receive a lash. I thought he would get the message. I was really kind to him, more than I had to be. But he thumbed his nose at me and the rules. He stayed longer by a full four minutes! So we were heading down now to the dungeon to administer the lashes."

The warden, an older man with a sympathetic face, addressed Shmuel.

"Is it true, lad?"

"There must be some mistake, sir," answered Shmuel. "When I entered my father's cell, I watched the clock closely. I knew that I had to be out in time. Although I hadn't seen my father in four years, I rushed through the visit as quickly as I could. I watched the clock every minute and we left with two minutes yet to go. But when we came out, the guard said we were late."

"*I didn't say it!*" roared Heinz, making the warden's office walls shake. "You saw the clock! Warden, you can send someone up to the cell and the anteroom; you'll see the clocks work perfectly fine. They are showing the exact same time!"

The warden gazed at Shmuel, and at little Lipa who hid timidly behind Shmuel. The warden seemed saddened by the situation.

"Heinz," he said. "Perhaps this time we can bend the rules a bit. Four lashes for four minutes seems too harsh."

Heinz raised himself straight in military fashion. He stared straight ahead formally, like a soldier.

"Warden, with great respect. The rules are the rules for all of us. I always go by the rules. This prison is the quietest one in Austria because every guard knows there is a Heinz walking by the cells, keeping strict watch. No one plays with Heinz. Why should we make an exception here—because he is a Jew?"

The warden's face darkened. "No impertinence, Heinz."

"I apologize, warden," answered Heinz contritely. "I'm just trying to do my job as best I can."

There was a heavy silence, and then suddenly a child's voice piped up. It was Lipa.

"You can't whip Samuel!" he announced.

The warden looked at him in amazement. "Oh, and why not, sonny?"

"Because he is under the protection of the French ambassador!"

There was a moment's startled silence, and then the room broke into gales of laughter. The warden chuckled, and Heinz broke out in a great, rumbling laugh, like from inside a beer barrel.

"And how does this Jewish lad happen to be under the protection of the French ambassador, may I ask?" the warden asked Lipa. "Can you prove it?"

Lipa tried to answer, but Shmuel turned and placed a finger over Lipa's mouth. There was no proof, and Lipa was just making them appear even more foolish.

The warden was still chuckling. "I'll tell you one thing—you have a good imagination, sonny."

Heinz was also in a more jolly mood at Lipa's outburst. He looked down from his great height at Lipa.

"I'll make you a bet, sonny. If this visitor is under the protection of the French ambassador, they can give *me* forty lashes—not four. How's that, now?" He suddenly glowered fiercely. "Now either prove it, or keep your mouth shut until I give you permission to talk, understand?!"

Lipa, utterly frightened of Heinz, and humiliated by the laughter, retreated behind Shmuel like a turtle into its shell. Again, Johannes secretly placed his hand on Lipa's shoulder to comfort him.

There was a moment's stillness, and the warden shrugged disconsolately. There was no more that he could do—he too, was afraid of Heinz.

Shmuel realized that his fate was sealed, and addressed the warden. "Sir, may I speak?"

"Go ahead."

"I see now that it is Heaven's will that I receive these lashes. It is not the guard, or the rules—it is from Whom we call 'Hashem.' I am innocent, my father is innocent—but Hashem has a reason for everything. However, one thing I will ask of you, if I can. It is already late afternoon. It is soon time for me to recite my afternoon prayers. I do not know whether I will be strong enough to pray after the lashes. I ask permission to pray first, and then, what happens, happens."

Heinz was infuriated. "It is a trick. He is trying to find a way to escape—"

"Quiet, Heinz," the warden silenced him. He turned to Shmuel. "How can you pray? There is no synagogue, and you have no prayer book."

"With your permission, I have a prayer book that I always keep in my pocket. I will use that."

"Let me see it."

Shmuel reached into his coat, retrieved the siddur, and handed it to the warden. It was wrapped in a thin sheet of paper, slightly shredded.

"What is this paper?" asked the warden.

"I wrap my prayer book in a paper so it remains protected wherever I go," Shmuel explained.

The warden unwrapped the paper, and lifted the thin prayer book. Suddenly, a card fell out of the book onto the desk.

"What's this?' asked the warden curiously. He lifted the card, peered at it, and his brows rose in astonishment. Shmuel stared at the snowy white card, with its French seal, unbelieving. *It was the French ambassador's official card*! Shmuel had accidentally slipped it into a page of the siddur, not alongside. The warden turned over the card, and read the ambassador's personal message:

The bearer of this card is under the protection of His Majesty's French ambassador to the Austrian Court. Signed, Ambassador: P. Turner

"Where did you get this?" asked the warden in amazement.

Quickly, Shmuel recounted the events that took place just the day before. As he spoke, Heinz's face grew pale.

The warden looked at Lipa, who was still hiding behind Shmuel. "Then, sonny, you were telling the truth!"

"Yes, sir," said Lipa, coming out from his hiding place.

"I have always tried to follow the rules, sir," Shmuel explained. "What happened with the clock was a misunderstanding; I don't know how it happened."

Meanwhile, Heinz suddenly softened his tone. "Yes, it might be, warden. Perhaps one of the clocks was fast, or slow—"

"Tell him the truth, Heinz!" Suddenly Johannes came forward

and stood before the warden's desk. "Heinz forced me to go into the rabbi's cell and put the clock back five minutes, so the boy would think he had an extra five minutes. That's why he came out late—"

"Johannes—" screamed Heinz. But it was too late. The warden ordered Heinz to stay silent.

"Will you testify to that before judges?" asked the warden.

"On ten Bibles, sir. I couldn't take this injustice any longer. This lad did nothing wrong."

"Johannes," he ordered, "summon the emergency security guard."

In a few minutes, the room was filled with a half-dozen helmeted guards carrying cudgels, swords, and a plethora of fearsome weapons.

The warden addressed Heinz sternly. "Heinz, you lost your bet. You said that if this lad was under the French ambassador's protection, you would take forty lashes. Well, he is. Do you want me to show you the card?"

"No, sir," answered Heinz, in barely a whisper.

"I can't hear you, Heinz!"

"No, sir!" answered Heinz loudly, even as his face grew deathly pale.

The warden turned to the captain of the emergency guard. "Do we have a cat-o'-nine-tails in the prison?" he asked.

"We will find one," the guard assured him. He also disliked Heinz thoroughly.

"Take him downstairs and administer the forty lashes immediately. I want him to feel each one! If he survives, throw him into a dungeon cell until I arrange for a trial for fabricating false evidence."

Heinz stood like a stone. His face had grown ghostly white. Indeed, Heinz was in shock. He didn't know what suddenly happened to him. The guards took him by each arm, broke him out of his trance-like state, and dragged him out of the office.

Outside in the hallway, Heinz suddenly broke out of his stupor. From the distance, they could hear his screams as he was being led away:

"The Jews did this to me! The Jews did this to me!"

A short time later, Shmuel and Lipa found themselves walking back toward the Jewish district. Shmuel was dazed—he did not know what to feel. He came within minutes of suffering terrible lashes given by a mammoth brute. Instead, it all turned over in an instant. He was free; the brute was even now suffering his lashes ten times over...

Baruch Hashem, baruch Hashem...

"Didn't I tell you that Hashem can help in a second?" he crowed to Lipa. "*Yeshuas Hashem k'heref ayin*" He stopped and turned to his young companion. "You know, it was all your doing. You set the whole thing rolling when you mentioned the French ambassador. I was afraid to say anything. Because of you, Heinz sealed his own fate."

Lipa beamed at Shmuel's words. He was so happy. It had taken all his courage to blurt out, first at Heinz, and then in the office in front of the warden. But he could not stand to see his beloved Shmuel suffer. The warden really liked him afterward. After Heinz was taken away and Johannes left, the warden summoned him to his side and congratulated him for his courage. Then he gave him a wink and a friendly tweak on his cheek. Even now, he rubbed the side of his face where his pinch had left a crimson mark.

They reached the road leading to the Jewish district. Shmuel's face turned troubled again. They had overcome Heinz, but his beloved father, the Tosfos Yom Tov, was still chained to his cell, facing the death penalty. Could the French ambassador help him? Would he? Maybe yes, maybe not. The Kaiser himself was angry—what could the ambassador do? Lipa saw Shmuel's sad visage, and suddenly was filled with secret apprehension.

"Shmuel, what will you do next?" he asked nervously.

Shmuel looked at Lipa, a distant gaze on his face. "You are a good boy, Lipa. I am glad you have been at my side."

"But what will you do next?" Lipa asked again.

Shmuel did not answer. They reached his uncle's street, and came to the synagogue where they had prayed that morning.

Shmuel turned to Lipa. "Lipa, I still have much to do today; there is still time to Minchah."

"I want to come with you."

Shmuel shook his head. "No, I must move very fast—I must run. Lipa, I need you to go inside the shul and say Tehillim for my father."

"Please, Shmuel. I want to come with you," Lipa pleaded.

Shmuel shook his head firmly. "No, Lipa. You will help me more by saying Tehillim that I may save my father. Come, let's go inside."

They walked up the front steps. Shmuel tried the front door, but it was locked. Minchah was not for another few hours. Shmuel was disappointed.

"Come," he said, taking Lipa by the hand. "Maybe there is a side door we can enter."

They turned into a narrow alley that separated the synagogue from the building next to it. It lay in deep shadow, and there was hardly any room to pass. There was no door there.

"There must be another way to get inside," Shmuel insisted. "People always want to learn. Let's try the back."

They followed the tall side of the shul until they arrived at the back. There was a small patch of bare earth, and three wooden steps that led to the back of the shul.

"Come," urged Shmuel, grasping Lipa's hand. Lipa wouldn't move. He was suddenly filled with childlike dread.

"Shmuel, I want to come with you," he pleaded.

Shmuel shook his head sadly. "I must go," he insisted, "alone."

"Will you come back for me?"

"*Im yirtzeh Hashem*, as soon as Hashem allows me. Come, Lipa, I have no time."

Shmuel walked quickly up the three steps and tried the back door. The handle moved—it was open. He raced back down. Lipa looked so sad and lonely. Shmuel gave him a tender pinch, right on his red mark.

"Go inside, Lipa—go."

Lipa slowly climbed the steps as Shmuel watched. He turned the handle, looked back one more time at his beloved companion, and entered the shul. It was dark inside, and the blinds were down. There stood…the familiar tables and benches of his father's shul.

Lipa was back in Jersey City. Vienna was gone, Shmuel was gone. He was all alone again…

Part Two

9
Gustavo

The summer began, and Lipa was bereft. His only friend Shmuel was gone, far away. Shmuel lived in the bustling Lower East Side, surrounded by his pals, while Lipa was abandoned alone in Jersey City, a lonely world apart. Lipa had nothing to do, no friends, no camp. He retreated into his backyard, spending hours daydreaming, throwing a rubber ball against the back of house, right over the tall outcrop of the *aron kodesh*. The backyard was a wonderful world for daydreaming, for it had no boundaries or limits. His imagination brought him anywhere; he could do anything, hit home runs, fly jet planes high in the sky, or captain a gigantic aircraft carrier. He was never alone, for Shmuel was always there at his side, sharing his heroic feats. Lipa's father watched him covertly from the upstairs kitchen window, Lipa's silly games, running here, running there, shouting excitedly to invisible companions. Rabbi Wallerstein puffed on his cigar and frowned. He sighed secretly—two out of three was not bad. Leon and Eva were terrific, but his youngest playing downstairs and talking to himself was not totally normal.

In truth, Lipa was never really alone. For, besides himself and his imaginary adventures, the backyard was populated by a large family of cats, three and four generations, the old male and female, their offspring, and their offspring's offspring. The family of twelve felines ran freely about the yard, and even into the house when the doors were open—it was their domain. The Wallerstein house had everything a cat family needed—a dark place to sleep inside the abandoned garages, a constant pool of rainwater where the pavement was sunken in, and above all—an abundant supply of leftovers. The minute they heard the upstairs kitchen window open above, the cats ran over, their eyes lifted expectantly. Soon a rain of chicken bones and leftover greasy potatoes poured down like manna. The cats ran after the pieces, fighting each other over the scraps, *kol d'alim g'var*, the stronger grabbing out of the paws of the weakest.

But the real frenzy was on Fridays, when Lipa cleaned the herring for kiddush. He opened the herring's stomach with a keen blade, extracting the long greasy milt sack, pulled out the spine with its needlelike bones, sliced off the tail, and peeled off the skin in one slimy sheet. Laden with these fragrant delicacies, Lipa entered the backyard to be accosted by a frenzy of cats driven wild by the salty fish smell. Some younger felines were so maddened by the herring smell that they tried to climb up his leg, scratching him with their needle-like claws.

Lipa stopped and looked down sternly. "You scratch me one more time, you won't get one piece!" he warned. Fearful of his voice, the young cats retreated.

Lipa waited until the cats calmed down, and then began the game of ripping apart pieces of the herring and flinging them to the farthest corners of the yard. The cats dashed madly toward the thrown morsel, but just then Lipa threw a second piece in the opposite direction. The cats behind in the race screeched to a halt, turned in their tracks, and raced toward the newest morsel. Those who were behind were now ahead. And so the game went, *v'rachamav al kol ma'asav*… Lipa was the king, doling out rewards, piece after piece, in every direction, sometimes hitting a cat who had nothing right over the nose, so that no cat went without. The greatest prize of all, the skin of the herring, he threw into the tall bush, so the cats had to climb up for it.

The herring feed was Lipa's high point of the week, and only then did Lipa feel Shabbos was truly coming.

One bright morning Lipa descended to his backyard refuge. His father had gone on hospital rounds, his mother was out shopping. He had the house and the backyard all to himself, free to imagine and daydream to his heart's content. No one could interrupt his magical world. He threw his ball over and over against the house, imagining that he and Shmuel were traipsing through a misty jungle with tigers and giant apes crouching behind each thick trunk.

Suddenly, Lipa halted his ball-throwing. He had a feeling that something unusual was going on. All the cats had suddenly disappeared and the yard was eerily silent. Where were the cats? He turned around and was startled to see the cats all lined up behind him in front of the garage doors, like students at class. They sat on their haunches silently, eyes glued upward, their heads turning from side to side in perfect unison. He had never seen them so silent and organized, like someone had hypnotized them. What were they staring at? Lipa gazed high up into the blue sky and saw what had garnered their rapt interest. High above the rooftop, a huge flock of pigeons flew around and around in a great circle. There were hundreds of birds, and they flew in perfect pattern, guided by an invisible master. Lipa had seen some birds last year, but now there were hundreds of birds, soaring higher and higher. The cats watched in fascination as the flock appeared and disappeared in great sweeps between Lipa's house and the apartment building next door. Lipa was drawn out of his reverie, and watched the beautiful spectacle with fascination. Not satisfied with the few seconds he could view them, Lipa raced down the driveway and into the street, where he could watch the immense flock unobstructed. Here, the full glory of the soaring birds was visible. They circled the air effortlessly, like a great white banner, their wings flapping in unison, climbing higher and higher, until they seemed like specks against the sky. They reached their apex, perhaps ten stories high, and then glided effortlessly, borne on warm summer thermals, wings outstretched.

Suddenly, Lipa gasped in horror. A half-dozen birds broke from the flock and began plummeting head over legs toward the ground. Lipa watched petrified as they tumbled over and over helplessly, nearing the top of his house, when abruptly they began beating their wings and soared back up toward their friends. In a few minutes, another group of birds repeated the dive, rolling over and over in dizzying somersaults, and then, at the last moment, flapping their wings and soaring swiftly back upward. It looked like some of the pigeons were showing off to the others. But what happened if they didn't catch themselves in time?

Whose pigeons are they? Lipa wondered. And what kept them in such perfect order, each bird knowing exactly its place in the flock? The epicenter of their circuits was the apartment house right alongside the driveway of Lipa's house. Lipa peered up to the rooftop, but saw no one. Eventually, the birds circled one last time, and as suddenly as they appeared, they were gone, leaving Lipa delighted and amazed.

How did Hashem teach the birds to fly like that? he wondered.

Lipa returned to his backyard. The cats realized they could not catch any of the birds for breakfast, and returned to their normal pursuits. But now Lipa had another scene to add onto his palette of make-believe, and he imagined adventures that included soaring birds and somersaulting pigeons.

July passed, and the dog days of August arrived. Lipa began counting the days until school resumed, and he could again sit next to Shmuel. Once, his father had taken him along to visit a hospital, but otherwise he was on his own. It was a hot afternoon, and Lipa was back playing behind the house. The cats went about their business of licking themselves clean, drinking from the waterhole, and lazing. Lipa threw the ball against the house, racing after it when it bounced afoul. Suddenly, he noticed that all the cats had sprung up in alert attention. It was curious, for they were usually lazy. Had someone opened up a window upstairs? Lipa stood back and looked to the kitchen. The window was closed. Besides, the cats were slinking off toward the driveway, away from the house. At first, Lipa did not take much notice—it was their own cat business. But then he realized the subject of their keen interest. There was a crumpled piece of newspaper that seemed to have a life of its own. There was no wind, but the paper fluttered from place to place, even skipping up from the little gutter that ran alongside the neighboring apartment house back up to his driveway. The cats were keenly interested in the skittering sheet, surrounding it stealthily. Lipa went to investigate this curiosity. He stepped into the cluster of cats, which should have driven them away instantly. But they were so intense in their pursuit that they did not scatter. Something had drawn their intense interest. Only when he approached the crumpled newspaper and shouted at them, did they grudgingly retreat—but only partially. Their eyes followed his every move as Lipa bent down to lift the newspaper. Lipa lifted the crumpled sheet and saw what had drawn their rapt interest. Entangled in the paper was a small pigeon, whitish gray with coal black tail feathers. Something was wrong with it. It tried to escape from Lipa, flapping one wing, but all it could do was skip a few feet before it stopped. One wing drooped down helplessly, and the bird's body tipped at an angle, the broken wing dragging on the pavement.

Lipa didn't know what to do. The injured bird tried again to fly away from him, but could only hop helplessly. Lipa glanced around. The cats were hard behind him, following him step for step, boring in on their prey silently. Lipa was afraid—he had never touched an injured bird before. If he walked away, the cats would jump on him in a moment. The cats grew even bolder, seeing his uncertainty. Lipa turned around angrily. "Get away from here!" he shouted at them. "Or you won't get a piece of herring again!"

But the cats were cats. They were born to hunt, and even Lipa's threats did not stop them. They drew closer to the injured bird. Lipa lifted his foot and stomped angrily at them, scattering them in all directions. Without further thought, Lipa lifted up the bird, newspaper and all, and held it to his chest. He thought the bird would hop back down, but it just rested there in his arms, breathing hard.

What should he do with the injured bird? Let the cats have it? *V'rachamav al kol ma'asav...* Where did the bird come from? Lipa looked up toward the apartment house. The bird must have been part of the flock, maybe one of the showoffs that tumbled down through the air, but didn't flap his wings in time before he struck something. It probably lived on the roof of the apartment house next door. Lipa knew what he should do. He carried the bird to the back steps where there was a pile of empty cartons. All the time, the cats dogged his every step, hoping for their prey—but they were out of luck. Lipa took a narrow carton, and placed the bird carefully inside, crumpled newspaper and all. All the time, the injured bird kept peering up at him, as though he understood that he was helping him. There was only one way Lipa could save the poor bird. He had to get to the roof of the apartment house and try to find the bird's owner.

Lipa had never once thought of entering the apartment house next door. It was just next door, but a foreign world. He didn't know anyone who lived there except the policeman who lived on the first floor facing the driveway. There were no Jews in this building, just gentiles. Lipa held the carton close to his chest and entered the building uneasily. The front hallway was dark, long and narrow, and a tall flight of stairs led to the second floor. The building smelled bad, all sorts of cooking aromas from foods that Jews did not eat. He was in an alien environment, although he was just a few feet from his own house. Lipa regretted having to smell the *treife* food that accosted him. Maybe he should retreat outside, leave the carton on the doorstep, and that was enough.

Just then, a little chirp came out of the carton. Lipa looked down. The little bird was crying to him: *Please bring me home*. After all, he wasn't eating the *treife* food, he just sniffed it—and hated it. It made him feel nauseous.

Don't worry, little bird, he answered, *we'll find your home*.

He climbed to the second floor and his eyes adjusted to the dim hallway light. Midway on each flight were two apartment doors, right and left. Lipa cautiously walked down the hallway, hoping he could tell where the bird's owner lived. He checked each door, but there were no names, no clue. If the bird flew from the roof, chances were that the owner lived on the top floor. Lipa climbed to the uppermost floor, and checked each door—*there it was*! On the right-side door was a plaque decorated with a songbird. *We're here*, Lipa reassured the bird.

Feeling proud of himself, Lipa knocked softly on the door. There was no answer. He knocked again, a little harder, but no one came to the door. Now what? It would be fair for him to lay the little bird in the doorway and run back out. Just then, the little bird rustled his one good wing, shaking the box. It was as though he read Lipa's mind and was protesting.

What else can I do? wondered Lipa. He noticed that at the end of the hallway, near a back window, was a rough wooden staircase that led up to the roof. The steps were plain wood planks, and there was no banister—it was almost like a ladder. Should he try to go up to the rooftop? He was afraid. The little bird chirped pleadingly. Lipa's curiosity and love of the unknown drew him carefully up the steep stairs. At the top of the stairs stood a narrow steel door. Holding the bird in one arm, Lipa pushed opened the door and entered the roof.

Lipa stood on the roof, breathless with wonder. There was only sky above, beautiful blue open sky, with the sun hanging like an orange lamp overhead. Was he really next door to his own house? It was so beautiful, so open, so clean! Was he really in Jersey City? The little bird began flapping its one wing excitedly, but it only caused it to spin around and around, dragging its broken limb. The roof was very wide, and in its center stood a large bird loft, formed out of plywood and mesh wire, with a tall post in its center, like a ship's mast, reaching straight up into the sky.

Lipa stood for a moment silently, absorbing this wondrous world that stood so close to his own house. Indeed, it was just a few feet across the driveway to his own bedroom. Who knew that a wonderful birdhouse existed so close to his own room? But from where he stood now atop the apartment roof, you would not even know his house lay just next door. The rooftop stretched under an endless sky, alone and silent.

Meanwhile, the little bird sensed that it was close to home, beating its wing wildly and tweeting feebly. Lipa broke out of his reverie and approached the wire mesh loft doorway, hoping to return the bird to its nest.

"Hey, what are you doing there!"

Lipa stopped in his tracks.

"What are you doing with my birds!" the angry voice yelled once more.

Lipa, frightened, turned around. Standing at the roof doorway was a heavyset man, burly and half shaven. He was glaring at Lipa, his face twisted in anger.

Lipa was too petrified to answer—the man was furious. Lipa was trapped on the high roof; the big man blocked his escape. The man approached Lipa quickly, a bat in his hand. Lipa desperately wanted to run away, but there was no way to escape—the man was between him and the door. Lipa stood there, trembling. The man approached Lipa angrily, his huge heavy bulk casting a menacing shadow over him.

"What are you holding?" he demanded. "Did you steal one of my birds?"

Lipa, trembling, shook his head. "No…sir. I found this bird downstairs in my driveway. It has a broken wing. I…I brought it up here. I thought maybe we can fix it."

The man stared at Lipa suspiciously and then peered into the open carton. He lifted the little bird. It flapped its one good wing, but very weakly. The man ran his fingers gently over the broken wing.

"Wait a second," he grunted.

He carried the bird to the front of the loft where there was a shallow bowl of water. He held the bird, and let it drink from the bowl. He returned to Lipa, his face a little softer.

"Where did you find him?" he asked

Lipa's trembling had ceased. "In my driveway, next door. The cats were going to eat it."

The man held the bird, smoothing its feathers gently. He examined the broken wing, then looked up and stared at Lipa for a long time, not saying anything. Lipa grew uncomfortable from his gaze.

The man stopped his brushing, surveying Lipa closely. "I know you—aren't you the rabbi's boy?"

Lipa nodded.

The man snorted loudly. "You must be the loneliest kid in the whole world!"

Lipa looked at him in shock. He tried to shake his head in denial.

"Don't you have any friends?" the man persisted. "I watch you from my apartment. You spend hours playing just by yourself. You are the loneliest kid I ever saw!"

"No—" Lipa tried to protest, but then the strangest thing occurred. Lipa started crying, hot, wet tears. He didn't want to, but he couldn't help it.

He was lonely—so lonely, and nobody knew except this man!

The man stared at him dumbfounded, not expecting his words would have this effect—the boy was crying like a baby.

Inside, Lipa was so happy—somebody realized how lonely he was, the first time in his life. Someone had laid a finger on his hurt.

"What are you crying about?" the man shouted uncomfortably. "It's no sin being lonely! Listen, I have to fix this bird's wing or he won't last. You want to help?"

Lipa wiped away his tears with his sleeve, nodding. He followed the keeper as he went to the birdhouse, which was raised slightly over the roof, and extracted from underneath a wooden box containing all sorts of supplies, scissors, tape, metal spoons, and wooden splints. He examined the bird carefully, measuring the injured wing between his thumb and forefinger, and extracted a small wooden splint, the size of the wing. He carefully joined the damaged wing together, pressed it against the splint, and wrapped it firmly with string.

He grunted with satisfaction. "This bird's only three months old. He'll heal pretty quick, give him a week or two. I'll give him some seed, and put him back in his nest."

All this time, Lipa had been following his silent, careful work with fascination, too afraid to speak. Finally, he broke his silence.

"Do you know every bird you have?" he asked.

"Why not?" he answered, completing the binding. "Every bird is different. You see this bird?" He lifted it gently in both hands, and held it in Lipa's face. "What do you see?"

Lipa felt the bird's feathers, studying its markings. "It's kind of gray, with black stripes running down its back."

The man snorted impatiently. "That's all? You'll never make a good birder. Look…look here—"

He held the bird right up close in front of Lipa, spreading the feathers at the end of one wing. "You see this?"

Lipa looked closely. At the very tip of the bird's wing were tiny blue feathers, scattered amid the black.

"I didn't see that," Lipa admitted.

"What else is special about this bird?"

Again, Lipa carefully ran his fingers over the bird's body, searching for a clue. He could not find any, and shook his head.

"Look here," the man pointed. "At the top of the head, a tiny bump, like he crashed his head on something. Every bird is different."

He suddenly stood up, dwarfing Lipa with his great bulk. "Follow me—I'm going to put him back in his nest."

He climbed the two wooden stairs leading to loft, unlocked it and threw the door open. Lipa hesitated at the entrance.

"Follow me," he ordered.

Lipa entered the bird loft, crowded with scores of cooing, twittering pigeons. The loft was very warm, and he was overcome with the heavy odor of bird leftovers. "*Uch*," he exclaimed, "it smells here!"

The man frowned at Lipa's outburst, but didn't answer. He walked halfway down the loft, surrounded on each side by row upon row of birds' nests, two birds to a box, and found the little pigeon's home.

The Shul Boy 237

"Here you are, birdy," he announced, "back where you belong."

Lipa watched proudly as he placed the little bird safely next to its mate. He had saved the bird's life, and it would fly again! *V'rachamav al kol ma'asav...* The man scattered a few kernels into the nest and the bird gobbled it quickly—the poor bird was famished.

"Let's go," the burly man ordered Lipa, pushing him ahead toward the entrance. They escaped into the fresher air, and Lipa breathed more easily. The man locked the mesh door behind, and placed his beefy hand on Lipa's shoulder.

"Sit down, sonny," he said. "I want to talk to you."

He sat Lipa down on the top step of the loft, and squeezed himself heavily next to him.

"What's your name, sonny?" he asked.

"Lipa."

"My name is—Gustavo. You did a good thing today, Lipa. Someone else would have just walked away and let the cats eat the bird. You didn't."

Lipa's face reddened. "Thank you, Mr. Gustavo."

"Not 'Mr.' Gustavo," he answered brusquely. "Just Gustavo."

"How did the bird get hurt?" asked Lipa.

"That stupid bird wants to be a tumbler, but he's not ready yet. It's my fault—I shouldn't have let him fly with the others."

"What's a tumbler?" asked Lipa.

"Tumblers like to tumble, do somersaults. Rollers swoop down like airplanes. High flyers fly high. Every pigeon is different. This bird tumbled too fast, and when he tried to fly back up, it was too late. He banged himself pretty bad, but he'll heal—thanks to you."

"I watch your birds flying from my backyard. They are really beautiful."

Gustavo nodded, pleased. "You like birds?"

"I like them all, cats, birds."

Gustavo didn't answer directly; he appeared to mull things slowly in his own head.

"Lipa, you are a good kid—the rabbi's boy. I've watched you for a long time. I don't know why your parents leave you alone so much—I wouldn't. You must be lonely there all by yourself."

This time Lipa nodded in agreement, without crying.

"You know, I can't fly my birds every day—otherwise the hawks will snatch them right out of the sky. I fly them a few days a week only, always different times. But it's a tough job keeping the loft clean, laying out just the right amount of seed, changing the water, cleaning nests. I could use some help. Do you want to work for me?"

Lipa's eyes lit up—he loved it up here!

"I'll pay you a quarter a week to come up here three days a week, the days I don't fly the birds, and help me care for the birds. Are you interested?"

Gustavo sounded almost pleading—for in truth, he too was lonely.

Lipa did not hesitate. "I would like that very much, Gustavo."

For the first time, the burly man who first appeared so threatening smiled slightly. He stuck out his hand. Lipa took his hand, sealing the deal. Then he added apologetically:

"Gustavo—I'm sorry what I said about the smell."

Gustavo did not answer—but the gruff smile did not leave his face.

Suddenly, Lipa's summer turned over—Hashem had rewarded him for saving the little bird's life. Lipa climbed the three flights of stairs to the upper floor, and then the steep wooden staircase to the roof. The roof was covered with blue shingles, so that when Lipa walked across to the loft, he felt like he was walking on water.

The Shul Boy 239

Gustavo was always there waiting for him, counting out feed pellets, changing the water, conversing with his birds. Lipa really did not have that much to do, but Gustavo always found a task for him, cleaning the feeding trays, moving nesting pairs from one compartment to another. Meanwhile, in his own rough way, Gustavo taught him a great deal about pigeons. There were not one, but dozens of types of pigeons, different sizes and shapes, natural wild rock pigeons, pretty gray toy Satinettes, Pouter pigeons which puffed up their crops and walked around pompously with inflated chests, colorful English Trumpeters, and high flying Srebrniaks. Gustavo knew each strain and where they came from, China, Persia, Italy, and explained it all to Lipa. Lipa realized after a few visits that help was not really so much needed… So why had Gustavo invited him up and offered him money? Was it because he was lonely and Gustavo wanted to be nice—or because Gustavo himself was lonely? Gustavo didn't appear to have any children or a wife—all he had was his pigeons.

Meanwhile, Lipa had developed a new attachment. Each time he visited the loft, he stopped at the nest of the little bird he had saved. The bird still had a tiny splint to mend his broken wing, but when he flapped his wings, both wings worked. Whenever Lipa approached the bird's nest, it began fluttering its wings excitedly, as though it recognized Lipa. Lipa stood in front of the little box, and the bird began chirruping happily, trying to raise itself in greeting. Lipa understood how Gustavo recognized each bird. Lipa could spot this little bird in a flock of hundreds. Each time he visited the bird, the bird flapped a greeting, and they grew more and more bonded. He was not just a bird—he was *Lipa's* bird. Even Gustavo admitted that the bird seemed to know Lipa, and he let Lipa remove him from his nest and hold him carefully in both hands. The little bird sat calmly in Lipa's hands, totally at ease. In a few weeks, the last bit of splint was removed and Lipa gently touched the repaired wing. Out of Gustavo's hearing, he leaned down and whispered to the bird: *"You are my Little Fleigel."*

From then on, this bird was different from all the others. The rest were pigeons, racing pigeons, homing pigeons, tumbling pigeons, high flying pigeons—but Little Fleigel was *Lipa's* pigeon.

August passed—school would start soon. Leon came home from camp, and Rabbi Wallerstein was already grumbling about having to pay tuition. Meanwhile, three days a week Lipa climbed up to the apartment house roof, helped clean the bird loft, arranged the pigeons, and fed them, so that he could already recognize some of them. But two days a week Gustavo strictly forbade him to visit—the days the birds flew. Instead, Lipa stood in the backyard of his house, surrounded by the cats, and watched as the pigeons soared high overhead, distant specks in the sky, circling over and over. Why wouldn't Gustavo let him on the roof when the birds flew? But Gustavo was adamant—no rooftop. Gustavo was a strange person, moody and changeable like the weather. He was heavyset and swarthy, with a slight Italian accent. Some days he was garrulous and cheerful, explaining everything to Lipa. Then the next time, Lipa would arrive and find him sullen and moody, barely saying a word as he went about his work. From time to time, Lipa would catch him staring up onto the mast above the loft with a distracted, faraway look.

Meanwhile, the family had caught wind of Lipa's new pigeon hobby. Rabbi Wallerstein did not mind his new interest as long as he took care of the shul. But Leon was gleeful to find a new way to torment his little brother, dubbing him the "Bird Man of Ulysses Avenue." On Shabbos Leon went from congregant to congregant, spreading the news about his brother's pigeon pursuit to general laughter. Lipa endured the laughter patiently. He did not know what else to do; after all, the men made the *minyan*.

It was ten days before Labor Day. Soon, Lipa would return to yeshivah and he would no longer be able to work for Gustavo. He told Gustavo the news, and Gustavo's face clouded with disappointment.

"You mean, you can't come up anymore?" he asked.

Lipa saw the unhappiness on Gustavo's face. He did not want to hurt him. "Maybe sometimes, when I don't have school," Lipa said.

Gustavo stared at him without answering, a long look that hid his feelings. But Lipa could read his face by now—Gustavo was hurt. He would truly miss him. He pressed his advantage.

"Gustavo, I only have a few more days to come up to the loft. Can I ask you a very big favor?"

Gustavo's eyes narrowed with suspicion. "What?"

"Can I stay up here and watch when you fly the birds?"

Gustavo shook his head emphatically. "No way."

But Lipa was emboldened by Gustavo's need for him.

"*Please*! Why not, Gustavo?"

"Because, no one is allowed to be up here when I fly my birds. It's something personal—a bond between me and the pigeons. You don't understand—you're too young. It will break my connection, you understand? When I fly my pigeons, I am like one of them. I have to be absolutely alone."

"You will be alone," promised Lipa. "I'll be so quiet, you won't know I'm even here. Make believe you don't see me, Gustavo. Please—just one time I want to be here when the birds fly. *Please*! Then I can come up to help you even when school starts—on days off!"

Gustavo's face grew uneasy. Lipa saw that he was wavering. He looked closely into the big man's face and whispered: "*Please, Gustavo—just one time.*"

Gustavo sighed. The little Jewish boy's friendship meant so

much to him. "You know, Lipa, you are the first person in my life that I am letting watch when I fly my birds. But it's on one condition—you must never tell anyone what you see me doing when the birds fly. Is that understood?"

What does he do? Lipa wondered, but he dared not ask.

Lipa nodded agreement quickly. He stuck out his hand, imitating Gustavo's first handshake.

"Let's shake on it, Gustavo."

Gustavo took Lipa's thin fingers in his beefy hand. He smiled, but he looked away embarrassed—he had surrendered too easily. But he really seemed pleased to have Lipa watch him.

"It's a deal," he grunted.

It was late afternoon. A hot August sun hung over Ulysses Avenue, causing heat waves to shimmer from the roof. Gustavo already stood outside the loft, waiting for Lipa. He seemed edgy. Lipa approached Gustavo cautiously—he did not know what his mood was. Maybe he was angry that Lipa had forced himself up on the roof to watch the pigeons fly.

"Hello, Gustavo," he greeted him.

Gustavo grunted his answer. *Perhaps it was a mistake for him to be here.* Lipa sought to give Gustavo an excuse to back out.

"Isn't it too hot for the birds?" he asked. "Maybe I should come back another time."

"The heat doesn't bother the birds. It makes thermals that help them fly." He sensed Lipa's hesitation. "Are you ready to help me or not?"

"Sure I'm ready! Is my bird flying also?"

"It's too soon. His wing's okay, but he's not strong enough to keep up with the rest. I put a net over his box so he can't get out.

Come on—"

He led Lipa around to the back of the loft, the first time he had been there. Gustavo had never allowed Lipa to go to the back of the loft or anywhere near the edge of the roof where he could peer down on his own house. Lipa saw there was a long narrow landing board set along the back loft wall under a large wire mesh window frame. The frame was attached to two chains that allowed it to be raised. Along the wall lay a wooden ladder which Gustavo raised up against the loft.

"I go up first, and then you'll follow," he announced. Gustavo climbed up the rough ladder gingerly, its narrow legs bending under his weight. Gustavo hoisted himself up onto the roof, and summoned Lipa to follow. Lipa suddenly panicked, like he was climbing over a great abyss. All he saw around him was endless blue sky. He took a step, and the ladder shook underneath him. He was afraid to climb higher, but Gustavo urged him on. Lipa climbed a few steps more, and then Gustavo reached down impatiently and hoisted Lipa right up onto the roof. Lipa stood atop the roof, frightened and thrilled all at once. He could see for miles and miles, nothing but blue sky and yellow sun, nothing between him and *Shamayim* above. Lipa grew afraid—there was nothing to stop him from falling over the narrow roof into the blue abyss below.

"Gustavo, I'm scared up here—" Lipa whimpered.

Gustavo showed patience. "Look, Lipa! If you fall, it's only a few feet to the roof of the apartment house. Nothing to be afraid of. If you want, you can hold on to the mast."

A tall pole rose from the middle of the roof reaching high up into the blue ether. Lipa took a step toward it, but its very presence calmed him—he could always grab it if he became light-headed. Having calmed Lipa, Gustavo raised a small, thin ladder that lay on the roof and set it against the mast, so that he could climb it up part ways. The roof of the loft resembled nothing less than a deck of a sailing ship, with its tall mast, and the rising heat from the roof waving like the sea.

Gustavo walked to the edge of the loft and raised open the back window by its chains. He lifted a pole that lay on the roof and pounded under him three times. From underneath in the loft came the sound of whirring wings, like a pot simmering. Lipa ran to the edge of the loft and watched as suddenly, right under his feet, a long flume of pigeons burst out of the loft, their wings beating wildly, and scattered into the air like a billowing cloud. They soared higher and higher, formed into a wing pattern, and began flying in wide circles, their wings flashing crimson and gold as the sun set their wings aflame. Gustavo climbed halfway up the mast, one foot set on the ladder, the other wrapped around the mast, and began waving a large white banner like a conductor. He directed the birds in their circuits. When he raised the banner the birds soared higher into the atmosphere, almost fifty feet above them. He signaled downward, and they swooped down like a giant winged roller coaster, their feathery wings outstretched effortlessly. Meanwhile, the tumblers and rollers performed their acrobatics, tumbling helplessly toward the ground, and then flapping their wings at the last instant, zooming back up to rejoin the flock.

Lipa looked up at Gustavo and could hardly recognize him—he had a different face, a child's face! All its roughness, its Italian swarthiness, had dissolved to that of a boy. Hanging from the tall mast, guiding his pigeons across the skies, Gustavo was as excited as a child. Lipa was seized up in Gustavo's infectious joy. Despite his promise to remain quiet, Lipa began waving his outstretched arms like a bird, twisting and turning around and around until he grew dizzy. Suddenly, he looked up and saw Gustavo staring at him. Lipa stopped short—he had broken his promise! But he had no reason to panic—Gustavo was smiling! Gustavo had feared that Lipa would mock his childish behavior, his ship deck on the roof. But now he saw that Lipa was not mocking him, but sharing in his make-believe world, a world of tall masts and soaring birds, infinite blue skies, a world where all dreams were possible.

10 *Little Fleigel*

Labor Day arrived. Lipa was set to begin yeshivah the next day and he would have little time for Gustavo's pigeons. Lipa was happy and sad. After a long summer, he would be reunited with his best friend, Shmuel—but he would also miss Gustavo. A little boy hid in Gustavo, and that little boy became Lipa's friend, as though he knew Gustavo forever.

Now Lipa sat in the front seat of Gustavo's battered pick-up truck, heading toward the bay. Lipa received permission from his father to go with Gustavo. His father had a busy schedule that day, reciting a prayer at the Jersey City Labor Day parade and visiting two hospitals. Rabbi Wallerstein was happy to have Lipa out of his hair. They drove past Ocean Avenue down toward the large railroad marshalling yards where trains passed on the way to New York City. Gustavo drove carefully. In the back of his pick-up, he carried a dozen crates containing some of his best pigeons, set for release. Lipa had his own precious cargo, Little Fleigel, who sat in a carton resting on his lap. It was still too early for Fleigel to fly, but Lipa took him along just for the company. Little Fleigel nestled contentedly in the box, peering up at Lipa and watching the trees pass by his window.

They cleared the last factory district and drove on to an empty field alongside the tracks. In the distance they could see Lower New

York harbor, with the green Statue of Liberty lifting her welcoming torch toward the ocean, her back to Jersey City. Gustavo exited the cab, and Lipa followed behind, Little Fleigel in hand. In the few days since Lipa had watched the pigeons fly up close, Gustavo had opened himself up to him, becoming almost garrulous. He taught Lipa many of his pigeon secrets, how to train them, how to make them fly off from the loft, and how to retrieve them. It was all in the feeding, he explained. Birds love to fly, but when they get hungry, they know where their food lies and they fly straight back home. Gustavo had trained the birds since they were fledglings, and his dream now was to train them for pigeon races.

Pigeon racing was treated very seriously, he explained. "You drive the birds to a starting station whose distance is measured from the loft. The birds are banded and then released to the exact second. Judges mark the time it takes each bird to fly back to its loft."

"But how do birds know their way home?" inquired Lipa.

Gustavo shrugged. "You're the rabbi's son, go ask him! It's a secret only G-d knows! Some say they use stars to navigate, even by day. Pigeons are amazing, you know. They used pigeons in the war to send messages back to headquarters in England all the way from Europe. One pigeon had her leg and half her head blown off—and she still made it back. Saved a whole battalion!"

Gustavo lifted the stacked crates and lay them flat across the floor of the pick-up. Just then, a thunderous rumble suddenly descended on them from just a few feet away. A huge locomotive thundered past them at breakneck speed, wheels clattering, whistle shrieking, hauling an endless line of freight cars. The train thundered past just a few feet away, and Lipa had to put his hands over his ears to protect himself from the noise. Then, as quickly as it had descended upon them, the train rolled off into the distance, and silence reigned again. After the terrible din, the silence afterward seemed almost palpable. Gustavo wet his finger and raised it into the air, judging wind direction. A calm breeze blew in off the bay.

"Perfect," Gustavo declared. "The winds will practically carry them back home."

He prepared to lift the crate lids, when he turned to Lipa. "Make sure you hold on to your bird," he warned. "I don't want him flying off with the others—he's not ready."

Lipa looked down at Little Fleigel who nestled contentedly in his hands. Little Fleigel wasn't going anywhere. Lipa brought a handful of sunflower seeds and Fleigel pecked contentedly on them. Gustavo opened the crate lids, tapped on the wall of the boxes, and one by one the pigeons shot upward, flapped their wings and flew off toward the loft. Suddenly, Lipa felt a stirring in his hands, and before Lipa could do anything, Little Fleigel flapped his wings and flew off to follow the others.

"Hey!" Lipa cried out desperately.

"Hold him!" Gustavo yelled.

But it was too late. Little Fleigel was airborne over the tracks. But unlike the others, he only reached a low altitude when he began to fall to the ground. Just then, another huge locomotive descended on them, roaring down the tracks. Little Fleigel fell onto the tracks right in front of the huge engine.

"Fleigel! Fleigel!" Lipa cried. "Little Fleigel!"

But it was too late. The huge train rolled over the poor little bird, two mammoth engines, endless freight cars, their huge iron wheels churning everything that lay beneath. Lipa began crying even as the train raced by, while Gustavo stood there speechless with shock.

It took forever, but finally the train passed. There was absolute stillness. Lipa didn't want to look. He opened his eyes. *There was Little Fleigel!* The little bird had hopped off the track just an instant in time to avoid disaster! Little Fleigel flapped his wings, and flying

The Shul Boy ∽ 249

in a straight line, flew straight at Lipa. Lipa grabbed him out of the air, his hands shaking.

"You are a bad bird, Fleigel!" he shouted angrily. "You are a very bad bird!"

He was so happy to have Little Fleigel back!

Finally, after an endless summer, school began. Lipa looked forward to it with excitement, not dread. His father had signed a peace treaty with the yeshivah's executive director. He agreed to pay a third of the regular tuition, based on his income as a Jewish chaplain. This time Lipa walked into class proudly, armed with an admittance pass. When the *rebbi* walked up and down the aisles to collect the card, he flashed his card boldly. He no longer had Rabbi Pesach Levy for a *rebbi*, but instead graduated to the class of famous Rabbi Hoenig, known for his discipline—but the boys hung on his every word. But where was Shmuel Praguer? Lipa searched around the room for his best friend—and he was nowhere to be seen. Was he sick? There was another eighth grade, but why should they move him there when everyone else was in the same class? Lipa was deeply disappointed, and could hardly concentrate on Rabbi Hoenig's first day's *Bava Kamma* class. Where was Shmuel?

Right there at recess, Lipa summoned his courage and walked up to the *rebbi* who was eating a snack and doing some papers. He looked up at Lipa silently, the famous Rabbi Hoenig stare. The boys said that for the first three months, anyone who approached Rabbi Hoenig shook with nervousness—and only later did his sweeter side appear.

"*Nu?*" asked Rabbi Hoenig.

"Rebbi, can I ask you something?"

"*Nu, nu—*"

"What happened to Shmuel Praguer—he's not in class."

"Why do you ask?"

"He...he was my *chavrusa* last year... We learned together, like friends."

The *rebbi* gave him a long look. "Shmuel Praguer is no longer in our yeshivah. He went to a yeshivah in Brooklyn."

Rabbi Hoenig turned back to his snack. Lipa stood there in shock. Shmuel Praguer, his only friend—was gone! He didn't say goodbye! Shmuel lived on the Lower East Side, so why would he go to Brooklyn? Lipa did not realize that he had done such a good job teaching Shmuel, that he decided to go to a yeshivah that taught more hours of Gemara. Lipa retreated to his desk, in shock. It was a glorious autumn day, and all the other boys were outside playing basketball in the courtyard. Lipa sulked in his seat, head buried glumly in his hands, and absorbed the shocking news. There was nothing he could do.

Days passed, but Lipa remained disconsolate. He had a new *chavrusa* now, a good boy, but it wasn't the same. He wasn't Shmuel. More than once Lipa dreamed of picking up the phone and calling—but he was too shy. What would he say? Shmuel probably forgot him already. Shmuel disappeared from the class, but not from Lipa's daydreams where they still studied together, knee to knee.

Meanwhile, even as Lipa dwelt in his lonesome world, Rabbi Wallerstein soared from success to success. He met the governor of New Jersey and local congressmen; he was liked in all the hospitals and prisons he visited. Even the non-Jewish staff appreciated him. There was talk that he would even be invited to give the invocation at the United States Senate. Rabbi Wallerstein was a happy man. He had his shul, he had enough *parnassah*, and every Friday night at the Shabbos meal, he gulped down a great *l'chaim*, sang *zemiros*, and thanked the *Ribono shel Olam* for his blessings.

It was fall, the holidays passed, and without Shmuel, Lipa was thrown headfirst into a valley of loneliness, without any break. During lunchtime, he wandered the canyons of the Lower East Side, with their grimy brick tenements looming on every side. Lipa knew every East Side street intimately, like his own Ulysses Avenue—Norfolk and Suffolk, Ludlow and Delancey, Essex, East Broadway, the East River Drive, all the great old shuls, the *mocher sefarim* book stores, the butcher shops and bakeries. How different the teeming, bustling Lower East Side, filled with its thousands of Jews and immigrants from all over, was from his own street, where the Jews could be counted on a few fingers. His daily wanderings went no further north than Delancey, for if he wandered further north to Houston, he would be late getting back to class. Meanwhile, he had passed his twelfth birthday and his bar mitzvah would be in the spring. His father had not yet told him what he was going to do in shul for his bar mitzvah, or discussed a *pshetl* that he would deliver at his celebration.

A few weeks before Chanukah, the science teacher, Mr. Fine, announced an important class project. Every student was to prepare a presentation on the subject of nature—trees, animals, rivers, mountains. The students were to bring their projects to class and give an oral presentation, explaining it. There were only two weeks allowed to prepare the projects. Immediately, the class broke into teams of twos and threes, deciding their subjects together. Lipa wished he could be part of a team, but he couldn't—it was not possible. All the other boys lived near each other, could visit each other's homes, work at the library together. But Lipa lived far away in Jersey City, the only student in his whole city who attended that yeshivah. He was all alone. When he went home, he entered a different world, a different planet—Jersey City. He explained to Mr. Fine why he could not team up with anyone.

Mr. Fine was a kindly, sensitive teacher who understood Lipa's isolation. "Pick a subject you like, keep it simple—and do the best you can."

Lipa liked Mr. Fine. Unlike Rabbi Hoenig who needed to keep strict discipline so the boys wouldn't run wild, Mr. Fine's science class was more unruly, but the teacher didn't care. After all, his subject was science, a fascinating new world to the boys, and whether he discussed astronomy, or the moon's cycles, or giant pythons in Brazil, or microbes in the drinking water, the boys listened, wide-eyed and open-mouthed.

Lipa went home, bent on finding an exciting project. But what? He had never done one before. His brother Leon was a good high school student and had done a dozen projects already. He approached his brother for ideas—what should he do? Leon was uninterested: "It's your project—you figure it out. Don't bother me." He couldn't go to his father or mother, for they wouldn't know either. So Lipa lay at night in bed, mulling over his project, staring out the dark window, when, *presto*! an awesome idea struck him. In fact, his project was right there—right outside his window!

It was Friday afternoon, and the day was short. Lipa hurried through his work, cleaning the shul, wiping the benches, running to Goldberg's to get herring. There were just two hours to Shabbos. Lipa entered the apartment house next door where he hadn't been since the summer. He climbed the three flights of stairs to the third floor, walked to the door with the little blue bird medallion, and knocked. At first there was nothing—maybe Gustavo was on the roof with his pigeons. But then he heard footsteps approaching from inside.

"Who's there?" Gustavo asked.

The Shul Boy 253

"Gustavo, it's me, Lipa."

There was a rattling of locks, and the door opened. "Well, look who's here—the rabbi's boy! I thought you forgot about me."

"Hello, Gustavo," Lipa answered. "I…I missed the birds. It's almost my Sabbath, but I wanted to see the pigeons—especially the one I saved. Could I?"

Gustavo was hurt. "You missed the birds—you didn't miss *me*?"

"I missed you *and* the birds," he corrected himself.

"It's not a good day for you to go up and visit the birds," Gustavo answered. "It's really cold up there on the roof now with the wind blowing. Maybe come back when the sun is shining."

"I can't, Gustavo. All the other days I don't come home until after six. I don't mind the cold. I have a coat."

Gustavo hesitated, and Lipa gave him one of his beseeching looks. In truth, Gustavo missed Lipa, who reminded him so much of himself. He gave a final warning: "But it's freezing, I tell you—and the roof ices up."

Gustavo went back inside, retrieved a heavy coat and locked the door behind him. Through the slightly open door, Lipa saw that Gustavo's apartment was crammed with all sorts of cartons and bags of bird feed. Pictures of birds cut out from magazines hung on his wall. His whole life was his birds.

Lipa followed Gustavo up the steep staircase and walked outside. Immediately, he was stung by the bitter November wind that swept across the roof. Gustavo turned around and shook his head. Lipa's face had turned cherry red in the cold.

"I told you it was freezing," he scolded.

How could pigeons survive on such a cold roof? Lipa wondered. But when they entered the loft, it was much warmer. The huddled birds created their own heat, and they sauntered about their compartments perfectly content.

"Where's my bird?" asked Lipa.

"You mean Fleigeli?"

Lipa giggled. Gustavo made Little Fleigel sound Italian. "I wonder if he still remembers me."

It did not take Lipa long to find out. The moment Little Fleigel spied Lipa, he beat his wings excitedly.

"He knows me, he knows me!" Lipa called out ecstatically. Lipa reached down and lifted Fleigel. The bird immediately settled comfortably in his hands.

Gustavo leaned over the pair. "He thinks you're his mother."

Lipa laughed, but Gustavo was serious. "I am not joking. Birds bond, you know. Fleigeli's bonded to you—he would follow you anywhere."

Lipa leaned down and murmured to Fleigel. "And this time—don't fly away!" Even as he held him just a few minutes, Lipa could tell that Fleigel had grown. He was heavier.

Now came the moment of truth. Lipa carefully returned Fleigel to his nesting box and then turned to Gustavo.

"Gustavo, can I ask you a favor, since we are friends?"

Gustavo eyed him suspiciously. "What is it?"

Lipa quickly described his class assignment to bring in a project. "I thought it would be really keen if I brought in Little Fleigel. I can show the class where his wing broke and you fixed it, and explain all about pigeons."

Gustavo was stunned. *Take a bird away from his loft?*

"No way, Lipa, no way!" he answered adamantly. "No bird of mine goes from this loft—especially this one! You think you're the only one who likes Fleigeli the best? He's special to me also. First of all, I fixed his wing and saved his life—thanks to you. But look at him—"

Gustavo reached in quickly and hoisted Fleigel back out in front

The Shul Boy ᔆ 255

of Lipa's face. "This bird is a beauty! Look how he's grown so perfect. You see those black stripes against his ivory tail, and the deep blue wing tips—it's the color of the sky! This bird is a beauty! By the way, where is your school, anyway?"

"New York City."

"New York City? How would you even get him there?"

"I could take him in one of your special containers. I wouldn't let him out of my sight. I can bring him on the Hudson Tubes."

Gustavo was aghast. "My birds riding in a train? Lipa, are you crazy? Never!"

"But Gustavo, *please*! Didn't I save him from the cats? I love Little Fleigel. I would watch him like he was the last pigeon in the world—every second! I'll show him to the class, show off his wings and beak, his tail feathers. I'll even tell about you—how you raise racing pigeons on your roof! You know, it'll be good luck for you, Gustavo. You see, you'll start winning races!"

Gustavo did not listen to Lipa's words, but watched the enthusiasm and excitement in his young, innocent face. Gustavo was also a young boy once, before his troubles started. He didn't swallow a word Lipa was saying, he just studied his boyish face.

Gustavo did not know what to do. He had never lent out one of his birds before. But this rabbi's boy was different. "Let me think about it," he finally answered. "When do you have to know by?"

"I have to know by next Friday, this time. Then, if you agree, I'll pick up Little Fleigel on Sunday night, keep him in my room overnight, and then bring him to school the next day. I'm sure the teacher will let me give my talk on Monday. Tuesday morning before school I'll bring Fleigel right back, I promise. Gustavo—please say *yes*."

Gustavo was almost ready to give in right there, but he was still unsure. "Let me think about it," he answered finally. "Maybe yes, maybe no. Come to me next Friday and I'll give you an answer."

He placed Little Fleigel back in his nest. Lipa leaned over and stroked Fleigel's head one last time. The pigeon lifted his wings in appreciation.

"Good Shabbos, Little Fleigel," he said. "I'll see you next Friday."

The week crept by too slowly for Lipa. He watched enviously as the other boys discussed their projects. It had taken over their whole imagination, and poor Rabbi Hoenig had to struggle to keep their heads in Gemara. For Lipa, there was no other plan. All his hopes rested on bringing Little Fleigel—a live exhibit. Friday afternoon came and Lipa didn't even run first to clean the shul. Instead, he ran straight up to Gustavo's apartment, praying all the time that the answer would be yes. Gustavo must have heard his footsteps racing up the stairs for when Lipa reached the top floor, he was already waiting outside his door.

"Can I have Fleigel?" Lipa asked impetuously, not even saying hello.

Gustavo did not answer at first, but he lifted his finger warningly: "Yes, you can borrow him for one day—only because you helped me during the summer! But if anything happens to him, Heaven help you!"

Lipa broke into a broad smile. "*Whooeee!*" he screamed happily, scaring the neighbors. He was so happy! His pigeon would beat all the other exhibits, he was sure. And nothing—*nothing*—would happen to Little Fleigel. He would not let go of him from the moment he took him to the minute he brought him back to Gustavo. Even moody-faced Gustavo broke into a smile. For the first time in many years, he felt warm inside, making this young boy so happy. A tiny portion of his own aching loneliness was healed.

Sunday night arrived. It was almost nightfall when Gustavo and

Lipa climbed up to the rooftop to collect Little Fleigel. They huddled against the cold wind and swirling snowflakes that blew across the roof. Gustavo had prepared a special perforated carton for Lipa to transport the pigeon. Gustavo lifted the bird carefully, inspected its repaired wing one last time, and placed it in the box. "Keep the lid on all the time. Hold the box straight up. Don't let it jiggle." Even so, Gustavo did not trust Lipa to carry the case across the icy roof or down the first set of steep stairs. Only when they reached the top floor, did Gustavo place the precious cargo into Lipa's hands. He seemed reluctant to give up the bird, even then. Lipa felt the gravity of the moment, and held the box tightly with both hands. He thanked Gustavo again, and carefully carried Fleigel down the three flights of stairs, holding the box close to his chest.

He crossed the sidewalk over to his own house, closed the door behind him, and immediately his mood lifted. *He had Little Fleigel all to himself!* Out of Gustavo's ponderous shadow, Lipa could not contain himself. "Abba, Ima, look what I brought home!"

He ran up the stairs with the carton and placed it on the kitchen table. Even Leon and Eva ran in to see what all the commotion was about. They all stood about, Rabbi Wallerstein, his mother, Leon and Eva, and Lipa opened the box. "Look, this is the bird I'm going to show off in class."

He proudly lifted up Little Fleigel, who sat in his hands, bewildered by the strange surroundings. The family was impressed. "What a beautiful bird!" Mrs. Wallerstein exclaimed.

"Can it really fly?" asked Eva.

"Sure," Lipa answered. "It's a racing pigeon!"

Rabbi Wallerstein seemed bemused by the bird's appearance. He took off his heavy framed glasses and examined it closely. "Looks, like he's wearing a *tallis*."

Lipa showed off Little Fleigel proudly. No one was making fun of him. He showed off the blue feathers, the little bulge on its head, and then placed him very carefully back into the carton.

"I'm going to take him up to my room," he announced.

Lipa had a quick supper, wrote down what he was going to say in class tomorrow, and prepared for bed. Outside, the wind rattled the windowpanes and snowflakes streaked down the outside of the glass. Inside Lipa's bedroom, it was warm and cozy. He donned his pajamas and gazed at the precious carton in the corner. For the first time since he had saved the little bird's life, Lipa was alone with Little Fleigel. Lipa checked carefully that the bedroom door was shut, the windows were sealed tight—there was no way for the bird to escape.

He went to the box and opened the top. He lifted Little Fleigel out and held him up on one hand, like a juggler. Little Fleigel beat his wings, happy to be free. Lipa gave him a little toss upward, and Fleigel began flying about the room. He flew to the dresser top, then into the open closet. Lipa chased after him, and Fleigel fluttered playfully to the top of the window shade. Lipa chased after him again, almost caught him, but Fleigel soared to the other side of the room. Fleigel understood the game of tag that Lipa was playing with him.

Finally, Lipa stood in place next to his bed. He lifted one arm and swept it down in an arc, in imitation of Gustavo. "Fleigel, fly downward!"

In an instant, Fleigel swept down from his perch and flew down onto the dresser top. The bird stood there, awaiting Lipa's next signal.

Lipa raised his arm upward. "Fleigel, fly up!" he ordered.

Instantly, Fleigel flapped his wings and flew upward, returning to his perch above the shade.

Lipa struck out both arms and turned in a circle. The bird followed his movements, flying around him in a perfect circle. Lipa twirled quickly a few times more until he became dizzy, and each time, Little Fleigel followed his signals perfectly.

"*Yay*, Fleigel!" Lipa exclaimed happily. He kept his voice low—he did not want anyone else in the family to know what was going on in his room. Then he cupped his hands in front of him: "Fleigel, fly to me!"

In an instant, the pigeon flew right into Lipa's hands, where he nestled contentedly. Lipa was ecstatic. It was true—Little Fleigel really listened to him! He lifted the bird close to his face and whispered:

"Fleigel, you're the *best*!"

Lipa returned the pigeon to its case, closed the lid and went to sleep joyfully. He couldn't wait for tomorrow—and to show off Little Fleigel to the class!

It was a cold morning, with blowing wind and snow flurries. Rabbi Wallerstein was touched by Lipa's project, and drove him to the Hudson Tubes himself so he and the bird would not have to wait for a bus outside in the cold. The trains were crowded Monday morning, and Lipa squeezed himself into a car, the carton held tightly against his chest, his briefcase dangling from one arm. He received more than one dirty look from passengers who were poked by the side of his carton, although no one seemed to realize that there was a live bird inside. Little Fleigel stayed quiet, enjoying the ride. Lipa was afraid that it might be too hot in the overcrowded train, and tried to fan Fleigel from outside the box, but the ride went quickly, and he was soon on the less crowded New York subway, the A Train and then D Train to East Broadway. Lipa was afraid to lift the lid to check on Fleigel, lest the bird escape inside the train—that would be fun, wouldn't it!

Lipa walked out onto the cold sidewalk at East Broadway, the chilly wind a refreshing break from the stuffy subway. Even Little Fleigel responded happily, hopping inside the box and flapping his wings. Lipa was very excited. Even his family was fascinated by Little Fleigel, and imagine when he showed him off to his class. But he still had to be careful. He didn't want anyone to see Fleigel before the science class, and he had Gemara all morning. So, during the whole morning, even as Rabbi Hoenig taught *Bava Kamma* and Lipa turned around afterward to learn with his *chavrusa,* he quietly hid Little Fleigel under his desk, squeezing the box between his feet, just fitting it in. Just before he stuffed the box below, he whispered to Fleigel to please stay quiet and not jump around too much. No one was to know there a was bird inside the box—it was Lipa's surprise for the science class, for Mr. Fine, whom he liked so much.

The morning Torah class finished. Lipa did not meander around the Lower East Side streets as usual, but remained in the classroom, ostensibly eating lunch and doing homework—but really guarding his secret below. From time to time, he bent down to make sure that Fleigel was okay.

Finally, the two o'clock bell rang and the English classes began, first math, then social studies, and finally late in the afternoon, the science class. It was past four o'clock, the skies were dark, and outside, snow beat against the windows. Mr. Fine entered, and there was the usual disorganized tumult. Mr. Fine called the class to order:

"Today, we will hear from three students about their projects," he announced.

He wrote the subjects on the boards: the first was *Alligators*, the second *Birds*, the third *Great Rivers*. Mr. Fine called up the first project. Two boys came up proudly clasping an oaktag sheet covered with pictures of alligators from four continents. They pointed to each picture and spoke about alligators at length; their size, what they ate, how they gave birth to a nest of little squirming alligators. The boys listened with interest, even as the embarrassed presenters tried keeping a straight face and not giggle as they spoke. After they completed their fifteen-minute presentation, one of the boys announced:

"Finally, we are going to pass around the room a real alligator skin wallet that my uncle bought in Miami."

With great pride, the other boy took a wallet out of his sweater pocket and handed it to pass down to the class. Each student felt the alligator hide, and passed it to the boy behind. The boys looked at Mr. Fine, who smiled at them, very pleased.

"Thank you, Barry and David—you may be seated."

With great ceremony, Mr. Fine lifted his roll book and wrote down a mark.

He looked up. "Now, we will hear from Lipa Wallerstein."

Proudly, Lipa lifted the carton that he had hidden under his seat. The boys were surprised by its presence—he had kept it totally out of their sight. He walked to the front of the class.

"Before I show you my project," he announced, "I need to have the classroom door shut." He looked to Mr. Fine for help. "No one can go in and out of the room until I'm finished. Also, we have to make sure the windows are shut tight."

Lipa's announcement gained everyone's curiosity.

"You hear that, boys," Mr. Fine announced. "Max, you stand by the door to make sure no one comes in or out. And let's make sure the windows are really closed."

Mr. Fine himself went to the side of the room and checked all the windows. They were closed tight against the swirling snow outside. "Okay, Lipa, you may proceed."

With great ceremony, Lipa placed the box on Mr. Fine's desk, opened the lid and extracted Little Fleigel. A surprised gasp rose from the class at the sight of the live bird in Lipa's hands. Little Fleigel, who was freed from his carrying case for the first time all day, flapped his wings, adding to the excitement. The boys all stood up, and despite Mr. Fine's protest, ran up and clustered around Lipa's bird. Little Fleigel was at his glorious best; his blue-tipped wings spread out, his black stripes glistening sharply across his back. He was skittish, not used to so many people surrounding him. But Lipa held him firmly in his hands.

Lipa began his presentation. He told of finding the injured bird in his backyard, and how he returned it up to its rooftop loft. He described how the bird keeper Gustavo had tied up the injured wing until it healed. Then he described in vivid detail how he watched the birds fly around and around in a flock, following the keeper's signals. Lipa knew so much about pigeons. He pointed out Fleigel's different parts, the crown with its tiny bulge, the wattle over the beak, the different parts of the wings, the crop, his feet. He showed off which part of the wing was used to fly, and which to land. The boys were enthralled. Even Mr. Fine laid down his roll book and listened to Lipa's presentation. Meanwhile, Fleigel rested comfortably in Lipa's hands, occasionally flapping his wings, causing *oohs* and *aahs*. The boys even reached out their hands to feel Fleigel's feathers. The whole class was so caught up in Lipa's presentation that no one noticed when two boys who were jealous of Lipa's presentation sneaked over to the front window and quietly opened it a few inches. They smirked to each other and quickly slipped back to join the class.

"You see," explained Lipa, "this bird has become used to me, like he knows me. It is one of the most beautiful birds in Gustavo's whole flock."

To show off its exceptional beauty, Lipa lifted it high in one hand, holding it by the tips of his fingers. Suddenly, Little Fleigel flapped his wings, lifted himself out of Lipa's hands and flew straight out the open window!

Lipa stood there for an instant, empty hand still raised. "Where is my pigeon?" he cried out.

"It flew out the window!" one of the boys screamed. "I saw him fly right out!"

Mr. Fine was furious. "Who opened that window?" he shouted angrily. No one knew—or if the boys knew, they weren't telling.

Lipa stood there in shock. "Where is my bird?" he cried out again. "Where did he go?"

He ran to the window, hoping that Fleigel was perched outside on the windowsill. But he was gone, vanished! Lipa remembered last time that Little Fleigel had taken off and landed just a few yards away. Maybe he was outside on the street! Without asking, Lipa threw open the door and raced down the four stories to the street below. The wind gusted, snow swirled around in his face—it was almost dark. Outside, the street was wet with melting snowflakes, trucks roared by, stray cats scurried among the parked cars.

"Fleigel! Fleigel!" Lipa cried. "Where are you?"

He ran back toward East Broadway, checked car hoods, underneath on the gutter, dodged in front of cars to look across the street from the yeshivah. Fleigel had completely disappeared. Lipa began to freeze in the cold. He retraced his steps and ran down to the other side of the school—maybe Fleigel had flown there. But there was no Fleigel. Fleigel was gone, vanished, lost in the Lower East Side!

Lipa climbed back up the stairs into the warm classroom. He sat down in his seat still clasping the empty box and began sobbing. *Fleigel was gone*! Gustavo would be so angry! Lipa had promised him over and over that he would watch Little Fleigel. The boys in the classroom watched Lipa with sincere sadness. They knew that someone among them had done this foolish prank. Those who saw it would not tell. The boys who had opened the window sat in their seats, shaking. They never realized the terrible consequence of their deed.

Mr. Fine stood before the somber, silent class. The usually mild mannered, bespectacled teacher barely contained his anger. "Boys, I know that someone here was responsible for doing this terrible thing to Lipa. It is not my wish to shame anyone in front of the class. But I'll tell you what I would do if it was I who did it. Very quietly, I would go over to Lipa and say: 'I'm sorry.' That's the grown-up thing to do—the manly thing. I am canceling the rest of today's class—I can't teach you anymore."

With that, he folded up his roll book and stalked out of the classroom. It was almost the end of the school day anyway—night had fallen. The boys grabbed their coats and marched out of the classroom silently. Lipa remained in his seat, unable to move. He wiped tears from his face. He felt like a baby, crying—but he couldn't help it. *Fleigel was gone*. He held the empty, worthless carton in his hands. He was about to leave when the door swung open. The two guilty boys approached Lipa.

"Lipa, we're sorry. It was really stupid what we did. Please be *moichel* us."

Lipa nodded, but tears ran down his cheeks. "Yes, I'm *moichel*," he intoned, "I'm *moichel*…"

But why did they have to do that?

―

Lipa traveled home in a state of shock. What would he say to Gustavo? He would be so angry. He didn't want him to take Fleigel, but Lipa had begged him, had promised to watch him, over and over. Lipa traveled home by three trains and the Norway Avenue bus. His head hung low as he stared at the empty carton, and his face was tearstained. Other passengers watched him worriedly. One nice woman rose from her seat on the Hudson Tubes and approached Lipa. Tears were coming down Lipa's face.

"Sonny, are you okay? Are you hurt?"

Lipa, ashamed, wiped the tears from his face and shook his head silently. He could barely speak. She returned to her seat, but continued to watch him anxiously. Finally, Lipa arrived home. He didn't want to talk to anyone. He was scared—Gustavo lived just next door. He ran up to his room without greeting anyone. His mother called up to his room.

"Lipa, I have chicken waiting for you."

Lipa called down, "Mommy, I'm not hungry. I just want to stay in my room."

He placed the empty carton on his dresser and sat down to think. Outside, the snow blew heavier, beating against his window. What should he do? He missed Little Fleigel so much. Last night they had been playing together in his room, and Fleigel was flying crazily all over. Now, who knew if Fleigel was alive? Maybe he was run over, or the cats got him. Lipa was very scared of Gustavo. He remembered the first day he saw him, how furious he could become. He was a big, strong man. Lipa promised to bring Fleigel back tomorrow morning. Maybe he should just go right now and tell him the truth, get it over with. But he was frightened. He even thought to run away, to hide. But he had no place to go, not even bus fare. Lipa spent a long time sitting on his bed, agonizing. Finally, after much anxious contemplation he thought of a possible solution—the only solution. He was afraid to meet Gustavo. Instead, he decided to write him a note and leave it with the empty carton outside Gustavo's door. He would explain everything. It was not really his fault that Fleigel flew away. He would apologize, ask forgiveness, and offer to pay for a new pigeon. What more could he do? Lipa looked at the clock. It was nearly ten, past his bedtime. But he needed to write the note. Then, maybe, maybe he would never have to see Gustavo again.

Lipa sat at his desk, his small lamp casting a yellow glow over his desk pad. He took out a sheet of paper, his good pen, and laid it flat. How should he begin? Outside, the snow beat even harder against the window. Poor Fleigel, he would freeze in the Lower East Side, or he would starve. Lipa lifted his pen and was about to begin writing, but the snow banging so noisily against the window distracted him. The beating snow grew louder and louder, *rat tat tat, rat tat tat.*

He began writing:

"Dear Gustavo: I have bad news—"

The pounding at the window became more insistent, like a beating drum, that Lipa had to stop. Lipa was curious. He lay down the paper, went to the window and peered out into the darkness. Sure enough, outside on the windowsill was a lump of snow, drumming against his window. *Oh, I hope this is not another night visitor,* he thought. At first he thought it was a small mound of snow that had piled up against the corner of his window, and was being blown back and forth by the wind. Lipa lifted the window a few inches to knock it off his ledge. But the little pile of snow shifted on its own. Lipa realized then that it was a little white bird buried in snow, begging to be let in. Lipa opened the window higher, hoping to brush the snow off the bird and let him fly off, when the bird burst in, scattering his heavy blanket of snow all over the room. The snowy cover scattered away, and there, flying around the room was—*Little Fleigel!*

Freed of his snowy load, Little Fleigel flew joyously around the room, landing atop the carton that lay on the dresser. Lipa ran to the window and shut it tight. *Little Fleigel!* Little Fleigel had flown all the way from the Lower East Side, crossed over the Hudson River, Statue of Liberty, through the snow storm—to him, to Lipa! He didn't fly to Gustavo's loft—but to Lipa's bedroom!

Yay, Fleigel!

"Fleigel, come to me!" Lipa ordered.

The pigeon skipped off the box and flew straight into Lipa's hands, beating his wings, tweeting happily.

He was back! Baruch Hashem, *Fleigel was back!*

Lipa could hardly talk. Tiny tears of happiness rolled down his cheeks. But how did it happen? How did Fleigel find his way at night through the storm back to Jersey City, to Ulysses Avenue, to his room?

Only Hashem knew.

In an instant, everything had changed. He didn't need to write any letter. Tomorrow morning, he would return Fleigel to Gustavo. Should he tell Gustavo what happened? And his classmates in school—should he tell them that his bird had flown back? Lipa closed his eyes, thinking. All the years of loneliness had honed his *neshamah* like a fine instrument. A voice inside murmured:

Hashem sent Little Fleigel to you... He is no regular bird, but a messenger flown down from Above. Three times he faced disaster—three times he survived. No one must know the awesome power of Little Fleigel—only Hashem must know!

Lipa lifted Fleigel up so he stared him straight in the face. "*Little Fleigel—who are you, really?*" he asked. But Fleigel did not answer.

Lipa placed the little pigeon carefully back into his carton, recited *Hamapil*, and fell happily asleep—little knowing what wondrous happenings lay ahead.

11
Pesachiah

Rabbi Wallerstein stood in his unlit synagogue and peered out the front window. It was a quiet Sunday morning, a gray December day. He leaned against his wooden *shtender*, a Tehillim in front of him, and puffed on his cigar. He ran his fingers contemplatively over the aging cover, and prepared to begin his weekly recital of the Psalms. But first he needed to think.

Lipa's bar mitzvah was coming in just three months. How different would be Lipa's bar mitzvah from Leon's bar mitzvah just a few years ago. Then, Rabbi Wallerstein was struggling to survive, barely making *parnassah*. Leon's bar mitzvah was simple. He recited the *Maftir*, there was a kiddush on Shabbos, and Sunday night Rabbi Wallerstein made a party for the family from New York and a few shul people. A *rebbi* from the yeshivah prepared a *pshetl* for Leon almost four pages long, and Leon read it clearly and fast, with self-confidence.

But now, things were different. Now he was the Jewish Chaplain of Hudson County. He had many important acquaintances; Harry Solomon, JVK, and the politicians he rubbed shoulders with. Lipa's bar mitzvah was a chance to make an impression on them — especially on JVK himself. Rabbi Wallerstein drew deeply on his cigar, blew smoke up to the ceiling, and considered his options. He thought of a plan, and smiled to himself, pleased. He finally laid down his cigar in the ashtray along the window and opened his Tehillim. Before he started reading, he fleshed out his ideas. He would make a Monday night meal at the Norway Avenue Shul. It had a large, beautifully decorated hall. There he could invite his most influential guests, leaders of the community, rabbis, even the politicians—JVK himself. It would cost a lot, but he was sure that he would make it back with the presents Lipa would receive.

At the thought of Lipa, a frown formed on Rabbi Wallerstein's face—*alyah v'kotz bah*. There was one thorn in his grand plans—the bar mitzvah boy himself. Lipa was a quiet, peculiar boy. He could imagine Lipa standing in front of a hundred people, mumbling a long *pshetl*, and no one would understand a word he said. No, he would have to make changes. Lipa wasn't Leon. The bar mitzvah boy would be seen but heard very little, just a brief Torah passage and a few words of welcome—*that's all*. Yes, that would work. The frown disappeared from Rabbi Wallerstein's face, and he began reciting Tehillim joyfully: "*Ashrei ha'ish…*"

Meanwhile, a subtle change had taken place in Lipa's standing among his classmates. After the incident of the flyaway bird, he was viewed as a tragic hero, even a tzaddik. The boys soon discovered who did the dastardly deed of opening the window, and that Lipa forgave them—truly forgave them. He was even nice to them—*imagine*! The guilty boys offered again and again to buy a pigeon in the place of the one that flew away, but Lipa would not accept a penny. Furthermore, Lipa became better and better in Gemara, and boys would approach Lipa before tests and ask him to explain lines. He was no longer so alone in class, although he still spent most lunchtimes alone, daydreaming.

It was only eight weeks until his bar mitzvah, and Lipa grew excited. Old Reverend Freidman taught him to lead Shacharis and recite *Maftir*. He learned quickly—Lipa had a high, sweet voice, still unchanged. But it was the Monday night bar mitzvah celebration that excited Lipa the most. At the Shabbos morning bar mitzvah, there would be just a few guests, plus the regular shul people. But at the Monday night affair he could invite his classmates, and above all—Shmuel. He still missed his old *chavrusa* very much, but was too shy to call him. But, if he found his address, he could send him an invitation. The bar mitzvah invitations finally arrived. Lipa was proud. They were very handsome, bold black Hebrew and English lettering embossed against a glistening white card. His father had gone all out—he explained that there would be very important people at this dinner.

Rabbi Wallerstein allotted Lipa just enough invitations for the boys in his class, although he doubted many would come all the way from New York City for Lipa. Lipa begged his father for one extra.

"Why?" his father demanded. "We hardly have enough for our guests."

"I have one special friend I want to invite," Lipa explained. Grudgingly, Rabbi Wallerstein gave up the extra invitation, but to Lipa, it was the most important one of all. Lipa carried the invitations up to his room, carefully inscribing the names of each classmate, including the two who had opened the window to let Little Fleigel escape. It was Lipa's very private secret—they didn't know what they made happen. But the most important invitation was to Shmuel Praguer. It was not easy getting his address. The school secretary would not give it to him, and Lipa had to ask the executive director himself, who understood boys better. Finally, he had Shmuel's address, and he mailed it, the first of all his invitations, praying that Shmuel would come. The rest of the invitations he gave out by hand.

The bar mitzvah drew closer. Return cards started pouring in, dozens of them. Rabbi Wallerstein was pleased to see that almost

The Shul Boy 271

everyone accepted, including most rabbis in the city, Harry Solomon, Abe Ravitz, community leaders, and above all, JVK himself. Rabbi Wallerstein ordered a special white yarmulke for him, embroidered with the initials JVK in gold letters. The bar mitzvah preparations were progressing smoothly, although he still needed a band.

One evening, just weeks before the bar mitzvah, Rabbi Wallerstein sat in his office and finished a speech he wrote out on a single sheet of lined paper. There was knock on the door.

"Come in," he called out, and Lipa entered the office.

"Ima said you needed to talk to me," Lipa said. It was the first time he had ever been summoned to talk to his father, and Lipa was happy.

Rabbi Wallerstein set down his cigar and cleared his throat. "Sit down, Lipa, sit down. I want to talk to you."

Lipa sat down in front of the desk. Right away he sensed his father was acting peculiar.

"Lipa," he father began, gazing out the window, "you know, I am making a really beautiful bar mitzvah for you, much bigger than Leon's."

"Thank you, Abba," Lipa answered gratefully.

"Now, there are going to be all sorts of people there, very important people, some who are not even Jewish. There will be a lot of speeches, not just yours."

"Will Mr. Ravitz speak?"

"Yes, he will be the master of ceremonies."

Lipa was so pleased. He liked Mr. Ravitz's speeches.

"Yes, it will be very nice. But you know, it means that there is no time for you to give a long *drashah* like Leon did. Those were different people, you understand?"

"Yes, Abba."

Rabbi Wallerstein swiveled his chair and faced his son directly. "So, I wrote out a speech for you to give at the dinner. Here—"

He handed the sheet he had just completed to Lipa. Lipa studied it and frowned. The speech was short, very, very short.

"But where is the rest of it, Abba?" he asked.

"There is no rest of it," Rabbi Wallerstein retorted. "There is no time for more, didn't I tell you?"

"But Abba, every bar mitzvah boy gives a *drashah* a few pages long. There is only one line of Torah in the whole speech—it won't look nice."

"'*Look nice? Look nice?*'" Rabbi Wallerstein raised his voice impatiently. "Lipa, I am spending ten times more on your bar mitzvah than I did on Leon's! The mayor of the city will be there! I'm buying you a new, beautiful suit. Of course it will look nice!"

"But Abba, all of my class will be there. Some had their bar mitzvahs already, and they all gave long *drashos*. Can't I do more?"

Rabbi Wallerstein lost his patience. He could not tell Lipa the real truth, that if he mumbled through three pages of Torah no one would understand a word he said and it would spoil the whole affair.

Rabbi Wallerstein tried to stay calm. "Listen, Lipa, there are things you don't understand. You are just a boy. I know who's coming, and this speech is just perfect for the dinner, not too long. Please don't argue!"

Lipa saw that his father was growing angry. But he made one last plea.

"But Abba, can't I add on something on my own?" he begged.

He won't add anything on his own, Rabbi Wallerstein knew. He sat back, like he considered the matter seriously. But he was impatient to go on to more pressing matters.

"Fine," he finally answered. "If you can add on a little something on your own, it's okay. But only on your own—no help from others, you understand?"

Lipa looked down resignedly at the one sheet of paper containing his whole bar mitzvah *pshetl* and nodded. This was to be his bar mitzvah *drashah*, and that was that. Meanwhile, his classmates returned their invitations. They were all coming! In fact, they were excited to visit Jersey City—it was like a foreign land. But the return he hoped for most did not come.

Rabbi Moshe Hoenig was an exceptional *rebbi*. He started off the year so strictly that the children trembled when he looked at them. Slowly, like a fish being played out on a line, he loosened his strictness. Even when he shouted at them, his words to the boys were always positive, encouraging. After Chanukah he slowly began to show another side, a funny side, and the boys responded. Now, with spring approaching, the boys worshipped him. He raised the bar high for them—*derech eretz*, *yiras Shamayim*, and above all a love of learning Torah. He imbued the boys not only with learning, but to *want* to learn Torah, to *want* to become *talmidei chachamim*. And the boys grew in his class. From the start of the year when they were silly, playful children, they began metamorphosing, like a caterpillar to a butterfly, into young *talmidei chachamim*.

Like the rest of the class, Lipa listened raptly to Rabbi Hoenig's talks that he gave on Fridays before school ended—always a passage from *Pirkei Avos*.

"*Yagata u'matzasa*, boys," he began each time, "it's all up to you! Listen—

"Listen… *Rabbi Elazar ben Chisma* says… *Kinnim*…*hein hein gufei halachos*… The laws of *Kinnim* are the real flesh and bones of the Torah… *Tekufos v'Gematrios—parpera'os la'chachmah*…

"You hear that, boys? *Tekufos*, *Gematrios*, they're okay, but they're just seasoning to the Torah, make it tasty. But *Kinnim*—that's the real thing, the meat and potatoes—"

All hands went up in the class. "Rebbi, what are *Tekufos* and *Gematrios*?"

"You don't know?" he asked back in shock. "Where have you been, boys, asleep? Don't you study the *Ba'al Haturim* with your fathers on Shabbos? *Gematria* is arithmetic… The Hebrew letters of one word in the Torah match up to the numbers of another word—and the connections are unbelievable! Study the *Ba'al Haturim* on Shabbos, boys—it's amazing!"

An excited buzz passed through the room. Suddenly, the *Ba'al Haturim* seemed the most wonderful thing to learn.

More hands went up. "Rebbi, what are *Tekufos*?"

Rabbi Hoenig tugged at his short blond beard. "*Tekufos*… I don't know if I should get into that—"

"Please, Rebbi!" the boys pleaded.

"It has to do with the rotation of the sun and the moon and the earth. It's very difficult astronomy, having to do with *Kiddush Hachodesh*… But remember—Rabbi Elazar said it's just *seasoning* compared to the real meat and potatoes—*Kinnim*!"

"*What's* Kinnim?" the class yelled out in chorus. They were having a grand time learning—Rabbi Hoenig had them eating out of his hand like little birds.

"*Don't even ask me!*" he shouted back. "It's too hard!"

"*Please!*" they shouted back,pleading.

Rabbi Hoenig smiled. "Enough! Class dismissed—have a good Shabbos!"

With faces full of smiles, the boys raced out of class, some boys shouting a quick good Shabbos to the *rebbi*. Only one boy remained behind as the *rebbi* put away his papers—Lipa. He approached Rabbi Hoenig shyly.

The Shul Boy 275

"Rebbi," he asked. "Please tell *me*—what *is* Kinnim?"

The *rebbi* looked at Lipa and smiled. "And why are you so interested, Lipa?"

"I think I once heard that word, but I don't remember how. *Kinnim* sounds so—keen… Does *Kinnim* have anything to with 'keen'—like a keen knife, or a keen game?"

The *rebbi* looked at this peculiar, shy student who he knew had once had his precious pigeon fly away and still forgave the miscreants, and smiled patiently.

"*Kinnim* is very keen, Lipa—very keen and very hard. It's too hard for me to explain it."

"Where is it? Is it a Gemara?"

Rabbi Hoenig shook his head at Lipa's ignorance. "No, not a Gemara, Lipa. It's in a mishnah, the last mishnah in *Seder Kadshim*."

Lipa wanted to ask more, but Rabbi Hoenig was in a rush to go home for Shabbos. In truth, Lipa was not even sure what *Seder Kadshim* was. But his curiosity was piqued, and he was determined to find out, somehow.

It was strange how *Kinnim* had so aroused Lipa's curiosity. Why? He did not know—but it was an itch that had to be scratched. It pulled at him. Rabbi Hoenig had declared: "*Kinnim* is 'meat and potatoes'!" But *what* was it? Lipa had no idea. Out of desperation, he even asked his brother Leon, but even he did not know. On Shabbos all the talk in shul was about Lipa's upcoming bar mitzvah. Lipa basked in all his fame, but underneath, *Kinnim* gnawed at him. He might have asked his father, but as the bar mitzvah drew closer, Rabbi Wallerstein grew more irritable and nervous—he had no time for anything. At the Friday night meal, he was short tempered and impatient, even after a *l'chaim*.

On Sunday afternoon, Lipa came home early from yeshivah and had more time to think. His thoughts dwelt completely on *Kinnim*. He did not understand why, but the need to learn *Kinnim* blossomed like a seed in his soul, sending out roots and branches, casting its shade over all else, even his bar mitzvah. He knew he had to find the section of *Kadshim,* and somewhere there was *Kinnim.* But then what? Rabbi Hoenig had warned that it was tremendously hard—then how could he ever understand it? At least, he had to look at the pages of *Kinnim*!

But then, a shiver of fright passed through Lipa's slender body. For he knew there was only one place where he could find *Kinnim*—it was part of Zeide's Mishnayos. But he was very frightened of the Mishnayos and what happened whenever he gazed in them. Each time he opened Zeide's Mishnayos, something wild and crazy happened. He was dragged into another world, and then just when things turned wonderful, he was cast back into his lonely world. He entered those magical worlds thrilled—he left brokenhearted. The friends he met in those beautiful worlds all vanished forever.

Lipa struggled inside himself. He so much wanted to learn *Kinnim*—but he was very afraid of what would happen to him—again.

He decided—forget *Kinnim.*

But how could he forget Kinnim?

A voice in him whispered constantly—"*Study* Kinnim!" And each time he heard it, he shivered in fear. He thought and thought, not sure what to do.

Then, one night on the way home from yeshivah, standing in the packed Hudson Tubes train clinging to a strap handle, the answer suddenly came to him. Other passengers must have wondered why the young boy was suddenly smiling to himself, but Lipa had finally figured out the perfect solution—and it came from standing in the crowded train car. Lipa suddenly realized why he was so frightened of his Zeide's Mishnayos, and what do about it.

The very next night, Thursday, Lipa rushed home from yeshivah as quickly as he could. It was the first week of March, less than two weeks before his bar mitzvah. The weather had turned spring-like, and a light rain fell, washing away the last slushy snow from the sidewalk. There was a low rumble of thunder in the distance, but it was almost a welcome guest, for it portended warmer weather to come. Lipa realized why he had been so frightened to open his Zeide's Mishnayos. Each time he had been enticed into strange worlds. But it was always the same, all by himself, lights out, the doors locked, down in the black coal bin. Or he heard eerie banging on the windows that lured him out into strange adventures. But now he was determined—no one would lure him away this time! The lights would stay on. He would not be cut off from everyone else, just like he was not cut off from people on the crowded train. He would be downstairs, but his family would be right upstairs, with the hallway door to upstairs open. Even if there were the loudest pounding on the windows, even if Eliyahu Hanavi himself came knocking on the door inviting him to follow, he would politely refuse.

"Eliyahu, I'll see you on Seder night!" he would announce.

Upstairs in the kitchen, the mood was already festive—everyone was excited about Lipa's bar mitzvah. Even his father was not so anxious anymore. Rabbi Wallerstein was thrilled that almost everyone had accepted his invitations, almost two hundred people! Eva was playing records in her room, and the sound of music echoed cheerfully throughout the house. Even Leon was treating Lipa with more respect. Lipa ate a fast supper and excused himself to go downstairs. His father read a Yiddish paper in the kitchen and his mother was preparing for Shabbos. He had the whole downstairs to himself.

Lipa did something he had never done before. He turned on all the downstairs lights—but *all* the lights. Usually, the shul lights stayed closed during the week—electricity cost money. But this time, Lipa turned on all the shul lights. All the *neshamos* hiding in the dark must have been startled by the bright lights, for they all suddenly disappeared. Instead, the shul was not frightening, but warm and cheerful, like Shabbos. If Lipa's father saw what he had done, he would not have been pleased. But Lipa had to do what he had to do. He turned on the front hall lights, the office lights, the lights to the *veibersher* shul, even the bathroom light. The whole downstairs was lit up like Rosh Hashanah. Lipa hoped that Hashem would forgive him for wasting so much money, but he was determined that this time no one was going to come out of the dark and knock on his door. Finally, he entered his father's office. It was not scary at all. Instead, the walls gleamed bright colors from the contact-paper covers that decorated so many *sefarim*. Outside, the rain fell heavier, and the rumble of thunder moved closer. Here and there a flash of lightning flickered in the distance.

He approached his Zeide's Mishnayos, with its old brown covers and faded gold lettering. It was hard to read the lettering. Lipa slipped his fingers over the backs of the volumes:

Zera'im, Moed, Nashim, Nezikin, Kadshim! Finally, he had found *Kadshim*. It was not easy extracting the volume from the rest of the set. All the books were squeezed together so tightly they stuck to each other. He extracted the *sefer* slowly, not wanting to damage the fragile cover. Tiny particles from the aging cover floated upward, making him want to sneeze. Finally, he freed the volume from the shelf. Where was *Kinnim*? He opened the *sefer* and began slowly turning the pages. The sections of Mishnah began to pass under his fingers in slow motion. It took many pages to complete even one section. *Zevachim...Menachos...Chullin...Bechoros...* Then the sections came quicker... *Arachin...Temurah—*

Suddenly, heavy thunder rumbled nearby, jolting Lipa. He

The Shul Boy 279

closed the *sefer* and recited: "...*Shekocho u'gevuraso malei olam...*"

The storm grew much fiercer outside, with deep thunder and bursts of lightning. Lipa could hear the rain streaming down the side of the house. But it did not matter. He was safe, far away from the windows. He turned back to the Mishnah. Where was *Kinnim*? He couldn't find it. Did the *rebbi* make a mistake? There were almost no more pages left. He moved on—*Kerisus...Me'ilah...* Just a few pages left... *Tamid...Middos*—*Kinnim*! He found *Kinnim*! He was overjoyed. A bolt of white lightning struck down just a few blocks away. Lipa did not care—he found *Kinnim*! *Now what*? This was the mishnah he was drawn to so much, that he needed to look at. He turned the pages and he frowned. It was so small. He flipped from the front of *Kinnim* to the back. *Was that all*? What was so special? He tried to read the first mishnah—he didn't understand one word. *Kinnim* had seemed so keen, but now, as he turned over its few pages, he almost cried with disappointment. It was so small, and he didn't understand one word. Just three tiny chapters: *Perek Aleph... Perek Beis... Perek Gimmel...*

Just one thing caught his eye. As he turned the pages on the third, final *perek*, he noticed that beside the *Bartenura* and the *Tosfos Yom Tov*, there was another commentary. He tried to read the title on top: *Yechin... Yachin... Yuchin...* He didn't know how to pronounce it. But the title on the other half he recognized easily: *Boaz...* One was called *Yuchin* something, and the other was called *Boaz...* He turned page after page of commentary in amazement. Who wrote all these thousands of tiny words? There were hundreds of lines, pages and pages. What was the writing about? He was in absolute awe. There were not even typewriters in those days. How could one person write so much with just a feather and ink?

He was in the midst of turning a page when an ear-shattering bolt of lightning suddenly struck the street lamp right outside his window, bursting the electrical transformer with a terrible blast. Everything went black, the house, the street, the whole neighborhood. Lipa's whole world was suddenly plunged into utter darkness. Lipa stood there petrified, still grasping the volume in his hand. The darkness was complete, palpable. Suddenly, the room grew strangely cold and the hair on Lipa's neck stood straight up. He trembled with fright. Without looking, he knew—*someone else was there in the room!*

"*Shalom aleichem,* young man!" a voice called.

Lipa stood stock still, afraid to turn around. He trembled in place, petrified.

"Young man, I said *shalom aleichem!*" the voice repeated impatiently. "Why don't you answer?"

Lipa could not just stand there. Full of fright, he slowly turned around. Seated at his father's desk was an elderly, gray bearded man. Two candles shone on the desk, casting a dim light onto his face. He wore thick spectacles and it was hard to see his eyes.

Lipa could barely speak. "Who…who are you?" he finally said.

The old man made a sour face. "I greet you with a nice *shalom aleichem*! Can't you even say '*aleichem shalom*' back before you start asking me questions?"

"Aleichem…aleichem shalom," Lipa answered in a quavering voice. "Please—who… who are you?"

The old man nodded, satisfied. "Come now, young man, don't look so scared! Take the *sefer* you're holding and sit down near me."

Lipa had forgotten that he was even still holding an open Mishnayos. He carried the large volume, still open to *Kinnim*, and sat down in front of the desk. Lipa's eyes adjusted to the darkness, and the glow of the two candles shone brighter, lighting up the old man's face. He seemed nice enough, but Lipa still trembled at this ghostly apparition.

The Shul Boy 281

The old man smiled pleasantly. "Young man, my name is Rabbi Israel Lipschitz—do you know who I am?"

Lipa shook his head firmly. The old man raised his voice impatiently. "You are holding my words in your hands and you don't even know who I am?"

Lipa looked down at the *sefer*. You…you wrote this—'*Yechin* and *Boaz*…'"

The old man snorted indignantly. "Not *Yechin*, young man. *Yachin*! My commentary is called *Yachin* and *Boaz*…"

"Oh, I am sorry…" said Lipa, embarrassed at his mistake. "*Yachin* and *Boaz*."

"And what is your name?" Rabbi Israel asked.

"Lipa."

"Lipa? Just Lipa?" the old man grumbled. "'Lipa' is not a name! What is your *real* name?"

"*Lipman*—Lipman Wallerstein."

"Ahh, Lipman! Now, that is a name! Do you know what 'Lipman' means?"

Lipa shook his head—no one had ever told him.

"Lipman means beloved, full of light—like 'Uri.' You don't know?"

"No one ever told me."

"Do not worry, Lipman, I will teach you. Do you know why I came here?"

Lipa shook his head. He felt stupid—he didn't know the answer to *anything*.

"I am here, because I am very, very pleased with you, young man! I saw you studying *Kinnim* and peering into my *peirush*. *Kinnim* is the hardest section of all Mishnayos! Do you know how hard I labored on my commentary to *Kinnim*? You see how many words, how many pages?"

Lipa peered down at the endless lines of commentary. It was truly awesome.

"I struggled so hard that the very milk I nursed from my mother squeezed out of my bones! And do you know how many people study my commentary to *Kinnim*?"

"How many?"

"Don't even ask!" retorted Rabbi Israel indignantly. "But you cared enough to study the *Mishnayos Kinnim*, and to gaze into my commentary. I was so pleased. Imagine—a young boy in Jersey City peering into my *Yachin* and *Boaz*! So I have come to reward you."

Lipa's faced colored with embarrassment and joy. *Reward*!? Suddenly, he was not so frightened of this old man, even though he appeared out of nowhere.

Lipa could not stand to be rewarded on a falsehood. He had to admit the truth. "Rabbi Israel, the truth is that I didn't understand even one word you wrote. I don't even understand the mishnah. I was just looking at the words, wondering how you wrote so many."

Rabbi Israel was pleased at Lipa's honesty. "I know you didn't understand, Lipman—I didn't expect you to. Bigger scholars than you don't understand a word I write! But at least you cared enough to look at my words!"

"Rabbi Israel," Lipa asked timidly. "May I ask you just one thing?"

"What?"

"*How did you get here*? And all the others I met when I looked into the Mishnayos—how did they all come to me?"

Rabbi Israel closed his eyes and swayed back and forth, deciding whether he should tell Lipa the secret. Finally, he opened his bespectacled eyes and peered at Lipa's innocent, shy face. How could he not tell him?

"Lipman, did no one ever teach you? When you study the words of a *Tanna* or an *Amora*, or any *talmid chacham*—that person sits right across from you, watching you learn. Did you ever study the words of Abaye?"

"Yes."

"Then Abaye was sitting right across from you, watching you and having *nachas*! And Rava, and Rabbi Meir—and all the rest! People don't see them unless they are special, and you, Lipman, *are* special! You have such an innocent imagination and pure *neshamah* that you were able to see me with your own eyes! That is how I have appeared!"

Lipa's face flushed with delight. "*Wow!*" he exclaimed.

Rabbi Israel grew impatient. "Young man, I have no time for '*wow*'—whatever that means! But here is your reward… You wondered how I was able to write such a long, long commentary. I am going to show you—right before your eyes! I have brought paper and a feather pen and even my inkstand. You see—"

For the first time, Lipa noticed all of Rabbi Israel's writing instruments laid out on the table. Just to prove, Rabbi Lipschitz spilled over the inkstand on its side. But it was so cleverly shaped that not a drop of ink spilled out. Rabbi Israel chuckled with amusement. It was good, for Lipa's father would not have been pleased.

"So here is what I am going to do," said Rabbi Israel. "I am going to write my commentary on *Kinnim* right before you, just as I did the first time! You will see how I did it. Mind you, I don't expect you to understand a word of it—but it doesn't matter. Even the great *Ra'avad* and the *Ba'al Hamaor* and the *Rosh* and everyone else scratched their heads how to understand these mishnahs, so I don't expect you to understand one word! But sit there quietly like a good boy, and you will watch me writing my commentary before your eyes! When I first wrote my commentary, I would not let even my own son stay in the room with me."

Rabbi Israel raised his pen, dipped it quickly into the inkwell, stretched out the writing sheet in front of him and was set to begin.

Lipa interrupted him. "Rabbi Israel—please, can I ask you just one question?"

The rabbi looked up impatiently, pen in hand. "*Nu?*"

"What's *Kinnim*?" asked Lipa.

Rabbi Israel sighed and laid down his pen. He was restless to begin but when he saw how eager Lipa was to know, he stopped to explain.

"When a woman had a baby, she counted forty days for a boy, or eighty days for a girl, and then brought two sacrifices to the Temple—a *Chatas* and an *Olah*. The *Chatas* was sacrificed at the bottom half of the Altar, under the *chut hasikra*, the red band that divided the Altar between upper and lower. The *Olah* was sacrificed at the top."

"What type of animals did she bring?"

Rabbi Israel grew impatient at Lipa's ignorance. "Not animals, Lipman—*birds*!"

"Birds?" asked Lipa. "What kind of birds?"

"Either *torim* or *bnei yonah*, they were a type of dove, like… like—pigeons—"

Lipa's eyes lit up excitedly. "*Pigeons*? I know pigeons!"

Rabbi Israel finally lost his patience. "Mazel tov, you know pigeons! Now, can I please begin my writing? I can't stay here forever."

Rabbi Israel began writing furiously. He bent over the sheet, his forehead perspiring with concentration, totally immersed. From time to time, he lifted his pen, tapped it against his lips, closed his eyes and struggled over a problem. Satisfied, he opened his eyes, plunged the feather quill back into the inkwell, swiftly wiped away the excess ink, and continued writing furiously. He wrote at a frantic pace, like the pen had a life of its own and wrote the words all on its own. Rabbi Israel's eyes were very weak. From time to time, he pulled off his glasses, and held the paper very close to his eyes, squinting. Satisfied, he donned his glasses and continued writing furiously. Lipa watched Rabbi Israel, enthralled. Rabbi Israel was such a great *talmid chacham*, but he was not scary at all. Lipa realized that he was truly a kindly man, just like his *Zeide*.

After a few minutes of absolute silence, except for the sound of the quill scraping on paper and the rain falling outside, Lipa's curiosity could no longer be contained. *What was Rabbi Israel writing?*

"Rabbi Israel," he asked, "what happened to all those pigeons?"

Rabbi Israel was so startled by Lipa's outburst he practically jumped out of his chair. He looked up sharply at Lipa, pen still suspended in his hand. Lipa was alarmed—had he angered Rabbi Israel? *I should have stayed quiet*, he thought.

But instead of being angry, Rabbi Israel just stared at Lipa silently, a mischievous smile on his face. He pointed the pen at Lipa and raised his voice in mock anger.

"*You*! You, Lipman Wallerstein who is not even bar mitzvah yet, want to know what happened to the pigeons? *Shalom aleichem*! The whole *world* wants to know what happened to those pigeons! The women who brought the pigeons want to know what happened to their pigeons! Even the *kohen* who is supposed to offer the pigeons on the *Mizbe'ach* wants to know what happened to his pigeons! And nobody knows for sure! They are all confused! And you, Lipman Wallerstein—you expect to know what happened to those birds?"

Despite his raised voice and impatient stare, there was an amused gleam in Rabbi Israel's eyes. Lipa's question had given him a little respite from his intense struggle to write.

Lipa gazed back steadily at this wonderful visitor and felt no fear. Rabbi Israel was like a second Zeide. He played the game, nodding firmly and holding his ground.

"Yes," he repeated firmly. "I, Lipman Wallerstein, want to know what happened to those pigeons… *Please*, Rabbi Israel!"

Rabbi Israel no longer played the role of pretending to be angry. He saw that Lipa was not to be denied. He treasured this earnest, innocent boy who was trying so hard to study Mishnah. He laid down his pen, leaned back in Rabbi Wallerstein's padded office chair, and tried to explain:

"Here is what happened, Reb Lipman. Six happy ladies who had babies came to the Beis Hamikdash to offer their *Kinnim*. Everyone carried cages that had two birds each, one bird a *Chatas* that is offered—"

He pointed at Lipa:

"*Chatas*—is offered below," answered Lipa sharply.

"Very good," said Rabbi Israel, nodding.

"The other an *Olah* that is offered—"

"On top."

"Good! Now what shall we call our six happy mothers? Let us call them something unusual: Sarah, Rivkah, Rachel, Leah, Bilhah, and Zilpah. You heard those names before?"

Lipa nodded, smiling. *Rabbi Israel is a great teacher*, he thought.

"Good. Now, here is the problem. Listen! Sarah brought one cage of *Kinnim*… Rivkah brought two cages… Rachel brought three cages… Leah brought four cages… Bilhah brought five cages…and Zilpah brought six cages—"

"You mean she had six babies all at once?" asked Lipa in amazement.

"And if she did? What does it bother you?" asked Rabbi Israel. "*Kein yirbu b'Yisrael… Let there be born Jewish children without end*! But listen to what happened, Reb Lipman! There was a terrible mix-up! Someone opened the cages too early! One bird from Sarah's

The Shul Boy 287

cage flew into Rivkah's cage of two sets of *Kinnim*… Then a bird from Rivkah's cage flew into Rachel's cage of three sets of *Kinnim*… Then one of Rachel's birds flew into Leah's cage of four sets of *Kinnim*… Then one of the birds in Leah's cage flew into Bilhah's cage of five sets of *Kinnim*…and then one of the birds in Bilhah's cage flew into—"

"Zilpah's cage of six *Kinnim*," interjected Lipa.

Rabbi Israel smiled. "So, are you mixed up yet?"

Lipa shook his head. "No, Rebbi," he answered confidently. "I can even tell you *why* it happened! When they took out the pigeons from their loft, they mixed up pigeons from different nests. Now the pigeons wanted to fly back to their mates."

Rabbi Israel looked at Lipa in amazement. "And how do you know that?"

Lipa smiled triumphantly. "*I know pigeons.*"

Rabbi Israel continued, trying hard to confuse Lipa. "But now, look what happened! After they were all mixed up together by flying out one way, so no one knew which was for a *Chatas* and which for an *Olah*, all the birds changed their minds and decided to fly backward! But we don't know which birds flew back! Maybe it was Sarah's first bird that escaped the first time, or maybe it's Rivkah's—or maybe a different bird! Who could tell? What a *mish-mash*!"

I bet Gustavo could tell, thought Lipa.

Rabbi Israel raised his voice in true dismay. "*Gevalt*! The birds flew this way and that, back and forth, up and down—and no one knew what to do! It took a Pesachiah to figure it out!"

"What's Pesachiah?" interrupted Lipa.

Rabbi Israel did not answer. He had had enough of explaining. He lifted his pen. "Listen, my young Lipman—I cannot remain here with you forever. There is so much more I still have to copy down and I want you to watch. And it gets even more confusing from here!"

Again, a profound silence descended in the office, just the sound of the holy *Tiferes Yisrael* inscribing his awesome commentary on *Kinnim*. Lipa closed his eyes, listening to the rain falling outside, and the scraping of ancient quill on paper. But for Lipa, *Kinnim* was not words. *He saw pigeons!* He could see Mother Sarah's pigeon skipping out of its cage looking for its missing mate in Mother Rivkah's cage. And Mother Rivkah's pigeon got jittery and escaped into Mother Rachel's cage! Each pigeon had a name, and each pigeon just wanted to fly home to its nest. But they had no Gustavo to guide them, they grew confused, and skipped back to their first cage. No wonder the *kohen* did not know what to do—he did not know pigeons!

Lipa closed his eyes, watching all the pigeons fluttering back and forth in front of him between the cages. He finally opened his eyes. Rabbi Israel was staring at him, eyes opened wide. But he did not see Lipa. He was completely lost in concentration, trying to puzzle out another mishnah. Finally, he snapped out of his trance and shook his head in dismay.

"Oh, little Reb Lipman, this is so difficult!" he cried out.

"What happened, Rebbi?" asked Lipa solicitously.

Rabbi Israel waved away Lipa's question impatiently, like it was a waste of time. It was too difficult to explain.

"Please, Rabbi Israel," Lipa persisted. "Remember, at least I peered into your commentary when no else did."

"You really want to know? All right then, Lipman—turn to the third *perek*, second *mishnah*."

Lipa was proud. At least now he could *find* the third *perek*, and after flipping a few pages, the second mishnah.

Rabbi Israel began reading: "*Achas l'zo*... Now, our wonderful mothers were back—mazel tov! Sarah had one set of *Kinnim*, Rivkah had two sets, Rachel had three sets, Leah had ten sets, and Bilhah

The Shul Boy 289

brought along one hundred sets of *Kinnim*—"

"*What!*" exclaimed Lipa. "Did Bilhah have a hundred babies!?"

"*Kein yirbu!*" Rabbi Israel answered back quickly. "*Let Jewish children flourish like grass of the field*! But—it does not mean that. Bilhah lived far away from Jerusalem. She was able to go to travel to the Beis Hamikdash, but her neighbors who had babies could not. So they all sent their *Kinnim* along with her. Bilhah was very nice, you understand, and did them a favor. Anyway, here we have five women—and how many *Kinnim*?"

Lipa reckoned for a split second, counting the birds that he could see standing right in front of him. "One hundred and sixteen *Kinnim*—that's two hundred and thirty-two birds."

Rabbi Israel sighed. "But what happened? Someone opened up the cages too early again and two hundred and thirty birds flew back and forth between the cages! What a mix-up! But the poor *kohen* didn't know enough to ask a *she'eilah*. He offered all the birds on top like an *Olah*, or all below like a *Chatas*, or maybe half on top and half below. Now what do we do?"

Lipa thought for a moment. "Ask Pesachiah!" he blurted out cheekily.

Rabbi Israel stared at Lipa, astonished. He almost dropped his pen. "Exactly—ask Pesachiah!"

"*But who is Pesachiah?*" asked Lipa. *Even as Rabbi Israel and Lipa studied* Kinnim *together, great things were stirring High Above.*

For there is a chut hasikra, *a holy line that divides the Worlds Above and the Worlds Below. High above the universe that we can discern and grasp, past the moon and sun, Jupiter and Saturn, above Aries and Gemini and Leo, beyond the belt of Orion and the jewel box of Pleiades, the Big Dipper and the Little Dipper, the Milky Way and the millions of galaxies beyond, suns born and unborn, worlds imploding and exploding…*

…Beyond the unfathomable vastness of the Hashem's seeable

universe—is a higher world of **neshamos**, *souls waiting to descend to earth. For although they dwell amid inconceivable purity, they long—like a baby longs for its mother's milk—they long to descend into our earthly realm. For only in our lowly, physical bound world can they give joy to Hashem by fulfilling His mitzvos. The real game is here, in our lowly world, below the* **chut hasikra.** *For didn't the holy Vilna Gaon, just a few hours before he died—the fifth day of Sukkos—hold a* **lulav** *and* **esrog** *in his hands and weep—for he knew that only here, in this dark and tangled world can mitzvos be performed. The* **neshamos** *gazed down yearningly, desperate to be born, to be brought into this world, to be clothed in flesh and blood, like a baby is dressed in swaddling, to be able to grasp a* **lulav** *and* **esrog** *someday. But they were not born—yet. Their mothers could not conceive—yet. Mothers prayed, fathers prayed—when would their yeshuah come?*

A Heavenly decree had left their doors locked. The **tzinnor,** *the channel by which* **neshamos** *descend into this world—was closed. Why? Who can answer? Who can fathom G-d's will?*

But who could open doors, undo the Divine decree?

Kinnim! *Humble* **Mishnayos Kinnim,** *like a tiny golden key, had the power to unlock the decree. For it contained the secrets of childbirth, and sacrifice, and new beginnings.*

And so now, in the candlelit glow of Rabbi Wallerstein's office, the Tiferes Yisrael explained to Lipa a little of the most difficult mishnah of **Kinnim**... *And as Rabbi Israel and Lipa studied, there was a great stirring of souls above... The locked doors above began rattling, and the blocked channels began blowing clear. The* **neshamos** *longing to be born stirred excitedly—was it their time?*

"Look below," they cried out in excitement, "they are studying **Kinnim!**"

Their heavenly wings fluttered, and they rose up expectantly, like passengers ready to depart through opened train doors, still clinging to hand straps, lined up to leave...

But a Heavenly voice announced: *"Wait...the doors are just opened slightly. Be patient,* **neshamos,** *for soon there will be a wondrous event that will throw all doors wide open!"*

Who was Pesachiah? Rabbi Israel did not answer Lipa's question.

Instead, Rabbi Israel pressed on, his head bent down in absolute concentration, his quill flying madly over the sheets like a living thing, word after word, line after line. The columns added up, and then the pages—there was no end. At the end of each section, Rabbi Israel snatched off his glasses quickly and scanned what he had written, holding the sheet up to his eyes. Satisfied, he put back on his glasses, and continued writing. The Tiferes Yisrael was so intent in his work that he did not hear anything, he did not see anything. Lipa watched him, and shivered with excitement. He was witnessing what no one else had witnessed, the great *talmid chacham* discharging his holy thoughts like a gushing fountain, the Torah he struggled so hard to master. A few times, Lipa timidly attempted to interrupt him, to ask him: *Rebbi, what you are writing? Teach me!* But he remained silent.

Finally, after watching Rabbi Israel compose page after page, Lipa forgot himself. The word "Rebbi—" sprung from his lips before he could catch it. Lipa threw his hand over his mouth in panic—how dare he interrupt the holy Tiferes Yisrael when he was writing! But it did not matter. Rabbi Israel heard nothing, saw nothing—he was glued to the holy words pouring forth from his pen, the candlelight glowing from his glistening face. Lipa gazed at Rabbi Israel intently. He felt so attached to him, even if he didn't understand one word he was writing. He saw Rabbi Israel's face begin to transform. When he had begun writing, his face was almost contorted with immense exertion to put his explanations into words. But as he wrote on, and especially now as he neared completion, his face lightened. There was a look of pure joy on his face. He nodded to himself from time to time happily, his smile of satisfaction growing wider. Suddenly, he stopped, raised his pen triumphantly into the air, and placed it firmly into the inkwell.

He looked up at Lipa, smiling broadly. "*Done!*" he proclaimed. "*All done!* Just like the last time! But now you, Lipman, were here to watch me!"

"*Wow!*" exclaimed Lipa.

Rabbi Israel stared at Lipa reprovingly. "Don't say '*wow*,' Reb Lipman! When you see a person has completed a mitzvah, you say '*yasher koach!*'"

"*Yasher koach!*" Lipa exclaimed, correcting himself. Rabbi Israel sat back in Rabbi Wallerstein's leather chair, resting after his arduous effort. He looked at Lipa, beaming. Lipa looked back, embarrassed at the attention. He loved this old man very much. He was such a world-famous *talmid chacham*, but he was so modest, so humble, even humorous.

They sat there a long time in silence. Lipa felt awkward—he felt Rabbi Israel was waiting for him to say something. Finally, he gathered his courage to speak.

"Rebbi," he asked, "may I ask you something?"

"Ask whatever you want, Lipman. You are my friend."

"How did you become such a great *talmid chacham*? That you could write so many pages about *Kinnim*? It's so hard."

Rabbi Israel tugged at his short, white beard. "Lipman, I did not write a commentary just on *Kinnim*," he corrected Lipa. He raised his finger emphatically. "*Baruch Hashem*, I have written a *peirush* on all the six sections of Mishnah, from *Brachos* to *Uktzin*!"

"But how, Rebbi?" Lipa persisted. "How did you become such a great *talmid chacham*? I also want to be a *talmid chacham*!"

Rabbi Israel looked down and smiled sadly. He sighed. "I was very fortunate, Lipman. I had a wonderful father of blessed memory, Rabbi Gedaliah. He was my father and my teacher. He spent hours and days with me in learning, Mishnah, Talmud, halachah—everything! If I had a question, I brought it to him. He was my father and my best friend! That is why whenever I quote my father, I write: '*My father, my teacher, the great* gaon, *the crown of my head.*' That is how I became a *talmid chacham*, Lipman."

Rabbi Israel paused and an extraordinary thing happened. Lipa began crying. Tears streamed from his eyes. Rabbi Israel looked at him with alarm. He leaned forward. "What is the matter, Lipman?" he asked. "Did I say something wrong?"

Lipa shook his head, sniffled loudly, and wiped his face dry. He looked up at Rabbi Israel, ashamed. "*I wish I had a father like that,*" he blurted out, half to Rabbi Israel, half to himself.

Rabbi Israel watched Lipa closely, studying him. He said nothing—he understood everything. *This is why he had come.* They sat silently like that until Lipa recovered. Time was growing late. In the distance were sounds of fire engines and emergency vehicles racing through the darkened streets.

"Rabbi Israel, can I ask you just one last question? *Who is Pesachiah?*" Rabbi Israel looked down, drummed his fingers on the desk, even fidgeted with his pen, lifting and dunking it back into the well. He looked up from time to time, gazing at Lipa. Lipa waited.

"Reb Lipman," he finally answered. "I will not tell you who Pesachiah is—but I will tell you where *you* can find Pesachiah. Pesachiah is a holy name, a jewel floating in the beautiful chapters of Mishnah. *Yagata u'matzasa*, Lipman! I can't feed you everything like a baby! You, Lipman! You must dive into the deep waters of the Mishnah and find him for yourself!"

"But where do I look—where do I start?"

Rabbi Israel looked at him sadly. The time was growing very short. "You start by closing the *Mishnah Kinnim* in front of you."

Lipa was shocked. *Close* Kinnim? An inexplicable shiver swept through Lipa's body. He did not want to close *Kinnim*.

"Rabbi Israel," he pleaded, "can't I leave it open just a little longer—so you will teach me?"

Rabbi Israel shook his head. He gazed at Lipa sadly.

"No, Lipa," he said. "The time has come to close *Kinnim*, put the *sefer* back on its shelf and begin Mishnayos from the start. Only then will you find Pesachiah."

Lipa hesitated. Rabbi Israel spoke firmly. "Now, Reb Lipman! Close *Kinnim*, and return it to its place. Go!"

With no choice, Lipa kissed the *sefer*, shut it and rose. He gazed at Rabbi Israel one last time, and the great scholar looked back at him also, lovingly. Lipa turned, walked quickly to the bookshelf and squeezed the volume back in its place.

Instantly, the lights came on in a brilliant flash. Everywhere, the hallway, the shul, the office, the lights blazed brightly. From upstairs, came the sound of music playing again. Lipa turned around—Rabbi Israel was gone! Lipa stared at the empty chair. *But was Rabbi Israel really gone?* Maybe he was still there, invisible, watching him? Lipa pulled out the first volume of Mishnah, flipped it open. Right there, on the first *daf* of *Brachos* was Rabbi Israel's *Yachin*—waiting for him.

Lipa lifted the open page high and showed it to the empty chair.

"Look, Rabbi Israel!" he announced proudly. "I found the first mishnah—I am ready to find Pesachiah!"

The holy Tiferes Yisrael sat unseen in the chair, invisible, and watched Lipa. He smiled happily: This one talmid will never leave me!

Rabbi Wallerstein sat in his office puffing contentedly on his cigar. It was just a week until Lipa's bar mitzvah, and everything was going very well. He scanned the list of those who accepted invitations—almost the whole city! The one final missing piece also fell in place, like a heavenly gift. He could not find a band willing to travel to Jersey City. But yesterday he received a call from a man named Chaim Galil who heard of the bar mitzvah and offered to bring his group. The band was modest, only three musicians, but the price was reasonable—and so now even that problem was solved. Everything, *baruch Hashem*, was in place. He gazed out his office window and felt a feeling of deep calm.

But Rabbi Wallerstein might not have felt so calm if he knew what lay ahead. For Lipa had decided what he wanted to add for his bar mitzvah *drashah*. And unbeknownst to anyone, he quietly slipped next door and went to see Gustavo.

12 Nishmas

It was the night before the great bar mitzvah dinner. Rabbi Wallerstein sat in his office working on final seating plans, when he received an unusual phone call.

"Rabbi Nosson Wallerstein?"

"Yes."

"*Shalom aleichem.* My name is Rabbi Gershon Seamansky. I was wondering if I could ask of you a favor, if it is not too difficult."

Rabbi Wallerstein thought for a moment. *Seamansky… Seamansky…*

"Tell me, are you *the* Rabbi Seamansky whom I have heard of?"

The voice on the other side laughed. "I am sorry. I am not '*the*' anything. I am plain Gershon Seamansky, period. Rabbi, I will tell you why I am calling—if it's not too much of a bother. I have to be in Jersey City tonight to see some people—you know, to help support my work. But it will be late, and it will be hard for me to travel back to New York. I was wondering—but only if it is not too much trouble—if you would have a place for me to sleep tonight?"

Rabbi Wallerstein was surprised, but did not hesitate. "You are very welcome to stay by us, Rabbi Gershon. I have heard a great deal about what you do all over. But I have to forewarn you—"

"Yes?"

"We don't have a fancy house. It'll be a plain room, a plain bed.

I don't want you to be uncomfortable."

There was a moment's silence. "Tell me, Rabbi Wallerstein... Does the bed have four legs? Will it have a sheet and pillow?"

Rabbi Wallerstein smiled. "Yes," he answered. "That much we can afford—and it will be a true *kavod* to have you. When do you think you will come?"

"That's the problem. I'm not sure how long I will take with these other people. I may have to *daven* Ma'ariv also."

"Rabbi Seamansky—I even have a shul to offer you!"

"*Yasher koach! Im yirtzeh Hashem*, we will meet later."

Rabbi Wallerstein hung up the phone. What a funny coincidence. Just the night that he was making his final preparation for Lipa's bar mitzvah, who should call him but the world-famous Rabbi Gershon Seamansky—who traveled the whole world making thousands of *ba'alei teshuvah*. *How did he know to call me?* Rabbi Wallerstein wondered. But he had his suspicion: it must have been the little Litvish Maggid, of *"Don't shoot the Maggid!"* fame. Who else stayed by him?

It didn't matter. There was an empty bedroom on the second floor, and the *chashuve* guest would be gone by the morning. Meanwhile, he continued shuffling the names in front of him. The right people had to sit next to the right people. His own shul people were no problem—wherever they sat was fine. His family from New York sat together. His most sensitive work was where to sit the politicians. He was so proud—three congressmen had accepted his invitation, members of city council, and above all, JVK himself. They needed a place of honor, but he did not want them too close up front—that would look like pandering. Then there were a half-dozen *rabbanim*, Rabbi Chaim Jacobs of Norway Avenue Synagogue, and a few elderly rabbis. Gazing at the guest list, Rabbi Wallerstein sighed with relief. He had felt slightly guilty that he had given Lipa such a short speech. But looking at this vast audience, politicians, businessmen, professionals, the cream of Jersey City—he knew he did the right thing. In truth, Lipa had done better than he expected on Shabbos in shul. He sang Shacharis and *Maftir* very nicely. But that was in shul, among shul people. Lipa was born to be a shul boy, to prepare herring, to prepare the tables, even to *daven* nicely. But in front of this huge crowd, he would be swallowed up.

Rabbi Wallerstein was so intent on the seating arrangements that he was startled when he heard a knock on the front door. He checked his watch—ten thirty already! It must be his distinguished guest. A little self-consciously, Rabbi Wallerstein rose and rushed to the front door.

"*Shalom aleichem*, Rabbi Wallerstein!"

Rabbi Wallerstein was startled at the visitor at the door. He had heard so much of Rabbi Gershon Seamansky. He expected an old, white-bearded tzaddik. Instead, standing before him was a strapping gentleman, tall, coal-black beard, brimming with life. Instead of a rabbinical briefcase, he had a large black knapsack, thrown jauntily over his back.

"Rabbi Seamansky?" he asked, just to make certain.

"Thank you for letting me stay at your house," Rabbi Gershon answered. He saw Rabbi Wallerstein staring at him, puzzled.

"Is something the matter? Have I come at a bad time?"

Rabbi Wallerstein shook himself out of his impolite stare. "No... But I heard so much about you and what you have done—I was expecting—you know—and older man, a rabbi with a white beard."

Rabbi Seamansky laughed. "I apologize. Give me a few more years, and I will come back with a gray beard."

Rabbi Wallerstein closed the door quickly behind his guest and ushered him into the hallway. He realized now why he had such a power—his warmth radiated like an oven. He tried to make up for his first awkwardness, offering to take Rabbi Seamansky's knapsack off his shoulder. But the guest refused.

"You should know, Rabbi Gershon," Rabbi Wallerstein said, "that it is a great honor for me to have you in my house. How did you hear of us?"

"Oh, the good word gets around," he answered lightly. "But I will tell you, Rabbi Wallerstein—"

"Please, please call me Nosson—"

"Reb Nosson… More than anything I need now is to *daven* Ma'ariv. I was running about all evening speaking to philanthropists in Jersey City. Who knows where I'll be tomorrow? You said… you have a shul for me?"

Rabbi Wallerstein had meant to lead him right upstairs, offer him supper, show him the bedroom. Instead, he led him into the shul. The lights were all off but for the *ner tamid* that shone over the *paroches*. In truth, Rabbi Wallerstein was embarrassed by how small his shul was. The politicians in city hall did not know whether his synagogue was big or not—but this famous tzaddik had to see how tiny his shul really was. Rabbi Gershon stood at the doorway, looking at the shul.

"It's very small," Rabbi Wallerstein apologized.

"It is very big," answered Rabbi Gershon. "It reaches all the way up to *Shamayim*."

Rabbi Wallerstein ran over to the light switch. "Let me at least turn on the lights for such a distinguished guest."

"No!" called out Rabbi Gershon, in a voice so firm that Rabbi Wallerstein was startled. "I feel the *Shechinah* here, just as the shul is—with the *ner tamid*. Please, leave the lights off."

Rabbi Wallerstein retreated from the light switch. "Rabbi Gershon, the siddurim are here on the shelf. I am going into my office next door. When you are done *davening* I will take you upstairs."

"*B'seder*," answered Rabbi Seamansky. "*Yasher koach.*"

Rabbi Wallerstein watched Rabbi Gershon lay down his knapsack casually on a back bench and walk toward the *bimah*. Meanwhile, Rabbi Wallerstein retreated to his office. There were still some seating arrangements to do, and by the time the guest was done *davening* he should be finished. He again scanned the list, and lifted his pen to write in table numbers when he heard a sound that left him fixed, unable to move. Rabbi Gershon began *davening* Ma'ariv no, he began *screaming* Ma'ariv. Rabbi Wallerstein sat stock still as the visitor began shouting out each word like it was his last.

"…*Asher bidvaro ma'ariv aravim*! *Who by His word brings on evenings*!

"*B'chachmah posei'ach she'arim*! *With wisdom opens gates*!

"*U'mesader es hakochavim b'mishmaroseihem b'rakia kirtzono*! *He orders the stars in their heavenly constellations as He wills*!"

Rabbi Wallerstein lowered his pen and sat listening. He was stunned. He had never heard a Ma'ariv like this; every word recited like it was his last breath on earth. Rabbi Gershon was not "*davening*"—he was crying out to the *Shechinah*; the *Shechinah* resided in his little shul…

Is such davening *happening in my shul*? thought Rabbi Wallerstein in wonder—and joy.

Rabbi Gershon moved on: "*V'nismach and we will rejoice—with the words of Your Torah and mitzvos for all eternity*!

"*Baruch Atah Hashem—oheiv amo Yisrael*!"

There was a second's silence and then a terrible cry:

"SHEMA YISRAEL HASHEM ELOKEINU HASHEM ECHAD!"

The visitor cried out like it was his last breath, like he was being cast into flames… Rabbi Wallerstein lowered his head and covered his eyes, almost weeping. He had never heard such a *Shema Yisrael* in his whole life. He bathed himself in Rabbi Gershon's *Shema Yisrael* like a *mikvah*. In the end, Rabbi Wallerstein had to cover his ears, for Rabbi Gershon's *davening* was almost too overwhelming. There was a deep silence as the visitor reached *Shemoneh Esrei*. How long did it take? Rabbi Wallerstein did not even know—he did not look at his watch. He just sat there, not doing any of his work, just feeling the holy silence. Finally, Rabbi Seamansky finished Ma'ariv. There was the sound of approaching footsteps, and then polite knocking at Rabbi Wallerstein's office door.

"May I come in?" the visitor asked.

Rabbi Wallerstein looked up at his guest. He tried not to stare at his visitor's face. But, in truth, there was nothing to see. Rabbi Seamansky stood there, a pleasant smile on his face, as though nothing unusual had transpired.

He hides everything, Rabbi Wallerstein thought. He stood up in his guest's honor, making believe that he had not heard anything.

"You must be tired from a long day," Rabbi Wallerstein said. "Come, I'll show you to your room."

He led Rabbi Gershon up the stairs to the second floor. It was strange having this world-famous person in his simple house. *What is he really doing here?* Rabbi Wallerstein thought to himself. He opened the bedroom door and showed him the modest, slightly cluttered room. "I'm sorry I can't offer you something more elegant," he apologized.

Rabbi Gershon placed his arm on Rabbi Wallerstein's shoulder, an arm so sturdy that it weighed heavily on him. "Rabbi Nosson, I cannot tell you how happy I am to be here tonight. You have made me feel at home."

"Where is your home?" asked Rabbi Wallerstein.

Rabbi Gershon smiled. "The whole world is my home. Tonight, this is my home."

Without thinking through or reckoning, Rabbi Wallerstein

turned to his famous visitor. "May I ask you a favor?" he blurted out.

"Ask what you want, Rabbi Nosson," Rabbi Seamansky answered.

"Tomorrow night, I am making a bar mitzvah for my son. If…if you could, it would be such an honor if you would attend."

"You mean Lipa?"

Rabbi Wallerstein looked at his guest in shock. "Yes, Lipa. How did you know?"

Rabbi Gershon just smiled. "You know, Reb Nosson—word gets around! I will have to change my schedule a bit, first go here, then there—but it will be my pleasure to join you. I am especially looking forward to hearing your son's *pshetl*!"

It was the night of the bar mitzvah—and Lipa had disappeared! The whole family piled into Rabbi Wallerstein's black Plymouth to head to the dinner. It was already five o'clock, and the guests would start coming in an hour. But no one could find Lipa. Rabbi Wallerstein was beside himself. He was so nervous. The biggest people in the city were coming; he still had to meet the head waiter. The photographer was waiting—but where was Lipa? Leon looked high and low in the house but could not find him. Finally, Eva reminded herself. "Lipa told me that he had to practice his speech," she finally remembered. "But I don't know where he went."

"What is there to practice?" fumed Rabbi Wallerstein. "It's one page! Who does he think he is, Winston Churchill?" He checked his watch. "Oh, my goodness—it's almost five thirty. Everyone is waiting for me!"

Rebbetzin Wallerstein tried to calm her husband. "Nosson, why don't you just drive to the shul. Lipa knows where the bar mitzvah is. The weather is mild and he can walk there or take a bus."

Rabbi Wallerstein shook his head in frustration. *How can he get lost at a time like this*! With no choice, he put the car in gear and drove off to the Norway Avenue Shul, biting anxiously on an unlit cigar. Norway Avenue Shul was the pinnacle of Jersey City Jewry. The wealthiest Jews in the city prayed there, and it was led by great rabbis; first Rabbi Bloch, and then the great scholar, Rabbi Chaim Jacobs. Rabbi Wallerstein took heart as he led his immaculately dressed family into the huge building. He was very proud—he had made the right choice. The bar mitzvah cost more than he could afford, but he was proud to invite his guests, the cream of the city and the most powerful politicians, to this splendid synagogue. They entered the *simchah* hall, and it was absolutely exquisite, palatial. The waiters were just finishing setting the dinner places. Each table had a centerpiece filled with a bouquet of rainbow-colored flowers, and each setting had an oversized chocolate cookie shaped like a bird with the words "mazel tov" etched in white frosting. A large, elegant golden chandelier glistened brightly under a domed, sky-blue ceiling; and two tall windows were left open high above allowing in fresh air.

Rabbi Wallerstein was accosted by the maître d', who introduced himself. "Good evening, Rabbi Wallerstein, mazel tov to your family! My name is Johnny V. I'm in charge of service tonight. I think the hall looks beautiful tonight, don't you? Is there anything else you need?"

Rabbi Wallerstein surveyed the beautiful hall, overcome. He never expected anything so elegant! He was so proud—it was much more magnificent than he had ever imagined. At first, he was so overwhelmed, he could hardly speak. Finally, he calmed down and found his voice. "It is really beautiful, thank you."

Johnny V. beamed. "The caterer told me to go all out for you tonight. He said you're someone special. We even added a few extras that you didn't order, at our own expense. So, where is the star of the night?"

Rabbi Wallerstein snapped out of his euphoria. "I don't know," he snapped. "We couldn't find him when we left. I'm sure he'll turn up eventually."

"Well, I'm sure he doesn't want to miss his own bar mitzvah!" the maître d' said. "Oh, I see the band has arrived."

Rabbi Wallerstein turned, saw the band enter, and his face clouded. It wasn't what he expected. The three musicians had arrived, but they were definitely not your regular New York City band. They had a decidedly Middle Eastern look about them. One of them was quite tan with long, twisted *peyos*. The others also looked Middle Eastern, although not so dark. The band leader approached, a broad smile on his face.

"*Shalom aleichem*, Rabbi Wallerstein, I'm Chaim Galil! Mazel tov on your son's bar mitzvah. Where is he?"

"He's not here yet. Tell me, is this your band?"

"For sure!" Chaim answered brightly. "Come, I want you to meet them."

Before Rabbi Wallerstein could say anything, Chaim Galil took him by the hand and led him to the other two musicians who were setting up their instruments on a small stage under the windows.

"This is Shlomo," he said, introducing the dark-skinned Yemenite. "He is excellent—he plays flute and clarinet."

Shlomo was very young. He smiled shyly, bowing politely in greeting.

"And this is Ovadiah. He came by way of Rome. He plays violin and harp."

"Mazel tov!" Ovadiah greeted Rabbi Wallerstein, smiling warmly.

Rabbi Wallerstein felt calmer, seeing what a cheerful, confident group of musicians they were. They acted like they were playing in Carnegie Hall. Even so, he had to explain certain things to Chaim Galil.

"Mr. Galil, I see that you have a talented band. But I have to tell you, this is not a *heimishe* audience like some shul in Brooklyn. We will have all sorts of Jews here, some are modern people. We will even have guests not of our faith, important politicians. You have to play music they can enjoy—do you understand?"

Chaim Galil placed a reassuring hand on Rabbi Wallerstein's shoulder. "I understand completely! Don't worry! Rabbi Wallerstein, listen! Go enjoy with your guests and leave the music to us!"

There was so much confidence and warmth in Chaim Galil's words that Rabbi Wallerstein felt reassured. What did it matter how they looked, long *peyos* and all? He addressed the musicians: "Thank you for coming here! I'll make sure you have plenty to eat!"

Rabbi Wallerstein turned to meet his guests who had begun trickling in. But where was Lipa? He had still not shown up. Rabbi Wallerstein sighed angrily—there was nothing he could do. Instead, he put on a brave face and began greeting the first arrivals. First to arrive were the shul people. The invitation had announced that the reception was at six thirty and the dinner would begin promptly at seven. A long table, laden with a vast selection of hors d'oeuvres and pastries, filled one whole wall. Nearby was the bar, where two waiters poured drinks. In a few minutes, the trickle quickly turned into a stream, and then a flood—the cream of Jersey City. For Rabbi Wallerstein, it was living in a good dream. He greeted each guest warmly, and they showered their congratulations. The great banquet hall was soon full with men and women enjoying steaming delicacies, sweet and sour meatballs, breaded chicken wings, pickled tongue, pastries and cakes of all sorts. And the real meal had not even begun yet.

Rabbi Wallerstein wished that Harry Kattel could be here and see what he had achieved without Willow Avenue Shul! Meanwhile, the band began playing softly. Fifteen minutes to the start of dinner and Lipa was still not there. Rabbi Wallerstein grew more anxious—where was he? Suddenly, a loud commotion rose from the entrance. Rabbi Wallerstein turned and saw a whole swarm of young boys enter. They were Lipa's classmates who had just arrived from New York, and they swooped boisterously into the hall, whooping with excitement. They were all fresh faces and youthful joy, and their enthusiasm filled the room. Even the most sophisticated guests watched these noisy New York intruders and smiled. Their joy was infectious. The boys were not given to subtleties. They spotted the hors d'oeuvres table and made a straight beeline for the food, almost jostling some of the guests in their rush. It was amusing to watch, and no one minded. Suddenly, two of the boys broke away from the others and approached Rabbi Wallerstein.

"Are you Lipa's father?" they asked. They had never seen Rabbi Wallerstein visit his son in the yeshivah.

"Yes," Rabbi Wallerstein answered. "*Shalom aleichem*, boys."

"We're Lipa's friends," they announced. In fact, they were the very two boys who had let Little Fleigel fly out the window.

"Where's Lipa?" they asked.

Rabbi Wallerstein's face clouded. "I don't know! He's supposed to be here already." He looked at his watch. It was late! The dinner was supposed to begin in less than ten minutes. There was no fooling around with tonight's schedule. It was a bar mitzvah, not a wedding. Nobody wanted it to stretch out too long. Seven o'clock the dinner began, eight thirty the speeches, and by nine o'clock, *Birkas Hamazon*.

Five minutes before the dinner started, there was an excited buzz in the hall. Rabbi Wallerstein looked around. JVK had arrived!

He was accompanied by a band of city aldermen, and behind them no less than three United States congressmen. Rabbi Wallerstein had no time to worry about Lipa. He rushed over to welcome JVK and the distinguished entourage.

"Mr. Mayor, I am so honored that you could make it," he gushed.

"Honor to be here, Rabbi," JVK answered, smiling slightly.

Rabbi Wallerstein welcomed each dignitary in turn, and personally led the group to the table that had been reserved for them in a place of honor, right in the center of the room.

Just as Rabbi Wallerstein was showing each official his seat, a voice called out: "Abba—I'm here!"

Rabbi Wallerstein looked up. It was Lipa—*finally*! Rabbi Wallerstein was filled with anger and relief. If he were not surrounded by all these important people, he would have yelled at Lipa for making him so worried. But all he did now was murmur *baruch Hashem* under his breath, glad that Lipa had arrived just in time. Satisfied that all his distinguished guests were properly seated, he headed toward the head table. Meanwhile, Lipa's friends spotted him, and they swarmed noisily around him, shaking hands like grown-ups and shouting mazel tovs. Then, on their own, they began chanting "*Siman tov u'mazel tov*" as they escorted Lipa to the head table like he was a *chassan* at a wedding. All the guests clapped along to the boys' singing, and even the band joined in, trying to find their key. The meal was finally about to begin.

Just before Lipa took his seat, Lipa scanned the room, leaned over and whispered to one of the boys, "Is Shmuel Praguer here?"

The boy shook his head—no. Despite all the great welcome, Lipa was heartbroken. He so much wanted his friend to be there tonight!

At the stroke of seven, the dinner began. Lipa sat at the middle of the head table next to his father. On his other side sat Abraham Ravitz, who was the toastmaster. Lipa's mother and two grandmothers sat on the other end of the table, which was bedecked with flowers. The only empty chair was next to Rabbi Wallerstein, at the very end. He had reserved it for his famous guest, Rabbi Gershon Seamansky, who had not arrived yet. Rabbi Wallerstein recited *Hamotzi*, and the meal proceeded. He gazed proudly at the sea of faces before him; powerful politicians, businessmen, even Harry Solomon, who was asked to say a few words. He could not believe that he had really succeeded—*baruch Hashem*! Everything was perfect. The hall was magnificent, and the food—outstanding. The caterer had gone out of his way to perfection. Lipa sat between his father and Mr. Ravitz, not saying a word, lost in his own world. Rabbi Wallerstein was not surprised—it was Lipa. Mr. Ravitz leaned over in his fatherly fashion, jowls shaking. "You should be very proud, Lipa. You've come a long way!" Lipa smiled at him shyly, but he was too caught up in his own thoughts to answer.

Rabbi Wallerstein was not comfortable sitting still at the head table like some dignitary. He stood up, moved among the tables, made jokes, welcomed everyone warmly, made sure that no one was hungry. Everyone laughed. He was who he was—plain spoken and humble, and the most distinguished people loved him for simple honesty. The meal proceeded on time, everyone appeared happy, but when Rabbi Wallerstein finally returned to his place and surveyed the crowd, he noticed an unusual hush had descended in the great hall. It was almost eerie—the room was too quiet for such a grand party. He listened carefully—*it was the music*. It was so beautifully strange. It was not Ashkenazic, it was not Sephardic, but something else, mystical in its beauty, turning the hall into an enchanted palace. The guests grew very quiet, listening spellbound as Shlomo played his flute so effortlessly that it sounded like a forest birdsong, and Ovadiah, who turned his harp strings into a singing waterfall. Chaim Galil himself accompanied the instruments just with his voice, a voice without words, a delicate humming, a holy sighing, causing a delicious shiver to course through the hall. All eyes were upon him, but Chaim never even noticed. His eyes were closed, and he was completely lost away in his own mystic world.

Abraham Ravitz leaned over Lipa and whispered to the rabbi, "Where did you ever find these musicians? I never heard anything so beautiful in my life!"

"I didn't find them," Rabbi Wallerstein whispered back. "They found me."

How did they find me? Rabbi Wallerstein wondered. He had never asked them.

Luckily for the mood of the *simchah*, the band took a break—giving the spellbound guests a chance to return to earth. The volume in the room rose sharply as people dove into the main course of roast chicken, vegetables, baby potatoes, all sorts of exotic salads. Suddenly, a hush fell in the hall. Rabbi Wallerstein looked up—Rabbi Gershon Seamansky had finally arrived! His very entrance drew stares. He strode across the hall, tall and princely, remarkably handsome, piercing blue eyes that darted from table to table like a captain surveying his crew. He appeared to return each gaze, one by one. Rabbi Wallerstein rose quickly to greet the famous orator who had turned thousands into *ba'alei teshuvah*.

"Rabbi Gershon, you made it!" he exclaimed happily. "Now my night is complete! I saved you a place right next to me."

Rabbi Seamansky raised his hands humbly. "What have I done to deserve such an honor?" he asked. "You could have sat me anywhere. I am joyous just to be here."

Rabbi Wallerstein would not hear of it. He sat Rabbi Seamansky alongside him at the head table. He had a waiter bring water and a towel so the honored guest could wash his hands. Rabbi Wallerstein handed him a great piece of the *mitzvah challah*. All eyes in the hall were turned to the new arrival. He made a profound impression even without saying a word.

"Please wish mazel tov to the bar mitzvah," Rabbi Wallerstein whispered to his guest.

Rabbi Seamansky's answer was surprising. "You mean Lipa?" he said offhandedly. "There is time for that." He did not even bother to look at the bar mitzvah, who was on the other side of the table. Rabbi Wallerstein was puzzled by his answer.

Meanwhile, the clock was moving. The main course was finished, and the time arrived for the speeches. Rabbi Wallerstein pressed his guest. "I would be honored if you would say a few words in honor of the bar mitzvah," he begged.

Rabbi Seamansky nodded without hesitation. "Yes, I would like to speak," he said.

Abraham Ravitz rose and began by clearing his throat. For the first time that evening, Rabbi Wallerstein turned and spoke to Lipa.

"Do you have your speech ready?" he asked.

Lipa removed the creased sheet his father had prepared, showing that he indeed had it. Rabbi Wallerstein was pleased. He sat back, enjoying himself, and waited for Abraham Ravitz to begin. Everything was going perfectly.

"Ladies and gentlemen," began Ravitz in his impressive, stentorian manner, "we are here to celebrate with our good friend, Rabbi Wallerstein and his dear wife, at the bar mitzvah of their son, Lipa. I have known the bar mitzvah since he was a baby. He is a fine boy! (*Applause*) I can't say that I have known Rabbi Wallerstein since he was baby also, but I am sure that he must have been a fine boy also—because he is a wonderful rabbi! (*Applause and laughter*) You all know that, I'm sure—and so, without further ado, I present tonight's host, our beloved Rabbi Nosson Wallerstein."

There was applause and smiles at Abraham Ravitz's short and amusing introduction. He had set the right light tone for the joyous occasion. Rabbi Wallerstein approached the lectern apprehensively—he was not used to addressing such a large audience. He lowered the microphone closer to his face. He gazed at the guests, clearing his throat nervously.

"Thank you, Abraham—you are indeed a true friend to our synagogue. Ladies and gentlemen! I cannot thank you enough, all of you, for being here tonight and joining our family's celebration, the bar mitzvah of our son, Lipa. Tonight, each and every one of you is like a member of our family—"

Rabbi Wallerstein paused, as his words were greeted unexpectedly with prolonged applause. He looked around in surprise. These people really liked him! He relaxed, and suddenly a warm smile crossed his face. He was no longer so frightened.

"I especially want to acknowledge the presence of the esteemed mayor of our city—the *Boss!*—my boss and your boss, Jersey City's boss—the honorable John V. Kenny! Thank you, Mr. Mayor, for being here!"

There were loud cheers, and a few sharp whistles by the aldermen. Everyone was having a grand time.

Rabbi Wallerstein dropped his voice and grew serious. "I want you all to know that tonight is very historic night for this city—"

He paused meaningfully, and silence filled the room. "Because tonight they served the best roast chicken that Jersey City ever ate in its history! Don't you all agree?"

There were gales of laughter, and amid the resounding tumult, Rabbi Wallerstein shouted: "Thank you all, and mazel tov!"

Rabbi Wallerstein sat down with tumultuous applause still echoing in his ears. He was beaming, and Abraham Ravitz gave him a hearty handshake. *Baruch Hashem, baruch Hashem*, Rabbi Wallerstein murmured to himself. *They all like me!*

Abraham Ravitz returned to the lectern and let the happy commotion die down. He waited until order was restored.

"That's our rabbi!" he said, "and that's why we love him. Now, to move on, I would like to invite Mr. Harry Solomon, president of the Jersey City Merchants Association, and a friend of the rabbi, to speak."

There was respectful quiet as Harry Solomon rose from his table and approached the podium. He seemed a little uncomfortable, after the humorous speech of the rabbi. Harry Solomon exuded dignity and responsibility, and his presence at the lectern quieted the hall. He gazed around, a deeply serious look on his face.

"Rabbi and Mrs. Wallerstein, esteemed rabbis, Mayor Kenny, aldermen, honored congressmen—ladies and gentlemen:

"I was asked to speak briefly tonight because of the association I have had with Rabbi Wallerstein over the past three years. I was, in a small way, helpful in his gaining the post of Chaplain of Hudson County. I am very proud of that, and above all, I thank you, Mayor Kenny, for making such a wise choice—"

Amid a round of applause, JVK smiled and waved his hand in acknowledgment. Solomon continued:

"Over the past two and a half years, Rabbi Wallerstein has distinguished himself by his humanity and warmth. He is a humble man who has dedicated himself to the sick and those in trouble. Wherever he has gone, he has shown himself a man of kindness and humility—an honor to our Jewish community."

An even louder round of applause swept through the hall. Rabbi Wallerstein blushed modestly in his chair.

"But—I did not come to speak mainly about Rabbi Wallerstein tonight. I came to speak about our bar mitzvah lad sitting alongside me, Lipa. You see, none of what you see here tonight, none of all the great deeds that Rabbi Wallerstein has accomplished would have happened without this wonderful lad here!"

Suddenly, all eyes were on Lipa, who blushed red.

"For a long time ago, Lipa and I made an important business deal. Lipa bought a three-button charcoal gray Armani suit, for which he negotiated a good price, like a real businessman. But I negotiated my own deal with him. I insisted that he pay for the suit one dollar a week—no more, no less. That was my deal. And so, every Friday afternoon for almost one year, he came to my office and paid me one dollar. But he paid me something more. Every time, before he left, he wished me: 'Good Shabbos, Mr. Solomon.'

"Ladies and gentlemen—that 'Good Shabbos' was more precious to me than all the money in the world. Do you know why? Because, when I was a little lad just like Lipa, I had a grandfather who went to synagogue every Saturday morning. My grandfather never took me with him, but every time he left he would look at me and say: 'Good Shabbos, Harry!' And when Lipa came to my office each week and left with his beautiful 'Good Shabbos,' I was that little boy again! I looked into Lipa's eyes and I saw my own eyes in his. And when Lipa told me about Rabbi Wallerstein's difficulties, it was for Lipa's sake that I tried all I could that his father might remain here in Jersey City. And tonight, ladies and gentlemen, you see the result! Lipa, the whole city owes you!"

Harry Solomon shook his head, embarrassed. He pulled out his pocket handkerchief and dried his eyes. The audience sat in respectful silence—many were misty-eyed themselves. They looked from Harry Solomon to Lipa, from Lipa to Harry Solomon. Lipa's face was red.

Harry Solomon finally recovered, cleared his throat and turned to Lipa. "Lipa, please come here."

Lipa was not sure what to do. Mr. Ravitz whispered in his ear. Lipa rose shyly and approached Harry Solomon.

"Lipa," Solomon said, looking at him. "I have a special bar mitzvah gift for you."

He reached into his coat pocket, and took out a worn white envelope. "Lipa, here—I am returning the forty one-dollar bills you gave me. I collected them each week like they were precious stones—for that is what they meant to me. Your 'Good Shabbos' each week made them the most precious currency in the world. With your 'Good Shabbos' you paid a hundred times over what the Armani suit was worth. Now take these precious one-dollar bills and use them to buy holy books and grow up to be a scholar and righteous man like your father!

"Lipa, we are all proud of you—mazel tov!"

Lipa accepted the worn envelope that Harry Solomon thrust in his hand. He smiled awkwardly, and just managed to say: "Thank you."

Harry Solomon stood a moment at the lectern, posed for the photographer, and returned quickly to his table, not looking at anyone. Strangely, there was hardly any applause. The audience was overcome by Harry's speech—he had tugged at their heartstrings. No one knew that the reserved, soft-spoken businessman bore such depth of feeling in him. Rabbi Wallerstein sat in his seat, confused. Until now, he had not realized fully the critical part that Lipa played in his success. The mood of the evening had suddenly turned from levity to great feeling. Rabbi Wallerstein did not know what to make of it. But there was no time to dwell on it. The time was getting late. Abe Ravitz rose and introduced Rabbi Gershon Seamansky.

"Ladies and gentlemen," Ravitz began, jowls bouncing impressively, "we have the privilege of having a world-renowned lecturer, Rabbi Gershon Seamansky, in our midst, who has traveled the globe to educate and inspire our people. It is an opportunity too good for us to overlook, and we have asked him to say a few words in honor of this special occasion. Please welcome our guest, Rabbi Gershon Seamansky."

Although only a few in the hall had heard of Rabbi Gershon and none had heard him speak, his striking appearance as he stood at the lectern made a profound impression. With his long, coal-black beard, and his piercing gaze, he looked like an ancient prophet, although he was not old. The audience sat in absolute silence, waiting. All eyes were glued on him. At first Rabbi Gershon did not say anything. He stood there silently, gazing outward, contemplating his next words. One could hear a pin drop.

Finally, Rabbi Gershon broke his silence, speaking in a voice so deep like the rumbling of waves at sea.

"Ladies and gentlemen, I would like to tell you a story tonight, a true story. But I am afraid—I am afraid you will not believe me! Perhaps I should forgo it. But no—I *must* tell you this story, and just tonight, no other time. If you do not believe me, I will understand. But *do* believe me—for what I will tell is true!

"I am a world traveler. My home is everywhere. My desire is to reach out to Jews everywhere. Why do I have this urge, this need? I know—but it is a secret that I cannot share. Believe me that I have visited and prayed in more than five hundred synagogues all over the world. The Al-mighty guides me, He guides my soul to where it must go to reach other *neshamos*, other souls. For we live in a world of *neshamos*—that is who we are, nothing else!

"And it so happened that the Al-mighty led me to this place called Jersey City. The *Boss* told me to come here—(*laughter*)—Not you, Mr. Mayor, but the *Boss* of *Bosses*!"

Rabbi Wallerstein peered nervously at JVK. He was smiling, apparently enjoying himself—thank goodness!

"Last night I found myself in your city and I needed a place to stay the night. Your wonderful host, Rabbi Wallerstein, invited me to sleep in his house. When I reached his home it was late, and I was deeply troubled for I had not yet recited the Ma'ariv evening prayers. 'No problem,' said my gracious host, 'you can pray in our synagogue...'"

Rabbi Gershon hesitated, gazing silently at his audience, as though deciding whether to continue. He took a deep breath.

"I entered Rabbi Wallerstein's synagogue alone. It was completely dark, except for the *ner tamid* lamp that shone over the ark. The moment I walked inside that shul I felt a holiness, a *kedushah, the likes that I never felt in all the other hundreds of synagogues I prayed in*! I did not know why—but I knew there was something here! I approached the ark and prepared to begin praying—and suddenly I knew that I was not alone. I turned quickly—and there behind me in the darkness I saw a room filled with *neshamos*, souls who were watching me pray.

"I was not frightened—why should I be? I have a *neshamah*—and they were *neshamos*. But what were they doing there?

"I addressed them: '*Neshamos*! Why are you here? What do you want?'

"One soul spoke for all. 'We are here,' he responded, 'because there is great joy for us in this shul.'

"'Why is that?' I asked. 'What makes this synagogue so very special that you gather just here, nowhere else?'

"And he answered: 'There is a boy who is in charge here—a shul boy. Each Friday afternoon before the Sabbath, he comes in and wipes these benches clean. And when he wipes his cloth over the benches, he also wipes away the dust that has settled over our souls from our misdeeds! He wipes the benches clean, and each time he wipes away a little more of the stains that trouble our *neshamos*—and we are cleansed also!'

"'What else does this boy do?' I asked.

"'After cleaning the benches, he carries out a great roll of white paper to cover the tables. He can't see, but we watch him at his game. He throws the roll hard ahead of him toward the end of the table, and then races to catch it before it falls over. He does not know—but *we* see—that two little angels run fast in front of him to stop the roll from falling over the sides. We *laugh*! The wooden tables that were so unsightly are suddenly transformed into beautiful snow white. And each time he throws the white paper roll, we look up and pray: Hashem, cover over our transgressions with Your great glistening *tallis* like this boy drapes the tables in white—so we will also be transformed in Your sight!'

"'And what else does that shul boy do?' I asked.

"'Then, when he is done wiping the benches and covering the tables, he proceeds to the women's table and prepares the herring for kiddush. He begins cutting the herring, and then he carefully cuts off all the extra parts, the skin and bones and milt. And he says: "This skin is for the old cat…and the bones for the younger ones… and I slice the milt into pieces to be shared by all the cats, for it says: *V'rachamav al kol ma'asav*! *His mercy is upon all His creatures*…" And we all look up Heavenward and pray: Like this boy shows mercy even on lowly cats, please, Hashem—show mercy upon our lowly souls!" And, in his merit, we are answered—each time!

"'That is why we sit here waiting all week, waiting for this lad who is so pure and so innocent and thinks he is alone. But he is not alone—*we are there*!'

"And I asked them: '*Mi hu zeh v'eizeh hu*…! Who is this special lad filled with such kindness and innocence that you await him each week?' And they all murmured his name: *Lipa*! *Lipa*!"

All eyes in the room were on Lipa. He looked down, his face

hidden behind the vase. Rabbi Wallerstein stared at his son, and at Rabbi Seamansky.

What is going on here tonight? he wondered. *This is so strange! What will people think?*

"So, ladies and gentlemen," Rabbi Gershon concluded, "this is my tale—a true tale. I have told it without exaggeration; I simply relate what I heard and what I saw. And tonight—tonight, is a night of nights! Lipa, here, is a boy of boys—a Shul Boy! May he be blessed, may you be blessed, and may the Redemption of Israel come soon, amen!"

There was breathless silence as Rabbi Seamansky returned to his seat. People looked at each other in wonder, asking: was this story *really* true? They all tried to glimpse Lipa, who hid behind the flower vase. Rabbi Wallerstein was unnerved. Lipa's bar mitzvah had taken such a strange turn—nothing the way he had planned. *What would JVK think?* Thank goodness...all that was left now was Lipa's short speech and then they could go straight to *Birkas Hamazon*.

Abe Ravitz finally rose. He also appeared rattled. He stood at the lectern, collected himself, and tried to smile. Then, with an exaggerated flourish, he proclaimed:

"Ladies and gentlemen, tonight's man of the hour, our bar mitzvah—Lipa Wallerstein!"

There was an expectant silence. Lipa finally rose. Mr. Ravitz looked at him with concern. Lipa's face was almost white. He was frightened of the great audience that sat before him, and of the strange story Rabbi Seamansky had just told. *Was it true?* Did invisible *neshamos* watch him every Friday afternoon? Lipa walked to the lectern in a daze, like he was walking in a dream. He peered at the hall. There were so many people out there! The mayor was there! But even more—there was his secret guest. Unbeknownst to anyone, another uninvited guest hid at the slightly opened exit

The Shul Boy 319

door—Gustavo. He stood there, peering, watching Lipa for the signal they arranged. But now Lipa stood at the lectern quaking with fear. He couldn't go through with it anymore. He nervously unfolded the speech his father had given him. That was all…he would read it just as his father wrote for him and sit down. The paper shook in his hands. Abe Ravitz saw Lipa's great nervousness and placed a reassuring hand on his shoulder. Lipa calmed a bit, and gave one final look over the vast hall before beginning.

Suddenly, he stopped short and stared. *There was Shmuel Praguer! He had come! Shmuel was finally here!* Lipa stood, staring beseechingly at his best friend. Shmuel saw him looking straight at him, and their eyes locked in greeting.

Shmuel Praguer came to his bar mitzvah! Lipa was so glad. It did not matter who else was there. The color flooded back joyously to his face, and his fright vanished. He gave one discreet glance to Gustavo, lurking behind the exit door. *I will do it!* he decided firmly.

He laid the wrinkled sheet flat on the lectern and began reading:

"*Chashuve rabbanim,* my honored parents and grandparents, Mayor Kenny, ladies and gentlemen, *morai v'rabosai!*

"We are taught in the first mishnah of *Pesachim*:

"*Ohr l'arba'ah assar bodkin es hachametz l'ohr haner…*

"*On the eve of the fourteenth night—that is the night before Passover—we search for the* chametz *by the light of the candle.*

"Our holy rabbis taught that that mishnah teaches us something special:

"*Ohr l'arba'ah assar…* When a boy starts his fourteenth year—that is, at his bar mitzvah—*bodkin es hachametz…* He must search for all the *chametz* that is in himself, all the bad habits and traits, *l'ohr haner*—by the light of the Torah, which is like a candle…

"Tonight is my bar mitzvah, *ohr l'arba'ah assar…* I pledge to search into myself, to rid myself of any bad habits, to try to live like a good Jew and be guided by the light of our holy Torah!

"I want to thank my father and mother for bringing me up until now and being such good parents. I want to wish mazel tov and long life to my two grandmothers who are here tonight, and I want to thank you all for being here at my *simchah*! Thank you!"

Lipa paused, and there was a loud wave of applause. Rabbi Wallerstein sat in his chair, beaming. Lipa had actually delivered his little speech better than he had expected. Rabbi Wallerstein took a deep breath. *Baruch Hashem*, it had all gone excellently, and now all that was left was the *Birkas Hamazon*.

But Lipa was not finished. Suddenly he announced: "Up to now, I have read the speech that my father prepared for me. But, tonight I would like to also say a *pshetl* of my own. I would like to teach a difficult mishnah in *Kinnim*—"

Rabbi Wallerstein blanched. *Kinnim? Kinnim?* What was Lipa talking about? He looked at the gathered tables, and there was a buzz of confusion. *What was* Kinnim? Rabbi Wallerstein looked at the clock. It was already way past nine. *What was Lipa doing*!

This had to be stopped! Rabbi Wallerstein stood up abruptly to pull away his son before he even started. He would apologize that it was too late. But in his haste to rise his arm brushed against a pitcher filled with water, hurtling it to the floor with an immense crash.

"Mazel tov!" some guests shouted in amusement. Rabbi Wallerstein turned red with embarrassment. It happened right in front of the mayor! The head waiter, Johnny V., was right at his side in a moment.

"Don't worry, Rabbi," he calmed him. "We'll get it cleaned up in a minute."

He summoned one of the waiters to his side. "Call out Big Hans to clean this up."

The Shul Boy 321

The guests waited politely as Big Hans was summoned. Lipa remained at the podium, eager to begin. Presently, the kitchen door opened, and a worker appeared at the door, shuffling quickly toward the shattered pitcher, broom and dustpan in hand. The audience watched him with curiosity. Big Hans was indeed a big man, strong looking and barrel chested. He once may have been very tall, but now he was bent over pitifully, like a lopsided letter "L", as though someone had lashed his back over and over into that grotesque shape. His rheumy eyes stared straight downward, and he had to raise his head from time to time to reach his goal. It was for the better that his gaze was cast down—so that he did not see all the eyes watching him pityingly. Hans worked quickly, mopping dry the spill, and sweeping the shattered glass into a pail. As quickly as he had emerged, Big Hans turned and shuffled back into the kitchen, broom and mop in hand.

Meanwhile, Lipa stood his ground stubbornly, waiting his turn. He rolled up his father's single sheet into a thin paper baton. Rabbi Wallerstein grew more and more agitated. This was terrible! He was already very embarrassed by the overturned pitcher, and now who knew what crazy things Lipa was going to say. More carefully now, he rose from his place to order Lipa back to his seat. He tried to stand up, but Rabbi Gershon immediately laid a powerful hand on his shoulder, forcing him back down.

"Let him speak, Rabbi Nosson," he ordered firmly. "The *Ribono shel Olam* is waiting for him to speak."

Rabbi Wallerstein was shocked by his guest's commanding tone. But he had no choice; Rabbi Gershon held him down firmly, almost like he was a prisoner. *Lipa*, he prayed, *please don't embarrass me*!

Lipa glanced one last time at Shmuel Praguer and was filled with confidence.

"There is a difficult mishnah called *Kinnim*... It is all about birds,

birds like pigeons—beautiful little pigeons. When a woman gave birth to a baby, she had to bring two pigeons to the Holy Temple, to the *Mizbe'ach* altar. The Altar had an upper part and a lower part. I would like everyone in the hall to look up to the windows near the ceiling—please!"

Lipa pointed upward with his baton, and the whole audience turned and gazed upward toward the windows. They were curious what would happen next. Some thought that a screen would drop, and Lipa would show a movie. But, no—

Suddenly, Lipa raised his voice. "So now, here come our two pigeons!"

At the flash of his baton, two pigeons suddenly streaked through the open window—it was Little Fleigel and his mate. They flew in together, wings flapping. At Lipa's signal, they parted sharply—Little Fleigel swinging upward, and his mate downward. They hovered there in place, wings beating rapidly.

"You must make believe that you see an imaginary *chut hasikra*, a bright red stripe that divided the Altar into two—up and down. My own pigeon, Little Fleigel—is flying on top, like an *Olah*. His partner down below is a *Chatas*. Can you see the *chut hasikra*? Do you see them hovering, above and below?"

There was an appreciative buzz of excitement from the audience; some laughed, and others clapped enthusiastically at the sight of these two pigeons following the young boy's orders. Glances flew from the birds to Lipa. Lipa saw that the people were pleased, and his confidence grew. He glanced quickly at Shmuel proudly. He was ready for the next stage, the teachings of the holy Tiferes Yisrael guiding him.

"And now, another lady came with her *Kinnim*, her set of birds—"

At these words, two new pigeons flew through the windows, wings flapping, hovering alongside the first pair. "But something strange happened—there was a mix-up! The two pairs of birds flew out of their cages, and became confused with each other!"

Lipa signaled, and the four pigeons, wings beating wildly, began an acrobatic dance in the air, over and under each other, in and out, weaving dizzying circles around each other. There was an amazed silence in the hall at the extraordinary sight of pigeons dancing like ballet. The three musicians, who had sat placidly during the speeches, rose quickly and took up their instruments again. They stood on the floor just below where the birds were performing their avian dances. Only Shlomo played, blowing gently into his ancient flute. It was high-pitched like a birdsong, like the birds themselves were cooing to each other. The hall fell under the spell of the dancing birds, and Shlomo's enchanted playing.

"You see," explained Lipa, "there were only four birds and everything was already mixed up. Which birds belonged to whom? And which pigeons belonged above and which pigeons below? There was only one great rabbi in the whole Temple who could answer—Pesachiah!"

Like a seasoned showman, Lipa clapped his hands dramatically, and the four birds zoomed out of the window as quickly as they were flown in. Rabbi Wallerstein, who was so nervous, breathed a sigh of relief. *Was this strange show finally over?* He rose to congratulate Lipa and pull him off the lectern, but Rabbi Gershon still held him down firmly.

"He's not done yet," he whispered.

With no choice, Rabbi Wallerstein sat back down. What was next?

Lipa glanced briefly at Shmuel, who was looking back at him, admiringly. Lipa was so happy. *I'm just getting started*!

"That was the first mishnah. But now, we had a greater problem—for not two, but *six* ladies had babies!"

An amused uproar rose from the audience.

"Their names were Sarah, Rivkah, Rachel, Leah, Bilhah, and Zilpah.

Sarah had one baby, so she brought two birds—"

Lipa waved his baton, and again two birds flew in, Little Fleigel at the head.

"Now the next lady, Rivkah, had two babies, so she brought in four birds—"

On signal, four birds now burst in, wings beating happily, and they aligned themselves in a perfect column of four, one above the other, alongside the first two pigeons. The pigeons beat their wings furiously to stay perfectly in formation.

"Now Rachel had three babies so she brought six pigeons, and Leah had four babies and brought eight birds—see!"

Right on cue, two more clusters of birds flew in, first six, then eight. They hovered right alongside the other waiting columns; the *Kinnim* columns rising higher and higher toward the ceiling, so they appeared like a feathery staircase, suspended in the air. The hall grew loud as the guests reacted with utter amazement at the scene above.

"But we're not done yet!" continued Lipa. "There were two more ladies, Bilhah and Zilpah. Bilhah gave birth to five babies, and Zilpah to six! And they *all* brought pigeons!"

Like magic, two small flocks of pigeons glided in through the windows, ten in one flock, twelve in the other. They joined the others, building the staircase higher and higher until the topmost bird almost touched the ceiling with its wings. The wall beneath the windows was now adorned with multiple pigeons, like feathery shields, wings beating gleefully. They held their staircase pattern, awaiting Lipa's next command.

Shlomo, who had lowered his flute as the birds entered, again took up his instrument while Ovadiah lifted his harp to his hands.

An expectant quiet fell on the room.

Lipa raised his paper baton. The birds began a dance, skipping up the feathery staircase, one over the other, column to column. A bird from Sarah's pair flew up to Rivkah's, and from Rivkah's to Leah's, and so on and on, up the winged steps... The birds soared upward, and then skipped back downward, a floating feathered escalator. From two flew to the four, and from four to the six, and then back again—just as the mishnah described. It was a winged ballet, back again, forward again, up, down, in and out, rising and collapsing and reforming again. Shlomo and Ovadiah accompanied their intricate movements, playing sweet harmonies set to the birds' intricate movements.

The hall fell into hushed silence, watching the pigeon ballet above, mesmerized also by the lush, enchanting melody that filled the room. From time to time, they turned their gaze from the birds to the remarkable young boy who stood confidently, directing it all. In the end, the birds flew such intricate, woven patterns that it was impossible to discern where each bird originally belonged, and to whom. Lipa lowered his wand, and the music stopped.

"You see how difficult this mishnah is?" he proclaimed. "Who could judge which birds could still be offered, and which could not? Only one great *talmid chacham* was wise enough to decide—Pesachiah!"

Lipa paused. The music grew ever quieter, and then fell still. Some calmness returned to the hall, and the guests caught their breath. Lipa waved his baton quickly, and in an instant the feathery staircase dissolved, and the flock of forty-two birds disappeared swiftly out the windows.

Rabbi Wallerstein was flabbergasted. He did not know what to think. *Was* this *the end of Lipa's* pshetl? Apparently not, for Rabbi Gershon still held him firmly, not letting him rise.

Meanwhile, high above, excited rustling had begun… Neshamos yearning to be born bestirred themselves excitedly… Was it time yet? Was it time yet?

For the first time since he had begun his strange presentation, Lipa paused, uncertain. Up to now, he had been a success—everything worked. Outside, Gustavo was waiting for his final signal. Lipa gazed out at the vast hall—they were all looking at him, waiting…such important people—even the mayor! He looked to Shmuel for encouragement. His friend sat, staring back, looking bewildered. He, too, wondered—what was next?

Lipa was frightened—but how could he stop now? He saw the holy face of the Tiferes Yisrael watching him, urging him on. *Explain the last mishnah*! he whispered to him.

Lipa took a deep breath and held his baton still.

"I have one more mishnah in *Kinnim* that I would like to present," he began unsteadily. "It is a…very difficult mishnah. I hope you will forgive me for keeping you so long!"

He gazed about the room. No one seemed in a rush to leave. All eyes were upon him. Lipa took heart.

"This mishnah teaches about…five women who came to the Temple with *Kinnim*. But some of these ladies brought not only their own birds, but the *Kinnim* of their neighbors as well! They were doing their friends a great favor."

There was a smattering of applause for the kindly women. What was next? Lipa raised his baton.

"The first lady brought one basket of *Kinnim*—two birds."

At these words, two lonely pigeons flew into the room. After the dramatic tumult of a few minutes ago, they hardly made any impression. Even so, Shlomo began playing softly on his flute—in

The Shul Boy

anticipation.

"Then came the second woman—and she brought two sets of *Kinnim*, four birds."

Again, four pigeons entered the windows, lining up next to the first two pigeons, so they all looked like they were standing horizontally on a telephone wire. But there was no wire—just the beating of their wings kept them firmly in place. Shlomo's flute grew louder.

"Now came the third lady. She brought three cages of *Kinnim*, six birds, and they came looking for the others."

Again, at Lipa's signal, six more pigeons flitted into the room, finding their place alongside the first six—on the invisible wire that held them all aloft. The wall was beginning to grow crowded with pigeons. But these were no ordinary pigeons. Gustavo had chosen his best, champion birds with puffed up chests, elaborately feathered legs, and a painter's palette of tinted wings.

"So now we have twelve birds all in a row," Lipa continued. "But now came a fourth lady, who was helping her friends. She brought in—ten *Kinnim*, all on her own!"

There was a startled eruption from the guests, as a flock of twenty pigeons entered swiftly through the two open windows. They hovered for a moment over the pigeons that were already there, seeming unsure where they belonged. But Lipa signaled with his paper baton, pointing upward. The birds responded immediately, forming themselves into a telephone wire row of twenty right above the twelve below. The guests marveled at the sight of thirty-two birds hovering in perfect order, their wings fluttering effortlessly like an invisible hand held them aloft. No one was more admiring than JVK himself, who was smiling and whispering animatedly to his neighbors. Eventually, the guests turned their gaze from the pigeons to the conjurer of this amazing achievement. Lipa stood there, appearing self-confident and calm. But in reality, Lipa was praying. For the hardest part was now to come.

Hashem, he whispered, *please let me succeed. Please let me not embarrass my father and mother*!

As the birds hovered silently above, Ovadiah joined Shlomo, playing with his harp. No more were these serene melodies, but songs of great joy and thanksgiving, as though they too flew among the feathery creatures, giving praise to Hashem. The hall was alive with excitement and anticipation. Rabbi Wallerstein sat in his seat, bewildered. What happened to his nice, normal bar mitzvah? Rabbi Gershon was in ecstasy. He even released his iron grip on Rabbi Wallerstein, for now no one dared move as Lipa stood anxiously, waiting for calm to return. This was the moment.

"Now…a fifth lady came. She was really very kind! Her neighbors knew that she was going to Jerusalem, and many owed *Kinnim* to the Altar. But they had no money for the trip, or they had to take care of their newborn babies. So they asked her: 'Please, bring our *Kinnim* to the Temple.' And she agreed, for she was very kind. And so she went to the Holy Temple and brought—"

Lipa paused, took one last anxious breath, and shouted out—"*One hundred* Kinnim!"

There was a shocked gasp from the audience, but before they could react, it began… Through the two open windows, a flume of two hundred pigeons swept into the domed hall. They entered in two sudden streams, half in each window. Once inside, they gathered like some great dark cumulus cloud, fluttering about in disorder. To add to the confusion, the two rows of organized pigeons below broke rank and flew upward to join the fluttering arrivals. For a moment, it looked like total chaos was at hand. For an instant, Lipa was afraid that he had overplayed his hand. But he swiftly lifted his thin baton and pointed it straight at—Little Fleigel! Little Fleigel emerged out of the confused flock and shot straight upward.

The Shul Boy 329

Lipa twirled the baton over his head and called out loudly:

"*Go, Fleigel!*"

Like a chief pilot, Little Fleigel burst out of the pile to the front of the flock and began circling the great center chandelier. The pigeons immediately fell into place behind him and followed. Like Gustavo on the rooftop, Lipa twirled his baton around and around, and the birds began flying graceful circuits around the chandelier, their feathers turning purples and greens and blues in the sparkle of the chandelier's luminescent crystals. Above, the pale blue roof rose like a summer's sky. Lipa was so delighted—he was the master of this giant flock! He lifted his wand and the birds soared higher, almost brushing the ceiling. He lowered the wand, and the birds swooped downward like a huge, waving feathery kite.

Meanwhile, the tumblers and rollers and puffers grew agitated, and began exhibiting their tricks, tumbling and falling crazily toward the floor, causing some guests to jump up in panic. But just above the heads of the guests, the pranksters somersaulted mid-air and zoomed back up to join the flock. The high flyers soared upward, flying as high as the domed ceiling allowed. There was utter tumult and wonder in the hall, a mixture of astonishment and panic and excited screaming. Who had ever seen a bar mitzvah like this? Shlomo and Ovadiah played furiously on their instruments, trying to match the soaring flight of the birds, wild, untamed music that left the guests breathless and dazed in their intensity. Only the leader, Chaim Galil, remained strangely aloof, eyes closed in deep contemplation, not playing, not singing.

At last, it was time for Lipa to explain this final mishnah. He signaled, and the two hundred and thirty-two pigeons—one hundred and sixteen *Kinnim*—now organized themselves in two long rows along the wall beneath the windows, their wings waving together in rhythm, their legs clasping an imaginary telephone wire. The guests, exhausted and dazed after the frenzied music of Shlomo and Ovadiah, turned in relief to listen to Lipa. A hush fell on the great hall.

Lipa began his *pshetl*: *"What happens if the* kohen *makes a mistake, and he offered all the pigeons—"*

Suddenly, a hum began wafting through the hall like a misty fog, interrupting Lipa. The extraordinarily pure voice, a strangely sweet but sad melody, had a hypnotizing effect. Lipa had to pause. Everyone turned toward the source of this beautiful sound. Chaim Galil stood, eyes shut, humming an enchanted melody, a melody without words. Then, abruptly, he stopped.

Lipa caught his breath—he did not expect this.

He began again: *"If the* kohen *offered all the pigeons above the* chut hasikra, *then only the number of pigeons—"*

The moment Lipa began speaking, Chaim began his humming again, stopping Lipa in mid-sentence. This time his voice was even more breathtaking, his melody even more yearning, like he was crying out—to someone, to something. But to whom? To what? The guests sat helpless, enthralled by the sound, their hearts trembling inside themselves. Again, Lipa had to stop—he could not speak. He held his wand midair, dazed, bewildered. *Why was Chaim singing just now, in the midst of the* Mishnah Kinnim? The guests remained transfixed, suspended dreamlike between heaven and earth, between the *chut hasikra* below and the *chut hasikra* above. High above, the pigeons flapped their wings gently, heads raised heavenward.

Lipa was growing dizzy, almost helpless. But this was his *pshetl*, and he needed to say it! After a few minutes, Chaim stopped once again. He stood, eyes shut tight, body trembling with anticipation.

Lipa seized his chance:

"...Then only the number of birds—"

Suddenly a great cry echoed through the room:

The Shul Boy

"*NISHMAS!*"

Chaim stood, eyes opened wide, staring upward.

"*NISHMAS!*" he sang out thunderously again.

Everyone turned to stare at him. They looked up toward the ceiling—what was he gazing at? Even Shlomo and Ovadiah appeared stunned. And then, as if stirring from a dream, Chaim awoke, and his face was filled with joy. He gazed at the assembled guests for an instant, as though he was astonished that they were still there. And then, in the sweetest voice, *kol dimamah dakah*, soft and tender, he looked heavenward and began reciting:

"*Nishmas kol chai…tevarech es shimcha Hashem Elokeinu!* The soul of every living thing…shall bless You, Hashem, our G-d!

"*NISHMAS!*"

Chaim's call echoed through the heavens like the roar of a mighty wave.

A heavenly Voice cried out:

"*Neshamos! Do you hear that call? Nishmas! Your time has come to descend beneath the chut hasikra!*"

The neshamos, *who had waited so long to descend to* Olam Hazeh, *to a world of flesh and blood and mitzvos and Torah study, cried out with joy. Finally! Their time had come. How did it happen?*

Only Chaim Galil saw: It was Lipa! *It was* Kinnim! *Lipa's mishnah had thrown open the sealed gates to birth! His mishnah of one hundred and sixteen* Kinnim—*exactly two hundred and thirty-two fluttering birds—had opened up broad, shining conduits between heaven and earth, through which the* neshamos—*who had waited so long—could descend.*

The truth—even Lipa himself did not know what Ineffable secrets that mishnah contained!

The neshamos *trembled with excitement! Finally! This was their time to enter* Olam Hazeh! *They wiped their souls one last time, so clean and pure that they shone!*

So now the neshamos *lined up like parachutists about to leap from a* plane, hand straps held at the ready, the angel of conception and birth standing at the doorway, ready to launch them on their great jump downward.

But before each soul was allowed to leave, it had to answer one final question from the great angel:

"When you enter Olam Hazeh, what will you be?"
"I shall be a tzaddik," the neshamah answered.
"Do you promise?"
"I promise!"
"Then fly, neshamah!"

The next neshamah approached:
"When you descend below, what will you do?"
"I shall study Torah day and night!"
"You promise?"
"I promise!"
"Then fly, neshamah!"

The next neshamah stood at the exit door:
"And what shall you do with your life?"
"I shall be a rebbetzin and raise a family of pious children!"
"Do you promise?"
"I promise!"
"Then fly, neshamah!"

"And you?"
"I shall do many acts of chessed!"
"Promise?"

"And you?"
"I shall make a thousand ba'alei teshuvah."

"How?"

"Hashem will help me."

"Promise?"

"So fly, neshamos*!"*

And so, the angel in charge of catapulting neshamos *down beneath the* chut hasikra, *sent each precious soul on its way, on its lifetime mission, leaving a glistening world of perfection and holiness, into a world of temptation, a world where lurked a clever* yetzer hara, *a world of troubles and confusion and sometimes joy.*

But there, just there, in a dangerous, bewildering world, could a Jewish neshamah *give the Al-mighty His greatest joy!*

Below, no one could see what transpired Above. There were no prophets and no vision. The world went about its usual humdrum way, buying, selling, shopping, cooking, learning, davening…

Until…

A phone rang…

"Mommy, guess what?"

"Yes?"

"I'm expecting!"

On the other side, there was no answer—just tears of joy. Finally— after three years!

Her mother raced over to the heavy Rabbi Meir Ba'al Haness pushkah *and gave it a kiss…*

It was Lipa It was Kinnim.

"Reb Meilech, you're wanted on the hall phone."

Reb Meilech was one of the older members of the kollel, *a* bar arayon, *a* masmid *who learned day and night.*

Reb Meilech looked up and frowned. "I am in the middle of learning with my chavrusa! I can't be interrupted by a telephone."

"But it's your wife!"

"Tell her I'll call her back."

"She says it is urgent, and you must come now."

"Wives!" snorted Reb Meilech. But she never called him during learning. Maybe something had happened, chas v'shalom.

He closed his Gemara, went to the hallway, and picked up the dangling phone.

"Nu?" he asked.

His wife could hardly speak above a whisper. "Meilech, I'm expecting a baby."

Meilech grew white with shock. "What?! Who says?"

"The doctor! I just got back from his office... Meilech, could you believe it?"

Meilech did not answer. He dropped the phone and began weeping. Fifteen years! Fifteen years they had been waiting for a yeshuah. And now—he looked heavenward, face awash with tears and thanksgiving.

"Ribono shel Olam!" he cried. "How did it happen?"

It was Lipa It was Kinnim.

"Hello, Esther?"

"Yes?"

"This is Dr. Abraham's secretary. He said it's urgent that you come see him."

Esther had seen the doctor just two days ago. She grew concerned. "Is everything all right?"

"I'm just the secretary. But we made an appointment for you for eight o'clock tomorrow morning."

That night Esther slept fitfully. She had been feeling peculiarly heavy for the last little while. Finally, morning came. She sent her husband off to shul and took a taxi to the doctor.

She sat down in his office anxiously. He sat down and opened her file. "Esther, I don't know if you are prepared for this."

"What, Doctor Abraham? Please tell me!"

"Mazel tov—you're expecting triplets!"

Triplets! *Esther was stunned. No one in her family or her husband's had ever had triplets. How did that happen?*

It was Lipa It was Kinnim.

And for those who had not yet given birth themselves?

Every man and woman in Klal Yisrael had a portion in these newly born neshamos! *For* kol Yisrael areivim zeh bazeh!

But such intensity could not last forever—the whole room would be consumed. Chaim Galil and his band finally paused and retired to their places. Lipa grabbed the moment. As quickly as he could speak, Lipa explained the complicated mishnah, pointing to the pigeons who rose and fell like piano keys at his command. At the end, he lowered his wand, clapped his hands loudly, and as swiftly as they entered, the pigeons flew out the windows in a rush of wings and were gone. The pigeon show was over. Rabbi Wallerstein sat bewildered, unable to move. *Was this his Lipa who had done all this?* He suddenly realized: he knew the whole city—*but he did not know his own son! Lipa was wonderful!*

Rabbi Gershon roused him back to life. "Rabbi Wallerstein, I think it is time for *Birkas Hamazon*," he whispered.

Rabbi Wallerstein nodded agreement, but he was still too stunned to act. *Birkas Hamazon?* Luckily, Abe Ravitz had the program schedule and invited one of the rabbis to lead the blessings. The dinner finally ended—the bar mitzvah was over.

During the *bentching*, Rabbi Wallerstein recovered somewhat.

He gazed around the room. Everyone seemed happy. Even JVK and the gentile politicians sat respectfully as the blessings were recited. By the time the *Birkas Hamazon* was over, some of the color had returned to his cheeks. Perhaps it was not so bad, after all.

The Grace ended, and as was the custom, Rabbi Wallerstein rose from his place, collected Lipa to his side, and stood alongside the head table, accepting mazel tov and gifts from the guests. *Baruch Hashem*—everyone seemed to have had a wonderful time! Harry Solomon approached, a proud smile on his face.

"Marvelous bar mitzvah, Rabbi, marvelous!" he exclaimed. "And you, Lipa, you were just outstanding!" He gave Lipa a loving pinch on his cheek.

They all came to wish congratulations. The cream of Jersey City, lawyers and doctors, big businessmen, presidents of shuls, admiring family from New York who saw what honor Rabbi Nosson Wallerstein had achieved in Jersey City. They were proud. Rabbi Wallerstein was back to himself. He greeted everyone warmly with a joke and a smile, accepted the presents on behalf of Lipa, who was pinched so many times on the cheek it was turning pink. It hurt—but it was worth it.

Suddenly, Rabbi Wallerstein's eyes lit up. JVK himself approached, followed by the aldermen. He stepped forward and greeted the mayor, shaking with both hands.

"Thank you for coming, Mr. Mayor," he blurted out. "It was such an honor to have you and the city council."

JVK smiled and nodded, but turned his attention to Lipa. "Young man, what you did was outstanding! You have to teach me how you trained those birds! I want you to come to my office with your father and meet Roosevelt and Truman!"

Who are Roosevelt and Truman? Lipa wondered. But he just smiled shyly, and said thank you.

The Shul Boy 337

"Thank you for inviting me to this event," the mayor said to Rabbi Wallerstein. "It was very meaningful."

JVK turned to leave. But Rabbi Wallerstein would not let him exit alone. Instead, he abandoned Lipa at the table, and personally escorted the mayor outside. Many of the guests departed or drifted away, and Lipa was left standing alone.

Now, his schoolmates rushed over to wish him mazel tov. They shook his hand, handed him envelopes or *sefarim*, and ran outside to find the van back to New York. Just two of his classmates stayed behind, waiting for the others to leave. When the others had gone, they approached Lipa hesitantly.

"Lipa, could we ask you something? That bird that flew in front of all the others around the chandelier… Wasn't that the bird who flew out the window in school—with the blue tail feathers?"

Lipa looked down and nodded. "Yes, that was Little Fleigel."

"But we thought he disappeared forever—how did he come back here?"

Lipa looked up at them, smiling enigmatically. "It is a secret. Hashem…brought him back."

"But how?"

"I can't tell you. It is a secret—only Hashem knows."

The two boys stared at Lipa, and they were suddenly filled with awe. *Lipa had a power*! They looked at each other wide-eyed, and ran off frightened, as quickly as their legs took them.

For a moment Lipa stood all by himself, and then, the one person who he was waiting for all night approached—Shmuel Praguer. He looked like a real yeshivah boy now, with a big black hat, and his *tzitzis* peering out from under his jacket.

Lipa was ecstatic. "Shmuel," he cried, "when did you come?"

"You didn't see me," explained Shmuel. "I came when Rabbi Gershon Seamansky walked in. You were probably watching him."

Lipa couldn't conceal his intense pleasure. "Shmuel, I'm so

happy you are here! I didn't think you would come!"

Shmuel looked at him with astonishment.

"How could you think that, Lipa? *Didn't I promise I would come back as soon as Hashem allowed me?* So here I am!"

Lipa suddenly felt dizzy, and his head began spinning. *When did Shmuel promise to come back?* He might have asked him, but there was no time. Shmuel had to join the others.

"Lipa, I have to go! Mazel tov!" He gave Lipa final quick handshake and ran off. Lipa raised his hand to his head to stop the spinning. The moment Shmuel disappeared, his dizziness vanished.

The guests were almost all gone now. Just the band members remained, having put away their instruments. They came to say goodbye to Lipa.

First to approach was Shlomo, a broad smile on his dark Yemenite face. He approached Lipa, arms outstretched.

"Mazel tov! Mazel tov, *bachur habar mitzvah*!" He embraced Lipa warmly, as though they were the oldest friends.

"Thank you," answered Lipa, overwhelmed by this friendly embrace. He was happy that Shlomo hadn't pinched his cheek.

Then Shlomo bent down and whispered in his ear. "Lipa, do you remember the birds that flew over the Kotel?"

Lipa was bewildered. *What Kosel? What was Shlomo talking about?* Again, his head began spinning slowly like a merry-go-round. This was all so strange... *What birds? What Kosel? When?*

Shlomo released Lipa from his embrace and quickly departed. Again, the minute he departed, the dizziness disappeared.

Now it was Ovadiah's turn. He approached quickly, hand outstretched. He was more reserved than Shlomo, but still he was filled with immense warmth. He held Lipa's hand in his, shaking it warmly. Then he bent down and whispered: "Lipa, do you remember Gustavi?"

Lipa stared up in wonder. *Who was Gustavi?* Maybe he meant

The Shul Boy ~ 339

Gustavo? Again, Lipa's head began spinning, but he tried to answer.

"You mean 'Gustavo'?"

"No, no, Lipa," Ovadiah insisted. "*Gustavi!*"

Gustavi? Lipa was growing dizzier and dizzier, the room taking off like a top. *Who was Gustavi?*

Before he could be asked, Ovadiah released his hand and disappeared. Immediately, the spinning came to a halt. Lipa stood, utterly confused by what he heard, even as Chaim Galil himself approached to say goodbye.

"Lipa, mazel tov!" he exclaimed heartily. "You did yourself proud tonight!" He took Lipa's hand in his. "Tell me," he asked confidentially, "who taught you all about those *Kinnim* pigeons tonight?"

"My friend, Gustavo—"

Chaim shook his head. He leaned down and whispered into Lipa's ear.

*"Don't you remember? I told you—your name is—*Pesachiah!"

Lipa stared at him in shock. *What was he talking about? Pesachiah?*

But it was too late. The moment Chaim mentioned Pesachiah, the walls around Lipa began spinning around and around. He felt like he was sliding down into a whirlpool, into Miriam's Well hidden deep in the Sea of Galilee. He closed his eyes to stop from falling, but the instant Chaim released his hand, the dizziness stopped. Lipa, trembling, shook his head clear and opened his eyes. Chaim and the other musicians were gone.

Lipa looked around. The great hall was empty. But no—still sitting at the table behind him was Rabbi Gershon Seamansky, watching him. He had not moved the whole time—waiting for the others to leave. Rabbi Gershon gazed at him, and Lipa looked back, very shy.

"Lipa," called Rabbi Gershon, "come here!"

Eyes cast down, Lipa approached Rabbi Gershon until he stood directly before him. Rabbi Gershon took Lipa's thin hands in his own hands. Rabbi Gershon's hands were hot like fire. Lipa would not look up—he was very shy.

"Lipa," Rabbi Gershon said, "look at me!"

Lipa shook his head.

"Lipa," Rabbi Gershon repeated, "look at me—don't be afraid!"

Very slowly, Lipa raised his head and looked up into Rabbi Gershon's face.

"Do you remember me?" he asked.

"Yes, Captain," Lipa answered.

"Do you remember the ship, and Henzel and Rabbi Ovadiah?"

"Yes."

"Do you remember when I revealed that I was really a Jew and would not change my ways? What did you say then?"

Lipa shook his head. He could not repeat those words now, in front of such a great tzaddik.

"You said: 'Captain Vincente—shame on you! If I, Lipa Wallerstein, was ready to feel the lashes of Henzel's whip—can you not have the courage to change?!' Lipa! Those brave words you uttered were like a flame that seared into my *neshamah*! They were beautiful, pure words of faith. Then, that time, in that world—I did not change. I was too weak and too ashamed. But when I was brought to the Heavenly Court for judgment, they saw that in my sinful *neshamah* there lay an immensely holy spark.

"'Where did that holy spark come from?' they asked.

"'It was your spark, Lipa! Your words!'

"And so the Angel of Mercy asked me: '*Gershon, do you desire your* neshamah *to descend back to earth again?*'

"'*Yes!*' I begged.

"'*And what will you accomplish there?*'

"'*I shall do* teshuvah—*and make many thousands of* ba'alei teshuvah!'

"'*Do you promise?*'

"'*I promise!*'

"'*Then fly*, neshamah!'

"And that, my young Lipa, is *why* I have done what I have done! And that is *how* I have done what I have done! It was you, Lipa! The ten thousand souls I have set aflame—came from your brave, holy words!

"Do you understand, Lipa—*you set the world aflame!*"

Lipa looked down, tears flowing. He could no longer look at Rabbi Gershon's face. He was too embarrassed, too shy, too overcome.

"Lipa, look at me!" Rabbi Gershon commanded. Lipa wiped his face on his sleeve, sniffled once, and looked up.

"Tonight is your bar mitzvah. What will be *your* life?"

"I will study Torah. I will become a *talmid chacham*."

"Yes, that is good for *you*. But what will you do for others? You are the grandson of Avraham Avinu who drew thousands under the wings of the *Shechinah*. You must do that also!"

"But how?" asked Lipa. "I am too shy! I am not a great speaker like you!"

"Lipa, Lipa, did you not once meet these holy *gedolim*?"

Suddenly, Lipa felt himself circling round and round, riding on a bright, painted carousel. At each new turn he saw a familiar, holy face. He saw Rabbi Ovadiah on the ship to Eretz Yisrael… He saw Rabbi Shlomo Adani sitting at the feet of Rabbi Chaim Vital… He saw Shmuel with his father, the Tosfos Yom Tov… And lastly, he glimpsed the face of the Tiferes Yisrael, bent over, furiously writing his holy commentary.

They all shared one immense power—the power of the pen!

"I shall be a writer," declared Lipa. "I shall write *sefarim* that will make Jews want to serve Hashem with all their hearts!"

Rabbi Gershon nodded in agreement, pleased. "Yes, Lipa! That is what your *neshamah* was sent to do!"

There was a moment of grave silence. Rabbi Gershon closed his eyes in concentration. Lipa stared into his holy face. He clasped Lipa's hands so fiercely that it almost hurt. Rabbi Gershon's hands burned like fire, and Lipa's hands turned oven-hot.

Rabbi Gershon finally opened his eyes, gazed at Lipa and prayed:

"May these ten innocent fingers become holy tools to set the world aflame!"

Rabbi Gershon rose, and without another word, raced quickly out of the hall. Lipa was left all alone.

Ohr l'arba'ah assar…the beginning of the rest of his life…

Lipa turned to leave. The party was over, and now he was left to begin his life. What would his life be like? Only Hashem knew, the *yegiah*, the struggle, the challenges—and the great triumphs!

Already, Lipa's mind was turning over: *What shall I write?*

Lipa did not know—the words were already there in Shamayim, ready to descend, holy words, mighty words, uplifting words.

And one day the words would descend like tiny neshamos—*into his head, into his heart, into the hearts of all Israel, amen!*